The Enchantress of Florence

The Enchantress of Florence

A NOVEL

Salman Rushdie

RANDOM HOUSE

NEW YORK

This is a work of fiction.
A few liberties have been taken with
the historical record in the interests
of the truth.

Published in the United States by Random House, an imprint of
The Random House Publishing Group, a division of
Random House, Inc., New York.

RANDOM HOUSE and colophon are registered trademarks
of Random House, Inc.

Grateful acknowledgment is made to the following for permission to reprint
previously published material:
SHAMSUR RAHMAN FARUQI: Excerpt from a poem by Mirza Ghalib as
translated by Shamsur Rahman Faruqi from the essay entitled
"A Stranger in the City: The Poetics of Sabk-I Hindi."
Reprinted by permission of Shamsur Rahman Faruqi.
A. S. KLINE: Excerpt from poem 90 from *The Canzoniere* by Petrarch,
translated by A. S. Kline.
Reprinted by permission of A. S. Kline.

ISBN 978-1-60751-430-5

Printed in the United States of America

To Bill Buford

Her way of moving was no mortal thing
but of angelic form: and her speech
rang higher than a mere human voice.

A celestial spirit, a living sun
was what I saw . . .

FRANCESCO PETRARCA
translated by A. S. Kline

If there is a knower of tongues here, fetch him;
There's a stranger in the city
And he has many things to say.

MIRZA GHALIB
translated by Shamsur Rahman Faruqi

I

{ I }

In the day's last light the glowing lake

In the day's last light the glowing lake below the palace-city looked like a sea of molten gold. A traveler coming this way at sunset—this traveler, coming this way, now, along the lakeshore road—might believe himself to be approaching the throne of a monarch so fabulously wealthy that he could allow a portion of his treasure to be poured into a giant hollow in the earth to dazzle and awe his guests. And as big as the lake of gold was, it must be only a drop drawn from the sea of the larger fortune—the traveler's imagination could not begin to grasp the size of that mother-ocean! Nor were there guards at the golden water's edge; was the king so generous, then, that he allowed all his subjects, and perhaps even strangers and visitors like the traveler himself, without hindrance to draw up liquid bounty from the lake? That would indeed be a prince among men, a veritable Prester John, whose lost kingdom of song and fable contained impossible wonders. Perhaps (the traveler surmised) the fountain of eternal youth lay within the city walls—perhaps even the legendary doorway to Paradise on Earth was somewhere close at hand? But then the sun fell below the horizon, the gold sank beneath the water's surface, and was lost. Mermaids and serpents would guard it until the return of daylight. Until then, water itself would be the only treasure on offer, a gift the thirsty traveler gratefully accepted.

The stranger rode in a bullock-cart, but instead of being seated on the rough cushions therein he stood up like a god, holding on to the rail of the cart's latticework wooden frame with one insouciant hand. A bullock-cart ride was far from smooth, the two-wheeled cart tossing and jerking to the rhythm of the animal's hoofs, and subject, too, to the vagaries of the highway beneath its wheels. A standing man might easily fall and break his neck. Nevertheless the traveler stood, looking careless and content. The driver had long ago given up shouting at him, at first taking the foreigner for a fool—if he wanted to die on the road, let him do so, for no man in this country would be sorry! Quickly, however, the driver's scorn had given way to a grudging admiration. The man might indeed be foolish, one could go so far as to say that he had a fool's overly pretty face and wore a fool's unsuitable clothes—a coat of colored leather lozenges, in such heat!—but his balance was immaculate, to be wondered at. The bullock plodded forward, the cart's wheels hit potholes and rocks, yet the standing man barely swayed, and managed, somehow, to be graceful. A graceful fool, the driver thought, or perhaps no fool at all. Perhaps someone to be reckoned with. If he had a fault, it was that of ostentation, of seeking to be not only himself but a performance of himself as well, and, the driver thought, around here everybody is a little bit that way too, so maybe this man is not so foreign to us after all. When the passenger mentioned his thirst the driver found himself going to the water's edge to fetch the fellow a drink in a cup made of a hollowed and varnished gourd, and holding it up for the stranger to take, for all the world as if he were an aristocrat worthy of service.

"You just stand there like a grandee and I jump and scurry at your bidding," the driver said, frowning. "I don't know why I'm treating you so well. Who gave you the right to command me? What are you, anyway? Not a nobleman, that's for sure, or you wouldn't be in this cart. And yet you have airs about you. So you're probably some kind of a rogue." The other drank deeply from the gourd. The water ran down from the edges of his mouth and hung on his shaven chin like a liquid beard. At length he handed back the empty gourd, gave a sigh of satisfaction, and wiped the beard away. "What am I?" he said, as if speaking to himself, but using the driver's own language. "I'm a man with a secret, that's what—a secret which only the emperor's ears may hear." The driver felt reassured: the fellow was a fool after all. There was no need to treat him with respect. "Keep your secret," he said. "Secrets are for children, and spies." The stranger got down from the cart outside the caravanserai, where all journeys ended and began. He was surprisingly tall and carried a carpetbag. "And for sorcerers," he told the driver of the bullock-cart. "And for lovers too. And kings."

In the caravanserai all was bustle and hum. Animals were cared for, horses, camels, bullocks, asses, goats, while other, untamable animals ran wild: screechy monkeys, dogs that were no man's pets. Shrieking parrots exploded like green fireworks in the sky. Black-smiths were at work, and carpenters, and in chandleries on all four sides of the enormous square men planned their journeys, stocking up on groceries, candles, oil, soap, and ropes. Turbaned coolies in red shirts and dhotis ran ceaselessly hither and yon with bundles of improbable size and weight upon their heads. There was, in general, much loading and unloading of goods. Beds for the night were to be cheaply had here, wood-frame rope beds covered with spiky horsehair mattresses, standing in military ranks upon the roofs of the single-story buildings surrounding the enormous courtyard of the caravanserai, beds where a man might lie and look up at the heavens and imagine himself divine. Beyond, to the west, lay the murmuring camps of the emperor's regiments, lately returned from the wars. The army was not permitted to enter the zone of the palaces but had to stay here at the foot of the royal hill. An unemployed army, recently home from battle, was to be treated with caution. The stranger thought of ancient Rome. An emperor trusted no soldiers except his praetorian guard. The traveler knew that the question of trust was one he would have to answer convincingly. If he did not he would quickly die.

Not far from the caravanserai, a tower studded with elephant tusks marked the way to the palace gate. All elephants belonged to the emperor, and by spiking a tower with their teeth he was demonstrating his power. Beware! the tower said. You are entering the realm of the Elephant King, a sovereign so rich in pachyderms that he can waste the gnashers of a thousand of the beasts just to decorate me. In the tower's display of might the traveler recognized the same quality of flamboyance that burned upon his own forehead like a flame, or a mark of the Devil; but the maker of the tower had transformed into strength that quality which, in the traveler, was often seen as a weakness. Is power the only justification for an extrovert personality? the traveler asked himself, and could not answer, but found himself hoping that beauty might be another such excuse, for he was certainly beautiful, and knew that his looks had a power of their own.

Beyond the tower of the teeth stood a great well and above it a mass of incomprehensibly complex waterworks machinery that served the many-cupolaed palace on the hill. *Without water we are nothing,* the traveler thought. *Even an emperor, denied water, would swiftly turn to dust. Water is the real monarch and we are all its slaves.* Once at home in Florence he had met a man who could make water disappear. The conjuror filled a jug to the brim, muttered magic words, turned the jug over and, instead of liquid, fabric spilled forth, a torrent of colored silken scarves. It was a trick, of course, and before that day was done he, the traveler, had coaxed the fellow's secret out of him, and had hidden it among his own mysteries. He was a man of many secrets, but only one was fit for a king.

The road to the city wall rose quickly up the hillside and as he rose with it he saw the size of the place at which he had arrived. Plainly it was one of the grand cities of the world, larger, it seemed to his eye, than Florence or Venice or Rome, larger than any town the traveler had ever seen. He had visited London once; it too was a lesser metropolis than this. As the light failed the city seemed to grow. Dense neighborhoods huddled outside the walls, muezzins called from their minarets, and in the distance he could see the lights of large estates. Fires began to burn in the twilight, like warnings. From the black bowl of the sky came the answering fires of the stars. *As if the earth and the heavens were armies preparing for battle,* he thought. *As if their encampments lie quiet at night and await the war of the day to come.* And in all these warrens of streets and in all those houses of the mighty, beyond, on the plains, there was not one man who had heard his name, not one who would readily believe the tale he had to tell. Yet he had to tell it. He had crossed the world to do so, and he would.

He walked with long strides and attracted many curious glances, on account of his yellow hair as well as his height, his long and admittedly dirty yellow hair flowing down around his face like the golden water of the lake. The path sloped upward past the tower of the teeth toward a stone gate upon which two elephants in bas-relief stood facing each other. Through this gate, which was open, came the noises of human beings at play, eating, drinking, carousing. There were soldiers on duty at the Hatyapul gate but their stances were relaxed. The real barriers lay ahead. This was a public place, a place for meetings, purchases, and pleasure. Men hurried past the traveler, driven by hungers and thirsts. On both sides of the flagstoned road between the outer gate and the inner were hostelries, saloons, food stalls, and hawkers of all kinds. Here was the eternal business of buying and being bought. Cloths, utensils, baubles, weapons, rum. The main market lay beyond the city's lesser, southern gate. City dwellers shopped there and avoided this place, which was for ignorant newcomers who did not know the real price of things. This was the swindlers' market, the thieves' market, raucous, overpriced, contemptible. But tired travelers, not knowing the plan of the city, and reluctant, in any case, to walk all the way around the outer walls to the larger, fairer bazaar, had little option but to deal with the merchants by the elephant gate. Their needs were urgent and simple.

Live chickens, noisy with fear, hung upside down, fluttering, their feet tied together, awaiting the pot. For vegetarians there were other, more silent cook-pots; vegetables did not scream. And were those women's voices the traveler could hear on the wind, ululating, teasing, enticing, laughing at unseen men? Were those women he scented upon the evening breeze? It was too late to go looking for the emperor tonight, in any case. The traveler had money in his pocket and had made a long, roundabout journey. This way was his way: to move toward his goal indirectly, with many detours and divagations. Since landing at Surat he had traveled by way of Burhanpur, Handia, Sironj, Narwar, Gwalior, and Dholpur to Agra, and from Agra to this, the new capital. Now he wanted the most comfortable bed that could be had, and a woman, preferably one without a mustache, and finally a quantity of the oblivion, the escape from self, that can never be found in a woman's arms but only in good strong drink.

Later, when his desires had been satisfied, he slept in an odorous whorehouse, snoring lustily next to an insomniac tart, and dreamed. He could dream in seven languages: Italian, Spanish, Arabic, Persian, Russian, English, and Portuguese. He had picked up languages the way most sailors picked up diseases; languages were his gonorrhea, his syphilis, his scurvy, his ague, his plague. As soon as he fell asleep half the world started babbling in his brain, telling wondrous travelers' tales. In this half-discovered world every day brought news of fresh enchantments. The visionary, revelatory dream-poetry of the quotidian had not yet been crushed by blinkered, prosy fact. Himself a teller of tales, he had been driven out of his door by stories of wonder, and by one in particular, a story which could make his fortune or else cost him his life.

{ 2 }

Aboard the Scottish milord's pirate ship

Aboard the Scottish milord's pirate ship *Scáthach,* named for a fabled warrior-goddess from Skye, a vessel whose crew had for many years been happily robbing and plundering up and down the Spanish Main, but which was presently bound for India on business of state, the languid Florentine stowaway had avoided being thrown summarily into the White River of southern Africa by pulling a living water-snake out of the boatswain's startled ear and tossing it overboard instead. He had been found under a bunk in the ship's forecastle seven days after the vessel rounded Cape Agulhas at the foot of the African continent, wearing mustard-colored doublet and hose and wrapped up in a long patchwork cloak made up of bright harlequin lozenges of leather, cradling a small carpetbag, and sleeping soundly, with many loud snores, making no effort to hide. He seemed perfectly ready to be discovered, and dazzlingly confident of his powers of charm, persuasion, and enchantment. They had, after all, brought him a long way already. Indeed, he turned out to be quite the conjuror. He transformed gold coins into smoke and yellow smoke back into gold. A jug of fresh water flipped upside down released a flood of silken scarves. He multiplied fishes and loaves with a couple of passes of his elegant hand, which was blasphemous, of course, but the hungry sailors easily forgave him. Crossing themselves hastily, to insure themselves against the possible wrath of Christ Jesus regarding the usurpation of his position by this latter-day miracle worker, they gobbled up their unexpectedly lavish, if theologically unsound, lunch.

Even the Scottish milord himself, George Louis Hauksbank,

Lord Hauksbank of That Ilk—which was to say, according to the Scottish fashion, Hauksbank of Hauksbank, a noble not to be confused with lesser, more ignoble Hauksbanks from inferior places— was speedily charmed when the harlequin interloper was brought to his cabin for judgment. At that time the young rogue was calling himself "Uccello"—"Uccello di Firenze, enchanter and scholar, at your service," he said in perfect English, with a low, sweeping bow of almost aristocratic skill, and Lord Hauksbank smiled and sniffed his perfumed kerchief. "Which I might have believed, wizard," he replied, "if I did not know of the painter Paolo of the same name and place, who created in your township's Duomo a *trompe l'oeil* fresco in honor of my own ancestor Sir John Hauksbank, known as Giovanni Milano, soldier of fortune, erstwhile general of Florence, victor of the battle of Polpetto; and if that painter had not unfortunately been dead these many years." The young rogue made a cheeky, clucking noise of dissent with his tongue. "Obviously I am not the deceased artist," he stated, striking an attitude. "I have chosen this *pseudonimo di viaggio* because in my language it is a word we have for 'bird,' and birds are the greatest travelers of all."

Here he plucked a hooded falcon from his breast, a falconer's glove from the empty air, and handed both to the astounded laird. "A hawk for the Hauksbank's lord," he said, with perfect formality, and then, once Lord Hauksbank had the glove on his hand and the bird upon it, he, "Uccello," snapped his fingers like a woman withdrawing her love, whereupon to the Scottish milord's considerable discomfiture they both vanished, the gloved bird and the birded glove. "Also," continued the magician, returning to the matter of his name, "because in my city, this veil of a word, this hidden bird, is a delicately euphemistic term for the organ of the male sex, and I take pride in that which I possess but do not have the ill grace to display." "Ha! Ha!" cried Lord Hauksbank of That Ilk, recovering his poise with admirable celerity. "Now that does give us something in common."

He was a much-traveled milord, this Hauksbank of That Ilk, and older than he looked. His eye was bright and his skin was clear but he had not seen his fortieth year for seven years or more. His swordsmanship was a byword and he was as strong as a white bull and he had journeyed by raft to the source of the Yellow River in the Kar Qu lake, where he ate braised tiger penis from a golden bowl, and he had hunted the white rhinoceros of the Ngorongoro Crater and climbed all two hundred and eighty-four peaks of the Scottish Munros, from Ben Nevis to the Inaccessible Pinnacle at Sgurr Dearg on the island of Skye, home of Scáthach the Terrible. Long ago in Castle Hauksbank he quarreled with his wife, a tiny barking woman with curly red hair and a jaw like a Dutch nutcracker and he had left her in the Highlands to farm black sheep and gone to seek his fortune like his ancestor before him and captained a ship in the service of Drake when they pirated the gold of the Americas from the Spanish in the Caribbean Sea. His reward from a grateful queen had been this embassy upon which he was presently embarked; he was to go to *Hindoostan* where he was at liberty to gather and keep any fortune he might be able to find, whether in gemstones, opium, or gold, so long as he bore a personal letter from Gloriana to the king and fetched home the *Mogol*'s reply.

"In Italy we say, *Mogor*," the young prestidigitator told him. "In the unpronounceable tongues of the land itself," Lord Hauksbank rejoined, "who knows how the word may be twisted, knotted, and turned."

A book sealed their friendship: the *Canzoniere* of Petrarch, an edition of which lay, as always, by the Scottish milord's elbow on a little *pietra dura* tabletop. "Ah, mighty Petrarca," "Uccello" cried. "Now there is a true magician." And striking a Roman senator's oratorical pose he began to declaim:

> *"Benedetto sia 'l giorno, et 'l mese, et l'anno,*
> *et la stagione, e 'l tempo, et l'ora, e 'l punto,*
> *e 'l bel paese, e 'l loco ov'io fui giunto*
> *da'duo begli occhi che legato m'ànno . . ."*

Whereupon Lord Hauksbank took up the sonnet's thread in English:

> "... and blessed be the first sweet suffering
> that I felt in being conjoined with Love,
> and the bow, and the shafts with which I was pierced,
> and the wounds that run to the depths of my heart."

"Any man who loves this poem as I do must be my master," said "Uccello," bowing. "And any man who feels as I do about these words must be my drinking companion," returned the Scot. "You have turned the key that unlocks my heart. Now I must share a secret that you will never divulge to anyone. Come with me."

In a small wooden box concealed behind a sliding panel in his sleeping quarters Lord Hauksbank of That Ilk kept a collection of beloved "objects of virtue," beautiful little pieces without which a man who traveled constantly might lose his bearings, for too much travel, as Lord Hauksbank well knew, too much strangeness and novelty, could loosen the moorings of the soul. "These things are not mine," he said to his new Florentine friend, "yet they remind me of who I am. I act as their custodian for a time, and when that time is ended, I let them go." He pulled out of the box a number of jewels of awe-inspiring size and clarity which he set aside with a dismissive shrug, and then an ingot of Spanish gold which would keep any man who found it in splendor for the rest of his days— "'tis nothing, nothing," he muttered—and only then did he arrive at his real treasures, each carefully wrapped in cloth and embedded in nests of crumpled paper and shredded rags: the silk handkerchief of a pagan goddess of ancient Soghdia, given to a forgotten hero as a token of her love; a piece of exquisite scrimshaw work on whalebone depicting the hunting of a stag; a locket containing a portrait of Her Majesty the Queen; a leather-bound hexagonal book from the Holy Land, upon whose tiny pages, in miniature writing embellished with extraordinary illuminations, was the entire text of the Qur'ān; a broken-nosed stone head from Macedonia, reputed to be a portrait of Alexander the Great; one of the cryptic "seals" of the Indus Valley civilization, found in Egypt, bearing the image of a bull and a series of hieroglyphs that had never been decoded, an object whose purpose no man knew; a flat, polished Chinese stone bearing a scarlet *I Ching* hexagram and dark natural markings resembling a mountain range at dusk; a painted porcelain egg; a shrunken head made by the denizens of the Amazon rain forest; and a dictionary of the lost language of the Panamanian isthmus whose speakers were all extinct except for one old woman who could no longer pronounce the words properly on account of the loss of her teeth.

Lord Hauksbank of That Ilk opened a cabinet of precious glassware that had miraculously survived the crossing of many oceans, took out a matched pair of opalescent Murano balloons, and poured a sufficiency of brandy into each. The stowaway approached and raised a glass. Lord Hauksbank breathed deeply, and then drank. "You are from Florence," he said, "so you know of the majesty of that highest of sovereigns, the individual human self, and of the cravings it seeks to assuage, for beauty, for value—and for love." The man calling himself "Uccello" began to reply, but Hauksbank raised a hand. "I will have my say," he continued, "for there are matters to discuss of which your eminent philosophers know nothing. The self may be royal, but it hungers like a pauper. It may be nourished for a moment by the inspection of such co-cooned wonders as these, but it remains a poor, starving, thirsting thing. And it is a king imperiled, a sovereign forever at the mercy of many insurgents, of fear, for example, and anxiety, of isolation and bewilderment, of a strange unspeakable pride and a wild, silent shame. The self is beset by secrets, secrets eat at it constantly, secrets will tear down its kingdom and leave its scepter broken in the dust.

"I see I am perplexing you," he sighed, "so I will show myself plainly. The secret you will never divulge to anyone is not hidden in a box. It lies—no, it does not lie, but tells the truth!—in here."

The Florentine, who had intuited the truth about Lord Hauksbank's concealed desires sometime before, gravely expressed proper respect for the heft and circumference of the mottled member that lay before him upon his lordship's table smelling faintly of fennel, like a *finocchiona* sausage waiting to be sliced. "If you gave up the sea and came to live in my hometown," he said, "your troubles would soon be at an end, for among the young gallants of San Lorenzo you would easily find the manly pleasures you seek. I myself, most regrettably . . ."

"Drink up," the Scottish milord commanded, coloring darkly, and putting himself away. "We will say no more about it." There was a glitter in his eye which his companion wished were not in his eye. His hand was nearer to the hilt of his sword than his companion would have liked it to be. His smile was the rictus of a beast.

There followed a long and lonely silence during which the stowaway understood that his fate hung in the balance. Then Hauksbank drained his brandy glass and gave an ugly, anguished laugh. "Well, sir," he cried, "you know my secret, and now you must tell me yours, for certainly you have a mystery in you, which I foolishly mistook for my own, and now I must have it plain."

The man calling himself Uccello di Firenze tried to change the subject. "Will you not honor me, my lord, with an account of the capture of the *Cacafuego* treasure galleon? And were you—you must have been—with Drake at Valparaiso, and Nombre de Dios, where he took his wound . . . ?" Hauksbank threw his glass against a wall and drew his sword. "Scoundrel," he said. "Answer me directly, or die."

The stowaway chose his words carefully. "My lord," he said, "I am here, I now perceive, to offer myself to you as your factotum. It is true, however," he added quickly, as the blade's point touched his throat, "that I have a more distant purpose too. Indeed, I am what you might call a man embarked on a quest—a secret quest, what's more—but I must warn you that my secret has a curse upon it, placed there by the most powerful enchantress of the age. Only one man may hear my secret and live, and I would not wish to be responsible for your death."

Lord Hauksbank of That Ilk laughed again, not an ugly laugh this time, a laugh of dispersing clouds and revenant sunshine. "You amuse me, little bird," he said. "Do you imagine I fear your green-faced witch's curse? I have danced with Baron Samedi on the Day of the Dead and survived his voodoo howls. I will take it most unkindly if you do not tell me everything at once."

"So be it," began the stowaway. "There was once an adventurer-prince named Argalia, also called Arcalia, a great warrior who possessed enchanted weapons, and in whose retinue were four terrifying giants, and he had a woman with him, Angelica . . ."

"Stop," said Lord Hauksbank of That Ilk, clutching at his brow. "You're giving me a headache." Then, after a moment, "Go on." ". . . Angelica, a princess of the blood royal of Genghis Khan and Tamerlane . . ." "Stop. No, go on." ". . . the most beautiful . . ." "Stop."

Whereupon Lord Hauksbank fell unconscious to the floor.

———⟨⟨⟨⟩⟩⟩———

The traveler, almost embarrassed about the ease with which he had inserted the laudanum into his host's glass, carefully returned the little wooden box of treasures to its hiding place, drew his parti-colored greatcoat about him, and hurried onto the main deck calling for help. He had won the coat at cards in a hand of *scarabocion* played against an astonished Venetian diamond merchant who could not believe that a mere Florentine could come to the Rialto and beat the locals at their own game. The merchant, a bearded and ringleted Jew named Shalakh Cormorano, had had the coat specially made at the most famous tailor's shop in Venice, known as *Il Moro Invidioso* because of the picture of a green-eyed Arab on the shingle over its door, and it was an occultist marvel of a greatcoat, its lining a catacomb of secret pockets and hidden folds within which a diamond merchant could stash his valuable wares, and a chancer such as "Uccello di Firenze" could conceal all manner of tricks. "Quickly, my friends, quickly," the traveler called in a convincing display of concern. "His lordship has need of us."

If, among this hardy crew of privateers-turned-diplomats, there were many narrow-eyed cynics whose suspicions were aroused by the manner of their leader's sudden collapse, and who began to regard the newcomer in a manner not conducive to his good health, they were partly reassured by the obvious concern shown by "Uccello di Firenze" for Lord Hauksbank's well-being. He helped to carry the unconscious man to his cot, undressed him, struggled with his pajamas, applied hot and cold compresses to his brow, and refused to sleep or eat until the Scottish milord's health improved. The ship's doctor declared the stowaway to be an invaluable aide, and on hearing that the crew went muttering and shrugging back to their posts.

When they were alone with the insensate man, the doctor confessed to "Uccello" that he was baffled by the aristocrat's refusal to awake from his sudden coma. "Nothing wrong with the man that I can see, praise God, except that he won't wake up," he said, "and in this loveless world it may be that it's wiser to dream than to awake."

The doctor was a simple, battle-hardened individual named Praise-God Hawkins, a good-hearted sawbones of limited medical knowledge who was more accustomed to removing Spanish bullets from his shipmates' bodies, and sewing up cutlass gashes after hand-to-hand combat with the Spaniard, than to curing mysterious sleeping sicknesses that arrived out of nowhere, like a stowaway or a judgment from God. Hawkins had left an eye at Valparaiso and half a leg at Nombre de Dios, and he sang, every night, mournful Portuguese *fados* in honor of a maiden on a balcony in the Ribeira neighborhood of Oporto, accompanying himself on some sort of gypsy fiddle. Praise-God wept copiously while he sang, and "Uccello" understood that the good doctor was imagining his own cuckolding, conjuring up, to torture himself, images of his port-wine-drinking beloved in bed with men who were still whole, fishermen stinking of their finny prey, lecherous Franciscan monks, the ghosts of the early navigators, and living men of every variety and hue, Dagos and Englishmen, Chinamen and Jews. "A man under the enchantment of love," the stowaway thought, "is a man easily distracted and led."

As the *Scáthach* made her way past the Horn of Africa and the isle of Socotra, and while she took on supplies at Maskat and then left the Persian coast to port and, blown along by the monsoon wind, headed southeast toward the Portuguese haven of Diu on the southern shore of the place Dr. Hawkins called "Guzerat," so Lord Hauksbank of That Ilk slumbered peacefully on, "a sleep so calm, praise God," according to the helpless Hawkins, "that it proves his conscience is clear and so his soul, at least, is in good health, ready to meet its Maker at any time." "God forbid," said the stowaway. "Praise God, let him not be taken yet," the other readily agreed. During their long bedside vigil "Uccello" often asked the doctor about his Portugee lady love. Hawkins needed little encouragement to discuss the subject. The stowaway listened patiently to adoring paeans to the lady's eyes, her lips, her bosoms, her hips, her belly, her rump, her feet. He learned the secret terms of endearment she used in the act of love, terms no longer so secret now, and he heard her promises of fidelity and her murmured oath of eternal union. "Ah, but she is false, false," the doctor wept. "Do you know this for a fact?" the traveler inquired, and when the lachrymose Praise-God shook his head, saying, "It has been so long, and I am now but half a man, so I must assume the worst," then "Uccello" coaxed him back to gaiety. "Well, let us now praise God, Praise-God, for you weep without cause! She is true, I'm certain of it; and waits for you, I doubt it not; and if you have a leg less, well then, she will have love to spare, the love allocated to that leg can be reassigned to other parts; and if you lack an eye, the other will feast twice as well upon her who has kept faith, and loves you as you love her! Enough! Praise God! Sing joyfully and weep no more."

In this fashion he dismissed Praise-God Hawkins nightly, assuring him that the crew would be desolate if they did not hear his songs, and nightly, when he was alone with the unconscious milord, and had waited a few moments, he made a thorough search of the captain's quarters, seeking out all their secrets. "A man who builds a cabin with one hidden cavity has built a cabin with at least two or three," he reasoned, and by the time the port of Diu was sighted he had plucked Lord Hauksbank as clean as any chicken, he had found the seven secret chambers in the paneled walls, and all the jewels in all the wooden boxes therein were safely in their new homes in the coat of Shalakh Cormorano, and the seven gold ingots, too, and yet the coat felt light as a feather, for the green-eyed Moor of Venice knew the secret of rendering weightless whatever goods were secreted within that magic garment. As for the other "objects of virtue," they did not interest the thief. He let them nest where they lay, to hatch what birds they could. But even at the end of his grand pilfering "Uccello" was not content, for the greatest treasure of all had eluded him. It was all he could do to conceal his agitation. Chance had placed a great opportunity within his grasp, and he must not let it slip. But where was the thing? He had looked over every inch of the captain's quarters, and yet it remained hidden. Damnation! Was the treasure under a spell? Had it been made invisible, to escape him thus?

After the *Scáthach*'s brief landfall at Diu she made haste for Surat, from which city (recently the site of a punitive visit by the emperor Akbar himself) Lord Hauksbank had intended to embark on his land journey to the *Mogol*'s court. And on the night that they reached Surat (which lay in ruins, still smoldering from the emperor's wrath), when Praise-God Hawkins was singing his heart out and the crew was rum-drunk and rejoicing at the end of the long sea voyage, the searcher belowdecks at last found what he was looking for: the eighth secret panel, one more than the magic number of seven, one more than almost any robber would expect. Behind that ultimate door was the thing he sought. Then after one last deed he joined the revelers on deck and sang and drank more heartily than any man aboard. Because he possessed the gift of staying awake when no other man's eyes could remain open, the time came, in the small hours of the morning, when he was able to slip ashore in one of the ship's dinghies and disappear, like a phantom, into India. Long before Praise-God Hawkins raised the alarm, having found Lord Hauksbank of That Ilk blue-lipped in his last sea-cot and released forever from the torments of his yearning *finocchiona,* "Uccello di Firenze" had gone, leaving only that name behind like the abandoned skin of a snake. Next to the nameless traveler's breast was the treasure of treasures, the letter in Elizabeth Tudor's own hand and under her personal seal, the missive from the Queen of England to the Emperor of India, which would be his open-sesame, his passe-partout, to the world of the Mughal court. He was England's ambassador now.

{ 3 }

At dawn the haunting sandstone palaces

At dawn the haunting sandstone palaces of the new "victory city" of Akbar the Great looked as if they were made of red smoke. Most cities start giving the impression of being eternal almost as soon as they are born, but Sikri would always look like a mirage. As the sun rose to its zenith, the great bludgeon of the day's heat pounded the flagstones, deafening human ears to all sounds, making the air quiver like a frightened blackbuck, and weakening the border between sanity and delirium, between what was fanciful and what was real.

Even the emperor succumbed to fantasy. Queens floated within his palaces like ghosts, Rajput and Turkish sultanas playing catch-me-if-you-can. One of these royal personages did not really exist. She was an imaginary wife, dreamed up by Akbar in the way that lonely children dream up imaginary friends, and in spite of the presence of many living, if floating, consorts, the emperor was of the opinion that it was the real queens who were the phantoms and the nonexistent beloved who was real. He gave her a name, Jodha, and no man dared gainsay him. Within the privacy of the women's quarters, within the silken corridors of her palace, her influence and power grew. Tansen wrote songs for her and in the studio-scriptorium her beauty was celebrated in portraiture and verse. Master Abdus Samad the Persian portrayed her himself, painted her from the memory of a dream without ever looking upon her face, and when the emperor saw his work he clapped his hands at the beauty shining up from the page. "You have captured her, to the life," he cried, and Abdus Samad relaxed and stopped feeling as if his head was too loosely attached to his neck; and after this visionary work by the master of the emperor's atelier had been exhibited, the whole court knew Jodha to be real, and the greatest courtiers, the *Navratna* or Nine Stars, all acknowledged not only her existence but also her beauty, her wisdom, the grace of her movements, and the softness of her voice. Akbar and Jodhabai! Ah, ah! It was the love story of the age.

The city was finished at last, in time for the emperor's fortieth birthday. It had been twelve hot years in the making, but for a long time he had been given the impression that it rose up effortlessly, year by year, as if by sorcery. His minister of works had not allowed any construction to go forward during the emperor's sojourns in the new imperial capital. When the emperor was in residence the stonemasons' tools fell silent, the carpenters drove in no nails, the painters, the inlay-workers, the hangers of fabrics, and the carvers of screens all disappeared from view. All then, it's said, was cushioned pleasure. Only noises of delight were permitted to be heard. The bells on the ankles of dancers echoed sweetly, and fountains tinkled, and the soft music of the genius Tansen hung upon the breeze. There was whispered poetry in the emperor's ear, and in the pachisi courtyard on Thursdays there was much languid play, with slave girls being used as living pieces on the checkerboard floor. In the curtained afternoons beneath the sliding punkahs there was a quiet time for love. The city's sensuous hush was brought into being by the monarch's omnipotence as much as by the heat of the day.

No city is all palaces. The real city, built of wood and mud and dung and brick as well as stone, huddled beneath the walls of the mighty red stone plinth upon which the royal residences stood. Its neighborhoods were determined by race as well as trade. Here was the silversmiths' street, there the hot-gated, clanging armories, and there, down that third gully, the place of bangles and clothes. To the east was the Hindu colony and beyond that, curling around the city walls, the Persian quarter, and beyond that the region of the Turanis and beyond that, in the vicinity of the giant gate of the Friday Mosque, the homes of those Muslims who were Indian born. Dotted around the countryside were the villas of the nobles, the art studio and scriptorium whose fame had already spread throughout the land, and a pavilion of music, and another for the performance of dances. In most of these lower Sikris there was little time for indolence, and when the emperor came home from the wars the command of silence felt, in the mud city, like a suffocation. Chickens had to be gagged at the moment of their slaughter for fear of disturbing the repose of the king of kings. A cartwheel that squeaked could earn the cart's driver the lash, and if he cried out under the whip the penalty could be even more severe. Women giving birth withheld their cries and the dumb show of the marketplace was a kind of madness: "When the king is here we are all made mad," the people said, adding, hastily, for there were spies and traitors everywhere, "for joy." The mud city loved its emperor, it insisted that it did, insisted without words, for words were made of that forbidden fabric, sound. When the emperor set forth once more on his campaigns—his never-ending (though always victorious) battles against the armies of Gujarat and Rajasthan, of Kabul and Kashmir—then the prison of silence was unlocked, and trumpets burst out, and cheers, and people were finally able to tell each other everything they had been obliged to keep unsaid for months on end. *I love you. My mother is dead. Your soup tastes good. If you do not pay me the money you owe me I will break your arms at the elbows. My darling, I love you too.* Everything.

Fortunately for the mud city, military matters often took Akbar away, in fact he had been away most of the time, and in his absences the din of the clustered poor, as well as the racket of the unleashed construction workers, daily vexed the impotent queens. The queens lay together and moaned, and what they did to distract one another, what entertainment they found in one another in their veiled quarters, will not be described here. Only the imaginary queen remained pure, and it was she who told Akbar of the privations the people were suffering because of the desire of overzealous officials to ease his time at home. As soon as the emperor learned this he countermanded the order, replaced the minister of works with a less dour individual, and insisted on riding through the streets of his oppressed subjects crying out, "Make as much racket as you like, people! Noise is life, and an excess of noise is a sign that life is good. There will be time for us all to be quiet when we are safely dead." The city burst into joyful clamor. That was the day on which it became clear that a new kind of king was on the throne, and that nothing in the world would remain the same.

The country was at peace at last, but the king's spirit was never calm. The king had just returned from his last campaign, he had slapped down the upstart in Surat, but through the long days of marching and war his mind wrestled with philosophical and linguistic conundrums as much as military ones. The emperor Abul-Fath Jalaluddin Muhammad, king of kings, known since his childhood as Akbar, meaning "the great," and latterly, in spite of the tautology of it, as Akbar the Great, the great great one, great in his greatness, doubly great, so great that the repetition in his title was not only appropriate but necessary in order to express the gloriousness of his glory—the Grand Mughal, the dusty, battle-weary, victorious, pensive, incipiently overweight, disenchanted, mustachioed, poetic, oversexed, and absolute emperor, who seemed altogether too magnificent, too world-encompassing, and, in sum, too *much* to be a single human personage—this all-engulfing flood of a ruler, this swallower of worlds, this many-headed monster who referred to himself in the first person plural—had begun to meditate, during his long, tedious journey home, on which he was accompanied by the heads of his defeated enemies bobbing in their sealed earthen pickle-jars, about the disturbing possibilities of the first person singular—the "I."

The interminable days of slow equestrian progress encouraged many languid wonderings in a man of speculative temperament, and the emperor pondered, as he rode, such matters as the mutability of the universe, the size of the stars, the breasts of his wives, and the nature of God. Also, today, this grammatical question of the self and its Three Persons, the first, the second, and the third, the singulars and plurals of the soul. He, Akbar, had never referred to himself as "I," not even in private, not even in anger or dreams. He was—what else could he be?—"we." He was the definition, the incarnation of the We. He had been born into plurality. When he said "we," he naturally and truly meant himself as an incarnation of all his subjects, of all his cities and lands and rivers and mountains and lakes, as well as all the animals and plants and trees within his frontiers, and also the birds that flew overhead and the mordant twilight mosquitoes and the nameless monsters in their underworld lairs, gnawing slowly at the roots of things; he meant himself as the sum total of all his victories, himself as containing the characters, the abilities, the histories, perhaps even the souls of his decapitated or merely pacified opponents; and, in addition, he meant himself as the apogee of his people's past and present, and the engine of their future.

This "we" was what it meant to be a king—but commoners, he now allowed himself to consider, in the interests of fairness, and for the purposes of debate, no doubt occasionally thought of themselves as plural, too.

Were they wrong? Or (O traitorous thought!) was he? Perhaps this idea of self-as-community was what it meant to be a being in the world, any being; such a being being, after all, inevitably a being among other beings, a part of the beingness of all things. Perhaps plurality was not exclusively a king's prerogative, perhaps it was not, after all, his divine right. One might further argue that since the reflections of a monarch were, in less exalted and refined form, doubtless mirrored in the cogitations of his subjects, it was accordingly inevitable that the men and women over whom he ruled also conceived of themselves as "we"s. They saw themselves, perhaps, as plural entities made up of themselves plus their children, mothers, aunts, employers, co-worshippers, fellow workers, clans, and friends. They, too, saw their selves as multiple, one self that was the father of their children, another that was their parents' child; they knew themselves to be different with their employers than they were at home with their wives—in short, they were all bags of selves, bursting with plurality, just as he was. Was there then no essential difference between the ruler and the ruled? And now his original question reasserted itself in a new and startling form: if his many-selved subjects managed to think of themselves in the singular rather than plural, could he, too, be an "I"? Could there be an "I" that was simply oneself? Were there such naked, solitary "I"s buried beneath the overcrowded "we"s of the earth?

It was a question that frightened him as he rode his white horse home, fearless, unvanquished, and, it must be conceded, beginning to be fat; and when it popped into his head at night he did not easily sleep. What should he say when he saw his Jodha again? If he were to say simply, "I'm back," or, "It is I," might she feel able to call him in return by that second person singular, that *tu* which was reserved for children, lovers, and gods? And what would that mean? That he was like her child, or godlike, or simply the lover of whom she too had dreamed, whom she had dreamed into being just as eagerly as he had dreamed her? Might that little word, that *tu,* turn out to be the most arousing word in the language? "I," he practiced under his breath. *Here "I" am. "I" love you. Come to "me."*

One final military engagement disturbed his contemplation on the homeward road. One more upstart princeling to slap down. A diversion into the Kathiawar peninsula to quell the obstinate Rana of Cooch Naheen, a young man with a big mouth and a bigger mustache (the emperor was vain about his own mustache, and took unkindly to competitors), a feudal ruler absurdly fond of talking about freedom. Freedom for whom, and from what, the emperor harrumphed inwardly. Freedom was a children's fantasy, a game for women to play. No man was ever free. His army moved through the white trees of the Gir forest like a silently approaching plague, and the pathetic little fortress of Cooch Naheen, seeing the advent of death in the rustling treetops, broke its own towers, ran up a flag of surrender, and begged abjectly for mercy. Often, instead of executing his vanquished opponents, the emperor would marry one of their daughters and give his defeated father-in-law a job. Better a new family member than a rotting corpse. This time, however, he had irritably torn the insolent Rana's mustache off his handsome face, and had chopped the weakling dreamer into garish pieces—had done it personally, with his own sword, just as his grandfather would have, and had then retreated to his quarters to tremble and mourn.

The emperor's eyes were slanted and large and gazed upon infinity as a dreamy young lady might, or a sailor in search of land. His lips were full and pushed forward in a womanly pout. But in spite of these girlish accents he was a mighty specimen of a man, huge and strong. As a boy he had killed a tigress with his bare hands and then, driven to distraction by his deed, had forever forsworn the eating of meat and become a vegetarian. A Muslim vegetarian, a warrior who wanted only peace, a philosopher-king: a contradiction in terms. Such was the greatest ruler the land had ever known.

In the melancholy after battle, as evening fell upon the empty dead, below the broken fortress melting into blood, within earshot of a little waterfall's nightingale song—*bul-bul, bul-bul* it sang—the emperor in his brocade tent sipped watered wine and lamented his gory genealogy. He did not want to be like his bloodthirsty ancestors, even though his ancestors were the greatest men in history. He felt burdened by the names of the marauder past, the names from which his name descended in cascades of human blood: his grandfather Babar the warlord of Ferghana who had conquered, but always loathed, this new dominion, this "India" of too much wealth and too many gods, Babar the battle machine with an unexpected gift for felicitous words, and before Babar the murderous princes of Transoxiana and Mongolia, and mighty Temüjin above all—Genghis, Changez, Jenghis, or Chinggis Qan—thanks to whom he, Akbar, had to accept the name of *mughal,* had to be the *Mongol* he was not, or did not feel himself to be. He felt . . . *Hindustani.* His horde was neither Golden, Blue, nor White. The very word "horde" struck his subtle ears as ugly, swinish, coarse. He did not want hordes. He did not want to pour molten silver into the eyes of his vanquished foes or crush them to death beneath the platform upon which he was eating his dinner. He was tired of war. He remembered the tutor of his childhood, a Persian Mir, telling him that for a man to be at peace with himself he must be at peace with all others. *Sulh-i-kul,* complete peace. No Khan could understand such an idea. He did not want a Khanate. He wanted a country.

It wasn't only Temüjin. He also sprang by direct descent from the loins of the man whose name was Iron. In the language of his forefathers the word for iron was *timur.* Timur-e-Lang, the limping iron man. Timur, who destroyed Damascus and Baghdad, who left Delhi in ruins, haunted by fifty thousand ghosts. Akbar would have preferred not to have had Timur for a forebear. He had stopped speaking Timur's language, Chaghatai, named after one of the sons of Genghis Khan, and adopted, instead, at first Persian and later also the bastard mongrel speech of the army on the move, *urdu,* camp-language, in which half a dozen half-understood tongues jabbered and whistled and produced, to everyone's surprise, a beautiful new sound: a poet's language born out of soldiers' mouths.

The Rana of Cooch Naheen, young, slender, and dark, had knelt at Akbar's feet, his face hairless and bleeding, waiting for the blow to fall. "History repeats itself," he said. "Your grandfather killed my grandfather seventy years ago."

"Our grandfather," replied the emperor, employing the royal plural according to custom, for this was not the time for his experiment with the singular, this wretch did not merit the privilege of witnessing it, "was a barbarian with a poet's tongue. We, by contrast, are a poet with a barbarian's history and a barbarian's prowess in war, which we detest. Thus it is demonstrated that history does not repeat itself, but moves forward, and that Man is capable of change."

"That is a strange remark for an executioner to make," the young Rana said softly, "but it is futile to argue with Death."

"Your time has come," the emperor assented. "So tell us truthfully before you go, what sort of paradise do you expect to discover when you have passed through the veil?" The Rana raised his mutilated face and looked the emperor in the eye. "In Paradise, the words *worship* and *argument* mean the same thing," he declared. "The Almighty is not a tyrant. In the House of God all voices are free to speak as they choose, and that is the form of their devotion." He was an irritating, holier-than-thou type of youth, that was beyond question, but in spite of his annoyance, Akbar was moved. "We promise you," the emperor said, "that we will build that house of adoration here on earth." Then with a cry—*Allahu Akbar,* God is great, or, just possibly, Akbar is God—he chopped off the pompous little twerp's cheeky, didactic, and therefore suddenly unnecessary, head.

In the hours after he killed the Rana, the emperor was possessed by his familiar demon of loneliness. Whenever a man spoke to him as an equal it drove him crazy, and this was a fault, he understood that, a king's anger was always a fault, an angry king was like a god who made mistakes. And here was another contradiction in him. He was not only a barbarian philosopher and a crybaby killer, but also an egotist addicted to obsequiousness and sycophancy who nevertheless longed for a different world, a world in which he could find exactly that man who was his equal, whom he could meet as his brother, with whom he could speak freely, teaching and learning, giving and receiving pleasure, a world in which he could forsake the gloating satisfactions of conquest for the gentler yet more taxing joys of discourse. Did such a world exist? By what road could it be reached? Was there such a man anywhere in the world, or had he just executed him? What if the Rana of the mustache had been the only one? Had he just slain the only man on earth he might have loved? The emperor's thoughts grew vinous and sentimental, his eyes blurring with drunken tears.

How could he become the man he wanted to be? The *akbar,* the great one? How?

There was nobody to talk to. He had ordered his stone-deaf body-servant Bhakti Ram Jain away, out of his tent, so that he could drink in peace. A body-servant who could not hear his master's ramblings was a blessing but Bhakti Ram Jain had learned to read his lips now, which undid much of his value, making him an eavesdropper like everyone else. *The king is mad.* They said that: everyone said that. His soldiers his people his wives. Probably Bhakti Ram Jain said that as well. They did not say it to his face, for he was a giant of a man and a puissant warrior like a hero out of the ancient tales, and he was also the king of kings, and if such a one wished to be a little nutty then who were they to argue. The king, however, was not mad. The king was not content with being. He was striving to become.

Very well. He would keep his promise to the dead Kathiawari princeling. In the heart of his victory city he would build a house of adoration, a place of disputation where everything could be said to everyone by anyone on any subject, including the nonexistence of God and the abolition of kings. He would teach himself humility in that house. No, now he was being unfair to himself. Not "teach." Rather, he would remind himself of, and recover, the humility that was already lodged deep in his heart. This humble Akbar was perhaps his best self, created by the circumstances of his childhood in exile, clothed now in adult grandeur but still present nonetheless; a self born not in victory but in defeat. Nowadays it was all victories but the emperor knew all about defeat. Defeat was his father. Its name was Humayun.

He didn't like thinking about his father. His father had smoked too much opium, lost his empire, only got it back after he pretended to become a Shiite (and gave away the Koh-i-noor diamond) so that the King of Persia would give him an army to fight with, and then died by falling down a flight of library stairs almost immediately after he regained his throne. Akbar didn't know his father. He himself had been born in Sind, after Humayun's defeat at Chausa, when Sher Shah Suri became the king Humayun should have been but wasn't capable of being, and then off the deposed emperor scurried to Persia, abandoning his son. *His fourteen-month-old son.* Who was found and raised by his father's brother and enemy, Uncle Askari of Kandahar, wild man Uncle Askari who would have killed Akbar himself if he could ever have got close enough, which he didn't, because his wife was always in the way.

Akbar lived, because his aunt wanted him to.

And in Kandahar he was taught about survival, about fighting and killing and hunting, and he learned much else without being taught, such as looking out for himself and watching his tongue and not saying the wrong thing, the thing that might get him killed. About the dignity of the lost, about losing, and how it cleansed the soul to accept defeat, and about letting go, avoiding the trap of holding on too tightly to what you wanted, and about abandonment in general, and in particular fatherlessness, the lessness of fathers, the lessness of the fatherless, and the best defenses of those who are less against those who are more: inwardness, forethought, cunning, humility, and good peripheral vision. The many lessons of lessness. The lessening from which growing could begin.

There were things, however, which nobody thought to teach him, and which he would never learn. "We are the Emperor of India, Bhakti Ram Jain, but we can't write our own damn name," he shouted at his body-servant at dawn, as the old man helped him with his ablutions.

"Yes, O most blessed entity, father of many sons, husband of many wives, monarch of the world, encompasser of the earth," said Bhakti Ram Jain, handing him a towel. This time, the hour of the king's levee, was also the hour of imperial flattery. Bhakti Ram Jain proudly held the rank of Imperial Flatterer First Class, and was a master of the ornate, old-school style known as cumulative fawning. Only a man with an excellent memory for the baroque formulations of excessive encomia could fawn cumulatively, on account of the repetitions required and the necessary precision of the sequencing. Bhakti Ram Jain's memory was unerring. He could fawn for hours.

The emperor saw his own face scowling back at him from his basin of warm water like an augury of doom. "We are the king of kings, Bhakti Ram Jain, but we can't read our own laws. What do you say to that?" "Yes, O most just of judges, father of many sons, husband of many wives, monarch of the world, encompasser of the earth, ruler of all that is, bringer together of all being," said Bhakti Ram Jain, warming to his task.

"We are the Sublime Radiance, the Star of India, and the Sun of Glory," said the emperor, who knew a thing or two about flattery himself, "yet we were raised in that shit-hole dump of a town where men fuck women to make babies but fuck boys to make them men—raised watching out for the attacker who worked from behind as well as the warrior straight ahead."

"Yes, O dazzling light, father of many sons, husband of many wives, monarch of the world, encompasser of the earth, ruler of all that is, bringer together of all being, Sublime Radiance, Star of India, and Sun of Glory," said Bhakti Ram Jain, who might have been deaf but who knew how to take a hint.

"Is that how a king should be raised, Bhakti Ram Jain?" the emperor roared, tipping over the basin in his wrath. "Illiterate, ass-guarding, savage—is that what a prince should be?"

"Yes, O wiser than the Wise, father of many sons, husband of many wives, monarch of the world, encompasser of the earth, ruler of all that is, bringer together of all being, Sublime Radiance,

Star of India, Sun of Glory, master of human souls, forger of thy people's destiny," said Bhakti Ram Jain.

"You are pretending you can't read the words on our lips," the emperor shouted.

"Yes, O more insightful than the Seers, father of many—"

"You are a goat who should have his throat slit so that we can eat his meat for lunch."

"Yes, O more merciful than the gods, father—"

"Your mother fucked a pig to make you."

"Yes, O most articulate of all who articulate, f—"

"Never mind," said the emperor. "We feel better now. Go away. You can live."

$\{4\}$

And here again with bright silks flying

And here again with bright silks flying like banners from red palace windows was Sikri, shimmering in the heat like an opium vision. Here at last with its strutting peacocks and dancing girls was home. If the war-torn world was a harsh truth then Sikri was a beautiful lie. The emperor came home like a smoker returning to his pipe. He was the Enchanter. In this place he would conjure a new world, a world beyond religion, region, rank, and tribe. The most beautiful women in the world were here and they were all his wives. The most brilliant talents in the land were assembled here, among them the Nine Stars, the nine most brilliant of the most brilliant, and with their help there was nothing he could not accomplish. With their help his wizardry would magick all the land, and the future, and all eternity. An emperor was a bewitcher of the real, and with such accomplices his witchcraft could not fail. The songs of Tansen could break open the seals of the universe and let divinity through into the everyday world. The poems of Faizi opened windows in the heart and mind through which both light and darkness could be seen. The governance of Raja Man Singh and the financial skills of Raja Todar Mal meant the empire's business was in the best of hands. And then there was Birbal, the best of the nine who were the best of the best. His first minister, and first friend.

The first minister and greatest wit of the age greeted him at the Hiran Minar, the tower of elephants' teeth. The emperor's sense of mischief was aroused. "Birbal," Akbar said, dismounting from his horse, "will you answer us one question? We have been waiting a long time to ask it." The first minister of legendary wit and wisdom bowed humbly. "As you wish, *Jahanpanah,* Shelter of the World." "Well then," said Akbar, "which came first, the chicken or the egg?" Birbal replied at once, "The chicken." Akbar was taken aback. "How can you be so sure?" he wanted to know. "*Huzoor,*" Birbal replied, "I only promised to answer one question."

The first minister and the emperor were standing on the ramparts of the city looking out at the wheeling crows. "Birbal," Akbar mused, "how many crows do you imagine there are in my kingdom?" "*Jahanpanah,*" Birbal replied, "there are exactly nine hundred and ninety-nine thousand, nine hundred and ninety-nine." Akbar was puzzled. "Suppose we have them counted," he said, "and there are more than that, what then?" "That would mean," Birbal replied, "that their friends from the neighboring kingdom have come to visit them." "And if there are fewer?" "Then some of ours will have gone abroad to see the wider world."

A great linguist was waiting at Akbar's court, a visitor from a distant Western land: a Jesuit priest who could converse and dispute fluently in dozens of languages. He challenged the emperor to discover his native language. While the emperor was pondering the riddle, his first minister circled the priest and all of a sudden kicked him violently in the backside. The priest let out a series of oaths—not in Portuguese, but in Italian. "You observe, *Jahanpanah,*" said Birbal, "that when it's time to unleash a few insults, a man will always choose his mother tongue."

"If you were an atheist, Birbal," the emperor challenged his first minister, "what would you say to the true believers of all the great religions of the world?" Birbal was a devout Brahmin from Trivikrampur, but he answered unhesitatingly, "I would say to them that in my opinion they were all atheists as well; I merely believe in one god less than each of them." "How so?" the emperor asked. "All true believers have good reasons for disbelieving in every god except their own," said Birbal, "and so it is they who, between them, give me all the reasons for believing in none."

The first minister and the emperor were standing at the Khwabgah, the Place of Dreams, looking out over the still surface

of the Anup Talao, the monarch's private, formal pool, the Pool
Without Peer, the best of all possible pools, of which it was said
that when the kingdom was in trouble its waters would send a
warning. "Birbal," said Akbar, "as you know, our favorite queen
has the misfortune not to exist. Even though we love her best of
all, admire her above all the others, and value her above even the
lost Koh-i-noor, she is inconsolable. 'Your ugliest, most sour-
natured shrew of a wife is still made of flesh and blood,' she says.
'In the end I will not be able to compete with her.'" The first
minister advised the emperor, "*Jahanpanah,* you must say to her
that it is precisely *in the end* that her victory will be apparent to
everyone, for in the end none of the queens will exist any more
than she does, while she will have enjoyed a lifetime of your love,
and her fame will echo down the ages. Thus, in reality, while it is
true that she does not exist, it is also true to say that she is the one
who lives. If she did not, then over there, behind that high window, there would be nobody waiting for your return."

Jodha's sisters, her fellow wives, resented her. How could the
mighty emperor prefer the company of a woman who did not
exist? When he was gone, at least, she ought to absent herself as
well; she had no business to hang around with the actually existing.
She should disappear like the apparition she was, should slide into
a mirror or a shadow and be lost. That she did not, the living
queens concluded, was the sort of solecism one had to expect from
an imaginary being. How could she have been brought up to
know her manners when she had not been brought up at all? She
was an untutored figment, and deserved to be ignored.

The emperor had put her together, they fumed, by stealing bits
of them all. He said she was the daughter of the prince of Jodhpur.
She was not! That was another queen, and she was not the Maharajah's daughter, but the sister. The emperor also believed his
fictitious beloved was the mother of his firstborn son, his long-

awaited firstborn son, conceived because of the blessing of a saint, that very saint beside whose hilltop hovel this victory city had been built. But she was not Prince Salim's mother, as Prince Salim's real mother, Rajkumari Hira Kunwari, known as Mariam-uz-Zamani, daughter of Raja Bihar Mal of Amer, of the Clan Kachhwaha, grievingly told anybody who would listen. So: the limitless beauty of the imaginary queen came from one consort, her Hindu religion from another, and her uncountable wealth from yet a third. Her temperament, however, was Akbar's own creation. No real woman was ever like that, so perfectly attentive, so undemanding, so endlessly available. She was an impossibility, a fantasy of perfection. They feared her, knowing that, being impossible, she was irresistible, and that was why the king loved her best. They hated her for her theft of their histories. If they could have murdered her they would have done so, but until the emperor tired of her, or died himself, she was immortal. The idea of the emperor's death was not beyond contemplation, but so far the queens were not contemplating it. So far they bore their grievances in silence. "The emperor is mad," they grumbled inwardly, but sensibly forbore to utter the words. And when he was galloping around killing people they left the imaginary consort to her own devices. They never spoke her name. *Jodha, Jodhabai.* The words never crossed their lips. She wandered the palace quarter alone. She was a lonely shadow glimpsed through latticed stone screens. She was a cloth blown by the breeze. At night she stood under the little cupola on the top story of the Panch Mahal and scanned the horizon for the return of the king who made her real. The king, who was coming home from the wars.

Long before the unsettling arrival in Fatehpur Sikri of the yellow-haired liar from foreign parts with his tales of enchantresses and spells, Jodha had known that her illustrious husband must have had witchcraft in his blood. Everyone had heard about Genghis Khan's necromancy, his use of animal sacrifice and occult herbs, and how with the help of the black arts he managed to sire eight hundred thousand descendants. Everyone had heard the tale of how Timur the Lame had burned the Qur'ān and after conquering the earth had tried to ascend to the stars and conquer the heavens too. Everyone knew the story of how the emperor Babar had saved the dying Humayun's life by circling his sickbed and luring Death away from the boy to the father, sacrificing himself so that his son might live. These dark pacts with Death and the Devil were her husband's heritage, and her own existence the proof of how strong the magic was in him.

The creation of a real life from a dream was a superhuman act, usurping the prerogative of the gods. In those days Sikri was swarming with poets and artists, those preening egotists who claimed for themselves the power of language and image to conjure beautiful somethings from empty nothings, and yet neither poet nor painter, musician nor sculptor had come close to what the emperor, the Perfect Man, had achieved. The court was also full of foreigners, pomaded exotics, weather-beaten merchants, narrow-faced priests out of the West, boasting in ugly undesirable tongues about the majesty of their lands, their gods, their kings. Through a stone screen covering a high window on the upper story of her quarters she looked down at the great walled courtyard of the Seat of Public Audience and watched the thronging aliens strut and preen. When the emperor showed her the pictures they brought with them of their mountains and valleys she thought of the Himalayas and Kashmir and laughed at the foreigners' paltry approximations of natural beauty, their *vaals* and *aalps,* half-words to describe half-things. Their kings were savages, and they had nailed their god to a tree. What did she want with people as ridiculous as that?

Their stories didn't impress her either. She had heard from the emperor a traveler's tale of an ancient sculptor of the Greeks who brought a woman to life and fell in love with her. That narrative did not end well, and in any case was a fable for children. It could not be compared to her actual existence. Here, after all, she was. She quite simply was. Only one man on all the earth had ever achieved such a feat of creation by a pure act of will.

She wasn't interested in the foreign travelers, though she knew they fascinated the emperor. They came in search of . . . what, exactly? Nothing of use. If they had possessed any wisdom, the inutility of their journeying would have been obvious to them. Travel was pointless. It removed you from the place in which you had a meaning, and to which you gave meaning in return by dedicating your life to it, and it spirited you away into fairylands where you were, and looked, frankly absurd.

Yes: this place, Sikri, was a fairyland to them, just as their England and Portugal, their Holland and France were beyond her ability to comprehend. The world was not all one thing. "We are their dream," she had told the emperor, "and they are ours." She loved him because he never dismissed her opinions, never swatted them away with the majesty of his hand. "But imagine, Jodha," he told her while they slapped down *ganjifa* playing cards one evening, "if we could awake in other men's dreams and change them, and if we had the courage to invite them into ours. What if the whole world became a single waking dream?" She could not call him a fantasist when he spoke of waking dreams: for what else was she?

She had never left the palaces in which she had been born a decade earlier, born an adult, to the man who was not only her creator but her lover. It was true: she was both his wife and his child. If she left the palaces, or so she had always suspected, the spell would be broken and she would cease to exist. Perhaps she could do it if he, the emperor, were there to sustain her with the strength of his belief, but if she were alone she wouldn't have a chance. Fortunately, she had no desire to leave. The labyrinth of walled and curtained corridors that connected the various buildings of the palace complex afforded her all the possibilities of travel she required. This was her little universe. She lacked a conqueror's interest in elsewhere. Let the rest of the world be for others. This square of fortified stone was hers.

She was a woman without a past, separate from history, or, rather, possessing only such history as he had been pleased to bestow upon her, and which the other queens bitterly contested. The question of her independent existence, of whether she had one, insisted on being asked, over and over, whether she willed it or not. If God turned his face away from his creation, Man, would Man simply cease to be? That was the large-scale version of the question, but it was the selfish, small-scale versions that bothered her. Was her will free of the man who had willed her into being? Did she exist only because of his suspension of disbelief in the possibility of her existence? If he died, could she go on living?

She felt a quickening of her pulse. Something was about to happen. She felt herself strengthen, solidify. Doubts fled from her. *He was coming.*

The emperor had entered the palace complex and she could feel the power of his approaching need. Yes. Something was about to happen. She felt his footfall in her blood, could see him in herself, growing larger as he walked toward her. She was his mirror because he had created her that way but she was herself as well. Yes. Now that the act of creation was complete she was free to be the person he had created, free, as everyone was, within the bounds of what it was in their nature to be and do. How strong she suddenly was, how full of blood and rage. His power over her was far from absolute. All she had to be was coherent. She had never felt more coherent. Her nature rushed into her like a flood. She was not subservient. He did not like subservient women.

She would scold him first. How could he stay away so long? In his absence she had had to combat many plots. All was untrustworthy here. The very walls were filled with whispers. She fought them all and kept the palace safe against the day of his return, defeating the small, self-serving treacheries of the domestic staff, confounding the spying lizards hanging on the walls, stilling the scurry of conspiratorial mice. All this, while she felt herself fading, while the mere struggle for survival required the exercise of almost the full force of her will. The other queens . . . no, she would not mention the other queens. The other queens did not exist. Only she existed. She too was a sorceress. She was the sorceress of herself. There was only one man she needed to enchant and he was here. He was not going to the other queens. He was coming to what pleased him. She was full of him, of his desire for her, of the something that was about to happen. She was the scholar of his need. She knew everything.

The door opened. She existed. She was immortal, because she had been created by love.

He was wearing a cockaded golden turban and a coat of gold brocade. He was wearing the dust of his conquered land like a soldier's badge of honor. He was wearing a sheepish grin. "'I' wanted to get home faster," he said. "'I' was delayed." There was something awkward and experimental about his speech. What was the matter with him? She decided to ignore his uncharacteristic hesitancy and proceed as she had planned.

"Oh, you 'wanted,'" she said, standing upright, in her ordinary day clothes, pulling a silken headscarf across the lower portion of her face. "A man doesn't know what he wants. A man doesn't want what he says he wants. A man wants only what he needs."

He was puzzled by her refusal to acknowledge his descent into the first person, which honored her, which was supposed to make her swoon with joy, which was his newest discovery and his declaration of love. Puzzled, and a little put out.

"How many men have you known, that you are so knowledgeable," he said, frowning, approaching her. "Did you dream up men for yourself while 'I' was away, or did you find men to pleasure you, men who were not dreams. Are there men that 'I' must kill." Surely this time she would notice the revolutionary, the erotic newness of the pronoun? Surely now she would understand what he was trying to say?

She did not. She believed she knew what aroused him, and was thinking only of the words she had to say to make him hers.

"Women think less about men in general than the generality of men can imagine. Women think about their own men less often than their men like to believe. All women need all men less than all men need them. This is why it is so important to keep a good woman down. If you do not keep her down she will surely get away."

She hadn't dressed up to receive him. "If you want dolls," she said, "go over to the dollhouse where they're waiting for you, prettifying and squealing and pulling one another's hair." This was a mistake. She had mentioned the other queens. His brow furrowed and his eyes clouded over. She had made a false move. The spell had almost broken. She poured all the force of her eyes into his and he came back to her. The magic held. She raised her voice and continued.

She didn't flatter him. "You already look like an old man," she said. "Your sons will imagine you're their grandfather." She didn't congratulate him on his victories. "If history had gone down a different path," she said, "then the old gods would still rule, the gods you have defeated, the many-limbed many-headed gods, full of stories and deeds instead of punishments and laws, the gods of being standing beside the goddesses of doing, dancing gods, laughing gods, gods of thunderbolts and flutes, so many, many gods, and maybe that would have been an improvement." She knew she was beautiful and now, dropping the thin silk veil, she unleashed the beauty she had kept hidden and he was lost. "When a boy dreams up a woman he gives her big breasts and a small brain," she murmured. "When a king imagines a wife he dreams of me."

She was adept at the seven types of unguiculation, which is to say the art of using the nails to enhance the act of love. Before he left on his long journey she had marked him with the Three Deep Marks, which were scratches made by the first three fingers of her right hand upon his back, his chest, and on his testicles as well: something to remember her by. Now that he was home, she could make him shudder, could actually make his hair stand on end, by placing her nails on his cheeks and lower lip and breasts, without leaving any mark. Or she could mark him, leaving a half-moon shape upon his neck. She could push her nails slowly into his face for a long time. She could make long marks on his head and thighs and, again, his always sensitive breasts. She could perform the Hopping of the Hare, marking the areolas around his nipples without touching him anywhere else on his body. And no living woman was as skilled as she at the Peacock's Foot, that delicate maneuver: she placed her thumb on his left nipple and with her four other fingers she "walked" around his breast, digging in her long nails, her curved, clawlike nails which she had guarded and sharpened in anticipation of this very moment, pushing them into the emperor's skin until they left marks resembling the trail left by a peacock as it walks through mud. She knew what he would say while she did these things. He would tell her how, in the loneliness of his army tent, he would close his eyes and imitate her movements, would imagine his nails moving on his body to be hers, and be aroused.

She waited for him to say it, but he didn't. Something was different. There was an impatience in him now, even an irritation, an annoyance she did not understand. It was as if the many sophistications of the lover's art had lost their charms and he wished simply to possess her and be done with it. She understood that he had changed. And now everything else would change as well.

—∞—

As for the emperor, he never again referred to himself in the singular in the presence of another person. He was plural in the eyes of the world, plural even in the judgment of the woman who loved him, and plural he would remain. He had learned his lesson.

{ 5 }

His sons riding their horses at speed

His sons riding their horses at speed, aiming lances at tent-pegs in the ground; his sons, still on horseback, excelling at the game of *chaugan,* swinging long sticks with curved feet and striking a ball into a netted goal; his sons playing polo at night with a luminous ball; his sons on hunting parties, being initiated into the mysteries of leopard shooting by the master of the hunt; his sons taking part in the "game of love," *ishqbazi,* an affair of racing pigeons . . . how beautiful they were, his sons! How mightily they played! See the Crown Prince Salim, at only fourteen already so expert an archer that the rules of the sport were being rewritten to accommodate him. Ah, Murad, Daniyal, my gallopers, the emperor thought. How he loved them, and yet what wastrels they were! Look at their eyes: they were already drunk. They were eleven and ten years old and they were already drunk, drunk in charge of horses, the fools. He had given strict instructions to the staff, but these were princes of the blood, and no servant dared gainsay them.

He was having them spied on, of course, so he knew all about Salim's opium habit and nightly feats of perverted lechery. Perhaps it was understandable that a young fellow in the first flush of his potency should develop a fondness for sodomizing wenches, but a word in his ear would soon be necessary, because the dancing girls were complaining, their bruised rears, their vandalized pomegranate buds, made it harder for them to perform, the little whores.

O, alas, alas for his debauched children, flesh of his flesh, heir to all his failings and none of his strengths! Prince Murad's falling sickness had thus far been concealed from the populace at large, but for how long? And Daniyal seemed good for nothing, seemed to not have any personality at all, though he had inherited the family good looks, an achievement in which he could take no legitimate pride, although, in his preening vanity, he did. Was it harsh to judge a ten-year-old boy in this way? Yes, of course it was, but these were not boys. They were little gods, the despots of the future: born, unfortunately, to rule. He loved them. They would betray him. They were the lights of his life. They would come for him while he slept. The little assfuckers. He was waiting for their moves.

The king wished, today as he did every day, that he could trust his sons. He trusted Birbal and Jodha and Abul Fazl and Todar Mal but he kept the boys under close surveillance. He longed to trust them so that they could be the strong supports of his old age. He dreamed of relying on their six beautiful eyes when his own grew dim, and on their six strong arms when his own lost their power, acting in unison at his behest, so that he would truly become as a god, many-headed, multilimbed. He wanted to trust them because he thought of trust as a virtue and wished to cultivate it, but he knew the history of his blood, he knew that trustworthiness was not his people's habit. His sons would grow up into glittering heroes with excellent mustaches and they would turn against him, he could already see it in their eyes. Among their kind, among the Chaghatai of Ferghana, it was customary for children to plot against their crowned sires, to attempt to dethrone them, to imprison them in their own fortresses or on islands in lakes, or to execute them with their own swords.

Salim, bless him, the bloodthirsty wretch, was already dreaming up ingenious methods of killing people. *If anyone betrays me, papa, I will slaughter an ass and have the traitor sewn up inside the animal's freshly flayed wet skin. Then I will sit him backward on a donkey and parade him through the streets at noon and let the hot sun do its work.* The cruel sun which would dry the carcass so that it slowly contracted, so that the enemy within died slowly of a strangled suffocation. Where did you come up with an idea as nasty as that? the emperor asked his son. *I made it up,* the boy lied. *And who are you to speak of cruelty, papa. I myself saw you draw your sword and cut off the feet of that man who stole a pair of shoes.* The emperor knew the truth when he heard it. If there was a darkness in Prince Salim, then it had been inherited from the king of kings himself.

Salim was his favorite son, and his most likely assassin. When he was gone these three brothers would fight like dogs in the street over the meaty bone of his power. When he closed his eyes and listened to the galloping hoofs of his children at play he could see Salim leading a rebellion against him, and failing like the puny runt he was. *We will forgive him, of course, we will let him live, our son, so fine a horseman, so shiny, with such a kingly laugh.* The emperor sighed. He did not trust his sons.

The question of love was rendered more mysterious by such matters. The king loved the three boys galloping before him on the maidan. If he were to die at their hands, he would love the arm that delivered the fatal blow. However, he did not plan to let the young bastards do him in, not while there was breath in his body. He would see them in Hell first. He was the emperor, Akbar. Let no man trifle with him.

He had trusted the mystic Chishti whose tomb stood in the courtyard of the Friday Mosque, but Chishti was dead. He trusted dogs, music, poetry, a witty courtier, and a wife he had created out of nothing. He trusted beauty, painting, and the wisdom of his forebears. In other things, however, he was losing confidence; in, for example, religious faith. He knew that life was not to be trusted, the world was not to be relied on. On the gate of his great mosque he had carved his motto, which was not his own, but belonged, or so he had been told, to Jesus of Nazareth. *The world is a bridge. Pass over it but build no house upon it.* He didn't even believe his own motto, he scolded himself, for he had built not just a house, but an entire city. *Who hopes for an hour hopes for eternity. The world is an hour. What follows is unseen.* It's true, he acknowledged silently, I hope for too much. I hope for eternity. An hour's not enough for me. I hope for greatness, which is more than men should desire. (That "I" felt good when he said it to himself, it made him feel more intimate with himself, but it would remain a private matter, one that had been resolved.) I hope for long life, he thought, and for peace, for understanding, and a good meal in the afternoon. Above all these things I hope for a young man I can trust. That young man will not be my son but I will make him more than a son. I will make him my hammer and my anvil. I will make him my beauty and my truth. He will stand upon my palm and fill the sky.

That very day a yellow-haired young man was brought before him wearing an absurd long coat made up of particolored leather lozenges, and holding a letter from the Queen of England in his hand.

In the early morning Mohini the sleepless whore of the Hatyapul brothel awoke her foreign guest. He came awake quickly and twisted her roughly into his arms, conjuring a knife from thin air and holding it against her neck. "Don't be stupid," she said. "I could have killed you a hundred times last night, and don't think I didn't think about it while you were snoring loud enough to wake the emperor in his palace." She had offered him two rates, one for a single act, the other, only slightly higher, for the whole night. "Which is better value?" he asked her. "People always say it's the all-night rate," she replied gravely, "but most of my visitors are so old or drunk or opium-stupid or incompetent that even doing it once is beyond a lot of them, so the rate for a single will almost certainly save you money." "I'll pay you double the all-night rate," he said, "if you promise to stay beside me all night. It's a long time since I spent the whole night with a woman, and a woman's body lying beside me sweetens my dreams." "You can waste your money if you want, I won't stop you," she said cold-heartedly, "but there hasn't been any sweetness left in me for years."

She was so thin that her name among the other whores was Skeleton, and those clients who could afford it often hired her together with her antithesis, the obese whore called Mattress, in order to enjoy the two extremes of what the female form had to offer, first the unyielding dominance of bone and then the flesh that engulfed. The Skeleton ate like a wolf, greedily and fast, and the more she ate the fatter Mattress became, until it was suspected that the two whores had made a pact with the Devil, and in Hell it would be Skeleton who was grotesquely overweight for all eternity while Mattress rattled bonily around with the nipples on her flat chest looking like little wooden plugs.

She was a *doli-arthi* prostitute of the Hatyapul, meaning that the terms of her employment stated that she was literally married to the job and would only leave on her *arthi* or funeral bier. She had had to go through a parody of a wedding ceremony, arriving, to the mirth of the street rabble, on a donkey-cart instead of the usual *doli* or palanquin. "Enjoy your wedding day, Skeleton, it's the only one you'll ever have," shouted one lout, but the other prostitutes poured a chamber pot of warm urine over him from an upstairs balcony, and that shut him up just fine. The "groom" was the brothel itself, represented symbolically by the madam, Rangili Bibi, a whore so old, toothless, and squinty that she had become worthy of respect, and so fierce that everyone was scared of her, even the police officers whose job it theoretically was to close her business down, but who didn't dare make a move against her in case she gave them a lifetime's bad luck by fixing them with the evil eye. The other, more rational explanation for the brothel's survival was that it was owned by an influential noble of the court— or else, as the city's gossips were convinced, not a noble but a priest, maybe even one of the mystics praying nonstop at the Chishti tomb. But nobles go in and out of favor, and priests as well. Bad luck, on the other hand, is forever: so the fear of Rangili

Bibi's crossed eyes was at least as powerful as an unseen holy or aristocratic protector.

Mohini's bitterness was not the result of being a whore, which was a job like any other job and gave her a home, and food and clothing, without which, she said, she would be no better than a pye-dog and would in all likelihood die like a dog in a ditch. It was aimed at one single woman, her former employer, the fourteen-year-old Lady Man Bai of Amer, currently residing at Sikri, a young hussy who was already receiving, in secret, the eager attentions of her cousin Crown Prince Salim. Lady Man Bai had one hundred slaves, and Mohini the Skeleton was one of her favorites. When the prince arrived perspiring from the hard work of galloping around killing animals in the heat of the day, Mohini was at the head of the retinue whose task it was to remove all his clothes and massage his pale skin with scented, cooling oils. Mohini was the one who chose the perfume, sandalwood or musk, patchouli or rose, and Mohini it was who performed the privileged function of massaging his man-hood to prepare him for her mistress. Other slaves fanned him and rubbed his hands and feet, but only the Skeleton could touch the royal sex. This was because of her expertise in preparing the unguents necessary for the heightening of sexual desire and the pro-longation of sexual congress. She made the pastes of tamarind and cinnabar, or dry ginger and pepper which, when mixed with the honey of a large bee, gave a woman intense pleasure without re-quiring much exertion from the man, and allowed the man also to experience sensations of warmth and a kind of squeezing palpitation that were extremely pleasurable. She applied the pastes sometimes to her mistress's vagina, sometimes to the prince's member, usually to both. The results were held by both parties to be excellent.

It was her mastery of the male drugs known as the "ones that made men into horses" that undid her. One day she ordered the castration of a male goat and boiled its testes in milk, after which she salted and peppered them, fried them in ghee, and finally chopped them up into a delicious-tasting mince. This preparation was to be eaten, not rubbed upon the body, and she fed it to the prince on a silver spoon, explaining that it was a medicine that would allow him to make love like a horse, five, ten, or even twenty times without losing his force. In the case of particularly virile young men it could facilitate one hundred consecutive ejaculations. "Delicious," said the prince, and ate heartily. The next morning he emerged from his mistress's boudoir, leaving her on the point of death. "Ha! Ha!" he shouted at Mohini on his way out. "That was fun."

It would be forty-seven days and nights before Lady Man Bai could even think about having sex again, and during that time the prince, when he visited her, was fully understanding of the damage he had wrought, behaved in a manner both contrite and solicitous, and fucked the slaves instead, asking, most often, for the favors of the skinny creature who had endowed him with such superhuman sexual powers. Lady Man Bai could not refuse him but inwardly she raged with jealousy. When it became plain after the notorious night of one hundred and one copulations that Mohini the Skeleton's tolerance for sex was infinite and that the prince was incapable of breaking her as he had almost broken his mistress, the slave girl's fate was sealed. The jealousy of Lady Man Bai grew implacable and Mohini was expelled from the household, leaving with nothing but her knowledge of the preparations that drove men mad with desire. She fell a long way, from palace to brothel, but her powers of enchantment served her well and made her the most popular of the women of the bawdy house at the Hatyapul. She hoped, however, for revenge. "If fate ever brings that little bitch into my power I will smear her with a paste so powerful that even the jackals will come to fuck her. She will be fucked by crows and snakes and lepers and water buffaloes and in the end there will be nothing left of her but a few soggy strands of her hair, which I will burn, and that will be the end of it. But she is going to marry Prince Salim, so pay no attention to me. For a woman like myself revenge is an unattainable luxury, like partridges, or childhood."

For some reason she was talking to the yellow-haired new-comer as she had never spoken to any of her tricks, perhaps because of his exotic appearance, his yellow hair, his cleansing alienness. "You must have put a spell on me," she said, in a disturbed voice, "because I never let any of my visitors even see me by daylight, much less tell them the story of my life." She had lost her virginity at the age of eleven to her father's brother, and the baby that was born was a monster which her mother took away and drowned without showing it to her for fear that if she saw it she would begin to hate the future. "She needn't have worried," Mohini said, "because as it happens I was blessed with an equable disposition and a fondness for the sex act which not even that thimble-cock ox of a despoiler could change. But I was never a warm person and since the injustice I suffered at the hands of Lady Man Bai the chill in my vicinity has increased. In the summer men like the cooling effect of my proximity but in winter I don't get so much work."

"Prepare me," said the yellow-haired man. "Because today I have to go to court on important business, and I must be at my best or perish."

"If you can afford it," she answered, "I'll make you smell as desirable as any king."

She began to turn his body into a symphony for the nose, for which she told him that the price would be one gold mohur coin. "I'm overcharging you, naturally," she warned him, but he simply shook his left wrist, and she gasped when she saw the three gold coins held between his four fingers. "Do a good job," he said, and gave her all three. "For three gold mohurs," she said, "people will believe you're an angel from Paradise if that's what you want them to think, and when you're finished up there doing whatever it is you have to do, you can have me and the Mattress together, satisfying your wildest dreams for a week for nothing extra."

She sent for a metal washtub and filled it herself, mingling hot and cold water in the ration of one bucket to three. Next she soaped him all over with a soap made from aloe, sandal, and camphor, "to make your skin fresh and open before I put on your royal airs." Then from beneath the bed she produced her magic box of fragrances wrapped up in a careful cloth. "Before you reach the emperor's presence you will have to satisfy many other men," she said. "So the perfume for the emperor will lie hidden at first beneath the fragrances that will please lesser personages, which will fade away when you reach the imperial presence." After that she got to work, anointing him with civet and violet, magnolia and lily, narcissus and calembic, as well as drops of other occult fluids whose names he did not even like to ask, fluids extracted from the sap of Turkish, Cypriot, and Chinese trees, as well as a wax from the intestines of a whale. By the time she had finished he was convinced he smelled like a cheap whorehouse, which was where he was, after all, and he regretted his decision to ask for the Skeleton's help. But out of courtesy he kept his regrets to himself. He took out of his little carpetbag clothes of a finery that made the Skeleton gasp. "Did you murder somebody to get those or are you really a somebody after all?" she wondered. He didn't answer. To look like a person of consequence on the road was to attract the attentions of men of violence; to look like a hobo at court was an idiocy of a different kind. "I have to go," he said. "Come back later," she told him. "Remember what I said about the free offer."

He put on his inevitable overcoat in spite of the budding heat of the morning and set off to do what he had to do. Miraculously the perfumes of the Skeleton went ahead of him and smoothed his way. Instead of shooing him off and telling him to go to the gate on the city's far side, to wait in line for permission to enter the Courtyard of Public Audience, the guards went out of their way to assist him, sniffing the air as if it bore good news and bursting into improbable welcoming smiles. The chief of the guardhouse dispatched a runner to fetch a royal adjutant, who arrived looking irritable about being summoned. As he approached the visitor there was a shift in the breeze and an entirely new scent filled the air, a scent whose subtlety was too delicate for the guards' coarse noses, but which made the adjutant think all of a sudden of the first girl he had ever loved. He volunteered to go personally to the house of Birbal to arrange things, and returned to say that all necessary approvals had been given, and he now had the authority to invite the visitor to enter the palace quarters. The visitor was asked, inevitably, for his name, and he answered without hesitation.

"You may call me Mogor," he said in immaculate Persian. "Mogor dell'Amore, at your service. A gentleman of Florence, presently on business for England's queen." He was wearing a velvet hat with a white feather in it, held in place by a mustard-colored jewel, and doffing this hat he bent down in a low bow that showed everyone watching (for he had attracted a substantial crowd, whose dreamy-eyed, grinning faces proved once again the omniscient power of the Skeleton's work) that he possessed a courtier's skill, politeness, and grace. "Mr. Ambassador," said the adjutant, bowing in return. "This way, please."

Yet a third fragrance had now been released as the earlier scents faded away, and this one filled the air with fantasies of desire. As he walked through the red world of the palaces the man who now went by the name of Mogor dell'Amore noticed the fluttering movements behind curtained windows and latticed screens. In the darkness of the windows he imagined that he could make out a host of shining almond eyes. Once he saw a jeweled hand making an ambiguous gesture that might have been an invitation. He had underestimated the Skeleton. In her way she was an artist to rival any that could be found in this fabled city of painters, poets, and song. "Let us see what she has in store for the emperor," he thought. "If it's as seductive as these early scents then I'm home and dry." He held on tightly to the Tudor scroll and his stride lengthened as his confidence grew.

At the center of the main chamber of the House of Private Audience was a red sandstone tree from which there hung what seemed to the visitor's untutored eye to be a great bunch of stylized stone bananas. Wide "branches" of red stone ran from the top of the tree trunk to the four corners of the room. Between these branches hung canopies of silk, embroidered in silver and gold; and under the canopies and bananas, with his back to the thick trunk of the stone tree, stood the most frightening man in the world (with one exception): a small, sugary man of enormous intellect and girth, beloved of the emperor, hated by envious rivals, a flatterer, a fawner, an eater of thirty pounds of food each day, a man capable of ordering his cooks to prepare one thousand different dishes for the evening meal, a man for whom omniscience was not a fantasy but a minimum requirement of life.

This was Abul Fazl, the man who knew everything (except foreign languages and the many uncouth tongues of India, all of which eluded him, so that he cut an unusual, monoglot figure in that multitongued Babel of a court). Historian, spymaster, brightest of the Nine Stars, and second-closest confidant of the most frightening man in the world (with no exceptions), Abul Fazl knew the true story of the creation of the world, which he had heard, he said, from the angels themselves, and he knew, too, how much fodder the horses in the imperial stables were allowed to eat each day, and the approved recipe for biryani, and why slaves had been renamed *disciples,* and the history of the Jews, and the order of the heavenly spheres, and the Seven Degrees of Sin, the Nine Schools, the Sixteen Predicaments, the Eighteen Sciences, and the Forty-two Unclean Things. He was also apprised, through his network of informants, of every single thing that went on in every language within the walls of Fatehpur Sikri, all the whispered secrets, all the treacheries, all the indulgences, all the promiscuities, so that every person within those walls was also at his mercy, or at the mercy of his pen, of which King Abdullah of Bokhara had said that it was more to be feared than even Akbar's sword: saving only the most frightening man in the world (with no exceptions), who was afraid of nobody, and who was, of course, the emperor, his lord.

Abul Fazl stood in profile like a king and did not turn to look at the newcomer. He remained silent for so long that it became plain that an insult was intended. The ambassador of Queen Elizabeth understood that this was the first test he had to pass. He too remained silent and in that dreadful hush each man learned much about the other. "You think you are telling me nothing," the traveler thought, "but I see from your magnificence and rudeness, from your corpulence and stern visage, that you are the exemplar of a world in which hedonism coexists with suspicion, violence— for this silence is a form of violent assault—walks hand in hand with the contemplation of beauty, and that the weakness of this universe of overindulgence and vindictiveness is vanity. Vanity is the enchantment in whose spell you are all held captive, and it is through my knowledge of that vanity that I will achieve my goal."

Then the most frightening man in the world (with one exception) spoke at last, as if in reply to the other's thoughts. "Excellency," he said, sardonically, "I perceive that you have perfumed yourself with the fragrance devised for the seduction of kings, and I deduce that you are not entirely innocent of our ways—in fact, not an innocent at all. I did not trust you when I first heard about you some moments ago, and now that I have smelled you I trust you even less." The yellow-haired Mogor dell'Amore intuited that Abul Fazl was the original author of the spell-book of unguents whose formulas Mohini the Skeleton had become adept at using, so that these olfactory enchantments had no power over him, and as a result they lost their influence over everyone else as well. The guards with goofy grins at the four entrances to the House of Private Audience suddenly came to their senses, the veiled slave girls waiting to serve the august company lost their air of dreamy eroticism, and the newcomer understood that he was like a man stripped naked beneath the all-seeing gaze of the king's favorite, and that only the truth, or something as convincing as the truth, would save him now.

"When the ambassador of King Philip of Spain came to visit us," Abul Fazl reflected, "he brought a full retinue, and elephants laden with gifts, and twenty-one gift horses of finest Arab stock, and jewels. By no means did he show up on a bullock-cart and spend the night in a whorehouse with a woman so thin that one can wonder whether she is a woman at all."

"My master, Lord Hauksbank of That Ilk, unfortunately joined God and his angels as we made landfall at Surat," the new-comer replied. "On his deathbed he bade me fulfill the duty with which Her Majesty had charged him. Alas, the ship's company was swarming with rogues, and before his body was cold they com-menced to plunder and ransack his quarters in search of whatever of value my good master may have possessed. I confess that it was only by good fortune that I escaped with my life and the queen's letter as well, for, knowing me to be my master's honest servant, they would have cut my throat had I stayed to defend Lord Hauks-bank's property. I fear, now, that his remains may not receive a Christian burial, but am proud to have arrived at your great city to discharge his responsibility, which has become mine."

"The Queen of England," Abul Fazl mused, "has been, I be-lieve, no friend to our friend the illustrious King of Spain."

"Spain is a philistine bully," the other improvised swiftly, "whereas England is the home of art and beauty and of Gloriana herself. Do not be blinded by the blandishments of Philip the Dull. Like must speak to like, and it is Elizabeth of England who is the true reflection of the emperor's greatness and style." Warming to his theme, he explained that the faraway redhead queen was noth-ing less than the Western mirror of the emperor himself, she was Akbar in female form, and he, the Shahanshah, the king of kings, could be said to be an Eastern Elizabeth, mustachioed, nonvir-ginal, but in the essence of their greatness they were the same.

Abul Fazl stiffened. "You dare to set my master no higher than a woman," he said softly. "You are fortunate indeed to be holding that scroll which bears, as I see, the authentic seal of the crown of England, and therefore obliges us to give you safe conduct. Other-wise it would be my inclination to reward such insolence by throwing you to the rogue elephant we keep tethered on a nearby lawn, to rid us of unacceptable swine."

"The emperor is famous throughout the world for his generous appreciation of women," said Mogor dell'Amore. "I am sure he will not be insulted, as the jewel of the East, to be likened to another great jewel, whatever her sex."

"The Nazarene sages sent to this court by the Portuguese of Goa speak poorly of your jewel." Abul Fazl shrugged. "They say she is against God, and a puny ruler who will surely soon be crushed. They say that hers is a nation of thieves and that you are in all probability a spy."

"The Portuguese are pirates," said Mogor dell'Amore. "They are buccaneers and scoundrels. No wise man should trust what they say."

"Father Acquaviva of the Society of Jesus is an Italian like yourself," Abul Fazl rejoined, "and Father Monserrate his companion comes from Spain."

"If they come here under the flag of the scurrilous Portugee," the other insisted, "then Portugee pirate dogs is what they have become."

Loud laughter broke out from a place above their heads, as if a god were mocking him.

"Have mercy, great *munshi,*" a huge voice boomed. "Let the young man live, at least until we have read the message he brings." The silken canopies fell away to the corners of the chamber and there, above them, seated on the cushioned top of the sandstone tree in the Position of Royal Ease, and dissolving into mirthful guffaws, was Abul-Fath Jalaluddin Muhammad Akbar, the Grand Mughal himself, revealed to view, and looking like a giant parrot on an outsize perch.

———

He had woken up in an oddly fretful mood, and not even his beloved's most skilled ministrations had calmed him. In the middle of the night a disoriented crow had somehow entered Queen

Jodha's bedchamber and the royal couple had been awoken by its terrified cawing, which the sleep-heavy emperor heard as an intimation of the end of the world. For one terrifying instant a black wing brushed his cheek. By the time the servants shooed the crow out again the emperor's nerves were jangling. After that his sleep was filled with portents. At one point he seemed to see the black beak of that apocalyptic crow reaching into his chest and pulling out his heart to eat it, as Hind of Mecca on the battlefield of Uhud had eaten the heart of the fallen Hamza, the Prophet's uncle. If that mighty hero could fall to a cowardly javelin then he, too, might be felled at any moment by an arrow from the dark, flying as the crow flies, ugly, deadly, and black. If a crow could get past all the defenses of his guards and flap its wings in his face, then might not a murderer be able to do the same?

Thus, full of forebodings of death, he was defenseless against the advent of love.

—·\\\·—

The arrival of the rogue calling himself the English ambassador had intrigued him and after he ordered Abul Fazl to have some sport with the fellow his spirits began to lighten. Abul Fazl, in reality the most companionable of men, was better at performing ferocity than anyone in Sikri, and as the emperor listened to the fun below him, hidden as he was above the heads of the two men, the interrogator and the interrogated, the clouds of the night dissipated at last, and were forgotten. "The charlatan has acquitted himself well," he thought. When he pulled the tasseled cords that released the silk canopies and revealed his presence to the men below, he was in a thoroughly affable frame of mind, but quite unprepared for the emotion that assailed him when his eyes met those of the yellow-haired visitor.

It was love, or felt like it. The emperor's pulse quickened like an infatuated young girl's, his breathing deepened, and the color rose in his cheeks. How handsome this young man was, how sure of himself, how proud. And there was something in him that could not be seen: a secret that made him more interesting than a hundred courtiers. How old was he? The emperor was not good at judging *farangi* faces. He might have been as young as twenty-five, or as old as thirty, "older than our sons," the emperor thought, "and too old to be a son to us," and then he wondered that such a thought had come into his head. Was the foreigner some sort of witch, he asked himself. Was he being enchanted by an occult charm? Well, he would go along with it, there was no harm in that, he was too wily to be caught by any hidden knife or to drink poison from a doctored cup. He would follow his feelings to see what had caused them. The absence of surprise is the necessary penalty of the life of power, the emperor had set up elaborate systems and machineries to make sure he was never surprised about anything, and yet this Mogor dell'Amore had caught him off guard, whether by accident or design. For that reason alone he deserved to be more fully known.

"Read us the queen's letter," Akbar commanded, and the "ambassador" bowed absurdly low, with theatrical flourishes of the wrist, and when he rose up again the scroll was hanging open even though neither Akbar nor Abul Fazl had witnessed the breaking of the seal. "A sleight-of-hand artist," the emperor thought. "We like that." The charlatan read the letter in English and then translated it smoothly into the Persian tongue. "Most invincible and most mightie prince," Queen Elizabeth wrote, "Lord Zelabdim Echebar, King of Cambaya, greeting." Abul Fazl gave a horsy snort of laughter. "'Zelabdim'?" he scoffed. "And who might this 'Echebar' be?" The emperor above him slapped his thigh for joy. "We are he," he chortled. "We are the *padishah* Echebar, lord of the fairy-tale kingdom of Cambaya. O poor benighted England, We pity thy people for that thy queen is an ignorant dunce."

The letter-reader paused to allow the laughter to subside. "Go on, go on." The emperor waved at him. "King 'Zelabdim' commands it." Then more laughter, and the discovery of a kerchief to wipe away his tears.

The "ambassador" bowed again, even more elaborately than before, and continued; and by the time he was done a second spell had been woven. "In matters of Trade and other purposes of mutual advantage we ask alliance," he read. "It has come to our notice that Your Majestie has declared himself Infallible, and we assure you we do not question the *auctoritas* of that mightie Claim. However, there is one Other who claims as much for Himself, and be in no doubt that we are assured that it is this Other who is the Fraud. We refer, great Monarch, to that unworthy Priest, the Bishop of Rome, the thirteenth Gregory of that inglorious Sequence, whose designs upon the Orient you would be Wise not to discount. If he sends priests to Cambaya, China, and Japan, this is not mere holiness, we do assure you. This same Bishop is presently preparing War against us, and his Catholic servants are treacherous presences at your Court, for they scheme his conquests to come.

"Beware these lackeys of your Rival! Make alliance with us, and we will defeat all foes. For I know I have the body of a weak and feeble woman, but I have the heart and stomach of a King, and of a king of England too, and I think foul scorn that any Pope in Rome should dare dishonor me, nor my allies neither. For I have not only my own *auctoritas,* but *potestas* as well, and that potency will make me the victor in the fight. And when they are all destroyed and blown to the four winds, then will you be glad you made common cause with England."

When the "ambassador" finished reading, the emperor realized that he had fallen in love for a second time within the space of a few minutes, because now he was possessed by a great desire for the author of the letter, England's queen. "Abul Fazl," he cried, "shall we not marry this great lady without delay? This virgin queen, Rani Zelabat Giloriana Pehlavi? We think we must have her at once."

"Excellent idea," said the "ambassador" Mogor dell'Amore.

"And here in this locket is her picture, which she sends you with her affectionate regard, and which will bewitch you with her beauty, which surpasses even the beauty of her words." With a flourish of the lace cuffs at his wrist he produced the golden charm, which Abul Fazl took with a look of profound suspicion. Abul Fazl was seized by the conviction that they were getting into deep water, and that the consequence of this Mogor's presence among them would be immense, and not necessarily to their benefit, but when he attempted to caution his master against this new involvement the world's most frightening man (with no exceptions) waved his worries away.

"The letter is charming and so is he who bears it," Akbar said. "Bring him to our private rooms tomorrow so that we can speak further." The audience was over.

The sudden infatuation of the emperor Zelabdin Echebar with his female mirror image Queen Zelabat Giloriana the First resulted in a stream of love letters which were carried to England by accredited royal messengers, and never answered. The rhapsodic letters bore the emperor's personal seal and were of an emotional intensity and sexual explicitness that was unusual in the Europe (and the Asia) of the period. Many of these letters failed to reach their destination because the messengers were waylaid by enemies along the way, and from Kabul to Calais these intercepted outpourings provided rich amusement for nobles and princes delighted by the Emperor of India's crazy declarations of undying affection for a woman he had never met, as well as his megalomaniac fantasies of creating a joint global empire that united the eastern and western hemispheres. Those letters that did arrive at Whitehall Palace were treated as forgeries, or the work of a pseudonymous crank, and their carriers were given short shrift, many of them ending up in jail as their poor reward for a long and dangerous journey. After a time they were simply refused admission and those who managed to limp back across the world to Fatehpur Sikri returned with embittered words. "That queen is a virgin because no man would wish to lie with so cold a fish," they reported, and after a year and a day Akbar's love vanished as swiftly and mysteriously as it had appeared, perhaps because of the revolt of his queens, who united for once behind his nonexistent beloved to threaten the withdrawal of their favors unless he stopped sending fancy letters to that Englishwoman whose silence, coming after her own initial blandishments had aroused the emperor's interest, proved the insincerity of her character and the folly of attempting to understand such an alien and unattractive personage, especially when so many more loving and desirable ladies were so much closer to hand.

Near the end of his long reign, many years after the time of the charlatan Mogor dell'Amore had passed, the aging emperor nostalgically remembered that strange affair of the letter from the Queen of England, and asked to see it again. When it was brought to him and translated by a different interpreter much of the original text had disappeared. The surviving document was found to contain no references to his own infallibility or the Pope's; nor did it ask for an alliance against common foes. It was in fact no more than a plain request for good trading terms for English merchants, accompanied by some routine expressions of respect. When the emperor learned the truth he understood all over again how daring a sorcerer he had encountered on that long-ago morning after the dream of the crow. By then, however, the knowledge was of no use to him, except to remind him of what he should never have forgotten, that witchcraft requires no potions, familiar spirits, or magic wands. Language upon a silvered tongue affords enchantment enough.

{ 6 }

When the sword of the tongue is drawn

When the sword of the tongue is drawn, the emperor thought, *it inflicts deeper cuts than the sharpest blade.* If he needed proof it was to be found in the war of the philosophers that took place each day in this very place: the embroidered and mirrorworked Tent of the New Worship. There was a constant hubbub here, the noise of the kingdom's finest thinkers gashing one another dreadfully with their words. Akbar had kept the vow he had made on the day he chopped up the insolent Rana of Cooch Naheen, and had created a debating chamber in which the adoration of the divine was reimagined as an intellectual wrestling match in which no holds were barred. He had invited Mogor dell'Amore to accompany him to the Tent so that he could show off his new invention, impress upon the newcomer the splendid originality and progressiveness of the Mughal court, and, not incidentally, demonstrate to the Jesuits sent by Portugal that they were not the only Westerners to have access to the imperial ear.

Inside the Tent the participants reclined on carpets and bolsters, grouped into two camps, the Water Drinkers and the Wine Lovers, who faced each other across a nave which was empty except for the seats of the emperor and his guest. The *manqul* party containing the religious thinkers and mystics drank only water, while their opponents the *ma'qul* celebrated pure philosophy and the sciences and poured wine down their throats all day long. Abul Fazl and Raja Birbal were here today, both seated as usual among the wine fanciers. Prince Salim, too, was visiting, a surly teenage presence alongside the puritanical water-only leader Badauni, a thin line of a man—one of those young men who seemed to have been born old—who detested the older Abul Fazl and was heartily loathed by that spherical worthy in return. Arguments raged between them, in terms so intemperate ("Fat sycophant!" "Tedious termite!") that the emperor found himself wondering how such discord could ever lead to the harmony he sought; was freedom indeed the road to unity, or was chaos its inevitable result?

Akbar had decided that this revolutionary temple would not be a permanent building. Argument itself—and no deity, however multilimbed or almighty—would here be the only god. But reason was a mortal divinity, a god that died, and even if it was subsequently reborn it inevitably died again. Ideas were like the tides of the sea or the phases of the moon; they came into being, rose, and grew in their proper time, and then ebbed, darkened, and vanished when the great wheel turned. They were temporary dwellings, like tents, and a tent was their proper home. Mughal tent-makers were geniuses in their own way, creating collapsible houses of great complexity and beauty. When the army marched it was accompanied by a second army of two and a half thousand men (to say nothing of elephants and camels) who raised and lowered the little tent-city in which the king and his men resided. These portable pagodas, pavilions, and palaces had even inspired the stonemasons of Sikri—but a tent was still a tent, a thing of canvas, cloth, and wood that well represented the impermanence of the things of the mind. One day, a hundred years from now when even his great empire was no more—yes! in this place he was willing to foresee even the destruction of his own creation!—his descendants would see the tent pulled down and all his glory vanish. "Only when we accept the truths of death," the emperor declared, "can we begin to learn the truths of being alive."

"Paradox, sire," Mogor dell'Amore answered cheekily, "is a knot that allows a man to seem intelligent even as it is trussing his brain like a hen bound for the pot. 'In death lies the meaning of life!' 'A man's wealth engenders his soul's poverty!' And so violence may become gentleness, and ugliness beauty, and any blessed thing its opposite. This is indeed a hall of mirrors, full of illusions and inversions. A man may wallow in the bogs of paradox until his last day without ever thinking a clear thought worthy of the name." The emperor felt within him a surge of the same blind fury that had caused him to tear off the Rana of Cooch Naheen's offensive mustache. Had his ears deceived him?—By what right did this foreign scoundrel . . . ?—How did he dare . . . ? The emperor realized that his face had purpled and that he had begun to spit and splutter in his wrath. The gathering fell into a silent terror, for Akbar in a rage was capable of anything, he could tear down the sky with his bare hands or rip out the tongues of everyone within hearing distance to make sure they could never talk about what they had witnessed or he could suck out your soul and drown it in a bowl of your bubbling blood.

It was Prince Salim, urged on by Badauni, who broke the scandalized silence. "Do you understand," he said to the interloper in the strange hot overcoat, "that you could die for what you have just said to the king?" Mogor dell'Amore looked (though perhaps he did not entirely feel) unabashed. "If I can die for such a thing in this city," he replied, "then it's not a city worth living in. And besides, I understood that in this tent it was reason, not the king, that ruled." The silence thickened like curdled milk. Akbar's face blackened. Then all of a sudden the storm passed, and the emperor began to laugh. He slapped Mogor dell'Amore on the back and nodded vigorously. "Gentlemen, an outsider has taught us a great lesson," he said. "One must stand outside a circle to see that it is round."

Now it was the turn of the Crown Prince to feel the rage of public rebuke, but he sat down without saying anything. The look on his rival Badauni's face pleased Abul Fazl so much that he began to warm toward the yellow-haired foreigner who had so unexpectedly charmed the king. As for the newcomer, he understood that his gamble had succeeded, but that in bringing off the

feat he had made a powerful enemy, who was all the more dangerous for being an immature and evidently petulant adolescent. *The
Skeleton is hated by the prince's lady and now the prince hates me,* he
thought. *This is not a quarrel that we are likely to win.* However, he
allowed none of his qualms to show, and accepted, with the most
flamboyant bows and flourishes he could muster, Raja Birbal's
offer of a glass of fine red wine.

The emperor too was thinking about his son. What a joy his
birth had been! But perhaps after all it had been unwise to place
him in the care of the mystics, the followers and successors of
Sheikh Salim Chishti after whom the prince had been named. The
boy had grown up to be a tangled mass of contradictions, a lover
of the delicacy and care of gardening but also of the indolence of
opium, a sexualist among the puritans, a pleasure lover who
quoted the most diehard thinkers and derided Akbar's favorites,
saying, *seek not for light from the eyes of the blind.* Not his own line of
course. The boy was a mimicking mynah bird, a puppet capable of
being used against him by whoever got hold of his strings.

Whereas, by contrast, and on the other hand, behold this foreigner so in love with argument that he dared fling a rationalist's
taunt at the emperor's amazed face, and to do it in public, which
was worse. Here, perhaps, was a man a king might talk to in ways
that his own flesh and blood would not understand, or would be
bored by. When he killed the Rana of Cooch Naheen he had wondered if he had murdered the only man who might have understood him and whom he might have been able to love. Now fate,
as if in answer to his grief, had perhaps offered him a second such
confidant, perhaps even an improvement on the first, for this was
not merely a talker but an adventurer too. A man of reason who in
reason's name took unreasonable risks. A paradoxical fellow who
disparaged paradox. The rogue was no less contradictory than
Prince Salim—no less contradictory, perhaps, than any man alive—
but these were contradictions that the emperor could enjoy. Could
he open his heart to this Mogor and tell him things that he had

never said, not even to Bhakti Ram Jain the deaf flatterer, or Birbal the wit, or omniscient Abul Fazl? Was this his confessor at last?

For there were so many things he wanted to talk about, things not even Abul Fazl or Birbal would fully understand, things he was not yet prepared to air in the open debate of the Tent of the New Worship. He wanted, for example, to investigate why one should hold fast to a religion not because it was true but because it was the faith of one's fathers. Was faith not faith but simple family habit? Maybe there was no true religion but only this eternal handing down. And error could be handed down as easily as virtue. Was faith no more than an error of our ancestors?

Maybe there was no true religion. Yes, he had allowed himself to think this. He wanted to be able to tell someone of his suspicion that men had made their gods and not the other way around. He wanted to be able to say, it is man at the center of things, not God. It is man at the heart and the bottom and the top, man at the front and the back and the side, man the angel and the devil, the miracle and the sin, man and always man, and let us henceforth have no other temples but those dedicated to mankind. This was his most unspeakable ambition: to found the religion of man. In the Tent of the New Worship the Winemen and the Waterers were calling one another heretics and fools. The emperor wanted to confess his secret disappointment in all mystics and philosophers. He wanted to sweep the whole argument aside, to erase the centuries of inheritance and reflection, and allow man to stand naked as a baby upon the throne of heaven. (If man had created god then man could uncreate him too. Or was it possible for a creation to escape the power of the creator? Could a god, once created, become impossible to destroy? Did such fictions acquire an autonomy of the will that made them immortal? The emperor did not have the answers, but the questions themselves felt like answers of a kind.) Could foreigners grasp what his countrymen could not? If he, Akbar, stepped outside the circle, could he live without its comforting circularity, in the terrifying strangeness of a new thought?

"We will go," he told his guest. "We have heard enough great thoughts for one day."

Because an eerie illusion of calm spread over the imperial complex as it shimmered in the heat of the day it became necessary to seek the true nature of the times in signs and auguries. When the daily shipment of ice was delayed it meant that there was trouble in the provinces. When green fungus clouded the clear water of the Anup Talao, the Best of All Possible Pools, it meant there was treason brewing at court. And when the king left his palace and rode in his palanquin down to the Sikri lake it was a sign that his spirit was troubled. These were all water portents. There were also auguries of air, fire, and earth, but the water prophecies were the most reliable. Water informed the emperor, it bore the truth to him upon its tides, and it also soothed him. It ran in narrow channels and broad pathways around and across the courtyards of the palace quarter and cooled the stone buildings from below. True, it was a symbol of abstemious puritans like Badauni's *manqul* party, but the emperor's relationship with the life-sustaining liquid was deeper than any religious bigot's.

Bhakti Ram Jain brought the king a steaming bowl of water for his ablutions each morning and Akbar would look deep into the rising steam and it would reveal to him the best course of action for the day. When he bathed in the royal hammam he leaned his head back and floated for a while like a fish. The hammam water whispered in his submerged ears and told him the innermost thoughts of everyone else who had taken a bath anywhere within a three-mile radius. Stationary water's powers of information were limited; for long-distance news it was necessary to immerse oneself in a river. However, the hammam's magic was not to be underestimated. It was the hammam that had told him, for example, about the hidden journal of the narrow-minded Badauni, a book so critical of the emperor's ideas and habits that if Akbar had admitted he knew of its existence he would have been obliged to execute Badauni at once. Instead he kept his critic's secret as close to his chest as any of his own, and each night when Badauni was asleep the emperor would send his most trusted spy, Umar the Ayyar, to the embittered author's study, to find and memorize the latest pages of the secret history of the emperor's reign.

Umar the Ayyar was as important to Akbar as water—so important that he was unknown to anyone except the emperor himself. Not even Birbal knew of his existence, and nor did Abul Fazl the master of spies. He was a young eunuch so slender and hairless of face and body that he could pass for a woman and so, at Akbar's command, he lived anonymously in the harem cubicle and pretended to be a humble servitor of the concubines he so strongly resembled. That morning, before Akbar took Mogor dell'Amore to the Tent of the New Worship, Umar had entered Akbar's chambers through the hidden door whose existence was unknown even to Bhakti Ram Jain, and informed his master of a murmur he had heard in the air, a faint wisp of a rumor emanating from the Hatyapul brothel. It was that the yellow-haired newcomer had a secret to tell, a secret so astonishing that it could shake the dynasty itself. Umar had not managed to find out what the secret was, however, and looked so ashamed of himself, so girlishly downcast, that the emperor had to console him for several minutes to make sure he didn't embarrass himself further by bursting into tears.

Because Akbar was so interested in this untold secret he behaved as if it did not matter, and found many ways to delay its telling. He kept the stranger close, but made sure they were never alone. He strolled with him to the pigeoncotes to inspect the royal racers, and allowed him to walk beside the imperial palanquin, next to the imperial parasol-bearer, as he rode down to the edge of the luminous lake. It was true that he was troubled in spirit. Not only was there this business of an undivulged secret that had crossed the world to find him, but also, in last night's lovemaking with his beloved Jodha, he had found himself less aroused than usual by the wife who had never failed him before, and had even found himself wondering whether the company of some of the prettier concubines might be preferable for a change. And then there was the matter of his growing disillusion with God. This was more than enough. It was time to float for a while.

As a gesture of nostalgia he had preserved and refurbished four of his grandfather Babar's favorite boats and given them the run of the lake. Ice from Kashmir came across the water on the largest boat, the flat-decked transportation vehicle named the Capacity, *Gunjayish,* passing the last leg of its quotidian journey from the high Himalayas to the drinking glasses of the court aboard the craft that had once been his namesake Sultan Jalaluddin's gift to the cruel, nature-loving First Mughal King. Akbar himself preferred to travel in the Comfort, or *Asayish,* with the little courier-skiff the *Farmayish,* or Command, in close attendance, to ferry orders and visitors back and forth from the shore. The fourth boat, the ornate *Arayish,* or Decoration, was a boat for romantic pleasures, only to be used at night. Akbar led Mogor dell'Amore into the main cabin of the *Asayish* and let out a low sigh of pleasure, as he always did when the subtleties of water replaced the banality of solid ground beneath his feet.

The foreigner looked as full of the unborn child of his secret as a woman on the verge of parturition, and as afraid of the dangers of the act. Akbar tormented his guest a little longer by asking the boat's crew to scurry around them performing a series of acts dictated by court protocol, procedures involving cushions, wine, and books. Any drink had to be tasted for poison three times before it reached the emperor's lips, and though the practice bored the emperor he did not gainsay it. As regarded books, however, Akbar had changed the protocol. According to the old ways, any book that reached the imperial presence had to be read by three different commentators and pronounced free of sedition, obscenity, and lies. "In other words," the young king had said on ascending the throne, "we are only to read the most boring books ever written. Well, that won't do at all." Nowadays all sorts of books were permitted, but the three commentators' reviews were relayed to the emperor before he opened them, because of the overarching, supreme protocol regarding the inappropriateness of royal surprise. And as for cushions, each of them had to be tested in case an ill-wisher had concealed a blade within. All this the emperor suffered to be done. Then, at last, he allowed himself to be with the foreigner out of earshot of any aide.

"Sire," said Mogor dell'Amore, and his voice seemed to tremble just a little as he spoke, "there is a matter I beg leave to reveal to you, and you alone."

Akbar burst into a great shout of laughter. "We think if we had made you wait any longer you might have died of it," he chuckled. "For over an hour now you have looked like a boil that needed to burst."

The foreigner colored brightly. "Your Majesty knows everything," he said, bowing. (The emperor had not invited him to sit.) "However, I venture to believe that the nature of my information cannot be known to you, even though its existence plainly is." Akbar composed himself and looked grave. "Well, get on with it, man," he said. "Let's have whatever it is you have to give."

"So be it, sire," began the foreigner. "There was once, in Turkey, an adventurer-prince named Argalia or Arcalia, a great warrior who possessed enchanted weapons, and in whose retinue were four terrifying giants, and he had a woman with him, Angelica . . ."

From the skiff *Farmayish,* which was racing toward the *Asayish* with Abul Fazl and a small crowd of men aboard, came a loud cry—"Beware! Save the emperor! Beware!"—and at once the crew of the king's boat rushed into the royal cabin and seized Mogor dell'Amore without ceremony. There was a thickly muscled arm around his throat, and three swords pointed at his heart. The emperor had risen to his feet and he, too, was quickly encircled by armed men, to defend him from harm.

". . . Angelica, the princess of India and Cathay . . ." the foreigner struggled to continue. The arm tightened around his windpipe. ". . . The most beautiful . . ." he added, painfully, and the grip on his throat tightened again; whereupon Mogor dell'Amore lost consciousness, and said no more.

{ 7 }

In the dark of the dungeon his chains

In the dark of the dungeon his chains weighed on him like his un-finished story. There were so many chains winding around him that he could imagine, in the darkness, that he had somehow been encased inside a larger body, the body of a man of iron. Movement was impossible. Light was a fantasy. The dungeon had been carved out of the living rock of the hill beneath the imperial palaces and the air in his cell was a thousand years old, and so perhaps were the creatures crawling over his feet and through his hair and into his groin, the albino roaches, the blind snakes, the transparent rats, the phantom scorpions, the lice. He would die without telling his story. He found this thought intolerable and so it refused to leave him, it crawled in and out of his ears, slid into the corners of his eyes and stuck to the roof of his mouth and to the soft tissue under his tongue. All men needed to hear their stories told. He was a man, but if he died without telling the story he would be some-thing less than that, an albino cockroach, a louse. The dungeon did not understand the idea of a story. The dungeon was static, eter-nal, black, and a story needed motion and time and light. He felt his story slipping away from him, becoming inconsequential, ceas-ing to be. He had no story. There was no story. He was not a man. There was no man here. There was only the dungeon, and the slithering dark.

When they came to get him he did not know if a day had passed, or a century. He could not see the rough hands that loos-ened his chains. For a time his hearing too was affected, and his powers of speech. They blindfolded him and took him naked to another place where he was scoured and scrubbed. As if he were a corpse being readied for burial, he thought, a dumb corpse who could not tell his tale. There were no coffins in this unchristian land. He would be sewn into a shroud and flung without a name into a hole in the ground. That, or burned. He would not rest in peace. In death as in life he would be full of unspoken words and they would be his Hell, tormenting him through all eternity. He heard a sound. *There was once.* It was his own voice. *There was once a prince.* He felt his heart begin to beat again, his blood to flow. His tongue was thick but it could move. His heart boomed like a cannon in his chest. *Who possessed enchanted weapons.* He had a body again, and words. They removed the blindfold. *Four terrifying giants and a woman.* He was in another cell but in this place there was a candle burning and a guard in the corner. *The most beautiful woman.* The story was saving his life.

"Save your strength," the guard said. "Tomorrow you stand trial for murder."

There was a question he was trying to ask. The words would not form. The guard took pity on him and answered it anyway.

"I don't know the name of the man who accuses you," he said. "But he is a godless foreigner like yourself, and he lacks an eye and half a leg."

The first trial of Mogor dell'Amore took place in the house of the sandstone banana tree, and his judges were the greatest grandees of the court, all nine of the Nine Stars, whose presence had been commanded by an exceptional imperial decree: Abul Fazl the wise and obese, Raja Birbal of the lightning wit, the finance minister Raja Todar Mal, Raja Man Singh the army chief, the unworldly mystic Fakir Aziauddin and the rather more worldly priest Mullah Do Piaza who preferred cookery to prayer and was accordingly a favorite of Abul Fazl's, the great poets Faizi and Abdul Rahim, and the musician Tansen. The emperor sat on the top of the tree as usual, but his mood was most unusual. His head was bowed, giving him the most unimperial appearance of an ordinary mortal suffering the misery of a dreadful personal calamity. For a long time he did not speak, but allowed the trial to take its course.

The crew of the pirate vessel *Scáthach* stood to one side in a tight, grumbling bunch, close behind the macabre figure of the one-legged, eyepatched doctor who was their appointed spokesman. This was not Praise-God Hawkins as the accused remembered him, the weepy cuckold whom he had so effortlessly bent to his will. This Hawkins was smartly dressed and grim of countenance, and when he saw the prisoner enter this courthouse he pointed at him and cried in a ringing voice, "There he stands, the vile Uccello, who murdered the ambassador for his gold!"

"Justice!" cried the sailors and, less nobly, "We want the money back!" The accused, wearing only a long white shirt, and with his hands tied behind him, took in the ominous scene—the emperor, the nine judges, the accusers, and the small gallery of lesser courtiers who had crowded into the small building to bear witness to the trial, among whom, distinctive in their black Jesuit garb, were the two Christian priests, Father Rodolfo Acquaviva and Father Antonio Monserrate, there to ensure that the men of the West received the justice and, perhaps, the money they had come so far to demand. The accused understood the size of his miscalculation. It had not occurred to him that this rabble would pursue him once their master was dead, and so he had not tried to cover his tracks. A tall yellow-haired man standing up in a bullock-cart in a leather coat of variegated colors was not a common sight on Indian roads. And they were many and he was one, and his case was doomed to fail. "In this place," Abul Fazl was saying, "he goes by a different name."

Father Acquaviva was permitted to speak through his Persian interpreter. "This *Mogor dell'Amore* is no name at all," he said, damningly. "It means, *a Mughal born out of wedlock*. It is a name that dares much and will offend many. By assuming it he implies that he wishes to be thought of as an illegitimate prince."

This statement caused consternation in the court. The emperor's head sank lower, until his chin was resting on his chest. Abul Fazl turned to face the accused. "What is your name?" he demanded. "For I am sure this 'Uccello' is only another disguise."

The prisoner remained silent. Then all of a sudden the emperor roared from above.

"Your name," he shouted, sounding like a more stentorian version of Praise-God Hawkins lamenting the infidelity of his Portuguese lady love. "The devil with it! Your name, *farangi,* or your life."

The prisoner spoke. "I am called Vespucci," he said quietly. "Vespucci, Niccolò."

"Another lie," Father Acquaviva interjected through his interpreter. "Vespucci, indeed." He laughed loudly, a vulgar Occidental laugh, the laugh of a people who believed they were the keepers of the world's laughter. "This is indeed a shameless, lying thief, and this time he has stolen a great Florentine name."

It was at this point that Raja Birbal intervened. "Sir," he said to the Jesuit, "we are grateful for your earlier remark, but spare us, please, these exclamations. A strange case is here before us. A Scottish nobleman is dead, that much is verified, and much regretted by all. The letter he bore for His Majesty has been delivered by the accused; this, too, we know, but a postman does not become a murderer by delivering a dead man's mail. The ship's crew states that after much research they located seven hidden chambers in the captain's cabin, and that all seven were empty. But who emptied them? We cannot say. Perhaps they contained gold, or jewels, but then again, perhaps they were empty to begin with. The ship's doctor Hawkins has given sworn deposition that he now believes the late milord to have suffered from the fatal consequence of laudanum poisoning, but as he himself tended to the sick man day and night until the hour of his death, he may be accusing another to cover his own guilt. The accusers hold the prisoner guilty of theft, yet he has faithfully delivered the one thing we know for certain that he removed, the parchment from the English queen; and as for gold, there is no sign of that, or of laudanum, among his effects." He clapped his hands and a servant entered, carrying the prisoner's clothes, including the lozenged leather coat. "We have searched his garments, and the bag he left at the Hatyapul house of ill fame, and we have found a trickster's hoard—playing cards, dice, deceptions of all sorts, even a living bird—but no great fortune in jewels or in gold. What then are we to think? That he is a skilled thief who has concealed his stolen goods; that he is not a thief, for there was nothing to steal; or that the thieves stand here, accusing an innocent man. These are our choices. The weight of numbers is against him, but if many accuse him, many may be rogues."

The king spoke heavily from on high. "A man who lies about his name will lie about much besides," he said. "We shall let the elephant decide."

Again, a loud murmuring in the room: a shocked, expectant hum. Raja Birbal looked distressed. "*Jahanpanah,*" he said, "Shelter of the World, consider this: do you recall the famous tale of the goatherd boy and the tiger?"

"As we recall it," Akbar replied, "the lying goatherd had falsely cried *tiger* so often, simply to annoy his village, that when the tiger truly attacked him no man came to his defense." "*Jahanpanah,*" said Birbal, "that is the story of a group of ignorant villagers. I am sure the king of kings would not wish a boy to be eaten by a tiger even if he was an untruthful, misbegotten rogue."

"Perhaps not," the emperor petulantly replied, "but on this occasion we would be glad to see him crushed beneath our elephant's feet."

Birbal, understanding that the emperor was behaving like a man whose beloved has proved unworthy of his love, was marshaling further arguments for clemency when the accused made a statement that placed him beyond salvation. "Before you kill me, great emperor," the foreigner boldly said, "I must warn you that if you do so you will be cursed, and your capital city will crumble, because a powerful wizard has placed a blessing upon me, which brings prosperity to my protectors, but rains down desolation upon any who do me harm."

The king looked at him as a man regards a slow insect he is about to squash. "That's very interesting," he replied, "because, Sir Uccello or Mogor or Vespucci, we have built this mighty city around the shrine of Sheikh Salim Chishti, the greatest saint in all India, and *his* blessing protects *us,* and rains down desolation upon *our* enemies. We wonder whose power is the greater, your wizard's or our saint's?"

"Mine was the most powerful enchantress in all the known world," the foreigner said, and at that the entire assembly could not restrain its laughter.

"Ah, a woman," the emperor said. "That is terrifying indeed. Enough of this! Throw the bastard to the mad elephant and let's see what his woman's wiles can do."

The second trial of the man with three names took place in the Garden of Hiran. It had been the emperor's whim to name his favorite elephant after a *hiran,* a deer, and maybe that was why after years of noble service the poor beast lost his mind and had to be restrained, because names were things of power, and when they did not fit the thing named they acquired a malign force. Even after the elephant went mad (and then blind) the emperor refused to allow him to be killed. He was kept and cared for in a place of honor, a special stall with padded walls to prevent him from harming himself in his rages, and from time to time he was brought out, upon the emperor's whim, to serve in a two-in-one capacity, as judge and executioner.

It was appropriate that a man who falsified his name should be judged by an elephant driven insane by his own whimsical naming. Hiran the mad blind elephant was tethered in the garden of judgment, prevented from running amok by a stout rope passing through a hole in a stone buried in the grass. He trumpeted and bellowed and kicked his legs and the tusks on his head flashed like swords. The court assembled to watch what happened to the man with three names, and the public, too, was admitted, and so there were many who witnessed the miracle. The man's hands were no longer tied behind his back, but their renewed freedom was not intended to save him, only to allow him to die with more dignity than a parcel. But he stretched out his hand toward the elephant, and all who were present saw the elephant become absolutely quiet and calm, and allow the man to caress him; all who were present, high-born and low, gasped aloud as the elephant tenderly wound his trunk around the prisoner and raised him up. Everyone saw the yellow-haired foreigner being set down like a prince upon Hiran's ample back.

The emperor Akbar observed the miracle from the five-storied pavilion called the Panch Mahal, with Raja Birbal by his side, and both men were greatly moved by what had occurred. "It is we who have been mad and blind and not our poor elephant," Akbar told his minister. "Arrest that crew of scoundrels right away and bring their innocent victim to our chambers as soon as he gets properly washed and dressed."

"The elephant did not kill him, it's true," Birbal said, "but does that mean he is innocent, *Jahanpanah*? Would the sailors have come all the way from the sea to accuse him if they themselves were the guilty ones? Would they not have been better advised simply to sail away?"

"Always rowing against the tide, eh, Birbal," Akbar replied. "Until a moment ago you were the fellow's prime advocate. Now that he is exonerated, your doubts move against him. Here, then, is an argument you will not be able to refute. The elephant's judgment is multiplied in potency if the emperor endorses it. If Akbar agrees with Hiran, then the elephant's wisdom is multiplied until it exceeds even yours."

Umar the Ayyar visited the crew of the *Scáthach* in their cells, wearing women's clothing. He was veiled, and his body moved softly, like a woman's, and the sailors were amazed at a lady's presence in this place of stone and shadow. "She" did not tell them "her" name or offer any explanation of "her" presence, but only presented them with a stark proposition. The emperor was not convinced of their guilt, the Ayyar said, and was consequently prepared to keep Signor Vespucci under careful surveillance until he betrayed himself, as all criminals eventually did. If they genuinely wished to serve the memory of their dead lord, they would accept the harsh prospect of waiting in the dungeon until the day of Vespucci's incrimination. If they bowed down before this unkind fate, Umar told them, their innocence would be demonstrated beyond a doubt, and the emperor would pursue Vespucci with all his might, and would surely get his man in the end. But there was no way of knowing whether the wait would be short or long, and the dungeon was the dungeon, that was undeniable; there was no way of sweetening its bitter days. "Nevertheless," Umar declared, "the only honorable course is to stay." Alternatively, he continued, he ("she") had been authorized to arrange for their "escape." If they chose this path, they would be escorted back to their ship and set free, but it would then become impossible to reopen the Vespucci case, since their flight would be the proof of their guilt; and if they ever returned to the kingdom they would be summarily executed for Lord Hauksbank's murder. "This is the choice which the emperor offers you in his wisdom," the eunuch solemnly, and femininely, intoned.

The crew of the *Scáthach* was almost immediately shown to be lacking in honor. "Keep the scurvy murderer," said Praise-God Hawkins, "we want to go home." Umar the Ayyar fought down a surge of contempt. The English had no future on this earth, he told himself. A race that rejected the idea of personal sacrifice would surely be erased from time's record before very long.

—⁓—

By the time the newly renamed Niccolò Vespucci was brought to the emperor's rooms, wearing his own clothes, and with the leather coat of many colors slung rakishly across his shoulders like a cape, he was entirely restored to himself and grinning mischievously, like a magician who has pulled off an impossible trick, such as making a palace disappear, or walking through a wall of flames unharmed, or making a mad elephant fall in love. Birbal and the emperor were struck by his cockiness. "How did you do it?" the emperor asked him. "Why didn't Hiran kill you?" Vespucci grinned more widely still. "Sire, it was love at first sight," he said. "Your elephant has served Your Majesty well, and no doubt he got, from me, so recently your friend and companion, a whiff of familiar perfume."

Is this what we all do? the emperor asked himself. This habit of the charming lie, this constant embellishment of reality, this pomade applied to the truth. Is the roguishness of this man of three names no more than our own folly writ large? Is the truth too poor a thing for us? Is any man innocent of embellishing it at times, or even of abandoning it entirely? Am "I" no better than he?

Vespucci, meanwhile, was thinking about trust. He, who trusted nobody, had trusted a woman, and she had saved him. *Rescued by a Skeleton,* he thought. A tale of wonder indeed. He took his treasures from their hiding places, the gold regaining its weight as it left the magic overcoat, the jewels heavy in the palm of his hand, and gave them all to her. "Thus I place myself in your power," he told her. "If you rob me I can do nothing about it." "You don't understand," she answered. "You have gained a greater power over me than I can overthrow." And in fact he did not immediately understand, and she did not know how to say the word "love," or how to explain the emotion's unexpected birth. So it was a mystery that saved him from being proven a thief, and when he was being prepared for the elephant, and had his hands untied, and was left to pray for a moment so that he could be in his Maker's good graces when he met him, he realized that she had foreseen this possibility as well, and now he drew out of that hiding place where no searcher cares to look the tiny vial of perfume that perfectly synthesized the emperor's own odor, and fooled the blind old elephant, and saved his life.

The emperor was speaking. The time he had hoped for had come. "Look here, fellow, whatever your name is," Akbar said. "This hinting and nudging must stop, and your story must at last be told. Out with it quick, before we lose our good mood."

When Hiran the elephant had placed the foreigner on his back as if he were a Mughal prince, the rider had suddenly understood how he had to begin. A man who always tells his story in the same words is exposed as a liar who has rehearsed his lie too well, he thought. It was important to begin in a different place. "Your Majesty," he said, "king of kings, Shelter of the World. I have the honor to inform you that I . . ." The words died on his lips and he stood before the king like a man struck dumb by the gods. Akbar was irritated. "Don't stop there, man," he said. "Once and for all, spit the damned thing out." The foreigner coughed, and began again.

"That I, my lord, am none other than . . ."

"What?"

"My lord, I find I cannot say it."

"But you must."

"Very well—though I fear your response."

"Nevertheless."

"Then, my lord, know now that I am, in fact . . ."

"Yes?"

(A deep breath. Then, the plunge.)

"Your relative by blood. In point of fact: your uncle."

{ 8 }

When life got too complicated for the men

When life got too complicated for the men of the Mughal court they turned to the old women for answers. No sooner had "Niccolò Vespucci" who called himself "Mogor dell'Amore" made his remarkable claim of kinship than the emperor sent messengers to the quarters of his mother Hamida Bano and Gulbadan Begum, his aunt. "As far as we know," he said to Birbal, "we have no uncles unaccounted for, on top of which this claimant to the title is ten years our junior, yellow-haired, and with no Chaghatai in him that we can perceive—but before we take the next step we will ask the ladies, the Keepers of the Tales, who will let us know for sure." Akbar and his minister fell into deep discussion in a corner of the room and ignored the probable impostor so thoroughly that he felt his sense of his own existence beginning to waver. Was he really there, in the presence of the Grand Mughal, claiming a tie of blood, or was this some opium hallucination from which he would be well advised to awake? Had he escaped an elephantine death only to commit suicide a few moments later?

Birbal said to Akbar, "The warrior Argalia or Arcalia the fellow has mentioned bears a name I do not know, and *Angelica* is a name of the foreigner's people, not of ours. Nor are we yet apprised of their part in this tall story, this 'golden tale.' But let us not write off these persons on account of their names, for a name, as we know, can be changed." Raja Birbal had begun his life as a poor Brahmin boy called Mahesh Das, and it was Akbar who had brought him to court and made a prince of him. While the two friends waited for the great ladies they fell into reminiscence, and were young again, and Akbar was hunting, and had lost his way. "Hey! Little fellow! Which of these roads goes to Agra?" the emperor cried, and Birbal, once again six or seven years old, replied gravely, "Sir, none of the roads goes anywhere." "That is impossible," Akbar chided him, and little Birbal grinned. "Roads do not move, so they go nowhere," he said. "But people, traveling to Agra, usually go down this one." This joke brought the boy to court and gave him a new name, and a new life.

"An uncle?" said Akbar, thoughtfully. "Our father's brother? Our mother's brother? The husband of our aunt?" "Or," said Birbal, in the interests of fairness, "to stretch it a little, the son of your grandfather's sibling." There was a merriment beneath their apparent gravity and the foreigner understood that he was being toyed with. The empire was at play while it decided his destiny. Things did not look well.

Crisscrossing the sprawling area of the imperial residences were curtained passageways down which the ladies of the court might move unobserved by inappropriate eyes. Along one such passage, the queen mother Queen Hamida Bano and the senior lady of the court, Princess Gulbadan, were gliding like two mighty boats passing through a narrow canal, with the queen's intimate confidante Bibi Fatima close behind. "Jiu," the queen said (it was her pet name for her older sister-in-law), "what madness is little Akbar up to now? Does he need more family than he already has?" "He already has," repeated Bibi Fatima, who had acquired the bad habit of becoming her mistress's echo. Princess Gulbadan shook her head. "He knows that the world is still mysterious," she said, "and the strangest story may turn out to be true." This remark was so unexpected that the queen fell silent and the two women and the servant floated to the emperor's rooms without exchanging another word.

It was a breezy day and the elaborately worked cloths shielding them from men's eyes flapped like anxious sails. Their own ornate garments, the wide skirts, the long shirts, the cloths of modesty wound around their heads and faces, were likewise teased by the wind. The closer they got to Akbar the more powerful the wind became. *Perhaps this is an omen,* the queen thought. *All our certainties are being blown away and we must live in Gulbadan's universe of mystery and doubt.* Hamida Bano, a fierce, commanding woman, was not attracted to the concept of doubt. It was her opinion that she knew what was what, had been brought up to know it, and it was her duty to convey that information to everyone as clearly as possible. If the emperor had lost sight of what was what then his mother was on her way to remind him. But Gulbadan seemed—oddly—to be of a different mind.

Since Gulbadan's return from the pilgrimage to Mecca she had seemed less certain of things than before. It was as though her faith in the fixed and unchanging truths of the divine cosmos had been weakened rather than strengthened by her mighty journey. To Hamida Bano's mind the women's *hajj,* organized by Gulbadan and composed almost entirely of the older ladies of the court, was itself an indication of the undesirably revolutionary nature of her son's monarchic style. A women's *hajj?* she had asked her son when the subject was first raised by Gulbadan. How could he permit such a thing? No, the queen had told him, she would not join it in any circumstance, most certainly not. But then her co-queen Salima had gone, and Sultanam Begum the wife of Askari Khan, who had saved Akbar's life when his parents abandoned him and went into exile—Sultanam who had been more of a mother to the child Akbar than Hamida herself; and Babar's Circassian wife, and Akbar's stepcousins, and Gulbadan's granddaughter, and various servants and such. Three and a half years away in the holy places! The queen's long Persian exile had more than satisfied her desires in the travel department, and three and a half years away was horrifying even in the contemplation. Let Gulbadan go to Mecca! The queen mother would reign on at home.

It was certainly the case that during those three and a half years of peace and quiet without Gulbadan's interminable chatter to put up with Hamida Bano's own influence over the king of kings had been without rival or hindrance. When women were required to broker a marriage or a peace she was the only great lady to hand. Akbar's own queens were just girls, except for the Phantom, of course, that ghostly sexpot who had memorized all the dirty books, and there was no need to think overmuch about *her*. But then Gulbadan had returned, and was now Gulbadan the Pilgrim, and there had been a shift in the balance of power. Which made it all the more irritating that the old princess spoke very little about God nowadays, and a good deal more about women, their un-tapped powers, their ability to do anything they chose, and how they should no longer accept the limitations men placed upon them but arrange their lives for themselves. If they could perform the *hajj* they could climb mountains and publish poetry and rule the world alone. It was a scandal, obviously, but the emperor loved it, any novelty was a delight to him, it was as if he had never stopped being a child and so fell in love with any shiny new notion as if it were a silver rattle in a nursery and not the serious stuff of a proper adult life.

Still: Princess Gulbadan was her senior in age, and the queen mother would always pay her the respect she was due. And oh, all right, it was impossible to dislike Gulbadan, she was always smiling and telling funny stories about some crazy cousin or other, and her heart was a good loving heart, even if her head was full of this new independent stuff. Human beings were not singular creatures, Hamida Bano would tell Gulbadan, they were plural, their lives were made up of interdependent forces, and if you willfully shook one branch of that tree who knew what fruit might fall on your head. But Gulbadan would just smile and go her own way. And everybody liked her. The queen mother liked her too. That was the most irritating thing. That, and Gulbadan's body of a young woman, as slender and lithe in its old age as it had been in its youth. The queen mother's body had succumbed comfortably and traditionally to the years, expanding to keep pace with her son's empire, and now it, too, was a continent of sorts, a realm with mountains and forests and above it all the capital city of her mind, which had not sagged, not at all. *My body is what an old woman's body should be like*, Hamida Bano thought. *It is usual.* Gulbadan's insistence on continuing to look young was further proof of her dangerous lack of respect for tradition.

They entered the emperor's rooms by the women's door and seated themselves as usual behind the filigreed walnut screen with marble inlays, and old Gulbadan, inevitably, got things going in the wrong way entirely. She should not have spoken directly to the stranger, but having heard that he spoke their language she insisted on getting right to the point. "Hey! Foreigner!" she shouted in a sharp, high voice. "Now then! What's this fairy tale you've crossed half the world to tell?"

———

This was the story as he had been told it, the foreigner swore. His mother was a princess of the true Chaghatai blood, a direct descendant of Genghis Khan, a member of the house of Timur, and the sister of the First Mughal Emperor of India, whom she called "the Beaver." (When he said this Gulbadan Begum sat up very straight behind the screen.) He knew nothing of dates or places, but only the tale as he had been told it, which he was honestly repeating. His mother's name was Angelica and she was, he insisted, a Mughal princess, and the most beautiful woman anyone had ever seen, and an enchantress without compare, a mistress of potions and spells of whose powers all were afraid. In her youth her brother the Beaver King had been besieged in Samarkand by an Uzbeg warlord named Lord Wormwood, who had demanded that she be given up to him as the price of the Beaver's safe conduct out of the city when he surrendered it. Then, to insult her, Lord Wormwood briefly gave her as a gift to his young water-carrier Bacha Saqaw, to use as he desired. Two days later Bacha Saqaw's body began to grow boils in every part, plague buboes hanging from his armpits and groin, and when they burst, he died. After that nobody tried to lay a finger on the witch—until at last she yielded to Wormwood's gauche amours. Ten years passed. Lord Wormwood was defeated by the Persian King Ishmael, in the battle of Marv by the shores of the Caspian Sea. Princess Angelica was once again a spoil of war.

(Now Hamida Bano too felt a quickening of the pulse. Gulbadan Begum leaned toward her and whispered a word in her ear. The queen mother nodded, and tears filled her eyes. Her servant Bibi Fatima cried as well, just to be supportive.)

The Persian king, in turn, was defeated by the Osmanli, or Ottoman, Sultan . . .

The women behind the screen could no longer be contained. Queen Hamida Bano was no less excited than her more readily excitable sister-in-law. "My son, come to us," she commanded loudly—"to us," Bibi Fatima echoed—and the king of kings obeyed. Then Gulbadan whispered in his ear and he became very still. Then he turned to Birbal, looking genuinely surprised. "The ladies confirm," he reported, "that a part of this story is already known. *Baboor,* which is to say 'Babar,' is an old-fashioned Chaghatai word for beaver, and this 'Wormwood' similarly translates into Shiban or Shaibani Khan, and the sister of my grandfather Babar, who was known to one and all as the greatest beauty of her age, was captured by Shaibani after Babar's defeat by that warlord at Samarkand; and Shaibani a decade later was defeated by Shah Ismail of Persia near the town of Marv, and Babar's sister fell into Persian hands."

"Excuse me, *Jahanpanah,*" said Birbal, "but that was Princess Khanzada, if I make no mistake? And of course Princess Khanzada's story is known. As I myself have learned, Shah Ismail returned her to Babar Shah as an act of friendship, and she lived with great respect in the bosom of the royal family until her sad demise. It is indeed remarkable that this foreigner has learned her story, but he cannot be her descendant. It is true she bore Shaibani a son, but the boy perished on the same day as his father, at the hands of the Persian Shah. And thus this fellow's story is disproved."

At this the royal ladies behind the screen shouted together, *"There was a second princess!"* And the servant echoed, *". . . cess!"* Gulbadan composed herself. "O radiant king," she said, "in our family's story there is a hidden chapter."

The man who had named himself "Mogor dell'Amore" stood quietly in the heart of the Mughal empire while its most exalted women rehearsed the genealogy of their line. "Allow me to remind you, O all-knowing king, that there were various princesses born to various wives and other consorts," Gulbadan said. The emperor sighed a little; when Gulbadan started climbing the family tree like an agitated parrot there was no telling how many branches she would need to settle on briefly before she decided to rest. But on this occasion his aunt was almost shockingly concise. "There was Mihr Banu and Shahr Banu and Yadgar Sultan." "But Yadgar's mother Agha was not a queen," Queen Hamida interrupted haughtily. "She was only a concubine." ". . . ncubine," said Bibi Fatima dutifully. "However," the queen added, "it must be conceded that even though Khanzada was first in years she was by no means first in looks, even though it was officially declared that she was. Some of the concubines' girls were prettier by far." "O most luminous king," Gulbadan continued, "I must inform you that Khanzada, alas, was always the jealous type."

This was the story old Gulbadan had kept secret for so long. "People said Khanzada was the pretty one because she was the eldest and it didn't do to cross her in any way. But in truth the youngest princess of all was the great beauty, and she had a pretty playmate and maidservant, too, a young slave girl who was just as beautiful and looked so much like her mistress that people started calling her 'the princess's mirror.' And when Khanzada was captured by Shaibani the little princess and the Mirror were captured too, and when Khanzada was liberated by Shah Ismail and sent home to Babar's court the hidden princess and the Mirror remained in Persia. This is why she was erased from our family history: she preferred life among foreigners to an honored place in her own home."

"La Specchia," the foreigner said suddenly. "The word for 'mirror' is a masculine noun, but they made up a feminine for her. *La specchia*, the little mirror girl."

The story was tumbling out so rapidly now that protocol was forgotten and the stranger was not rebuked for his interjection. It was Gulbadan who did the telling in her high-speed, high-pitched voice. The tale of the hidden princess and her Mirror was insisting on being told.

But Hamida Bano was lost in memories. The queen was young again with a baby boy in her arms and with her husband Humayun in the hour of his defeat she was fleeing from the most dangerous men in the world: his brothers. It was so cold in the badlands of Kandahar that when she poured soup from a pot into a bowl it froze at once and could not be drunk. One day they were so hungry that they killed a horse and had to cut it up so that pieces of meat could be cooked in a soldier's helmet, which was their only pot. And then they were attacked, and she had to flee, and leave her baby boy behind, her baby boy, to take his chances in a combat zone, her baby boy, to be raised by another woman, the wife of Askari, her husband's brother and enemy, Sultanam Begum, who did what Hamida Bano could not do for her son, the emperor, her son.

"Forgive me," she whispered (". . . me," said Bibi Fatima), but the emperor wasn't listening, he was rushing on with Princess Gulbadan into unknown waters. "The hidden princess did not return with Khanzada because—yes!—she was in love." In love with a foreigner, so besotted that she was prepared to defy her brother the king and to scorn his court, which was where her duty and her higher love should have reminded her she belonged. In his fury Babar the Beaver cast his younger sibling out of history, decreeing that her name be stricken from all records and never spoken again by any man or woman in his realm. Khanzada Begum herself obeyed the order faithfully in spite of her great love for her sister, and slowly the memory of the hidden princess and her Mirror faded. So they became no more than a rumor, a story half heard in a crowd, a whisper on the wind, and from that day until this one there had been no further word.

"The Persian king, in turn, was defeated by the Osmanli, or Ottoman, Sultan," the foreigner continued. "And in the end the princess reached Italy in the company of a mighty warrior. Argalia and Angelica were their names. Argalia bore enchanted weapons, and in his retinue were four terrifying giants, and by his side rode Angelica, the princess of Cathay and India, the most beautiful woman in the world, and an enchantress beyond compare."

"What *was* her name?" the emperor asked, ignoring him. The queen mother shook her head. "I never heard it," she said. And Princess Gulbadan said, "She had a nickname that's on the tip of my tongue, but her real name has faded from my memory completely."

"Angelica," said the foreigner. "Angelica was her name."

Then from behind the screen he heard Princess Gulbadan say, "It's a good story, and we should find out how the fellow learned it, but there is a problem, and I do not know if he can solve it to our satisfaction."

Birbal had understood, of course. "It is a question of dates," he said. "Of dates, and people's ages."

"If Khanzada Begum were alive today," said Princess Gulbadan, "she would be one hundred and seven years old. Her youngest sister, eight years Babar's junior, would perhaps be ninety-five. This foreigner who stands here telling us the story of our buried past is no more than thirty or thirty-one. So if the hidden princess reached Italy, as the fellow says, and if he is her son, as he further asserts, then at the time of his birth she would have been approximately sixty-four years of age. If that miraculous act of childbearing did indeed occur, then he would surely be Your Majesty's uncle, the son of your grandfather's sister, and would merit recognition as a prince of the royal house. But it is impossible, obviously."

The foreigner felt the grave yawning at his feet and knew he would not be listened to much longer. "I told you I knew nothing of dates and places," he cried. "But my mother was beautiful, and young. She was no sexagenarian crone."

The women behind the screen were silent. His fate was being decided in that hush. Finally Gulbadan Begum spoke again. "It is a fact that he has told us things which have been buried very deep. Had he not spoken up then we old women would have taken the story to our graves. So he deserves the benefit of a little doubt."

"But as you have shown us," the emperor objected, "no conceivable doubt remains."

"On the contrary," Princess Gulbadan said. "There are two possible explanations."

"The first one being," the queen mother, Queen Hamida Bano, found herself saying, "that the hidden princess truly was a supreme enchantress, and learned the occult secrets of eternal youth, so that she was still a young woman in body and mind when she gave birth, even though she was almost seventy years old."

The emperor pounded his fist against a wall. "Or perhaps you have all lost your minds, and that is the reason why you credit such arrant nonsense," he bellowed. Princess Gulbadan hushed him as one hushes a small child. "You have not heard my second explanation," she said.

"Very well then," the emperor growled. "Speak up, aunt." Gulbadan Begum said, with pedantic emphasis, "Let us suppose that the fellow's story is true, and that the hidden princess and her warrior went to Italy long ago. It may also then be true that this fellow's mother was not the warrior's royal mistress . . ."

". . . but the princess's daughter," Akbar understood. "But who, then, was his father?"

"Thereby," replied Birbal, "I do believe, hangs the tale."

The emperor turned to the foreigner with a sigh of resigned curiosity. His unexpected affection for the stranger was soured by the distaste of emperors for outsiders who know too much. "The Hindustani storyteller always knows when he loses his audience," he said. "Because the audience simply gets up and leaves, or else it throws vegetables, or, if the audience is the king, it occasionally throws the storyteller headfirst off the city ramparts. And in this case, my dear Mogor-Uncle, the audience is indeed the king."

{ 9 }

In Andizhan the pheasants grew so fat

In Andizhan the pheasants grew so fat that four men could not finish a meal cooked from a single bird. There were violets on the banks of the Andizhan River, a tributary of the Jaxartes or Syr Darya, and tulips and roses bloomed there in the spring. Andizhan, the Mughals' original family seat, was in the province of Ferghana *"which lay,"* his grandfather had written in his autobiography, *"in the fifth clime, on the edge of the civilized world."* The emperor had never seen the land of his forefathers but he knew it from Babar's book. Ferghana stood on the great Silk Road in Central Asia to the east of Samarkand, north of the mighty peaks of the Hindu Kush. There were fine melons and grapes for wine, and you could feast on white deer and pomegranates stuffed with almond paste. There were running streams everywhere, good pasture meadows in the nearby mountains, red-barked spirea trees whose wood made excellent whip-handles and arrows, and turquoise and iron in the mines. The women were considered beautiful, but such things, the emperor knew, were always a matter of opinion. Babar the conqueror of Hindustan had been born there, and Khanzada Begum as well, and also (though all records of her birth had been obliterated) the princess without a name.

When he first heard the story of the hidden princess Akbar summoned his favorite painter Dashwanth to meet him at the Place of Dreams by the Best of All Possible Pools. When Akbar came to the throne at the age of not-quite-fourteen Dashwanth had been an apparently ignorant and shockingly gloomy boy of his own age whose father was one of the emperor's palanquin bearers.

Secretly, however, he was a great draftsman whose genius was bursting out of him. At night when he was sure nobody was looking he covered the walls of Fatehpur Sikri with graffiti—not obscene words or images, but caricatures of the grandees of the court so cruelly accurate that they all became determined to hunt him down as soon as possible and cut off those satirical hands. Akbar called Abul Fazl and the first master of the royal art studio, the Persian Mir Sayyid Ali, to meet him at the Place of Dreams. "You'd better find him before his enemies, whoever he is," he told them, "because we do not want such a talent extinguished by an angry nobleman's sword." A week later Abul Fazl returned, holding a small, dark, scrawny youth by the ear. Dashwanth was wriggling and protesting loudly, but Abul Fazl dragged him up to Akbar while the emperor was playing human pachisi. Mir Sayyid Ali followed close behind the miscreant and his captor, managing to look simultaneously delighted and grim. The emperor glanced briefly away from his human pieces, the pretty black slave girls standing on the pachisi board, commanded Dashwanth to join the imperial art studio immediately, and forbade any person in the court to do him harm.

Not even the emperor's wicked aunt and chief nurse Maham Anaga dared plot against Dashwanth in the face of such an order, even though the portrait he had drawn of her and her son Adham had been not only the most cruel but the most prophetic of all his works. The caricature of Maham Anaga appeared on the outside wall of the Hatyapul brothel. She was depicted to the general approval of the common people as a cackling blue-faced hag surrounded by bubbling potions, while the sniveling, murderous Adham was drawn as a reflection in one large glass retort, falling from the castle ramparts onto his head. Six years later, when Adham, in a delirious bid for power, physically attacked Akbar and was sentenced by the emperor to be hurled headfirst to his death off the city walls, the monarch remembered Dashwanth's prophecy with amazement. But Dashwanth said he didn't recall doing it, and the picture had been cleaned off the brothel wall long before, so the emperor was left to question his memory and wonder how much of his waking life had been infected by dreams.

Dashwanth quickly became one of the brightest stars of Mir Sayyid Ali's studio and made his name painting bearded giants flying through the air on enchanted urns, and the hairy, spotted goblins known as *devs,* and violent storms at sea, and blue and gold dragons, and heavenly sorcerers whose hands reached down from the clouds to save heroes from harm, to satisfy the wild, fantastic imagination—the *khayal*—of the youthful king. Over and over again, he painted the legendary hero Hamza on his three-eyed fairy horse overcoming improbable monsters of all types, and understood better than any other artist involved in the fourteen-year-long Hamza cycle which was the atelier's pride and joy that he was painting the emperor's dream-autobiography into being, that although his hand held the brush it was the emperor's vision that was appearing on the painted cloths. An emperor was the sum of his deeds, and Akbar's greatness, like that of his alter ego Hamza, was not only demonstrated by his triumphs over enormous obstacles—recalcitrant princes, real-life dragons, *devs,* and the like—it was actually created by those triumphs. The hero in Dashwanth's pictures became the emperor's mirror, and all the one hundred and one artists gathered in the studio learned from him, even the Persian masters, Mir Sayyid Ali and Abdus Samad. In their collaborative paintings of the adventures of Hamza and his friends, Mughal Hindustan was literally being invented; the union of the artists prefigured the unity of the empire and, perhaps, brought it into being. "Together we are painting the emperor's soul," Dashwanth told his collaborators sadly. "And when his spirit leaves his body it will come to rest in these pictures, in which he will be immortal."

In spite of all his artistic achievements, Dashwanth's depressive personality never changed for the better. He never married, lived the celibate life of a *rishi,* and as the years passed his moods darkened further and there were long periods when he was unable to work at all, but sat in his little cubicle at the art studio staring for hours at an empty corner, as if it contained one of the monsters he had depicted with such mastery for so many years. In spite of his increasingly odd behavior, however, he continued to be recognized as the finest of the Indian painters who had learned their trade under the two Persian masters who had accompanied Akbar's father Humayun home from exile years earlier. So it was Dashwanth whom Akbar summoned when he had his idea about undoing his grandfather's harsh deed and restoring the hidden princess to the history of her family at last. "Paint her into the world," he exhorted Dashwanth, "for there is such magic in your brushes that she may even come to life, spring off your pages, and join us for feasting and wine." The emperor's own life-giving powers had been temporarily exhausted by the immense effort of creating and then sustaining his imaginary wife Jodha, and so in this instance he was unable to act directly, and had to rely on art.

Dashwanth at once began to paint the life of Akbar's lost great-aunt in a series of extraordinary folios that put even the Hamza pictures in the shade. All Ferghana sprang to life: the three-gated, water-swallowing fortress of Andizhan—nine streams flowed into it but none flowed out—and the twelve-peaked mountain above the neighboring town of Osh, and the desert wilderness where the twelve dervishes lost each other in a fierce wind, and the region's many snakes, bucks, and hares. In the very first picture Dashwanth completed he showed the hidden princess as a beautiful four-year-old girl wandering with a little basket in the gorgeous woodlands of the Yeti Kent mountains, collecting belladonna leaves and roots, to add brilliance to her eyes and perhaps also to poison her enemies, and also discovering large expanses of the mythical plant the locals called *ayïq otï*, otherwise known as the mandrake root. The mandrake—or "mandragon"—was a relative of the deadly nightshade and looked quite like it above ground; but below the earth its roots had the shapes of human beings and they screamed when you pulled them up into the air just as human beings would scream if you buried them alive. Its powers of enchantment needed no explanation and everyone who saw that first painting realized that Dashwanth's exceptional powers of intuition were revealing the hidden princess as a born Enlightened One, who instinctively knew what to do to protect herself, and also to conquer men's hearts, which so often turned out to be the same thing.

The painting itself worked a kind of magic, because the moment old Princess Gulbadan looked at it in Akbar's private rooms she remembered the girl's name, which had been weighing down the tip of her tongue for days and making it difficult for her to eat. "Her mother was Makhdum Sultan Begum," Gulbadan said as she bent low over the glowing page, speaking so softly that the emperor also had to bend down to hear. "Makhdum, yes, that was the mother's name, the last true love of Umar Sheikh Mirza. And the girl was Qara Köz!—Qara Köz, that was it!—and Khanzada hated her poisonously, until, of course, she decided to love her instead."

Gulbadan Begum remembered the tales of the vanity of Khanzada Begum. Every morning as Lady Khanzada arose for the day (she told the emperor) her chief lady-in-waiting was instructed to say, "Lo, she wakes, Khanzada Begum; the most beautiful woman in the world opens her eyes and regards her beauty's domain." And when she went to pay her respects to her father Umar Sheikh Mirza, "Lo, she is come, your daughter, the most beautiful woman in the world," the heralds cried, "she is come, who rules in beauty as you rule in might," and on entering her mother's boudoir, Khanzada heard something similar from that dragon-queen herself; Qutlugh Nigar Khanum, breathing fire from her eyes and smoke from her nose, trumpeted her firstborn child's arrival. "Khanzada, most beautiful daughter in the world, come to me and let me feast my poor fading eyes."

But then the youngest princess was born to Makhdum Sultan Begum. From the day of her birth she was nicknamed Qara Köz, which was to say Black Eyes, on account of the extraordinary power of those orbs to bewitch all upon whom they gazed. From that day forward, Khanzada noticed a change in the timbre of her daily adorations, which began to contain a higher level of insincerity than was acceptable. In the years that followed there were a number of murder attempts on the little girl, none of which was ever traced back to Khanzada. There was poison in a cup of milk which Lady Black Eyes drank down; she was unharmed, but her lapdog, to whom she gave a final few sips, died instantly, writhing with pain. Later there was another drink to which someone had added a quantity of crushed diamonds, to inflict on the beautiful child the dreadful death known as "drinking fire," but the diamonds passed through her without harming her and the murder attempt only came to light when a nursemaid slave, cleaning the royal toilet, found the stones twinkling in the princess's feces.

When it became plain that Lady Black Eyes was the possessor of superhuman powers the murder attempts ceased, and Khanzada Begum, swallowing her pride, decided to change her tactics and began to coddle and cosset her infant rival instead. It wasn't long before the older half-sister had fallen under the younger girl's spell. It began to be said in the court of Umar Sheikh Mirza that his youngest daughter might be the reincarnation of the legendary Alanquwa, the Mongol sun-goddess who was the ancestor of Temüjin or Chingiz or Genghis Khan, and who, because she controlled all light, could also make the spirits of darkness subservient to her by threatening to enlighten, and so obliterate, the shadows where they hid. Alanquwa was the mistress of life and death. A religious cult of sun-worshippers began to spring up around the growing child.

It didn't last long. Her beloved father the *padishah* or king soon met with a cruel fate. He had gone to the Akhsi fortress near Andizhan—ah, Akhsi, where the delicious *mirtimurti* melons grew!—Akhsi, painted by Dashwanth as being built on the very edge of a deep ravine—and while he was visiting his pigeons in their pigeoncote the ground gave way beneath his feet and the *padishah,* the pigeons, and the pigeoncote all tumbled into the ravine and were lost. Lady Black Eyes' half-brother Babar became king at the age of twelve. She herself was still only four years old. In the midst of family tragedy and the chaos that followed it, the subject of Qara Köz's power of occult Enlightenment was forgotten. Alanquwa the sun-goddess retreated once again to her proper place in the sky.

The fall of Umar Sheikh Mirza, the great-grandfather of the king of kings, was depicted with panache in one of Dashwanth's finest works. The *padishah* was shown upside down against the blackness of the ravine, its stone walls rushing past him on either side, with the details of his life and character woven into the intricately abstract borders of the image: a short, fat man, good-natured and talkative, a backgammon player, a just man, but also a man who picked fights, a scarred paladin who knew how to punch, and, like all his descendants, like Babar, Humayun, Akbar, and Akbar's sons Salim, Daniyal, and Murad, a man excessively fond of wine and hard liquor, and of the candy or sweetmeat called *majun* that was made from the cannabis plant and had led to his sudden demise. In a *majun* haze he had chased a pigeon too close to the edge of the cliff and then down he went, to that netherworld in which it mattered not if you were short or fat or good-natured or talkative or just, in which there were no backgammon partners or opponents to fight, and where the delirious haze of *majun* could surround a man through all eternity.

Dashwanth's picture looked deep into the abyss and saw the demons waiting to welcome the king to their kingdom. The image was plainly an act of *lèse-majesté,* because even to suggest that the emperor's ancestor might have fallen into the inferno was a crime punishable by death, containing as it did the suggestion that His Majesty might be headed the same way, but when Akbar saw the picture he simply laughed and said, "Hell sounds like a much more enjoyable place to me than all that tedium of angels by the side of God." When the Water Drinker Badauni was told about this saying he concluded that the Mughal empire was doomed, because God would surely not tolerate a monarch who was turning into a Satanist before their very eyes. The empire survived, however, not forever, but for long enough; and so did Dashwanth, but for a much shorter time.

The next few years in the life of little Lady Black Eyes were an unsettled, wandering time, during which her brother and protector Babar galloped back and forth, winning battles, losing battles, gaining territory, losing it again, being attacked by his uncles, attacking his cousins, being rounded upon by his cousins, and attacking his uncles again, and behind all these ordinary family matters there waited the figure of his greatest enemy, the savage Uzbeg orphan, soldier of fortune and plague of the house of Timur, Wormwood—which is to say "Shaibani"—Khan. Dashwanth painted the five-, six-, and seven-year-old Qara Köz as a supernatural being cocooned in a little egg of light while all around her the battle raged. Babar captured Samarkand but lost Andizhan, then lost Samarkand, then recaptured it, and then lost it again, and his sisters with it. Wormwood Khan besieged Babar in that great city, and around the Iron Gate, the Needlemakers' Gate, the Bleachers' Gate, and the Turquoise Gate there was much hard fighting done. But in the end the siege starved Babar out. Wormwood Khan had heard the legend of the beauty of Babar's elder sister Khanzada Begum and sent a message saying that if Khanzada was surrendered to him then Babar and his family could leave in peace. Babar had no choice but to accept, and Khanzada had no choice but to accept Babar's choice.

Thus she became a sacrificial offering, human booty, a living pawn like the slave girls of Akbar's pachisi court. However, in that last family gathering in the royal chambers of Samarkand, she added a choice of her own. Her right hand fell upon her little sister's left wrist like the claw of a roc. "If I go," she said, "I will take Lady Black Eyes to keep me company." Nobody present could decide whether she spoke out of malice or love, because in Khanzada's dealings with Qara Köz both emotions were always present. In Dashwanth's picture of the scene Khanzada cut a magnificent figure, her mouth wide open as she cried her defiance, while Lady Black Eyes looked at first like a frightened child. But then those dark eyes drew you in and you saw the power lurking in their depths. Qara Köz's mouth was open, too—she too was crying out, lamenting her misery and announcing her strength. And Qara Köz's arm was extended also; her right hand, too, was fastened around a wrist. If Khanzada was to be Wormwood Khan's prisoner, and she, Qara Köz, was to be Khanzada's, then the little slave girl, the Mirror, would be hers.

The painting is an allegory of the evils of power, how they pass down the chain from the greater to the lesser. Human beings were clutched at, and clutched at others in their turn. If power was a cry, then human lives were lived in the echo of the cries of others. The echo of the mighty deafened the ears of the helpless. But there was a final detail to be observed: Dashwanth had completed the chain of hands. The Mirror, the slave girl, her left wrist captured in her young mistress's firm grasp, with her free right hand had seized hold of Khanzada Begum's left wrist. They stood in a circle, the three lost creatures, and by closing that circle the painter suggested that the clutch or echo of power could also be reversed. The slave girl could sometimes imprison the royal lady. History could claw upward as well as down. The powerful could be deafened by the cries of the poor.

As Dashwanth painted Qara Köz growing into the fullness of her young beauty during her captivity, it became plain that some higher power had captured his brush. The beauty of his canvases was so intense that Birbal, looking at them for the first time, presciently said, "I fear for the artist, for he is so deeply in love with this bygone woman that it will be hard for him to return to the present day." The girl, the adolescent, the lambently beautiful young woman Dashwanth brought, or rather restored, to life in these masterpieces was, Akbar suddenly realized as he examined the work, almost certainly the *qara ko'zum,* the dark-eyed beauty celebrated by the "Prince of Poets," the supreme versifier of the Chaghatai language, Ali-Shir Nava'i of Herat. *Weave a nest for yourself in the depths of my eyes. O your slender body that resembles a young tree growing in the garden of my heart. At the sight of a bead of sweat on your face I may suddenly die.* Dashwanth had actually painted a part of the last verse into the pattern of the fabric of Qara Köz's garment. *I may suddenly die.*

Herat, the so-called "Florence of the East," fell to Shaibani or Wormwood Khan soon after his capture of Samarkand, and it was where Khanzada, Qara Köz, and the Mirror spent most of their captive years. The world was like an ocean, people said, and in the ocean was a pearl, and the pearl was Herat. "If you stretch your feet in Herat," Nava'i said, "you are sure to kick a poet." O fabled Herat of mosques, palaces, and flying-carpet bazaars! Yes, it was a wonderful place, no doubt, the emperor thought, but the Herat which Dashwanth was painting, irradiated by the beauty of the hidden princess, was a Herat which no actually existing Herat could match, a dream-Herat for a dream-woman, with whom, as Birbal had divined, the artist was hopelessly in love. Dashwanth painted day and night, week in and week out, neither seeking nor accepting a day of rest. He became even scrawnier than usual and his eyes began to bulge. His fellow painters feared for his health. "He looks so *drawn,*" Abdus Samad murmured to Mir Sayyid Ali. "It's as if he wants to give up the third dimension of real life and flatten himself into a picture." This, like Birbal's remark, was a piece of sharp observation, the truth of which quickly became apparent.

Dashwanth's colleagues began to spy on him, because they had begun to fear he might do himself harm, so profound had his melancholy become. They took turns to watch him, and it wasn't hard because he only had eyes for his work. They saw him succumb to the final madness of the artist, heard him pick up his pictures and embrace them, whispering *Breathe.* He was working on what would turn out to be the final picture of the so-called *Qara-Köz-Nama,* the Adventures of Lady Black Eyes. In this swirling transcontinental composition Wormwood Khan was dead in a corner, bleeding into the Caspian Sea, which swarmed with finny monsters. In the remainder of the picture Wormwood's conqueror Shah Ismail of Persia greeted the Mughal ladies in Herat. The face of the Persian king bore an expression of wounded melancholy which reminded the emperor of Dashwanth's own characteristic way of looking, and he surmised that this dolorous countenance might be the artist's way of inserting himself into the tale of the hidden princess. But Dashwanth had gone further than that.

The simple fact was that in spite of the almost constant scrutiny of his peers he had somehow managed to vanish. He was never seen again, not in the Mughal court, nor anywhere in Sikri, nor anywhere in all the land of Hindustan. His body did not wash up on the shores of the lake, nor was it found hanging from a beam. He had simply disappeared as if he had never been, and almost all the pictures of the *Qara-Köz-Nama* had vanished with him, except for this last picture, in which Lady Black Eyes, looking lovelier than even Dashwanth had managed to make her look before, came face to face with the man who would be her destiny. The mystery was solved, inevitably, by Birbal. A week and a day after Dashwanth's disappearance the wisest of Akbar's courtiers, who had been scrutinizing the surface of the last remaining picture of the hidden princess in the hope of finding a clue, noticed a strange technical detail which had thus far gone undetected. It seemed as if the painting did not stop at the patterned borders in which Dashwanth had set it but, at least in the bottom left-hand corner, continued for some distance beneath that ornate two-inch-wide frame. The picture was returned to the studio—the emperor himself accompanied it, along with Birbal and Abul Fazl—and under the supervision of the two Persian masters the painted border was carefully separated from the main body of the work. When the hidden section of the painting was revealed the onlookers burst into cries of amazement, for there, crouching down like a little toad, with a great bundle of paper scrolls under his arm, was Dashwanth the great painter, Dashwanth the graffiti artist, Dashwanth the palanquin bearer's son and the thief of the *Qara-Köz-Nama,* Dashwanth released into the only world in which he now believed, the world of the hidden princess, whom he had created and who had then uncreated him. He had pulled off an impossible feat which was the exact opposite of the one achieved by the emperor when he conjured up his imaginary queen. Instead of bringing a fantasy woman to life, Dashwanth had turned himself into an imaginary being, driven (as the emperor had been driven) by the overwhelming force of love. If the borderline between the worlds could be crossed in one direction, Akbar understood, it could also be crossed in the other. A dreamer could become his dream.

"Put the border back," Akbar commanded, "and let the poor fellow have some peace." When this had been done the story of Dashwanth was left to rest where it belonged, in the margins of history. At the center of the stage were the rediscovered protagonist and her new lover—the hidden princess Lady Black Eyes or Qara Köz or Angelica, and the Shah of Persia—standing face to face.

II

{ 10 }

A hanged man's seed falls to the ground

A hanged man's seed falls to the ground," il Machia read aloud, "and there the mandrake will be found." When Nino Argalia and his best friend Niccolò—"il Machia"—were boys together in Sant'Andrea in Percussina in the state of Florence they dreamed of having occult power over women. Somewhere in the woods of the region a man must have been hanged sometime or other, they decided, and for many months they hunted for mandrakes on Niccolò's family property, the Caffagio oak wood and the *vallata* grove near Santa Maria dell'Impruneta, and also in the forest around the castle of Bibbione a little way away. They found only mushrooms and a mysterious dark flower that made them come out in a rash. At some point they decided the semen for the mandrake didn't necessarily have to come from a hanged man, and after much rubbing and panting they managed to spill a few impotent drops of their own upon the uninterested earth. Then on Easter Sunday in their tenth year the Palazzo della Signoria was festooned with the swinging dead, eighty of the defeated Pazzi conspirators hanged from its windows that weekend by Lorenzo de' Medici, including the archbishop in full regalia, and as it happened Argalia was staying in town with il Machia and his father Bernardo at their family house across the Ponte Vecchio, only three or four blocks away, and when they saw everyone running they could not be restrained.

Bernardo ran with the two boys, scared and excited at the same time, just like they were. Bernardo was a bookish man, boyish, sweet, and blood was distasteful to him, but a hanging archbishop was different, that was a sight worth seeing. The boys carried tin cups with them in case of useful drips. In the Piazza they ran into their pal Agostino Vespucci blowing loud raspberries at the murderous dead and making obscene masturbatory gestures at their corpses and shouting "Fuck you! Fuck your *daughter*! Fuck your *sister*! Fuck your *mother* and your *grandmother* and your *brother* and your *wife* and *her* brother and *her* mother and *her* mother's sister too" at them as they twisted and stank in the breeze. Argalia and il Machia told Ago about the mandrake rhyme and he grabbed a cup and went and stood under the archbishop's dick. Afterward in Percussina the three boys buried the two cups and recited what they imagined to be Satanic verses and then began a long, fruitless wait for the burgeoning of the plants of love.

"What begins with pendant traitors," the emperor Akbar said to Mogor dell'Amore, *"will be a treacherous tale."*

In the beginning there were three friends, Antonino Argalia, Niccolò "il Machia," and Ago Vespucci. Golden-haired Ago, the most voluble of the trio, was one of a throng, a jostle, an argument of Vespuccis living cheek by jowl in the crowded Ognissanti district of the city, trading in olive oil, wine, and wool across the Arno in the *gonfalone del drago,* the district of the dragon, and he had grown up foul-mouthed and loud because in his family you had to be like that to get heard over the racket of all the fire-breathing Vespuccis yelling at one another like apothecaries or barbers in the Mercato Vecchio. Ago's father worked for Lorenzo de' Medici as a notary, so after that Easter of stabbings and hangings he was relieved to come out on the winning side. "But the fucking Pope's army will come after us now because we killed the fucking priest," Ago muttered. "And the fucking King of Naples's army too." Ago's cousin, the wild twenty-four-year-old Amerigo or Alberico Vespucci, was soon packed off with his uncle Guido to get help for the Medici government from the King of France. From the light in Amerigo's eyes as he set off for Paris it was easy to see that he was more interested in the journey than the king. Ago wasn't the traveling kind. "I know what I'm going to be when I grow up," he told his friends in the Percussina mandrake woods in which there were no mandrakes. "I'll be a fucking sheep salesman or a booze merchant or else, if I get into the public service somehow, I'll be a fucking ledger-scribbling no-account no-hope no-future fucking clerk."

In spite of the bleakness of his clerical future Ago was full of stories. His stories were like Polo's adventures, they were fantastic voyages, and nobody believed a word he said, but everybody wanted to listen, especially to his tall tales about the most beautiful girl in the whole history of the city, or possibly since the earth was formed. It was just two years since Simonetta Cattaneo, who married Ago's cousin Marco Vespucci, known behind his back as Horned Marco or Marco the Fool of Love, had died of consumption and plunged all Florence into mourning, because Simonetta possessed a pale, fair beauty so intense that no man could look at her without falling into a state of molten adoration, and nor could any woman, and the same went for most of the city's cats and dogs, and maybe diseases loved her too, which was why she was dead before she was twenty-four years old. Simonetta Vespucci was married to Marco but he had to share her with the whole town, which he did, at first, with a resigned good grace that only proved his lack of brains to the citizens of that conniving, crafty locale. "Such beauty is a public resource," he would say, with an idiotic innocence, "like the river, or the gold in the treasury, or the fine light and air of Tuscany." The painter Alessandro Filipepi painted her many times, before and after she died, painted her clothed and naked, as the Spring and the goddess Venus, and even as herself. Whenever she posed for him she called him "my little barrel," because she always mistook him for his older brother, whom people called *"Botticelli"*—"Little Barrels"—on account of his bulbous shape. The younger Filipepi, the painter, didn't look like a barrel at all, but if that was what Simonetta wanted to call him it was all right by him, and so he started answering to the name.

Such was the effect of Simonetta's powers of enchantment. She would turn men into whatever she wanted them to be, gods or lap-dogs or little barrels or footstools or, of course, lovers. She could have ordered boys to die to prove their love of her and they would have done so gladly, but she was too good-natured for that, and never used her immense powers for ill. The cult of Simonetta grew until people were secretly praying to her in church, mumbling her name under their breath as if she was a living saint, and rumors grew of her miracles: a man struck blind by her loveliness as she passed him in the street, a blind man given sight when her sad fingertips were placed in a sudden gesture of pity upon his troubled brow, a crippled child rising to his feet to chase after her, another boy sud-denly paralyzed when he made obscene gestures behind her back. Both Lorenzo and Giuliano de' Medici were crazy about her and held a jousting tournament in her honor—Giuliano carried a ban-ner bearing her portrait, painted by Filipepi and bearing the French legend *la sans pareille,* proving that he had beaten his brother to her hand—and they moved her into a suite of rooms in the palace, at which point even stupid Marco noticed that something was wrong in his marriage, but he was warned that if he protested it would cost him his life. After that Marco Vespucci became the only man in the city capable of resisting the beauty of his wife. "She is a whore," he would say in the taverns he began to frequent to drown the knowl-edge of his cuckolding, "and to me she is as ugly as the Medusa." Total strangers would beat him up for impugning the beauty of *la sans pareille* and in the end he had to stay home in Ognissanti and drink alone. Then Simonetta fell sick and died and it was said on the streets of Florence that the city had lost its enchantress, that a part of its soul had died with her, and it even became a part of the common parlance that one day she would rise again—that Florentines would never truly be themselves until her second coming, at which time she would redeem them all, like a second Savior. "But," hissed Ago in the *vallata* wood, "you have no idea what Giuliano did to try to keep her alive: he turned her into a vampire."

According to her cousin-in-law, the best vampire hunter in the city, a certain Domenico Salcedo, was summoned to Giuliano's chamber and ordered to find a member of the blood-drinking undead. The following night Salcedo brought the vampire to the room in the palace where the sick girl lay, and the vampire bit her. But Simonetta refused to face eternity as a member of that sad, pale tribe. "When she realized she was a vampire she jumped from the top of the tower of the Palazzo Vecchio and impaled herself on the pike of a guard at the gate. You can imagine what they had to do to hush *that* up." So, according to her cousin-in-law, perished the first enchantress of Florence, perished beyond hope of a return from the dead. Marco Vespucci lost his mind with grief. ("Marco was a fool," Ago said unkindly. "If I was married to a piece of hot stuff like that, I'd keep her locked up in the highest tower where nobody could do her harm.") And Giuliano de' Medici was stabbed to death by a conspirator on the day of the Pazzi plot, while Filipepi the little barrel went on painting her, over and over, as if by painting her he could raise her from the dead.

"The same as Dashwanth," the emperor marveled.

"This may be the curse of the human race," responded Mogor. "Not that we are so different from one another, but that we are so alike."

The three boys were in the woods most days now, climbing trees and masturbating for mandrakes and telling each other insane stories about their families and complaining about the future to hide their fear, because right after the crushing of the Pazzi conspiracy the plague came to Florence and the three friends had been sent to the country for safety. Niccolò's father Bernardo stayed in the city and caught the disease, and when he became one of the few people to have had the plague and lived his son told his friends it was on account of his mother Bartolomea's magical way with cornmeal. "Whenever we get sick she covers us in porridge," he pronounced solemnly, whispering so that the wood-owls couldn't hear. "Depending on the sickness she uses the regular sweet yellow polenta but if it's something serious she buys the white Friuli kind. For something like this she probably puts kale and tomatoes into it as well and I don't know what other magical stuff. But it works. She makes us take off all our clothes and she ladles the hot porridge over every part of us and never mind the mess. The porridge sucks up the sickness and that's that. Seems even the plague was no match for Mamma's sweet polenta." After that Argalia started calling il Machia's crazy family the "Polentini" and made up songs about an imaginary sweetheart called Polenta. "If she was a florin, I would have spent her," he sang, "and if she was a book, then I would have lent her." And Ago joined in, "If she was a bow, then I would have bent her, and if she was a courtesan then I would rent her—my sweet Polenta." In the end il Machia stopped being annoyed and joined in. *If she was a message I would have sent her. If she was a meaning I would have meant her.* But when news came that both Nino Argalia's parents had caught the plague all the polenta magic in the world proved useless. Argalia became an orphan before he was ten years old.

The day Nino came to the oak wood to tell il Machia and Ago that his parents were dead was also the day they found the mandrake. It was hiding under a fallen branch like a scared animal. "All we need now," said Ago sadly, "is the spell that turns us into men, because without that what's the point of having ladies besotted with us, anyhow?" Then Argalia arrived and they saw in his eyes that he had found the spell of manhood. They showed him the mandrake and he shrugged. "That sort of thing doesn't interest me anymore," he said. "I'm running away to Genoa to join the Band of Gold." It was the autumn of the *condottieri,* the soldiers of fortune with personal, mercenary armies who rented out their services to the city-states of Italy, which were too cheap to maintain standing armies of their own. All Florence knew the story of the city's own Giovanni Milano, who had been born Sir John Hauksbank in Scotland a hundred years before. In France he was "Jean

Aubainc," in the German-speaking cantons of Switzerland he was "Hans Hoch," and in Italy it was Giovanni Milano—"Milano" because a *milan* was a hawk—leader of the White Company, erstwhile general of Florence, and victor, on Florence's behalf, of the battle of Polpetto against the hated Venetians. Paolo Uccello had worked on his funerary fresco and it was in the Duomo still. But the age of the *condottieri* was coming to an end.

The greatest remaining mercenary fighter, according to Argalia, was Andrea Doria, leader of the Band of Gold, who just then were busy with the liberation of Genoa from French control. "But you are Florentine, and we are allied with the French," Ago cried, remembering his relatives' mission to Paris. "When you are a mercenary," Argalia said, feeling his chin to see if any hairs might be growing there, "the allegiances of your birth go by the board."

Andrea Doria's soldiers were armed with "hook-guns"— harquebuses or arquebuses—which you had to support on a tripod when you were shooting, like a little portable cannon. Many of them were Swiss, and the Swiss mercenaries were the worst killing machines of all, men with no faces or souls, invincible, terrifying. When he was done with the French and had gained command of the Genoese fleet, Doria intended to take on the Turk himself. Argalia liked the idea of sea battles. "We never had any money anyway," he said, "and my father's debts will eat up our house in the city and our little bit of property out here, so I can either beg in the street like a pauper's dog or die trying to make my fortune. The two of you will grow fat with power and fill a couple of wretched women full of babies and you'll leave them home to listen to the little bastards scream while you go off to the whorehouse of La Zingaretta or some such pillowy high-class tart who can recite poetry while you bounce up and down on her and fuck yourselves silly, and meanwhile I'll be dying on a burning caravel outside Constantinople with a Turkish scimitar in my gut. Or who knows? I might turn Turk myself. Argalia the Turk, Wielder of the Enchanted Lance, with four huge Swiss giants, Muslim converts, in my retinue. Swiss Mohammedans, yes. Why not. When you're a mercenary it's gold and treasure that talk, and for that you have to go east."

"You're just a kid like us," il Machia reasoned with him. "Don't you want to grow up before you get yourself killed?"

"Not me," said Argalia, "I'm off to heathen lands to fight against strange gods. Who knows what they worship out there, scorpions or monsters or worms. They'll die the same as us, though, I'll bet on that."

"Don't go to your death with your mouth full of sacrileges," said Niccolò. "Stay with us. My father loves you at least as much as he loves me. Or, think how many Vespuccis there are in Ognissanti already. They won't even notice an extra one if you prefer to live at Ago's place."

"I'm going," said Argalia. "Andrea Doria has almost driven the French out of the city and I want to be there to see the day of freedom when it comes."

"And you, with your three gods, a carpenter, a father, and a ghost, and the carpenter's mother for a fourth," the emperor asked Mogor with some irritation, "you from that holy land which hangs its bishops and burns its priests at the stake, while its greatest priest commands armies and behaves as brutally as any common general or prince—which of the wild religions of this heathen land do you find most attractive, or are they all one to you in their vileness? In the eyes of Father Acquaviva and Father Monserrate, we are sure, we are all what your Argalia thought us to be, which is to say, godless swine."

"Sire," said Mogor dell'Amore, calmly, "I am attracted toward the great polytheist pantheons because the stories are better, more numerous, more dramatic, more humorous, more marvelous; and because the gods do not set us good examples, they are interfering, vain, petulant, and badly behaved, which is, I confess, quite appealing."

"We have the same feeling," the emperor said, regaining his composure, "and our affection for these wanton, angry, playful, loving gods is

very great. We have set up a force of one hundred and one men to count and name them all, every worshipped divinity of Hindustan, not only the celebrated, high gods, but all the low ones too, the little spirits of place, of sighing woodland grove and laughing mountain stream. We have made them leave their homes and families and embark on a journey without end, a journey that will only end when they die, for the task we have set them is an impossible one, and when a man takes on the impossible he travels every day with death, accepting the journey as a purification, a magnification of the soul, so that it becomes a journey not toward the naming of the gods but toward God himself. They have barely begun their labors, yet they have already collected one million names. Such a proliferation of divinity! We think there are more supernatural entities in this land than people of flesh and blood, and are happy to live in so magical a world. And yet we must be what we are. The million gods are not our gods; the austere religion of our father will always be ours, just as the carpenter's creed is yours."

He was no longer looking at Mogor, and had fallen into a reverie. Peacocks danced on the morning stones of Sikri and in the distance the great lake shimmered like a ghost. The emperor's gaze traveled past the peacocks and the lake, past the court of Herat and the lands of the fierce Turk, and rested on the spires and domes of an Italian city far away. "Imagine a pair of woman's lips," Mogor whispered, "puckering for a kiss. That is the city of Florence, narrow at the edges, swelling at the center, with the Arno flowing through between, parting the two lips, the upper and the lower. The city is an enchantress. When it kisses you, you are lost, whether you be commoner or king."

Akbar was walking the streets of that other stone city in which nobody ever seemed to want to stay indoors. The life of Sikri took place behind drawn curtains and barred gates. The life of this alien city was lived under the cathedral dome of the sky. People ate where the birds could share their food and gambled where any cutpurse could steal their winnings, they kissed in full view of strangers and even fucked in the shadows if they wanted to. What did it mean to be a man so completely among men, and women too? When solitude was banished, did one become more oneself, or less? Did the crowd enhance one's selfhood or erase it? The emperor felt *like the Caliph of Baghdad Harun al-Rashid walking round his city at night to learn how his citizens lived. But Akbar's cloak was cut from the cloths of time and space and these people were not his. Why, then, did he feel so strong a sense of kinship with the denizens of these braying lanes? Why did he understand their unspeakable European tongue as if it were his own?*

"The questions of kingship," the emperor said after a time, "concern us less and less. Our kingdom has laws in place to guide it, and officials worthy of trust, and a system of taxation that raises enough money without making people unhappier than is prudent. When there are enemies to defeat we will defeat them. In short, in that field we have the answers we require. The question of Man, however, continues to vex us, and the related problem of Woman, almost as much."

"It is in my city, sire, that the question of Man has been answered for all time," Mogor said. "And as to Woman, well, that is the very sum and matter of my story. For, many years after the death of Simonetta the first enchantress of Florence, the foretold second enchantress did indeed arrive."

{ 11 }

Everything he loved was on his doorstep

Everything he loved was on his doorstep, according to Ago Vespucci; it wasn't necessary to go questing across the world and die among guttural strangers to find your heart's desire. Long ago in the octagonal gloom of the Battistero di San Giovanni he had been baptized twice, as was customary, once as a Christian and again as a Florentine, and to an irreligious bastard like Ago it was the second baptism that counted. The city was his religion, a world as perfect as any heaven. The great Buonarroti had called the Baptistery doors the gates of Paradise and when little baby Ago emerged from that place with a wet head he had understood at once that he had entered a walled and gated Eden. The city of Florence had fifteen gates and on their inner faces were pictures of the Virgin and various saints. Voyagers touched the gates for good luck, and nobody starting on a journey through those gates did so without consulting astrologers. In the opinion of Ago Vespucci the absurdity of such superstitions only proved the folly of long-distance travel. The Machiavelli farm in Percussina was at the outer rim of Ago's universe. Beyond that the cloud of unknowing began. Genoa and Venice were as distant and fictional as Sirius or Aldebaran in the sky. The word *planet* meant *wanderer*. Ago disapproved of the planets and preferred the fixed stars. Aldebaran and Venice, Genoa and the Dog Star might be too far away to be completely real, but at least they had the good grace to stay where they were.

As it turned out the Pope and the King of Naples didn't attack Florence after the defeat of the Pazzi plot, but when Ago was in his early twenties the King of France did show up, and entered the city in triumph—a short little red-haired homunculus whose insufferable Frenchness made Ago feel like throwing up. Instead he went to a whorehouse and worked strenuously to improve his mood. On the threshold of manhood Ago had agreed with his friend Niccolò "il Machia" on one thing: whatever hardships the times might bring, a good, energetic night with the ladies would put everything right. "There are few woes in the world, dear Ago," il Machia had advised him when they were still only thirteen, "that a woman's fanny will not cure." Ago was an earnest boy, good-hearted beneath his pose of a foul-mouthed rapscallion. "And the ladies," he asked, "where do they go to cure their woes?" Il Machia looked perplexed, as if he had never considered the matter, or, perhaps, as if to indicate that a man's time should not be wasted on the consideration of such things. "To each other, no doubt," he said with an adolescent finality that sounded to Ago like the last word on the matter. Why should women not seek consolation in each other's arms at a time when half the young men of Florence did the same thing?

The widespread popularity of sodomy among the flower of Florentine manhood had earned the city the reputation of being the world capital of the act. "Sodom Reborn," Niccolò at thirteen renamed his hometown. Even at this early age he was already able to reassure Ago that the ladies were more interesting to him, "so you don't have to worry about me jumping you in the woods." Many of their contemporaries were of the opposite temperament, however—for example, their classmates Biagio Buonaccorsi and Andrea di Romolo—and as an answer to the problem of the growing fashionability of homosexual practices the city, with the full support of the Church, established a Decency Office, whose job it was to build and subsidize brothels and recruit prostitutes and pimps from other parts of Italy and Europe to supplement the local tarts. The Vespuccis of Ognissanti, spotting an opportunity, diversified their businesses and began to offer women for sale as well as olive oil and wool. "Maybe I won't even be a clerk," Ago gloomily told Niccolò when they were sixteen. "I'll end up running a bawdy house instead." Il Machia told him to look on the bright side. "Clerks never get fucked," he pointed out, "but you'll be the envy of us all."

The path of Sodom never appealed to Ago either, and the truth was that underneath all his dirty talk Ago Vespucci was a youth of overweening modesty. Il Machia, however, seemed to be the reincarnation of the god Priapus, always ready for action, always chasing the ladies, both professionals and amateurs, and he dragged Ago to his damnation several times a week. In the early days of their adolescent potency, when Ago accompanied his friend into the raucous brothel night, he would always choose the youngest whore in il Machia's preferred establishment, who called herself "Scandal" but seemed almost demure: a skeletal creature from the village of Bibbione who never spoke, and looked as scared as he did. For a long time he actually paid her to sit still on the edge of the bed while he stretched out and pretended to sleep until il Machia stopped heaving and grunting in the room next door. Then he began to try to improve her mind by reading poetry to her, which she kindly pretended to appreciate, even though she was secretly so bored that she thought she might die of it, and even a little repelled by what sounded to her like the noises men make when they tell accomplished lies.

One day she decided to change things. Her solemn features broke into a shy smile and she came to Ago and put one hand over his Petrarch-filled mouth and the other in another place. When she exposed his manhood Ago blushed violently, and then began to sneeze. He sneezed for an hour without stopping, and by the end of it there was blood pouring from his nose. The skeletal whore thought he was dying and ran for help. She came back with the biggest naked woman Ago had ever seen and the moment his nose smelled her it stopped misbehaving. "I get it," said the giantess, who went by the name of La Matterassina, "you think you like them skinny, but in fact you're a boy for flesh." She turned to her bony co-worker and told her, in plain terms, to get lost; where-upon, without any warning, Ago's nose exploded again. "Mother of God," the giantess exclaimed, "so you're a greedy bastard under all that terror. You won't be satisfied unless you have us both."

After that there was no stopping Ago, and even il Machia had to applaud. "Slow starter, strong finisher," he said approvingly. "For a fellow who's nothing much to look at you have the instincts of a champion."

When Ago was twenty-four his love of the city was put to the test as never before. The Medici family was expelled, the brothels were all closed, and the stink of religious sanctimony filled the air. This was the time of the rise to power of the cult of the Weepers, the narrow-minded fanatics of whom Ago would say to il Machia, under his breath, that they might have been born Florentines but when the baptismal water hit their heads it must have boiled off before it could anoint them, because they were all blazing with hellfire heat. "The Devil sent us these devils to warn us against devilry," he said on the day the long darkness came to an end. "And they bedeviled us for four fucking years. The cassock of ho-liness cloaks the codpiece of evil, every fucking time."

He didn't need to whisper anymore on the day he said this, be-cause his adored hometown had just been reborn, like the fabled phoenix, thanks to a healing fire. The Head Weeper, the monk Girolamo who had made everyone's life a living hell, was roasting nicely in the middle of the Piazza della Signoria, on the exact spot where his lachrymose crew had tried to turn beauty to ashes sev-eral years earlier, dragging paintings and female adornments and even mirrors out there and setting them alight, under the erro-neous impression that human beings' love of loveliness, and even Vanity herself, could be destroyed in hypocritical flames. "Burn, you shit-blood prick," Ago yelled, capering around the burning monk in a manner that did not befit his imminent sober employ-ment as a city clerk. "That bonfire gave us the idea for this one!" The musky stench of Girolamo Savonarola's burning flesh did nothing to spoil Ago's good mood. He was twenty-eight years old, and the brothels were reopening.

———※———

"Mercatrice, meretrice." The city of wealthy traders was also according to ancient custom a city of fabulous whores. Now that the Weepers' day was done the true nature of that city of lubricious sensualists reasserted itself. The world of the whorehouse came flooding back. The big Macciana brothel, in the center of town near the Mercato Vecchio and the Battistero, took down its shutters and offered short-term discount rates to re-establish its preeminence, and in the Piazza del Frascato at the brothel's heart the dancing bears and dwarf jugglers reappeared, the monkeys dressed up in uniform who were trained to "die for their country" and the parrots that remembered the names of the brothel's clients and shouted them out to greet their owners whenever they showed up. And of course the women came back too, the wild Slav harlots, the melancholy Polish doxies, the loud Roman strumpets, the thick German tarts, the Swiss mercenaries as ferocious in bed as their male counterparts were on the field of battle, and the local girls, who were the best of all. Ago didn't believe in traveling, even in bed. He found his favorite girls again, fine Tuscan goods, both of them: and as well as the whore called Scandal and her sidekick La Matterassina he took a shine to a certain Beatrice Pisana who took the name of Pantasilea, the Queen of the Amazons, because she had been born with only one breast which, by way of compensation, was the most beautiful breast in the city, which was to say, as far as Ago was concerned, in all the known world.

As daylight failed and the fire in the Piazza went out, its job well done, music rose up from the Macciana and its rival pleasure-zone, the Chiasso de' Buoi or Alley of the Cows, and blessed the city like an angel pronouncing the rebirth of joy. Ago and il Machia decided to make a night of it, a great night which would also be the last night of their carefree youth, because while Savonarola was still burning the new ruling Council of Eighty had called Niccolò into the Palazzo and appointed him secretary of the Second Chancery which handled the foreign affairs of the Republic of Florence.

Niccolò immediately told Ago he was giving him a job as well. "Why me?" Ago asked. "I hate fucking foreigners."

"In the first place, *furbo,*" il Machia replied, "I'll fuck with the foreigners and just leave all the most tedious paperwork to you. In the second place, you're the one who prophesied this, so don't bitch about it now that your dream is coming true."

"Fuck, *bugiarone,* you really are an asshole," said Ago, unhappily, and rudely made a fig at his friend with his left hand by sticking his thumb between his first and second fingers. "Let's go get a drink to celebrate my clairvoyant powers."

A *furbo* was a fellow with street smarts. A *bugiarone* was a less complimentary and in Niccolò's case also a less accurate thing to be called. It remained the case that neither Ago nor il Machia were sodomites, or not often, but that night, while Weepers were running for their lives or, if they couldn't run fast enough, being strung up in side-alleys and horse-barns, the true Florence was emerging from its hiding places, and that meant that men were once again holding hands and kissing each other almost anywhere you cared to look. "Buonaccorsi and di Romolo can stop hiding their love at last," il Machia said. "By the way, I think I'm going to hire them as well, so you can watch them going at it in the office while I'm away on official business."

"There's nothing those two sex maniacs can show me," Ago replied, "that I haven't already seen, and that includes the pathetic little prunes in their pants."

Renewal, regeneration, rebirth. In Ago's local church in Ognissanti, a building he only willingly entered when word got out that some great courtesan was present to advertise her charms, the faithful swore that Giotto's stern Madonna spent the night grinning all over her face. And that evening outside the church of Orsanmichele where the grandest courtesans were once again at prayer, once again wearing their finest Milan fashions and the jewels of their protectors, Niccolò and Ago were accosted by a *ruffiana,* Giulietta Veronese, the midget agent and some said also the Sapphic lover of the most celebrated night-lady in all of Florence, Alessandra Fiorentina. The Veronese invited them to the gala re-opening night of the House of Mars, the city's leading salon, named after the lost statue of the war god which used to stand on the riverbank until the flooding Arno bore it away. The House stood on the north bank of the river near the Bridge of the Graces. This invitation was an extraordinary event. La Fiorentina's network of informants was unquestionably excellent and quick, but even if she had already heard about il Machia's new position the rank of secretary of the Second Chancery scarcely merited his inclusion in that most select and exclusive company, and as for dragging the even less significant Ago Vespucci along, that was an unprecedented privilege.

They had seen Alessandra's picture, of course, they had drooled over her image in a volume of miniatures, her long blond hair evoking the memory of the departed Simonetta, after whose death her deranged husband Horned Marco had unsuccessfully begged for admission to La Fiorentina's salon. He had hired one of the city's leading *mezzano* agents to negotiate with Alessandra's *ruffiana.* The agent had written love letters on Horned Marco's behalf, and sung serenades beneath Alessandra's evening casement, and even had a sonnet by Petrarca written out in gold calligraphy as a special Twelfth Night gift. The door of the salon remained barred. "My mistress," Giulietta Veronese told the *mezzano,* "is not interested to be a crackpot cuckold's necrophiliac fantasy. Tell your master to go put a hole in a picture of his late wife and fornicate with that instead."

A week after this final refusal Marco Vespucci hanged himself. His body dangled from the Bridge of the Graces, but Alessandra Fiorentina never saw it. She braided her long golden tresses at her window and it was as if Marco the Fool of Love were an invisible man, because Alessandra had long ago perfected the art of seeing only what she wanted to see, which was an essential accomplishment if you wanted to be one of the world's masters and not its victim. Her seeing constructed the city. If she did not see you then you did not exist. Marco Vespucci dying invisibly outside her window died a second death under her erasing gaze.

Once, a decade ago in the glory of her youth, Niccolò and Ago had worshipped Alessandra as she lounged at an open balcony, looking out at the Arno and leaning forward on a red velvet cushion so that the whole world could admire her noble *décolletage,* pretending all the while to read a book that was probably Boccaccio's *Decameron.* The puritan years did not seem to have damaged her beauty or her standing. She had her own palazzo now, was the queen of the so-called House of Mars, and would hold court that evening on the *piano nobile.* "The lower orders," said Giulietta Veronese, "are able to entertain themselves in the casino on the ground floor." During the nine years of Weeper rule Giulietta the midget had been obliged to scrape a living as a hairdresser, fortune-teller, and concocter of love potions. She was rumored to have robbed graves and stolen the umbilical cords of dead babies, and cut away the hymens of dead virgins, and popped the eyes of the dead out of their sockets, for use in her nefarious spells. Ago wanted to tell her that she was scarcely the person to be talking about the lower fucking orders but il Machia pinched him just in time, hard enough to make him forget what he was going to say and decide to kill Niccolò Machiavelli instead. This, too, he quickly forgot, because the Veronese hag was giving them instructions. "Bring her poetry," she said. "Poetry is what she likes, not flowers. She has enough of flowers. Bring her the latest thing by Sannazaro or Cecco d'Ascoli, or learn well one of Parabosco's madrigals and offer to sing it for her. She is formidable. If you sing badly she will slap you in the face. Do not bore her, or some of her favored young gentlemen may toss you out of a window like a tiresome toy. Do not importune her, or her protector will have you stabbed in the heart in an alley before you get home tomorrow. You are being invited for one reason only. Do not trespass on territory that is not yours to walk upon."

"Why are we being invited, then," il Machia asked her.

"She will tell you," said the Veronese crone spitefully, "if she feels like it."

—————\\\—————

Akbar the Great was informed of the rapid rise of the sex workers known as Skeleton and Mattress from lowly whores at the Hatyapul gate to fully fledged courtesans with a villa of their own by the lakeside. "Their success is being seen by the people as a sign of the ascendancy of the ladies' favorite, the foreigner Vespucci, who prefers the problematic title of Mogor dell'Amore," Abul Fazl told him. "As to the source of the capital needed to initiate such an enterprise, one can only speculate." Umar the Ayyar independently confirmed the popularity of the so-called House of Skanda, named after the Hindu god of war, "because," the saying went in the noblemen's mansions in Lower Sikri, "when you grapple with those ladies it's more like fighting a battle than making love." Umar reported that the court's musical genius Tansen had gone so far as to create a raag in the two courtesans' honor, the raag deepak, *so called because when he played it for the first time in the House of Skanda the sorcery of the melody made unlit lamps burst into flame.*

In his dreams the emperor himself visited the brothel, which in the night country stood on the banks of an unknown foreign river instead of the shores of his own lake. It was plain that Mogor dell'Amore was also in the grip of a waking dream, because it was he who had transported these whores across the world to the Arno in his tale. "All men lie about whores," Akbar thought, and forgave him. He had more serious things to worry about.

To dream of searching for love was a sure sign that a love had been lost, and when he awoke the emperor was perturbed. The next night he sought

out Jodha and possessed her with a fury that had been lacking in their cou-
plings ever since he returned from the wars. She wondered, when he left to
listen to the foreigner's story, if this wild passion was a sign of his return,
or a gesture of farewell.

———

"For a woman to please a man," the emperor said, "it is necessary that
she be able to sing. She should know how to play musical instruments, and
dance, and do all three things together when requested: singing, dancing,
and piping on a flute or fiddling a tune upon a string. She should write
well, draw well, be adept in the giving of tattoos, and be prepared to receive
them in whatsoever place the man should desire. She should know how to
speak the language of flowers when decorating beds or couches, or even
when decorating the ground: the cherry is for loyalty, the narcissus for joy,
the lotus for purity and truth. The willow is the woman and the peony the
man. Pomegranate buds bring fertility, olives bring honor, and pine cones
are for long life and wealth. The morning glory should always be avoided
because it speaks of death."

In the emperor's harem the concubines were boxed in red stone cubicles
softened by fat pillows. Around a central courtyard, above which a mirrorwork marquee shielded the harem from the sun and unworthy eyes, the cubicles stood in serried ranks, like an army of love, or livestock. One day
Mogor was accorded the privilege of accompanying Akbar into this hidden
world. He was followed by a slender eunuch whose body was undefiled by a
single hair. This was Umar the Ayyar; he had no eyebrows, his head shone
like a helmet, his skin was unwrinkled and soft. It was impossible to tell his
age but Mogor intuited instantly that this silken boy would kill a man without a qualm, would cut off his best friend's head if that were the emperor's
desire. The women of the harem moved around them in patterns that reminded Mogor of the journeys of the stars, the loops and swirls of heavenly
bodies moving around—yes!—the sun. He told the emperor about the new,
heliocentric model of the universe, speaking in a low voice, because it was a
concept which could still get a man burned at the stake for heresy back home.

It was not a thing to shout about, even though it was improbable that the Pope could hear him here, in the harem of the Grand Mughal.

Akbar laughed. "This has been known for hundreds of years," he said. "How backward your reborn Europe seems to be, like a baby throwing a rattle out of its bassinet because it doesn't want the rattle to make a noise." Mogor accepted the rebuke and changed the subject. "I meant only to say that Your Majesty is the sun and these your satellites," he said. The emperor thumped him on the back. "In the field of flattery, at least, you can teach us a thing or two. We will tell our champion flatterer Bhakti Ram Jain to come and pick up some pointers from you."

Silently, slowly, like mind-creatures in a dream, the concubines circled and swayed. They stirred the air around the emperor into a magic soup flavored with the spices of arousal. There was no hurry. The emperor ruled over everything. Time itself could be stretched and paused. There was all the time in the world.

"In the arts of staining, dyeing, coloring, and painting her teeth, her clothes, her nails, and her body a woman should be beyond compare," the emperor said, his speech now sluggish with lust. Wine was brought in golden glass pitchers and he drank in large, unwise gulps. A pipe was brought forward and then there was opium smoke in his pupils. The concubines were closer now, circling inward, their bodies beginning to brush against those of the emperor and his guest. In the emperor's company one was emperor for a day. His privileges became yours as well. "A woman should know how to play music on glasses filled to different heights with liquids of various sorts," said the emperor, slurring his words. "She should be able to fix stained glass into a floor. She should know how to make, trim, and hang a picture; how to fashion a necklace, a rosary, a garland, or a wreath; and how to store or gather water in an aqueduct or tank. She should know about scents. And about ornaments for the ear. And she should be able to act, and to lay on theatrical shows, and she should be quick and sure in her hands, and be able to cook and make lemonade or sherbet, and wear jewels, and bind a man's turban. And she should, of course, know magic. A woman who knows these few things is almost the equal of any ignorant brute of a man."

The concubines had blended into a single supernatural Woman, a composite Concubine, and She was all around the two men, besieging them with love. The eunuch had slipped away outside the circle of the planets of desire. The single woman of many arms and infinite possibilities, the Concubine, silenced their tongues, her softness touching their hardness. Mogor gave himself up to her. He thought of other women far away and long ago, Simonetta Vespucci and Alessandra Fiorentina, and the woman whose story he had come to Sikri to tell. They were part of the Concubine too.

"In my city," he said much later, reclining on cushions, amid the melancholy of women after love, "a woman of breeding should be prudent and chaste, and should not be the object of gossip. Such a woman must be modest and calm, candid and benign. When she dances she should not make energetic movements and when she plays music she should avoid the brazenness of brass, and the drumness of drums. She should be painted sparingly and her hairstyle should not be elaborate." The emperor, even though he was mostly asleep, made a noise of disgust. "Then your men of breeding must die of boredom," he pronounced. "Ah, but the courtesan," said Mogor, "she fulfills all your ideals, except, possibly, for the business about the stained glass." "Never make love to a woman who is bad with stained glass," the emperor said solemnly, giving no indication of humorous intent. "Such a woman is an ignorant shrew."

—⁓—

That was the night Agostino Vespucci fell in love for the first time, and understood that adoration was a journey too, that however determined he might be not to leave his native city he was doomed like all his footloose friends to walk down roads he did not know, the heart's pathways that would oblige him to enter places of danger, confront demons and dragons, and run the risk of losing not only his life but his soul as well. He caught a glimpse through an idly open door of La Fiorentina in her private sanctum, reclining on a gilded chaise in the midst of a small group of the city's very finest men, and idly permitting her patron Francesco del Nero to kiss her left breast while a little hairy white lapdog licked at her right nipple, and in that instant he was done for, and knew that she was the only woman for him. Francesco del Nero was a relative of il Machia's and maybe that was why they had been invited, but at that moment Ago didn't care, he was ready to strangle the bastard on the spot, yes, and the fucking lapdog too. To conquer La Fiorentina he would have to defeat many such rivals, yes, and make his fortune too, and as the road to his future rolled out before him like a rug he felt the insouciance of his youth slip away from him. In its place a new resolve was born, as sharp and tempered as any Toledo blade.

"She will be mine," he murmured to il Machia, and his friend looked amused. "On the day I am elected Pope," he said, "Alessandra Fiorentina will invite you into her bed. Look at you. You are not a man with whom beautiful women fall in love. You are a man who runs errands for them, and on whom they wipe their feet."

"Go to hell," Ago replied. "It's your curse to see the world too fucking clearly, and without a shred of kindness, and then you can't keep it to yourself, you just have to spit it out, and to hell with people's feelings. Why don't you go and masturbate a diseased goat."

Il Machia raised his bat's-wing eyebrows, as if to concede that he had gone too far, and kissed his friend on both cheeks. "Excuse me," he said in a repentant voice. "You are right. A young man of twenty-eight who is not particularly tall, who is already losing his hair, whose body is a collection of soft pillows stuffed into a case that's slightly too small to hold them, who remembers no verses except filthy ones, and whose tongue is a byword for obscenity— that's exactly the fellow who will part Queen Alessandra's legs." Ago shook his head unhappily. "I'll tell you how big a prick I am," he said. "I don't just want her flesh. I want her fucking heart."

In the high-ceilinged salon of Alessandra Fiorentina, under a domed ceiling frescoed with flying cherubs in a blue sky attending upon the cloud mattress where Ares and Aphrodite were making love, listening to the celestial music of the German Heinrich Zink, the greatest player of the *cornetto curvo* in all Italy, Ago Vespucci felt as if he had been illuminated by a ray of the sun at midnight, and turned once again into that petrified virgin of years before who had sat on a skinny tart's bed reading her the verses of the great poets of the day and blushing and sneezing when she decided to get to the point. La Fiorentina was nowhere to be seen and in her absence he stood cap in hand by a little fountain, unable to join in the orgy all around him. Il Machia abandoned him for a time and ran off into a *trompe l'oeil* wood with a pair of nude dryads. Ago's body weighed heavily upon him. He was a phantom at the feast. He was the only living man in a house of orgiastic ghosts. He felt ponderous, sad, and alone.

Nobody in the reborn city slept that night. Music crowded the air, and the streets, the taverns, the houses of ill repute and those of good reputation too, the markets, the nunneries, all were full of love. The statues of the gods came down from their flower-decked alcoves and joined in the fun, pressing their cold marble nudity against warm human flesh. Even the animals and birds got the idea and went at it with a will. Rats rutted in the shadows of bridges, and bats in their belfries did whatever it is that bats like to do. A man ran through the streets naked and tolling a merry bell. "Wipe your eyes and unbutton your pants," he shouted, "for the time of tears is done." Ago Vespucci in the House of Mars heard that bell ringing in the distance and was filled with an inexplicable fear. A moment later he understood that it was the terror of his life passing, his life slipping through his fingers while he stood paralyzed and alone. He felt as though twenty years might pass in that instant, as if he might be borne away by the music, carried helplessly into a future of paralysis and failure, when time itself would stop altogether, crushed under the burden of his pain.

Then, at last, the *ruffiana* Giulietta Veronese beckoned him. "You are a lucky such-and-such," she said. "Even though she has had a big night, a magnificent night, La Fiorentina says she will see you now, and your sex-crazy friend as well." Ago Vespucci burst with a yell into the bedchamber of the painted woods, dragged il Machia off his dryads, threw his clothes at him, and pulled him, still dressing, toward the enchanted chamber where Alessandra the Beauty was waiting.

In the sanctum of the great courtesan, the city's grandees were asleep, sated, in *déshabillé* on velvet couches, their limbs flung wantonly across the prone bodies of naked hetaerae, Alessandra's junior troupe, her supporting act, who had danced naked for the dignitaries until they forgot their dignity and turned into howling wolves. La Fiorentina's bed, however, was empty, its sheets pristine, and Ago's heart gave a little leap of stupid hope. *She has no lover. She is waiting for you.* But radiant Alessandra was not thinking about sex. She lounged across her unused bed eating grapes from a bowl, clothed in nothing but her golden hair, and gave only the most minute indication of having noticed their entry into her boudoir in the company of her midget watchdog. They stood and waited. Then after a few moments she spoke, softly, as if telling herself a bedtime story.

"In the beginning," she said, absently, "there were three friends, Niccolò 'il Machia,' Agostino Vespucci, and Antonino Argalia. Their boyhood world was a magic wood. Then Nino's parents were taken by the plague. He left to seek his fortune and they never saw him again."

When they heard these words both men forgot about the present and were plunged into memories. Niccolò's own mother Bartolomea de' Nelli, who cured sicknesses with the help of porridge, had died suddenly not long after the nine-year-old orphan Argalia had headed to Genoa to seek employment in the arquebus-armed militia commanded by the *condottiere* Andrea Doria. Niccolò's father Bernardo had done his best to cook up a polenta cure but Bartolomea had died anyway, burning up and shivering, and Bernardo had never been the same since. These days he spent his time on the farm in Percussina, scratching out a living and blaming himself for lacking the skills in the kitchen that could have saved his wife's life. "If I had just paid attention," he said a hundred times a day, "I could have learned the proper recipe. Instead I just covered her poor body in a useless hot muck and she left me in disgust." And while il Machia was thinking about his dead mother and his ruined father, Ago was remembering the day Argalia left them looking like any destitute tramp, with a bundle of possessions hanging on a shouldered stick. "The day he left," he said aloud, "was the day we stopped being children." But that wasn't what he was thinking, or not all of it. *And it was the day we found the mandrake root,* he added silently, and a fantasy began to take shape in his head, a plan that would make Alessandra Fiorentina his love-slave for life.

Their distraction irritated Alessandra, but she was far too grand to show it. "What a pair of cold-hearted good-for-nothings you are," the courtesan chided them without raising her low, smoky, indifferent voice. "Does the name of your lost, best friend mean nothing to you, though you have not heard it for nineteen years?"

Ago Vespucci was too tongue-tied to reply, but the truth was that nineteen years was a long time. They had loved Argalia and lost him and for months, even years, they had hoped for news. Finally they had both stopped mentioning him, both separately convinced that Argalia's silence must mean their friend was dead. Neither of them wanted to face that truth. So each of them had hidden Argalia away within themselves, because as long as he was a taboo subject he might still be alive. But then they grew up and he got lost inside them, he faded, and became no more than an unspoken name. It was hard to call him back to life.

In the beginning there were three friends, who each went on a journey. Ago, who detested travel, was destined to go down the rocky path of love. Il Machia was far more desirable than he, but was most interested in the quest for power, which was a surer aphrodisiac than any magic root. And Argalia, Argalia was lost in the heavens, he was their wandering star . . . "Is it bad news?" Niccolò was asking Alessandra. "Forgive us. We have feared this moment for most of our lives."

Alessandra gestured toward a side door. "Take them to her," she told Giulietta Veronese. "I'm too tired to answer any of these questions right now." With that she slipped into sleep, her head resting on her outstretched right arm, and from her perfect nose there emerged the faintest little ghost of a snore. "You have heard her," Giulietta the midget said roughly. "It's time to go." Then, relenting a little, she added, "You will get all your answers in here."

Behind the door was another bedchamber, but the woman in this place was neither naked nor recumbent. The room was poorly lit—a single candle burned low in its holder on a wall—and as they accustomed their eyes to the gloom they saw standing before them an odalisque of royal bearing, bare of midriff, wearing a tight bodice and loose pantaloons, and with her hands clasped in front of her chest. "Silly bitch," said Giulietta Veronese, "she thinks perhaps that she is still in the Ottoman harem, and has not become accustomed to the facts." She went up close to the odalisque, who was almost twice her height, and shouted up at her from the level, approximately, of her navel. "You were captured by pirates! *Pirates!* Already two weeks ago—*il y a déjà deux semaines*—you have been sold at a slave market in Venice! *Un marché des esclaves!* Understand? You hear what I say to you? *Est-ce que tu comprends ce que je te dis?*" She turned back to Ago and il Machia. "The owner, he offers her to us on approval, and we still make up our minds. She's a looker all right, the breasts, the ass, these are good"—here the midget fondled the stationary woman lasciviously—"but this is a strange one, for sure."

"What is her name?" Ago asked. "Why do you address her in French? Why does she look as if she has been turned to stone?"

"We have heard a story of a French princess kidnapped by the Turk," said Giulietta Veronese, circling the silent woman like a predator. "But it is only a legend, we have thought. Maybe this is she. Maybe not she. She speaks French, that is sure. However, she will not answer to a real name. When you ask her what she's called she says, *I am the memory palace.* Ask her yourself. Go ahead. Why not? Are you afraid?"

"*Qui êtes-vous, mademoiselle,*" il Machia asked in his kindest voice, and the stone woman replied, "*Je suis le palais des souvenirs.*" "You see?" Giulietta crowed in triumph. "Like she's not a person anymore. Like she's more of a place."

"What does she have to do with Argalia?" Ago wanted to know. The odalisque stirred, as if on the verge of speech, but then became still once more.

"It's like this," said Giulietta Veronese. "When she came here she wouldn't speak at all. A palace with all the doors and windows locked, she was. Then the mistress said, *do you know where you are?* I repeated it, obviously, *est-ce que tu sais où tu es,* and when the mistress added, *you are in the city of Florence,* it was like turning a key. 'There is a room in this palace containing that name,' she said, and she began to make small, incomprehensible movements of the body, like a person walking without moving, as if she was going somewhere in her head. And then she said the thing that made my mistress command me to bring you here."

"What did she say?" Ago demanded.

"Listen for yourself," Giulietta Veronese replied. Then, turning to the shrouded woman, she said, "*Qu'est-ce que tu connais de Florence? Qu'est-ce que se trouve dans cette chambre du palais?*" At once the slave girl began to move, as if she were walking down corridors, turning corners, passing through doorways, without ever leaving the spot where she stood. Then, at last, she spoke. "In the beginning," she said, in perfect Italian, "there were three friends, Niccolò il Machia, Agostino Vespucci, and Antonino Argalia. Their boyhood world was a magic wood."

Ago began to tremble. "How does she know that? How can she possibly have heard it?" he asked in amazement. But il Machia had guessed the answer. A part of it lay in the books in his father's small, highly prized library. (Bernardo was not a rich man and books were always a struggle to afford, so the decision to purchase a volume was not lightly made.) Next to Niccolò's favorite book, the *Ab Urbe Condita* of Titus Livius, stood Cicero's *De Oratore,* and next to that was the *Rhetorica ad Herennium,* a slim volume by an anonymous author. "According to Cicero," Niccolò said, remembering, "this technique was invented by a Greek, Simonides of Ceos, who had just left a dinner party full of important men when the roof fell in and killed everyone. When he was asked who was there he managed to identify all the dead by remembering where they had sat at the dinner table."

"What technique?" Ago asked.

"In the *Rhetorica* it's called by the same name, the memory palace," il Machia answered. "You build a building in your head, you learn your way around it, and then you start attaching memories to its various features, its furniture, its decorations, whatever you choose. If you attach a memory to a particular location you can remember an enormous amount by walking around the place in your head."

"But this lady refers to herself as the palace," Ago objected. "As if her own physical person is the edifice to which these memories have been attached."

"Then somebody has gone to a great deal of trouble," said il Machia, "to build a memory palace the size of an entire human brain. This young woman has had her own memories removed, or consigned to some high attic of the palace of memory which has been erected in her mind, and she has become the repository of everything her master needed to have remembered. What do we know of the Ottoman court? This may be a common practice among the Turks, or it may have been the tyrannical whim of a specific potentate, or one of his favorites. Suppose now that our friend Argalia was that favorite—suppose that he himself was the architect, at least of this particular chamber in the memory palace—or suppose, even, that the architect was someone who knew him well. In either case we must conclude that this beloved companion of our youth is still, or was until recently, very much alive."

"Look," said Ago, "she's getting ready to speak again."

"There was once a prince named Arcalia," the palace of memories announced. "A great warrior who possessed enchanted weapons, and in whose retinue were four terrifying giants. He was also the most handsome man in the world."

"Arcalia or Argalia," said il Machia, very excited now. "That sounds like our friend all right."

"Arcalia the Turk," said the memory palace. "Wielder of the Enchanted Lance."

"That complete bastard," said Ago Vespucci, admiringly. "He did what he said he'd do. He went over to the other side."

{ 12 }

On the road to Genoa an empty inn

On the road to Genoa an empty inn stood with darkened windows and open doors, abandoned by the innkeeper, his wife, his children, and all the guests on account of the Partly-dead Giant who had recently moved in upstairs. According to Nino Argalia, whose tale this was, the giant was partly-dead because while he was completely dead in the daytime he came to fearsome life at night. "If you spend a night in there you will surely be gobbled up," the neighbors told the boy Argalia when he passed that way; but Argalia wasn't afraid and went indoors and ate a hearty meal all alone. When the giant came to life that night he saw Argalia and said, "Aha! A snackerel! Excellent!" But Argalia replied, "If you eat me you will never know my secret." The giant was curious, and also stupid, as is often the way with giants, so he said, "Tell me your secret, my little snackerel, and I promise I won't eat you until it's told." Argalia bowed deeply, and began. "My secret is up that chimney," he said, "and whoever gets up there first will be the richest boy in the world." "Or giant," said the Partly-dead Giant. "Or giant," Argalia agreed, sounding doubtful. "But you are so huge that you won't be able to fit." "Is it a big treasure?" the giant asked. "The biggest on earth," Argalia replied. "That is why the wise prince who amassed it hid it up the chimney of a humble roadside inn, because nobody would suspect that so grand a monarch would use such a stupid hiding place." "Princes are dumb," said the Partly-dead Giant. "Not like giants," Argalia added thoughtfully. "Exactly," said the giant, and tried to stuff himself up the chimney. "Too big," Argalia sighed. "Just as I feared. Too bad." The giant cried out, "By the gods, I'm not done yet," and tore off one of his arms. "Not so wide now, am I?" he said, but still he couldn't get up the chimney. "Maybe if you bit off the other one," Argalia suggested, and at once the giant's great jaws chewed up his remaining arm as if it were a mutton shank. But even that didn't make the great brute narrow enough. "I have an idea," said Argalia, "suppose you just send your head up there to see what can be seen?" "I don't have any arms anymore, snackerel," the giant said, sorrowfully, "so although your idea is excellent, I can't very well detach my head by myself." "Permit me," Argalia replied smartly, and, picking up a kitchen cleaver, he jumped up on a table and cut through the behemoth's neck— *snickersnee! snackersnee!*—with a single fluent stroke. When the innkeeper, his wife, his family, and all the guests (who had spent the night sleeping in a nearby ditch) learned that Argalia had beheaded the Partly-dead Giant, so that he was now totally deceased, by night as well as by day, they asked if he would help them out one more time and also behead the rapacious Duke of nearby U., who had been making their lives a misery. "Solve your own problems," Argalia said. "That's none of my business. I only wanted to have a quiet bed for the night. Now I'm on my way to sail with Admiral Andrea Doria and make my fortune." And with that he left them flat and went off to find his destiny . . .

The story was completely untrue, but the untruth of untrue stories could sometimes be of service in the real world, and it was tales of this sort—improvised versions of the endless stream of stories he had learned from his friend Ago Vespucci—that saved little Nino Argalia's own neck after he was found hiding under a bunk in the forecastle of the flagship of Andrea Doria's fleet. His information had been out of date—the French had been dispatched by the Band of Gold some time ago—and when he heard that Doria was about to set off to fight the Turk he knew it was time for desperate measures. The eight triremes full of ferocious mercenaries armed to the teeth with arquebuses, cutlasses, pistols, garrotes, daggers, whips, and bad language had already been at sea for five days when the starving wretch of a stowaway was dragged by the ear into the presence of the great *condottiere* himself. Argalia looked like a dirty rag doll, dressed in rags and clutching a bundle of rags to his chest. Now, Andrea Doria was not a man of good character. He lacked all scruple and was capable of acts of extreme vindictiveness. He was tyrannical and vain. His bloodthirsty army of soldiers of fortune would have risen up against him long ago except that he was a great commander, a grand master of strategy, and was also entirely lacking in fear. He was, in short, a monster, and when he was displeased he looked as dangerous as any giant, whether half-deceased or not.

"You have two minutes," he said to the boy, "to give me a reason why I should not throw you overboard immediately."

Argalia looked him straight in the eye. "You would be most unwise to do so," he lied, "for I am a person of strange and varied experience. I have sought my fortune far and wide and on these journeys I have executed a giant—*snickersnee! snackersnee!*—and slain the Soulless Sorcerer and learned the secrets of his spells, and mastered the language of snakes. I have met the king of the fishes and lived in the house of a woman with seventy sons and only one kettle. I can turn myself at will into a lion, an eagle, a dog, or an ant, so I can serve you with the strength of a lion, spy for you with the eye of an eagle, be as loyal to you as a dog, or conceal myself from you by becoming as small as an ant, so that you will never see the assassin who crawls into your ear and poisons you. In short, I am not to be crossed. I am small, but still worthy to be of your company, because I live my life according to the same profound principle as you yourself follow."

"And what is that principle, might one inquire?" Andrea Doria asked, with some amusement. He had a protruding beard, a sardonic mouth, and a glittering eye that missed nothing.

"That the end justifies the means," Argalia replied, recalling something il Machia liked to say about the ethics of using the mandrake root to seduce otherwise unattainable females.

"The end justifies the means," Doria repeated in surprise. "Now that is damnably well expressed."

"I made it up myself," Argalia said, "for I am an orphan like you, rendered penniless in my youth as you were, forced into this line of work just like you; and orphans know that their survival requires them to be prepared to do whatever is necessary. That there are no limits." What was it il Machia had said after the day of the hanged archbishop? "That only the fittest survive."

"The survival of the fittest," mused Andrea Doria. "A second infernally potent idea. Did you come up with that one, too?" Argalia inclined his head in a gesture of modest pride. "Because you were orphaned too," he continued, "you know that while I may look like a child, I am no helpless babe. A 'child' is a safe and pampered thing, cocooned from the truth of the world, allowed to waste years in mere play—a creature who believes that wisdom can be acquired in school. 'Childhood' is a luxury I cannot afford, just as you could not. The truth about 'childhood' lies hidden in the most untrue stories in the world. Children face monsters and demons and only survive if they are fearless. Children starve to death unless they free a magic fish who grants them their heart's desires. Children are eaten alive by trolls unless they manage to delay the creatures until the sun rises, whereupon the vile things turn to stone. A child must learn how to cast beans to tell the future, how to cast beans to bind men and women to his will, and how to grow the beanstalk upon which such magic beans are found. An orphan is a child writ large. Our lives are lives of fable and extremes."

"Give this loudmouth philosopher something to eat," Admiral Doria told his boatswain, an intimidating ox of a sailor named Ceva. "He may be useful to us before our journey's done, and his goblin lies will entertain me until that time comes."

The boatswain kept a firm hold of Argalia's ear as he led him out of the captain's cabin. "Don't think you got away with this because of your fancy blather," he said. "You are alive for one reason only." "Ouch," said Argalia, "and what is that?"

Ceva the boatswain twisted his ear harder. There was a scorpion tattooed on the right side of his face and he had the dead eyes of a man who had never smiled. "The reason is that you somehow found the guts, or the gall, to look him in the eye. If a fellow don't look him in the eye he tears their liver out and feeds it to the gulls."

"Before I'm finished," Argalia replied, "I will be the commander making judgments of that sort, and you? You'd better look *me* in the eye, or else."

Ceva cuffed him on the side of the head, without a trace of affection. "You'll have to wait your turn, runt," he said, "because right now your eye is only high enough to stare at my fucking cock."

Whatever Ceva the Scorpion said, Argalia's tall stories must have had something to do with his survival too, because it turned out that the monstrous Admiral Andrea Doria had a weakness for such tales, just like any dumb giant. In the evenings when the sea was black and the stars burned holes in the sky the Admiral would smoke an opium pipe below decks and call for the story-filled boy. "As your Genoan ships are all triremes," Argalia would say, "you should carry cheese on one deck, breadcrumbs on another, and rotting flesh on the third. When you come to the Island of Rats, give them the cheese; the breadcrumbs will please the denizens of the Isle of Ants; and as for the rotting flesh, the birds of Vulture Island will appreciate it. After that you will have mighty allies. The rats will gnaw through all obstacles for you, even through mountains, and the ants will perform all those duties that are too delicate for human hands. The vultures, if you ask them nicely, will even fly you to the top of the mountain where the spring of eternal life gushes out." Andrea Doria grunted. "But where are these infernal islands?" he wanted to know. "Admiral," the boy replied, "you're the navigator, not I. They must be on your charts somewhere." In spite of such cheeky remarks he lived to tell another tale another day—*once upon a time there were three oranges and inside each one a*

*beautiful girl who would die if you didn't give her water the moment she
came out of the orange*—and the Admiral, wreathed in coils of
smoke, would mumble confidences to him in return.

The sea was full of murder. The caravels of the Barbary pirates
marauded through these waters, plundering and kidnapping, and
since the fall of Constantinople the galleys of the Osmanli Turk or
Ottoman navy were active here as well. Against all these maritime
infidels Admiral Andrea Doria had set his pockmarked face. "I will
drive them from the *Mare Nostrum* and make Genoa mistress of the
waves," he boasted, and Argalia did not dare to offer any contrary
or irreverent word. Andrea Doria leaned toward the silent boy, his
eyes milky with *afim*. "What you know and I know the enemy
knows as well," he whispered, half lost in his opium dream. "The
enemy, too, follows the orphan's law." "What orphan?" Argalia
asked him. "Mahomet," Andrea Doria replied. "Mahomet, their
orphan god."

Argalia had not known that he shared his orphan status with
the Prophet of Islam. "The end justifies the means," Andrea Doria
went on in a thickening, slow voice. "See? They go by the same
rule as we do. The One Commandment. *Whatever it takes is the
choice we makes.* So their religion is the same as ours." Argalia took
a deep breath and asked dangerous questions. "If that is correct,"
he said, "then are they truly our enemies? Is our proper adversary
not our antithesis? Can the face we see in a mirror be our foe?"
Admiral Andrea Doria was close to unconsciousness. "Quite
right," he mumbled as he slumped back in his chair, beginning to
snore. "And, anyway, there is one enemy I hate more than any
Mohammedan pirate scum."

"Who is that?" Argalia asked.

"Venice," he said. "I'm going to fuck up those pretty-boy
Venetian bastards as well."

As the eight Genoan triremes sailed in battle formation, hunting down their prey, it became plain to Argalia that religion had
nothing to do with anything. The corsairs from the Barbary states

weren't bothered about conquering anybody or spreading the faith. They were interested in ransom, blackmail, and extortion. As for the Ottomans, they knew that the survival of their new capital city of Stamboul depended on getting food into the port from elsewhere, and so the shipping lanes had to be kept open. They had also begun to have acquisitive notions and had sent ships to attack ports along and beyond the shores of the Aegean Sea; and they didn't like Venetians, either. Power and wealth and possessions and wealth and power. As for Argalia, at night his dreams, too, were full of exotic jewels. Alone in his fo'c'sle bunk he swore a private vow. "I will never return to Florence as a pauper, but only as a treasure-laden prince." His quest was really very simple. The nature of the world had become clear.

When things seemed clearest, however, they were invariably at their most treacherous. After a victorious engagement with the pirate ships of the Barbarossa brothers of Mytilene, the Admiral was dripping satisfactorily with Saracen blood, and having presided over the execution of the captured pirates—they were coated with pitch and burned alive in the main square of their own hometown—he conceived the daring notion of entering the Aegean and taking the battle to the Osmanlis in their own "home" waters. But as the Band of Gold entered that legendary sea and faced the Ottoman galleys head-on an occult fog arose from nowhere and blotted the whole world from view; as if some Olympian mischief was at work, as if the ancient gods of the region, bored with the long tedium of an age in which they no longer held sway over men's affections and loyalties, had decided to toy with them, to ruin their plans, just for old times' sake. The eight Genoan triremes attempted to hold their battle line, but the fog was disorienting, it was filled with the howls of ghouls and the shrieks of witches and the stink of disease and the wailing of the drowned, and even those hardened mercenaries soon enough began to panic. The system of foghorns which Admiral Doria had instituted against just such a day quickly broke down. Each of his ships had been given its own individual signal of short and long blasts, but as the mercenaries panicked in that miasma of death and superstition their communications lost all clarity, and so did the foghorns of the Ottomans, until nobody knew where they were, or who was friend and who was deadly foe.

Cannon fire broke out abruptly from the sides of the triremes and from the mighty swiveling cannons mounted on the decks of the Ottoman galleys, and the red flames and bright flashes of the big guns in the fog looked like small pieces of Hell in the midst of this formless Limbo. Rifle fire blossomed all around, a flickering garden of deadly red flowers. Nobody knew who was firing at whom, or how to act for the best, and a great catastrophe was imminent. Then all of a sudden, as if both sides understood their peril at exactly the same moment, a silence fell. No gun fired, no voice called out, no foghorn sounded. Stealthy movements began everywhere in the empty white. Argalia, standing alone on the deck of the flagship, felt his destiny grip him by the shoulder, and was surprised to note that destiny's hand was trembling with fear. He turned to look. No, it was not Fate standing behind him, but Ceva the boatswain, no longer grim and terrifying, but an unnerved, beaten dog. "The Admiral needs you," he whispered to the boy, and led him below decks to where Andrea Doria waited, holding in his hand the great horn of the flagship of the fleet. "Today is your day, little man, my storyteller," the Admiral said softly. "Today you will achieve greatness by deeds instead of words."

The plan was for Argalia to be lowered into the water and set adrift in a small dinghy, which he was to row away from the flagship as fast as possible. "On every hundredth stroke of the oars," the Admiral said, "blow hard on this horn. The enemy will mistake subtlety for arrogance, he will accept the challenge of Andrea Doria's *cornetto*, and will turn his ships toward you, thinking to capture a great prize—which is to say, my own person!—and in the meanwhile I will have the advantage of him and will strike him fatally from a quarter from which he expects no wound." It seemed like a bad plan to Argalia. "And I?" he asked, staring at the horn in his hand. "When the ships of the Infidel are bearing down upon my little vessel, what am I supposed to do?" Ceva the Scorpion picked him up bodily and dropped him into the dinghy. "Row," he hissed. "Little hero. Row for your fucking life."

"When the fog clears and the enemy is vanquished," said the Admiral, a little vaguely, "we'll pick you up again." Ceva gave the dinghy a hard push. "Yeah," he hissed. "That's what we'll do."

Then there was only the whiteness of the fog and the sound of the sea. Land and sky began to feel like ancient fables. This blind floating was the universe entire. For a time he did as he had been ordered to do, a hundred strokes of the oars, then a blast on the horn, twice, three times he did it, and never heard any answering noise. The world was mute and lethal. Death would come upon him in a noiseless watery rush. The Ottoman ships would bear down on him and crush him like a bug. He stopped blowing the horn. It became plain to him that the Admiral was uninterested in his fate and had sacrificed his "little storyteller" as casually as a man spitting a mouthful of phlegm over the side of a ship. He was no more than that gob of sputum, bobbing for an instant on the waves before he drowned. He tried to tell himself stories to keep his spirits up but could only think of frightening ones, a leviathan rising from the deep to crunch a boat in its gigantic jaws, the uncoiling of deep-sea worms, the breathing of underwater dragonfire. Then after a further time all the stories faded away as well and he was left without defenses or recourse, a lonely human soul drifting vaguely into the white. This was what was left of a human individual when you took away his home, his family, his friends, his city, his country, his world: a being without context, whose past had faded, whose future was bleak, an entity stripped of name, of meaning, of the whole of life except a temporarily beating heart. "I am absurd," he told himself. "A cockroach in a steaming turd has more significance than I." Many years later, when he met Qara Köz the hidden

Mughal princess and his life finally acquired the meaning which destiny had in store for it, he saw the look of abandoned despair in her eyes and understood that she, too, had had to face the profound absurdity of the human condition. For that, if for no other reason, he would have loved her. But he had other reasons too.

The fog thickened around him, around his eyes, his nose, his throat. He felt himself beginning to choke. Maybe he would die now, he thought. His will had been broken. Whatsoever Fate brought, he would accept. He lay down in his little boat and remembered Florence, saw his parents as they had been before the plague deformed them, remembered boyhood escapades in the woods with his friends Ago and il Machia, was filled with love by these memories, and, a moment later, fainted.

When he awoke, the fog had vanished, and so had the eight triremes of Admiral Andrea Doria. The great *condottiere* of Genoa had simply turned tail and fled, and the foghorn in the dinghy had been a simple diversionary measure. Argalia's little craft bobbed helplessly right in front of the assembled Ottoman navy like a mouse cornered by half a dozen hungry cats. He stood up in the boat and waved to his conquerors and blew the Admiral's foghorn as loudly as he could.

"I surrender," he shouted. "Come and get me, you godless Turkish swine."

{ 13 }

In the children's prison camp at Usküb

In the children's prison camp at Usküb *(said the memory palace)* there were many tongues but only one God. Each year the press gangs roamed the expanding empire to levy the devshirmé tax, the child tribute, and took the strongest, cleverest, best-looking boys into slavery, to be changed into instruments of the Sultan's will. The principle of the Sultanate was governance by metamorphosis. *We will take your finest offspring from you and we will transform them utterly. We will make them forget you and turn them into the force that keeps you under our heel. By your own lost children will you be ruled.* In Usküb where the process of change began there were many tongues but only one uniform, the baggy-trousered garb of the Ottoman recruit. The hero's rags were taken from him and he was washed and fed and given clean water to drink. Then Christianity was taken from him as well and he was obliged to put on Islam like a new pair of pajamas. There were Greeks and Albanians in Usküb, Bosnians and Croats and Serbs, and there were *mamlúk* boys, white slaves, from up and down the Caucasus, Georgians and Mingrelians, Circassians and Abkhazas, and there were Armenians and Syrians as well. The hero was the only Italian. Florence did not pay the child tribute, though it was the opinion of the Osmanlis that that would change with time. His captors pretended to have difficulty with his name, *al-ghazi,* the conqueror, they called him for a joke, or *al-khali,* the empty one, the vessel. But his name wasn't important. Argalia, Arcalia, Arqalia, Al-Khaliya. Nonsense words. They didn't matter. It was his soul that had to be placed under new management just like everyone else's. On the parade ground in their new outfits the sullen children stood in ranks before a man in a frock, whose white hat was as tall as his white beard was long, the one rising three feet above his brow and the other falling an equal distance from his chin, giving him the appearance of possessing a head of immense length. This was a holy man, a dervish of the Bektashi order, and he had come to convert them to Islam. In their many accents the angry, frightened boys parroted the necessary Arabic sentence about the one God and his Prophet. Their metamorphosis had begun.

※

While he was traveling in the service of the republic il Machia never stopped thinking about the palace of memories. In July he galloped down the Ravenna road to Forlì to persuade Countess Caterina Sforza Riario to let her son Ottaviano fight alongside the Florentine forces for considerably less money than she wanted, because if she refused she would lose Florence's protection and be at the mercy of the terrible Duke Cesare Borgia of Romagna, the son of the Borgia Pope Alexander VI. The "Madonna of Forlì" was a woman so beautiful that even il Machia's friend Biagio Buonaccorsi broke off from sodomizing Andrea di Romolo to ask Niccolò to bring home a drawing of her. But Niccolò was thinking about the nameless Frenchwoman standing like a marble figure in her boudoir at Alessandra Fiorentina's House of Mars. "Hey, Machia," Ago Vespucci wrote, "we need you back here fast because without you there's nobody to organize our nights of boozing and cards, and besides that, this Chancery of yours is full of the bitchiest assholes in Italy, all trying to get us fired—so all this riding about of yours is bad for business too." But Niccolò wasn't thinking about intrigue or wild living, or, rather, there was just one woman's body he was hoping to debauch, if he could just find the key that unlocked her secret self, the suppressed personality hidden beneath the memory palace.

Il Machia sometimes saw the world too analogically, reading

one situation as an analogue of another, quite different one. So when Caterina refused his proposal he saw it as a bad omen. Maybe he would fail with the palace of memories as well. Soon afterward, when Cesare Borgia attacked and conquered Forlì exactly as predicted by Niccolò, Caterina stood on the ramparts and showed the Duke of Romagna her genitals and told him to go fuck himself. She ended up a prisoner of the Pope in Castel Sant'Angelo but il Machia interpreted her fate as a good sign. That Caterina Sforza Riario was a prisoner in Pope Alexander's castle made her like a mirror of the woman kept in a darkened room at Queen Alessandra's House of Mars. That she had exposed herself to Borgia meant that maybe the palace of memories would agree to do the same to him.

He returned to the House of Mars where the *ruffiana* Giulietta grudgingly agreed to let him have unrestricted access to the memory palace, because she, too, hoped he could wake that somnambulant lady up, so that she could start acting like a proper courtesan instead of a talking statue. And il Machia's reading of the omens turned out to be accurate. When he was alone in the boudoir with her he led her gently by the hand and laid her down on the fourposter bed with its suitably French draperies of pale blue silk embroidered with golden fleurs-de-lys. She was a tall woman. Things would be easier if she was lying down. He lay beside her and caressed her golden hair and whispered his questions in her ear while he unbuttoned her seraglio inmate's bodice. Her breasts were small. That was all right. Her hands were clasped at her waist, and she made no objection to the movements of his hand. And as she recited the memories that had been buried in her mind she seemed to be unburdening herself, and as the weight of the memories lessened the lightness of her spirits rose. "Tell me everything," il Machia whispered in her ear while he kissed her newly exposed bosom, "and then you will be free."

After the child tribute had been gathered *(the memory palace said)* it was taken to Stamboul and distributed among good Turkish families to serve them and to be taught the Turkish language and the intricacies of the Muslim faith. Then there was military training. After a time the boys were either taken as pages into the Imperial Seraglio and given the title of *Ich-Oghlán,* or else they entered the Janissary Corps as *Ajém-Oghlán.* Raw recruits. At the age of eleven the hero, the mighty warrior, the Wielder of the Enchanted Lance and the most handsome man in the world, became, God be praised, a Janissary; the greatest Janissary fighter in the history of the Corps. Ah, the feared Janissaries of the Osmanli Sultan, may their renown spread far and wide! They were not Turks, but the pillars of the Turks' empire. No Jews were admitted, for their faith was too strong to be altered; no gypsies, because they were scum; and the Moldavians and Wallachians of Romania were never harvested. But in the time of the hero the Wallachians had to be fought, under Vlad Dracula, the Impaler, their king.

While the memory palace had been telling him about the Janissaries il Machia's attention had wandered to her lips. She told him how the cadets were inspected naked on arrival in Stamboul and he thought only about the beauty of her mouth as it formed the French word *nus.* She spoke of their training as butchers and gardeners and he traced the outlines of her moving lips with his index finger as she said the words. She said their names were taken from them and their family names as well and they became Abdullahs or Abdulmomins or other names beginning with *abd,* which meant slave and indicated their status in the world. But instead of worrying about the deformation of these young lives he only thought that he didn't like the shapes her lips made when she spoke those Oriental syllables. He kissed the corners of her mouth as she told him of the Chief White Eunuch and the Chief Black Eunuch who trained boys for imperial service and told him that the hero, his friend, had begun as chief falconer, an unheard-of rank for a cadet. He knew that his lost friend, the boy without a childhood, was growing up as she spoke, growing up in her telling of him, having whatever it is that children have instead of a childhood when they don't have a childhood, changing into a man, or into whatever a child without a childhood becomes when he grows up, maybe a man without a manhood. Yes, Argalia was acquiring martial skills that caused other men to admire and fear him, he was gathering around himself a coterie of other young warriors, child-tribute cadets from the far frontiers of Europe, as well as the four albino Swiss giants, Otho, Botho, Clotho, and D'Artagnan, mercenaries captured in battle and auctioned off in the slave markets of Tangier, and a wild Serb named Konstantin who had been captured at the siege of Novo Brdo. But in spite of the importance of this information he found himself drifting into a reverie as he watched the small movements of the memory palace's face as she spoke. Yes, Argalia had grown up somewhere, and achieved various feats, and all of this was information he should have, but in the meanwhile here were these slow undulations of lips and cheek, the articulate movements of tongue and jaw, the glow of alabaster skin.

Sometimes in the woods near the farm in Percussina he lay on the leaf-soft ground and listened to the two-tone song of the birds, high low high, high low high low, high low high low high. Sometimes by a woodland stream he watched the water rush over the pebbled bed, its tiny modulations of bounce and flow. A woman's body was like that. If you watched it carefully enough you could see how it moved to the rhythm of the world, the deep rhythm, the music below the music, the truth below the truth. He believed in this hidden truth the way other men believed in God or love, believed that truth was in fact always hidden, that the apparent, the overt, was invariably a kind of lie. Because he was a man fond of precision he wanted to capture the hidden truth precisely, to see it clearly and set it down, the truth beyond ideas of right and wrong, ideas of good and evil, ideas of ugliness and beauty, all of which were aspects of the surface deceptions of the world, having little to do with how things really worked, disconnected from the what-ness, the secret codes, the hidden forms, the mystery.

Here in this woman's body the mystery could be seen. This apparently inert being, her self erased or buried beneath this never-ending story, this labyrinth of story-rooms in which more tales had been hidden than he was interested to hear. This tooth-some sleepwalker. This blank. The rote-learned words poured out of her as he looked on, and while he unbuttoned and caressed. He exposed her nudity without compunction, touched it without guilt, manipulated her without any feelings of remorse. He was the scientist of her soul. In the smallest motion of an eyebrow, in the twitch of a muscle in her thigh, in a sudden minuscule curling of the left corner of her upper lip, he deduced the presence of life. Her self, that sovereign treasure, had not been destroyed. It slept and could be awakened. He whispered in her ear, *"This is the last time you will ever tell this story. As you tell it, let it go."* Slowly, phrase by phrase, episode by episode, he would unbuild the palace of memories and release a human being. He bit her ear and saw a tiny answering tilt of the head. He pressed her foot and a toe moved gratefully. He caressed her breast and faintly, so faintly that only a man looking for the deeper truth would have seen it, her back arched in return. There was nothing wrong in what he did. He was her rescuer. She would thank him in time.

At the siege of Trebizond it rained every day. The hills were full of Tar-tars and other heathen. The road down from the mountains turned to mud, so deep that it reached the bellies of the horses. They destroyed the supply wagons and carried the bags on camels' backs instead. A camel fell and a treasure chest broke open, sixty thousand pieces of gold lying on the hill-side for all to see. At once the hero, with the Swiss giants and the Serb, drew swords and mounted guard around the Sultan's fallen wealth until he, the emperor, arrived on the scene. After that the hero was better trusted by the Sultan than the king's own kin.

At last the stiffness had gone from her limbs. Her body lay loose and inviting upon the silken sheets. The stories she was telling now were of recent date. Argalia had grown up and was almost as old as il Machia and Ago. Their chronologies were united once again. Soon she would have finished and then he would wake her up. The *ruffiana* Giulietta, an impatient creature, goaded him to take her while she slept. "Just stick it in there. Get on with it. No need to be gentle. Give it to her good. That'll open her eyes." But he had decided not to ravish her until she awoke of her own accord, and won the assent of Alessandra Fiorentina in the matter. The memory palace was an exceptional beauty and would be handled delicately. She might be no more than a slave in a courtesan's house but she would receive this much respect.

Against Vlad III the voivode of Wallachia—Vlad "Dracula," the "dragon-devil," the Impaler Prince, Kazikli Bey—no ordinary power could have prevailed. It had begun to be said of Prince Vlad that he drank the blood of his impaled victims as they writhed in their death throes upon their stakes, and that drinking the living blood of men and women gave him strange powers over death. He could not die. He could not be killed. He was also a brute of brutes. He cut off the noses of the men he killed and sent them to the prince of Hungary to boast about his prowess. These stories made the army fear him and the march into Wallachia was not a happy one. To encourage the Janissaries the Sultan distributed thirty thousand gold pieces and told the men that if they won they would be given property rights and regain the use of their names. Vlad the Devil had already burned down the whole of Bulgaria and impaled twenty-five thousand people on wooden stakes, but his forces were smaller than the Ottoman army. He retreated and left scorched earth behind him, poisoning wells and slaughtering cattle. When the Sultan's army was marooned in desolation without food or water the Devil King launched surprise attacks. Many soldiers were killed and their bodies stuck onto sharpened sticks. Then Dracula retreated to Tirgoviste and the Sultan declared, "This will be the devil's last stand."

But at Tirgoviste they saw a terrible sight. Twenty thousand men, women, and children had been impaled by the devil on a palisade of stakes around the town just to show the advancing army what awaited them. There were babies clinging to their impaled mothers in whose rotting breasts you could see the nests of crows. At the sight of the forest of the impaled the Sultan was disgusted and withdrew his unnerved troops. It seemed that the campaign would end in catastrophe, but the hero stepped forward with his loyal group. "We will do what must be done," he said. One month later the hero returned to Stamboul with the head of the devil in a jar of honey. It turned out that Dracula could die after all, in spite of the rumors to the contrary. His body had been impaled as he had impaled so many others and left for the monks of Snagov to bury as they pleased. This was when the Sultan understood that the hero was a superhuman being whose weapons possessed enchanted powers and whose companions were more than human also. He was accorded the highest honor of the Osmanli Sultanate, the rank of Wielder of the Enchanted Lance. In addition, he became a free man once again.

"From now on," the Sultan told him, "you are my right hand as my right hand is, and a son to me as my sons are, and your name is not a slave name, for you are no longer any man's mamlúk or abd, your name is Pasha Arcalia, the Turk."

A happy ending, il Machia thought drily. Our old friend made his fortune after all. As good a place as any for the palace of memories to conclude her account. He lay down beside her and tried to picture Nino Argalia as an Oriental pasha fanned by bare-chested Nubian eunuchs and beset by harem lovelies. Feelings of revulsion arose in him at the image of this renegade, a Christian convert to Islam, enjoying the fleshpots of lost Constantinople, the new Konstantiniyye or Stamboul of the Turks, or praying in the Janissaries' mosque, or walking without a care by the fallen, broken statue of the emperor Justinian, and reveling in the growing power of the enemies of the West. Such a treasonous transformation might impress a good-natured innocent like Ago Vespucci, who saw Argalia's journey as the kind of exciting adventure he himself was not interested in having, but to Niccolò's mind it broke the bonds of their friendship, and should they ever meet face to face they would do so as foes, for Argalia's defection was a crime against the deeper truths, the eternal verities of power and kinship that drove the history of men. He had turned against his own kind, and a tribe was never lenient with such men. However, it did not occur to il Machia then, or for many years afterward, that he would ever see his boyhood companion again.

The midget Giulietta Veronese stuck her head round the door. "Well?" Niccolò nodded judiciously. "I think, signora, that she will presently be awake and restored to herself. As for me, for my small part in the renewal of her personhood—of the human Dignity which, great Pico tells us, stands at the very heart of our humanity—I admit I feel a little glow of pride." The *ruffiana* blew exasperated air through a corner of her mouth. "It's about time," she said, and withdrew.

Almost at once the palace of memories began to murmur in her sleep. Her voice strengthened and Niccolò realized she was telling the last story, the story that was embedded in the very doorway of the memory palace that had colonized her brain, the tale that had to be told as she passed out through that doorway and reawakened to ordinary life: her own story, which unfolded backward, as if time were running in reverse. With growing horror he saw rising before him the scene of her indoctrination, saw the necromancer of Stamboul, the long-hatted long-bearded Sufi mystic of the Bektashi order, adept in the mesmerist arts and the building of memory palaces, working at the behest of a certain newly minted Pasha to commit that Pasha's exploits to this captive lady's memory—to erase her life to make room for Argalia's no doubt self-aggrandizing version of himself. The Sultan had given him the gift of this enslaved beauty and this was the use he had made of her. Barbarian! Traitor! He should have died of the plague along with his parents. He should have drowned when Andrea Doria cast him into that rowboat. To be impaled on a stake by Vlad Dracula of Wallachia would not have been too harsh a punishment for such misdeeds.

Il Machia's mind was full of these and other angry thoughts

when from nowhere there rose up an unwanted image from the past: the boy Argalia teasing him about his mother's porridge cures for sickness. "Not the Machiavelli but the Polentini." And Argalia's old song about an imaginary porridge girl. If she were a sin then I would repent her. If she were to die then I would lament her. Il Machia found tears running down his cheeks. He sang the song to himself, *And if she were a message then I would have sent her,* singing softly, so as not to disturb the flesh and blood damsel he had brought back from the palace of distress. He was alone with the memory of Argalia, with only his new sense of outrage and the old, sweet memory of childhood for company, and he wept.

My name is Angélique and I am the daughter of Jacques Coeur of Bourges, merchant of Montpellier. My name is Angélique and I am the daughter of Jacques Coeur. My father was a trader and brought nuts and silks and carpets from Damascus to Narbonne. He was falsely accused of poisoning the King of France's mistress and fled to Rome. My name is Angélique and I am the daughter of Jacques Coeur who was honored by the Pope. He was made captain of sixteen papal galleys and sent to the relief of Rhodes but he fell ill on the way and died. My name is Angélique and I am of the family of Jacques Coeur. While my brothers and I were trading with the Levant I was abducted by pirates and sold into slavery to the Sultan of Stamboul. My name is Angélique and I am the daughter of Jacques Coeur. My name is Angélique and I am the daughter of Jacques. My name is Angélique and I am the daughter. My name is Angélique and I am. My name is Angélique.

He slept beside her that night. When she awoke he would tell her what had happened, he would be gentle and kind, and she would thank him like the lady she had once been, a girl of well-bred mercantile stock. He pitied her for her bad luck. Twice taken by Barbary pirates, once from the French, a second time from the Turks—who knew what assaults she had been subjected to, how many men had had her, or what she would remember of such matters, and even now she was not free. She looked as refined as any aristocrat but she was just a girl in a house of pleasure. But if her brothers were alive they would surely rejoice to have her returned, their hidden sister, their lost beloved Angélique. They would buy her back from Alessandra Fiorentina and she could go home, to wherever home might be, Narbonne or Montpellier or Bourges. Maybe he could fuck her before that happened. He would discuss that with the *ruffiana* in the morning. The House of Mars was in his debt for increasing the value of its formerly damaged asset. Lovely Angélique, Angélique of the sorrows. He had done a fine and almost selfless thing.

That night he had a strange dream. An Oriental *padishah* or emperor sat, at sunset, under a little cupola at the apex of a pyramid-like five-story building made of red sandstone, and looked out over a golden lake. To his rear there were body-servants wielding large feathered fans, and beside him stood a European man or woman, a figure with long yellow hair wearing a coat of colored leather lozenges, telling a tale about a lost princess. The dreamer only saw this yellow-haired figure from behind, but the Padishah was plainly visible, a big, fair-skinned man with a heavy mustache, handsome, much bejeweled, and tending a little to fat. Evidently these were dream-creatures he had conjured up, for this prince was certainly not the Turkish Sultan, and the yellow-haired courtier did not sound like the new Italian Pasha. *"You speak only of the love of lovers,"* the Padishah said, *"but we are thinking of the love of the people for their prince. For we have a great desire to be loved."*

"Love is fickle," the other man answered. *"They love you today, but they may not love you tomorrow."*

"What then?" the Padishah asked. *"Should I be a cruel tyrant? Should I act in such a way as to engender hatred?"*

"Not hatred, but fear," the yellow-haired man said. *"For only fear endures."*

"Don't be a fool," the Padishah told him. *"Everyone knows that fear rubs along very nicely with love."*

He awoke to screaming and light and open windows, women running everywhere while the midget Giulietta screeched into his ear, *"What did you do to her?"* Courtesans without their finery, their hair a-straggle, their faces unpainted and dirty, their night-clothes askew, ran shouting from room to room. All the doors had been flung open and daylight, enchantment's antidote, poured brutally through the House of Mars. What harridans these women were, what poxy, uncouth rodents with bad breath and ugly voices. He sat up and struggled into his clothes. *"What did you do?"* But he had done nothing. He had helped her, cleansed her mind, set her spirit free, and barely laid a finger upon her. Certainly he didn't owe the *ruffiana* any money. Why was she harassing him so? Why the commotion? He should leave at once. He should find Ago and Biagio and di Romolo and have some breakfast. And no doubt there was work to be done. *"You stupid fool,"* Giulietta Veronese was shouting, *"to meddle in what you didn't understand."* Something had happened here. He was presentable now and moved through the un-magicked House of Mars with as much dignity as he could muster. The courtesans fell silent as he passed. Some of them pointed. One or two were heard to hiss. There was a shattered window in the *grand salon,* on the side that overlooked the Arno. He needed to know what had happened. Then the house's mistress stood before him, La Fiorentina, still beautiful without a shred of cosmetic assistance. "Mr. Secretary," she said with icy formality. "You will never be welcome in this house again." Then she left him in a flurry of petticoats and the crying, the lamentation started up again. "God damn you," said Giulietta the *ruffiana.* "It was impossible to stop her. She ran from that room where you slept on like a rotting corpse, and nobody could get in her way."

While you were anesthetized to the tragedy of your life you were able to survive. When clarity was returned to you, when it was painstakingly restored, it could drive you mad. Your reawakened memory could derange you, the memory of humiliation, of so much handling, of so many intrusions, the memory of men. Not a palace but a brothel of memories, and behind those memories the knowledge that those who loved you were dead, that there was no escape. Such knowledge could make you come to your feet, gather yourself, and run. If you ran fast enough you might be able to escape your past and the memory of everything that had been done to you, and the future as well, the inescapable bleakness ahead. Were there brothers to rescue you? No, your brothers were dead. Perhaps the world itself was dead. Yes, it was. To be a part of the dead world it was necessary that you die as well. It was necessary that you run as fast as possible until you reached the edge between the worlds and then you didn't stop you ran on across that border as if it wasn't there as if glass was air and air was glass, the air shattering around you like glass as you fell. The air slicing you to pieces as if it were a blade. It was good to fall. It was good to fall out of life. It was good.

—⁓—

"Argalia, my friend," Niccolò said to the phantom of the traitor, "you owe me a life."

{ 14 }

After Tansen sang the song of fire

After Tansen sang the song of fire, the *deepak raag,* and made lamps at the House of Skanda run by the Skeleton and Mattress burst into flame by the power of his music, he was found to be suffering from serious burns. In the ecstasy of the performance he hadn't noticed his own body beginning to show scorch marks as it heated up under the fierce blaze of his genius. Akbar sent him home to Gwalior in a royal palanquin, telling him to rest and not return until his wounds had healed. In Gwalior he was visited by two sisters, Tana and Riri, who were so distressed by his injuries that they began to sing *megh malhar,* the song of the rain. Soon a gentle drizzle began to fall on Mian Tansen even though he was lying in the shade. Nor was this any ordinary rain. As Riri and Tana sang they removed the bandages from his wounds and as the rain washed his skin it became whole again. All Gwalior was agog with the story of the miracle of the rain-song and when Tansen returned to Sikri he told the emperor about the marvelous girls. At once Akbar dispatched Birbal to invite the sisters to the court and sent them gifts of jewels and clothes to thank them for their feat. But when Tana and Riri met Birbal and heard what he wanted they grew solemn and withdrew to discuss the matter, refusing all the emperor's gifts. After a time they emerged and told Birbal they would give him their reply the next morning. Birbal spent the night feasting and drinking as the guest of the Maharajah of Gwalior in his great fortress but when he returned to Tana and Riri's house the next day he found everyone plunged into deep mourning. The sisters had drowned themselves in a well. As strictly observant Brahmins they had not wanted to serve the Muslim king, and feared that if they refused then Akbar would treat the rebuff as an insult and their families would suffer the consequences. To avoid such an outcome they had preferred to sacrifice their own lives.

The news of the suicide of the sisters with the enchanted voices plunged the emperor into a deep depression, and when the emperor was depressed the whole city held its breath. In the Tent of the New Worship the Water Drinkers and Wine Lovers found it impossible to continue with their arguments and the royal wives and concubines stopped squabbling as well. When the heat of the day had passed Niccolò Vespucci who called himself Mogor dell'Amore waited outside the royal quarters as he had been directed but the emperor was not in the mood for his tales. Then near sunset Akbar burst from his rooms accompanied by guards and punkah-wallahs and headed toward the Panch Mahal. "You," he said when he saw Mogor, in the voice of a man who has forgotten about his visitor's existence, and then, turning away, "Very well. Come on." The bodies of the men guarding the emperor's person moved apart a little and Mogor was drawn into the circle of power. He had to walk quickly. The emperor was moving at speed.

Under the little cupola at the apex of the Panch Mahal the Emperor of Hindustan looked out over Sikri's golden lake. To his rear there were body-servants wielding large feathered fans, and beside him stood the yellow-haired European man who wanted to tell him a tale about a lost princess. "You speak only of the love of lovers," the emperor said, "but we are thinking of the love of the people for their prince, which we confess we much desire. Yet these girls died because they preferred division to unity, their gods to ours, and hatred to love. We conclude, therefore, that the love of the people is fickle. But what follows from that conclusion? Should we become a cruel tyrant? Should we act in such a way as to engender universal fear? Does only fear endure?"

"When the great warrior Argalia met the immortal beauty

Qara Köz," Mogor dell'Amore replied, "a story began which would regenerate all men's belief—your belief, grand Mughal, husband of husbands, lover of lovers, king of kings, man of men!—in the undying power and extraordinary capacity of the human heart for love."

By the time the emperor descended from the top of the Panch Mahal and retired for the night the cloak of sadness had slipped from his shoulders. The city let out a collective sigh and the stars shone a little more brightly overhead. The sadness of emperors, as everyone knew, threatened the safety of the world, because of its capacity for metamorphosis into weakness, or violence, or both. The emperor's good mood was the best guarantee of an uneventful life, and if it was the stranger who had restored Akbar's spirits then much credit was due to him, and he had earned the right to be thought of as a friend in need. The stranger, and perhaps also the subject of his story, the Lady Black Eyes, Princess Qara Köz.

—⁙—

That night the emperor dreamed of love. In his dream he was once again the caliph of Baghdad, Harun al-Rashid, wandering incognito, this time, through the streets of the city of Isbanir. All of a sudden he, the caliph, developed an itch that no man could cure. He returned swiftly to his palace in Baghdad, scratching himself all over throughout the twenty-mile journey, and when he got home he bathed in asses' milk and asked his favorite concubines to massage his whole body with honey. Still the itch drove him mad and no doctor could find the cure, though they cupped him and leeched him until he was at the very gates of death. He dismissed those quacks and when he regained his strength decided that if the itch was incurable the only thing to do was to distract himself so thoroughly that he stopped noticing it.

He summoned the most famous comedians in his realm to make him laugh, and the most knowledgeable philosophers to stretch his brain to the limit. Erotic dancers aroused his desires and the most skillful courtesans satisfied them. He built palaces and roads and schools and race tracks and all of these things served well enough but the itching continued without the slightest sign of improvement. He had the whole city of Isbanir placed in quarantine and fumigated its gutters to try to attack the itching plague at its source but the truth was that very few people seemed to be itching as badly as he was. Then on another night when he went cloaked and secret through the streets of Baghdad he saw a lamp at a high window and when he looked up he glimpsed a woman's face illuminated by the candle so that she seemed to be made of gold. For that single instant the itching stopped completely but the moment she closed her shutters and blew out the candle it returned with redoubled force. It was then that the caliph understood the nature of his itch. In Isbanir he had seen that same face for a similar instant looking down from another window and the itching had begun after that. "Find her," he told the vizier, "for that is the witch who has hexed me."

Easier said than done. The caliph's men brought seven women a day before him on each of the next seven days, but when he obliged them to bare their faces he saw at once that none of them was the one he sought. On the eighth day, however, a veiled woman came to the court unbidden and asked for an audience, saying she was the one who could ease the caliph's pain. Harun al-Rashid had her admitted right away. "So you are the sorceress," he cried. "I am nothing of the sort," she answered him. "But ever since I caught a glimpse of a man's hooded face in the streets of Isbanir I have been itching uncontrollably. I even left my hometown and moved here to Baghdad hoping the move would ease my affliction, but it was no use. I have tried to occupy myself, to distract myself, and have woven great tapestries and written volumes of poetry, all to no avail. Then I heard that the caliph of Baghdad was looking for a woman who made him itch and I knew the answer to the riddle."

With that she boldly cast off her veiling garment and at once the caliph's itches disappeared completely and were replaced by an entirely different sentiment. "You too?" he asked her and she nodded. "No more itching. Something else instead." "And that, too, is an affliction no man can heal," said Harun al-Rashid. "Or, in my case, no woman," the lady replied. The caliph clapped his hands and announced his forthcoming mar-

*riage; and he and his Begum lived happily ever after, until the coming of
Death, the Destroyer of Days.*

Such was the emperor's dream.

—— ෴ ——

As the story of the hidden princess began to spread through the
noble villas and common gullies of Sikri a languid delirium seized
hold of the capital. People began to dream about her all the time,
women as well as men, courtiers as well as guttersnipes, sadhus as
well as whores. The vanished Mughal enchantress of faraway
Herat, which her lover Argalia afterward dubbed "the Florence of
the East," proved that her powers were undiminished by the passage of the years and her probable death. She even bewitched the
queen mother Hamida Bano, who ordinarily had no time for
dreams. However, the Qara Köz who visited Hamida Bano's
sleeping hours was a paragon of Muslim devotion and conservative
behavior. No alien knight was allowed to sully her purity; her sep-
aration from her people caused her great anguish and was, it had to
be said, probably her older sister's fault. Old Princess Gulbadan, by
contrast, had dreamed up a completely different Qara Köz, a free-
spirited adventuress whose irreverent, even blasphemous gaiety
was a little shocking but entirely delightful, and the tale of her liaison with the most handsome man in the world was simply delicious, Princess Gulbadan would have envied her if she could, but
she was having too much fun living vicariously through her several
nights a week. For the Skeleton, chatelaine of the lakeside House
of Skanda, Qara Köz was the personification of female sexuality
and performed impossible gymnastic feats nightly for the courtesan's voyeuristic pleasure. But not all the dreams of the hidden
princess were fond. Lady Man Bai, lover of the heir to the throne,
thought of the absurd kerfuffle about the lost lady as a distraction
from herself, the next queen of Hindustan, who should by right of
youth and destiny be the object of her future subjects' fantasies.

And Jodha, Queen Jodha alone in her chambers, unvisited by her creator and king, understood that the coming of the hidden princess gave her an imagined rival whose power she might not be able to withstand.

Plainly Lady Black Eyes was becoming all things to all people, an exemplar, a lover, an antagonist, a muse; in her absence she was being used as one of those vessels into which human beings pour their own preferences, abhorrences, prejudices, idiosyncrasies, secrets, misgivings, and joys, their unrealized selves, their shadows, their innocence and guilt, their doubts and certainties, their most generous and also most grudging response to their passage through the world. And her narrator, Niccolò Vespucci the "Mughal of Love," the emperor's new favorite, swiftly became the city's most sought after guest. By day all doors were open to him, and by night an invitation to his chosen place of recreation, the House of Skanda, whose two queens, those emaciated and corpulent twin deities, had reached the point at which they could pick and choose among Sikri's finest, was the most coveted symbol of status to be had. Vespucci's own monogamous attachment to the bony, inexhaustible Skeleton, Mohini, was considered admirable. She herself found it hard to credit. "Half the ladies of Sikri would open their back doors for you," she told him, wonderingly. "Can I really be all you desire?" He enfolded her in a reassuring embrace. "What you should understand," he said, "is that I have not come all this way just to screw around."

Why, indeed, had he come? It was a question that vexed many of the city's keenest minds, and some of its most spiteful intelligences as well. The citizenry's growing interest in the drink-sodden daily life and sex-crazed nocturnal culture of faraway Florence, as Mogor dell'Amore described it over a long series of banquets in aristocratic villas and drinks of rum in the lower order's recreational dives, led some to suspect a hedonistic conspiracy to weaken the people's moral fiber and to erode the moral authority of the One True God. Badauni, the puritanical leader of the Water Drinkers and mentor of the increasingly rebellious Crown Prince Salim, had hated Vespucci ever since his twitting by the foreigner in the Tent of the New Worship. Now he began to see him as an instrument of the Devil. "It is as if your increasingly godless father has conjured up this Satanic homunculus to assist him in corrupting the people," he told Salim, and added, menacingly, "Something must be done, if there is anyone man enough to do it."

Now Prince Salim's reasons for his alliance with Badauni were entirely adolescent; he sided with Abul Fazl's adversary because Abul Fazl was his father's close confidant. Puritanism was not his style, for he was a sybarite whose capacities would have horrified Badauni had the thin man been allowed to know of them. Salim was therefore unimpressed by Badauni's theory that the emperor had somehow raised a demon of lust from Hell. He disliked Vespucci because, as patron of the House of Skanda, the foreigner was the only man permitted the freedom of Madame Skeleton's person; and in spite of the increasingly frenzied ministrations of Lady Man Bai the Crown Prince's yen for Mohini had only increased with the passage of time. "I am the next king," he told himself furiously, "and yet that arrogant pleasure-house denies me the woman I require." As for Lady Man Bai, her fury on learning that her fiancé was still desperate to fuck her former slave was very great. It merged with her resentment of the dream-princess that Vespucci had sneakily inserted into the dreams of everyone she knew, and formed an ugly suppurating boil on her psyche, which needed, somehow, probably violently, to be lanced.

When Salim next deigned to visit her she put on her most alluring manner and held grapes between her teeth for him to remove with his tongue. "If this Mogor persuades the emperor of his parentage," she murmured to her beloved, "or if, which is more likely, the emperor pretends to believe him for reasons of his own, do you understand the consequences, my love, the complex and dangerous consequences for yourself?" Prince Salim usually needed other people to work out things like complex consequences on his behalf, so he asked her to spell them out. "Don't you see, O King of Hindustan in waiting," she purred, "that it would permit your father to say that another's claim to the throne was better than yours? And even if that proves too far-fetched to believe, what if he decides to adopt that sycophant as his son? Does the throne no longer matter to you, or will you fight for it, my dearest? As the woman who wants nothing more than to be your queen, I would be sorry to learn that you were not a king in the making but only a spineless bug."

Even those closest to the emperor had growing reservations and suspicions, about Mogor dell'Amore's presence and true purposes at court. The queen mother Hamida Bano thought him an agent of the infidel West, sent to confuse and weaken their holy kingdom. In the opinion of both Birbal and Abul Fazl he was almost certainly a scoundrel, probably on the run from some dreadful deed back home, a confidence man needing to worm his way into a new life because the old one had ceased to be viable. Maybe he faced being burned to death, or hanged, or drawn and quartered, or at the very least tortured and jailed if he returned whence he came. "We should not be the innocent, gullible Easterners he takes us for," said Abul Fazl. "In the matter of the death of Lord Hauksbank, for example, I have never ceased to be convinced of his guilt." Birbal's concern was for the emperor himself. "I do not think he means you any harm," he said, "but he has woven a spell around you that may do you harm in the end, by distracting you from the great matters that should be your proper concern."

The emperor was unconvinced, and inclined to be compassionate. "He is a homeless man looking for a place in the world," he told them. "Down the hill at the House of Skanda he has created a kind of domesticity in a house of pleasure and made a sort of wife of a skeletal whore. How hungry for love he must be! Loneliness is the wanderer's fate; he is a stranger wherever he goes, existing only through the power of his own will. When did a woman last praise him and call him her own? When did he last feel cherished, or worthy, or valuable? When a man is not yearned for there is a thing in him that begins to die. Optimism fades, our wise Birbal. Abul Fazl, our cautious protector, a man's strength is not inexhaustible. A man needs other men to turn toward him by day and a woman to fold herself into his arms by night. We think he has not had such nourishment for a long time, our Mogor. There is a light in him that was almost extinguished when we met him, but it grows stronger by the day in our company, or in hers, the little Skeleton, Mohini. Maybe she is saving his life. It is true we do not know what that life has been. His name, Father Acquaviva told us, is illustrious in his own city, but if so then he has been excluded from its protection. Who knows why he was cast out? We find that we enjoy him and do not care, for the present, to unravel his mysteries. Maybe he has been a criminal, maybe even a murderer, we cannot say. What we know is that he has crossed the world to leave one story behind and to tell another, that the story he has brought us is his only baggage, and that his deepest desire is the same as poor vanished Dashwanth's—that is, he wants to step into the tale he is telling and begin a new life inside it. In short, he is a creature of fables, and a good *afsanah* never did anybody any real damage."

"Sire, I hope we do not live to learn the folly of that remark," Birbal gravely replied.

The reputation of the late Khanzada Begum, elder sibling of the hidden princess, deteriorated as the city's infatuation with her younger sister increased. That grand lady, who had become a heroine of the court of Akbar's grandfather Babar when she returned home in triumph after her years of captivity with Shaibani Khan, and who had subsequently become a potent force in the Mughal household, consulted on all matters of state, now became, instead, the archetype of all cruel sisters, and her name, once so much revered, became an insult women flung at each other in anger when they wanted to make accusations of vanity, jealousy, pettiness, or betrayal. Many people began to harbor the belief that it was her treatment at the hands of Khanzada, as much as her infatuation with a foreign pasha, that had pushed the hidden princess away from her family, a choice that had led down enigmatic, unknown roads toward utter obscurity. As time went by the public mood of revulsion against the "wicked sister" began to have a more worrying consequence. Something quarrelsome rose out of the story, a green stenchy wisp of discord floated up out of the tale and infected the women of Sikri, so that reports began to reach the palace of bitter quarrels between previously loving sisters, suspicions and accusations, irreparable breaches and bitter estrangements, cat-fights and even knife-fights, the bubbling up of dislikes and resentments of which the women in question had barely been aware until the unmasking of Khanzada Begum by the foreigner with the yellow hair. Then the trouble spread more generally until it affected first cousins, then more distant relations, and finally all females, whether related or not; and even in the harem of the emperor the hubbub of enmity rose to unprecedented and wholly unacceptable levels.

"Women have always moaned about men," Birbal said, "but it turns out that their deepest complaints are reserved for one another, because while they expect men to be fickle, treacherous, and weak, they judge their own sex by higher standards, they expect more from their own sex—loyalty, understanding, trustworthiness, love—and apparently they have all collectively decided that those expectations were misplaced." Abul Fazl, with a sardonic edge to his voice, additionally remarked that the king's belief in the alleged harmlessness of stories was becoming a more embattled position to defend. All three men, the courtiers and the king, knew that the war of the women was impossible for men to end. The queen mother Hamida Bano and old Princess Gulbadan were summoned to the Place of Dreams. They arrived jostling and shoving each other, each old lady complaining loudly of the secret perfidy of the other, and it became evident that the crisis had run out of control.

One of the few places in Sikri that remained immune to the phenomenon was the House of Skanda, and finally the Skeleton and Mattress marched up the hill and demanded an audience with the emperor, insisting that they had the solution to the problem. Self-preservation was their powerful motive for this outrageous act. "We have to do something," the Skeleton had whispered to Mogor in bed at night, "otherwise five minutes from now somebody will decide that this whole commotion is your fault and then we'll all be done for." The emperor was both amused enough by the whores' daring and worried enough about the situation to grant their request for an audience and summoned them to the edge of the Best of All Possible Pools. He sat in cushioned comfort on the *takht* in the middle of the pool and told the courtesans to get on with it. "*Jahanpanah,* Shelter of the World," said the Skeleton, "you have to order all the women in Sikri to take all their clothes off." The emperor sat up. This was interesting. "*All* their clothes?" he asked, just to make sure he had heard correctly. "Every stitch," said the Mattress in deadly earnest. "Underwear, socks, even the ribbons in their hair. Let them walk around the city stark naked for one day and you'll have no more of this nonsense."

"The reason the trouble hasn't spread to the whorehouses," the Skeleton explained, "is that we ladies of the night have no secrets from each other, we wash each other's private parts and we know exactly which bitches have the pox and which are clean. When the ladies of the city see each other naked in the street, naked in the kitchen, naked in the bazaar, naked everywhere, visible from every angle, all their faults and secret hairiness on display, they will start laughing at themselves and realize what fools they are being to think that these weird, funny creatures could be their foes."

"As for the men," said Mohini the Skeleton, "you must command them all to be blindfolded, and you yourself must do the same. For one day no man in Sikri will look upon a woman, while the women, seeing each other unhidden, so to speak, are coming to terms with one another once again."

"If you think I'm doing that," said Hamida Bano, "then that foreigner's stories have truly softened your brain." The emperor Akbar looked his mother in the eye. "When the emperor commands a thing," he said, "the punishment for disobedience is death."

—— \\\ ——

The skies were kind on the day of the nakedness of the women. Clouds covered the sun all day, and a cool breeze blew. The men of Sikri did not work that day, no stores opened, the fields were empty, the doors to the studios of the artists and craftsmen were barred. Noblemen stayed in bed, musicians and courtiers alike turned their faces to the wall. And in the absence of the men the women of the capital learned all over again that they were not made of lies and treasons but only of hair and skin and flesh, that they were all as imperfect as each other, and that there was nothing special they were hiding from one another, no poisons, no plots, and that even sisters can, in the end, find a way of getting along. When the sun set the women dressed again, and the men removed their blindfolds, and a meal was eaten similar to the repast taken at the breaking of a fast, a supper of water and fruits. From that day on the house of the Skeleton and the Mattress became the only nocturnal establishment to be granted the emperor's personal seal of approval, and the ladies themselves became honored advisers to the king. There were only two pieces of bad news. The first had to do with Crown Prince Salim. In his cups, that night, he boasted to anyone who would listen that he had ignored his father's decree, removed his blindfold, and ogled the entire female population for hours. The news reached Akbar, who ordered his son's immediate arrest. It was Abul Fazl who suggested the most appropriate punishment for the prince's crime. The next morning in the open space outside the royal harem he had Salim stripped naked and then beaten by guards from the harem, both eunuchs and women built like male wrestlers. They pelted him with sticks, small stones, and clods of earth until he begged for mercy and forgiveness. After that it was inevitable that the drunkard, opium-addled prince would one day attempt to be avenged on Abul Fazl and on the Emperor of Hindustan as well.

The second sad consequence of the nakedness of the women was that old Princess Gulbadan caught a chill and subsided rapidly toward death. At the very last she summoned the emperor and attempted to rehabilitate the reputation of the late Khanzada Begum. "When your father returned from his long Persian exile and found you again," she said, "it was Khanzada Begum who had been looking after you, because Hamida Bano was not there, of course. Khanzada loved you very much, don't forget it. She would kiss your hands and feet and say they reminded her of the feet and hands of your grandfather. So whatever the story is about her dealings with Qara Köz, remember that this is also true. A bad sister can be a loving great-aunt." Gulbadan had always sought precision in her memory of the past, but now she began to slip into confusion, sometimes calling Akbar by his father's name, *Humayun,* and sometimes even by his grandfather's. It was as though all the first three Mughal emperors had gathered at her bedside, contained in Akbar's body, to stand guard over her soul's passage out of this world. After Gulbadan died, Hamida Bano was filled with dreadful remorse. "I jostled her," she said. "I shoved her so that she almost fell, and she was my senior. I did not honor her and now she is gone." Akbar comforted his mother. "She knew you loved her," he said. "She knew that a woman may be a bad jostler and a good friend as well." But the queen mother was inconsolable. "She always seemed so young," she said. "The angel made a mistake. I am the one who was just waiting to die."

After the forty days of mourning for Gulbadan were over, Akbar summoned Mogor dell'Amore to the Place of Dreams.

"You're taking too long," he told him. "You can't draw this out forever, you know. It's time you got on with your account. Just tell the whole damn story as fast as you possibly can—and do it, please, without stirring the ladies up all over again."

"Shelter of the World," said Mogor, bowing deeply, "there is nothing I desire more earnestly than for my whole tale to be told, for it is what men long for above all things. But to bring the Lady Black Eyes into the embrace of Argalia the Turk, I must first explain certain military developments involving the three great powers standing between Italy and Hindustan, that is to say, Wormwood Khan the Uzbeg warlord, Shah Ishmael or Ismail the Safavid king of Persia, and the Ottoman Sultan."

"A curse on all storytellers," said Akbar irritably, drinking deeply from a red and gold goblet of wine. "And a pox on your children too."

{ 15 }

By the Caspian Sea the old potato witches

B y the Caspian Sea the old potato witches sat down and wept. Loudly they sobbed and wildly keened. All Transoxiana was in mourning for the great Shaibani Khan, mighty Lord Wormwood, ruler of wide Khorasan, potentate of Samarkand, Herat, and Bukhara, scion of the true bloodline of Genghis Khan, erstwhile vanquisher of the Mughal upstart Babar . . .

"It is probably not a good idea," said the emperor gently, "to repeat in our presence that scoundrel's boasts about our grandfather."

. . . Shaibani the hateful, that savage rogue, who fell in the battle of Marv and was slain by Shah Ismail of Persia, who set his skull in a bejeweled, red and gold wine goblet, and sent parts of his body around the world to prove that he was dead. So perished that seasoned, though also appalling, uneducated, and barbaric warrior of sixty: quite appropriately, and humiliatingly, decapitated and dismembered by a green youth of only twenty-four.

"That's much better," said the emperor, regarding his own wine goblet with satisfaction. "For it cannot be called skill to kill one's fellow citizens, to betray friends, to be without faith, without mercy, without religion; by these means one can acquire power, but not glory."

"Niccolò Machiavelli of Florence could not have said it better," the storyteller agreed.

Potato witchcraft was born in Astrakhan on the banks of the River Atil, afterward called Volga, brought into being by the apocryphal Witch Mother Olga the First, but its exponents had long since been divided as the world had been divided, so that now on the west coast of the Caspian Sea which they called the Khazar, near Ardabil where Shah Ismail's Safavid dynasty had its roots in Sufi mysticism, the witches were Shiites and rejoiced in the triumphs of the new Twelver Persian empire, while on the east coast where the Uzbegs lived they were—some of them, poor, misguided wretches!—on the side of Wormwood Khan. Afterward, when Shah Ismail tasted defeat at the hands of the Ottoman army, these Sunni potato witches of the east Khazar Sea claimed that their curses had proved more powerful than the magic of their Shiite sisters in the west. *For the Khorasani potato is omnipotent,* they cried many times, in the words of their holiest creed, *and all things may by it be accomplished.*

By proper use of Sunni-Uzbeg potato-based spells it was possible to find a husband, chase off a more attractive love rival, or cause the downfall of a Shiite king. Shah Ismail had fallen victim to the rarely used Great Uzbeg Anti-Shiite Potato and Sturgeon Curse, which required quantities of potatoes and caviar which were not easy to amass, and a unity of purpose among the Sunni witches which was likewise difficult to achieve. When they heard the news of Ismail's rout, the eastern potato witches wiped their eyes, ceased their wailing, and danced. A pirouetting Khorasani witch is a rare and particular sight, and few who saw the dance ever forgot it. And the Caviar and Potato Curse created a rift between the sisterhood of potato witches which has not been healed to this day.

There may, however, have been more prosaic reasons for the outcome of the battle of Chaldiran: that the Ottoman army greatly outnumbered the Persian; or that the Ottoman soldiers bore rifles, which the Persians thought of as unmanly weapons and refused to carry, so that they were dispatched in large numbers to inevitable but undeniably manly deaths; or that at the head of the Ottoman forces was the invincible Janissary general, slayer of Vlad the Impaler, the Dragon-Demon of Wallachia, namely Argalia the Florentine Turk. Great as Shah Ismail believed himself to be—and he was second to no man in his high opinion of himself—he could not stand for long against the Wielder of the Enchanted Lance.

Shah Ismail of Persia, the self-appointed representative on earth of the Twelfth Imam, was by repute arrogant, egotistical, and a fanatic proselytizer of *Ithna Ashari,* that is to say Twelve Shiite Islam. "I will break the polo sticks of my adversaries," he boasted, in the words of the Sufi saint Shaykh Zahid, "and then the field will be mine." Then he made a larger claim, in his own words. "I am Very God, Very God, Very God! Come now, O blind man who has lost the path, behold the Truth! I am the Absolute Doer of whom men speak." He was called *Vali Allah,* the vicar of God, and to his "red-headed" *qizilbash* soldiers he was indeed divine. Modesty, generosity, kindness: these were not his most renowned characteristics. And yet, when he marched south from the battlefield of Marv, accompanied by the head of Shaibani Khan in a jar of honey, and entered Herat in triumph, those were the exact words used to describe him by the princess whom history forgot, Lady Black Eyes, Qara Köz. Shah Ismail was her first infatuation. She was seventeen years old.

"So it's true," the emperor cried. "The foreigner who was the reason for her refusal to return with Khanzada to my grandfather's court, the reason for her removal from the record by my noble grandfather—the seducer of whom our beloved aunt Gulbadan spoke—was not your Arcalia or Argalia, but the Shah of Persia himself."

"They were both chapters in her story, O Shelter of the World," the storyteller replied. "One after the other, the victor and then the victor's vanquisher. Women are not perfect, one must admit, and it would appear that the young lady had a weakness for being on the winning side."

Herat, pearl of Khorasan, abode of painter Behzad, the creator of matchless miniatures, and the poet Jami, the deathless philosopher of love, and last resting place of the patroness of beauty, the great Queen Gauhar Shad, which is to say, Happy or Shining Jewel! "You belong to Persia now," Shah Ismail said aloud as he rode through its conquered streets. "Your history, oasis, baths, bridges, canals, and minarets are all mine." Watching him from a high palace window were the two captured princesses of the Mughal house. "Now we will either die or be set free," said Khanzada, not allowing her voice to tremble. Shaibani Khan had made her his wife and she had borne him a son. She beheld the sealed urn being carried behind the conqueror's horse slung on a common spear and understood what it contained. "If the father is dead," she said, "then my son is doomed as well." Her analysis was correct; by the time Shah Ismail presented himself at the princesses' door the boy had already been dispatched to join his father. The Persian king bowed his head before Princess Khanzada. "You are the sisters of a great brother," he said, "and so I set you free. I have it in mind to return you with many gifts of friendship to Lord Babar, who is at present in Qunduz; and you ladies will be the greatest gifts of all."

"Until just now," Khanzada replied, "I was not only a sister but also a mother and a wife. Since you have destroyed two-thirds of me the last part may as well go home." After nine years as Wormwood Khan's queen and eight as the mother of a prince, her heart was torn to pieces. But at no time did Khanzada Begum allow her face or voice to betray her true emotions, so that she struck Shah Ismail as unfeeling and cold. At twenty-nine she was a great beauty, and the Persian was greatly tempted to look behind her veil, but, restraining himself, he turned to the younger girl instead. "And you, madame," he said with as much courtesy as he could muster, "what do you have to say to your liberator?"

Khanzada Begum took her sister by the elbow as if to lead her away. "Thank you, my sister and I are of one mind," she said. But Qara Köz shook off her sister's hand, threw off her veil, and looked the young king right in the face.

"I would like to stay," she said.

There is a weakness that comes over men at the battle's end, when they become aware of the fragility of life, they clutch it to their bosoms like a crystal bowl they almost dropped, and the treasure of life scares away their courage. At such a time all men are cowards, and can think of nothing but women's embraces, nothing but the healing words only women can whisper, nothing but the joy of losing themselves in the fatal labyrinths of love. In the grip of this weakness a man will do things which unravel his best-laid plans, he can make promises which change his future. So it was that Shah Ismail of Persia drowned in the seventeen-year-old princess's black eyes.

"Then stay," he replied.

"The need for a woman to cure the loneliness of murder," the emperor said, remembering. *"To wipe away the guilt of victory or the vainglory of defeat. To still the tremble in the bones. To dry the hot tears of relief and shame. To hold you while you feel the ebbing tide of your hatred and its replacement by a form of higher embarrassment. To sprinkle you with lavender to hide the scent of blood on the fingertips and the gore stinking in the beard. The need for a woman to tell you that you are hers and to turn your mind away from death. To quell your curiosity about how it might be to stand at the Judgment Seat, to take away your envy of those who have gone before you to see the Almighty plain, and to soothe the doubts twisting in your stomach, about the existence of the afterlife and even of God Himself, because the slain are so utterly dead, and no higher purpose seems to exist at all."*

Afterward, when he had lost her forever, Shah Ismail spoke of sorcery. There was an enchantment in her gaze that was not wholly human, he said; a devil was in her, and had goaded him to his doom. "That a woman so beautiful should not be tender," he said to his deaf-mute body-servant, "this I did not expect. I did not expect her to turn away from me so casually, as if she were changing a shoe. I expected to be the beloved. I did not expect to be *majnun-Layla,* driven mad by love. I did not expect her to break my heart."

When Khanzada Begum returned to Babar in Qunduz without her sister she was greeted with a great celebration of soldiery and dancers, of trumpets and song, and Babar himself on foot to embrace her as she descended from her litter. But in private he was incensed, and it was at this time that he ordered the removal of Qara Köz from the historical record. For a time, however, he allowed Shah Ismail to believe that they were friends. He minted coins with Ismail's head on them to prove it, and Ismail sent troops to help him drive the Uzbegs out of Samarkand. Then suddenly he could bear it no more, and told Ismail to take his troops and go home.

"This is interesting," said the emperor. "For our grandfather's decision to send the Safavid army home after the recapture of Samarkand has always been a mystery. It was at this time that he stopped writing the book of his life, which he did not take up again for eleven years, so his own voice is silent on the topic. After the Persians departed he at once lost Samarkand again and was obliged to flee into the East. We had thought his rejection of Persian assistance was because he didn't care for Shah Ismail's religious bombast: his interminable proclamations of his own divinity, his Twelver Shiite aggrandizements. But if Babar's slow anger about the hidden princess was the real reason, then how many great matters have followed from her choice! For it was because he lost Samarkand that Babar came into Hindustan, and established his dynasty here, and we ourselves are third in that line. So if your story is true, then the beginning of our own empire is the direct consequence of the willfulness of Qara Köz. Should we condemn or praise her? Was she a traitor, forever to be held in contempt, or our genetrix, who shaped our future?"

"She was a beautiful, willful girl," said Mogor dell'Amore. "And her power over men was so great that perhaps even she did not at first know the force of her enchantments."

Qara Köz: see her now in the Safavid capital city of Tabriz, caressed by the Shah's fine carpets, like Cleopatra rolled in Caesar's rug. In Tabriz even the hills were carpeted, for it was on the hillsides that the great rugs were spread out to dry in the sun. In her royal chambers Lady Black Eyes rolled over and over on the rugs of Persia as if they were the bodies of lovers. And always in a corner a samovar, steaming. She ate voraciously, chicken stuffed with prunes and garlic, or shrimp with tamarind paste, or kebabs with fragrant rice, and yet her own body remained slender and long. She played backgammon with her maidservant the Mirror and became the greatest player in the Persian court. She played other games with the Mirror too; behind locked doors in her bedchamber the two girls giggled and shrieked and many courtiers believed them to be lovers, but no man or woman dared say as much, for it would have cost the gossip a head. When she watched the young king at polo Qara Köz sighed a sigh of erotic ecstasy each time he swung his stick and people began to believe that these grunts and cries actually placed an enchantment on the ball, which inevitably found its way to the goal while the sticks of defenders flailed forlornly at empty air. She bathed in milk. She sang like an angel. She did not read books. She was twenty-one years old. She had not conceived a child. And one day when her Ismail spoke of the growing strength of his rival to the west, the Ottoman Sultan Bayezid II, she murmured deadly advice.

"Just send him that goblet of yours," she said, "the one made with the skull of Shaibani Khan, to warn him what will happen if he does not remember his place."

She found his vanity seductive. She was in love with his faults. A man who believed himself to be a god was perhaps the man for her. Perhaps a king was not enough. "Very God!" she cried when he took her. "Absolute Doer!" He liked that, of course, and being susceptible to praise he did not consider the autonomy of her great beauty, which no man could own, which owned itself, and which would blow wherever it pleased, like the wind. Though she had abandoned everything for him, had changed her world in a single glance, leaving sister, brother, and clan to travel west in a handsome stranger's company, Shah Ismail in the immensity of his self-love thought such a radical act perfectly natural, for, after all, it had been done for him. As a result he did not see the wandering thing in her, the unrooted thing. If a woman turned so easily from one allegiance she might just as readily turn away from the next.

There were days when she wanted badness: his badness and her own. In bed she whispered to him that she had another self inside her, a bad self, and when that self took over she was no longer responsible for her actions, she might do anything, anything. This aroused him beyond endurance. She was more than his equal in love. She was his queen. In four years she had not given him a son. No matter. She was a banquet for the senses. She was what men killed for. She was his addiction and his teacher. "You want me to send Bayezid the Shaibani goblet," he said thickly, as if intoxicated. "To send him another man's skull."

"For you to drink out of your enemy's skull is a great victory," she whispered. "But when Bayezid drinks from the head of your enemy's defeated foe it will put fear in his heart." He understood that she had placed a spell of terror on the goblet. "Very well," he said. "We will do as you suggest."

—⁓—

Argalia's forty-fifth birthday had come and gone. He was a tall pale man, and in spite of the years of war his skin was as white as a woman's; men and women alike marveled at its softness. He was a lover of tulips, and had them embroidered onto his tunics and cloaks, believing them to be bringers of good fortune, and of the fifteen hundred varieties of Stamboul tulip six in particular were to be found thronging his palace rooms. The Light of Paradise, the Matchless Pearl, the Increaser of Pleasure, the Instiller of Passion, the Diamond's Envy, and the Rose of the Dawn: these were his favorites, and by them he was revealed as a sensualist beneath his warrior's exterior, a creature of pleasure hiding inside a killer's skin, a female self within the male. He had, too, a woman's taste for finery: when not in battle-dress he lounged in jewels and silks and had a great weakness for exotic furs, the black fox and lynx of Muscovy which came down to Stamboul through Feodosiya in the Crimea. His hair was long and black as evil and his lips were full and red as blood.

Blood, and its shedding, had been his life's concern. Under Sultan Mehmed II he had fought a dozen campaigns and won every battle in which he raised his arquebus to the firing position or unsheathed his sword. He had drawn a platoon of loyal Janissaries around him like a shield, with the Swiss giants Otho, Botho, Clotho, and D'Artagnan as his lieutenants, and though the Ottoman court was full of intrigues he had foiled seven assassination attempts. After Mehmed's death the empire came close to civil war between his two sons, Bayezid and Cem. When Argalia learned that the Grand Vizier, in defiance of Muslim tradition, had refused to bury the dead Sultan's body for three days so that Cem could reach Stamboul and seize the throne, he led the Swiss giants to the Vizier's quarters and killed him. He led Bayezid's army against the would-be usurper and drove him into exile. Once that was done he became the new Sultan's commander-in-chief. He fought the Mamluks of Egypt by land and sea and when he vanquished the alliance of Venice, Hungary, and the papacy his reputation as an admiral equaled his fame as a warrior on dry land.

After that the main problems came from the *qizilbash* peoples of Anatolia. They wore red hats with twelve pleats to show their fondness for Twelver Shiism and as a result they were attracted to Shah Ismail of Persia, the self-styled Very God. Bayezid's third son Selim the Grim wanted to crush them utterly but his father was more restrained. As a result Selim the Grim began to think of his father as an appeaser and a weakling. When the goblet from Shah Ismail arrived in Stamboul, Selim took it as a mortal insult. "That heretic who calls himself by God's name should be taught his manners," he declared. He picked up the cup as a duelist picks up the glove that has struck him in the face. "I will drink Safavid blood from this cup," he promised his father. Argalia the Turk stepped forward. "And I will pour that wine," he said.

When Bayezid refused permission for the war, things changed for Argalia. A few days later he and his Janissaries had joined forces with Selim the Grim, and Bayezid was forced from power. The old Sultan was banished into enforced retirement, sent back to his birthplace of Didymoteicho in Thrace, and died of a broken heart on the way, which was just as well. The world had no room for men who had lost their nerve. Selim, with Argalia at his side, hunted down and strangled his brothers Ahmed, Korkud, and Shahinshah, and killed their sons as well. Order was restored and the risk of a coup eliminated. (Many years later, when Argalia told il Machia about these deeds, he justified them by saying, "When a prince takes power he should do his worst right away, because after that his every deed will strike his subjects as an improvement on the way he started out," and on hearing this il Machia grew silent and thoughtful and, after a time, slowly nodded his head. "Terrible," he told Argalia, "but true.") Then it was time to face Shah Ismail. Argalia and his Janissaries were sent to Rum, in north-central Anatolia, arrested thousands of *qizilbash* residents, and slaughtered thousands more. That kept the bastards quiet while the army marched across their land to deliver Selim the Grim's letter to the Shah. In this message Selim said, "You no longer uphold the commandments and prohibitions of the divine law. You have incited your abominable Shiite faction to unsanctified sexual union. And you have shed innocent blood." One hundred thousand Ottoman soldiers made camp at Lake Van in eastern Anatolia on the way to push these words down Shah Ismail's blasphemous throat. Among their ranks were twelve thousand Janissary musketeers under Argalia's command. There were also five hundred cannons, chained together to form an impassable barrier.

The battlefield of Chaldiran was to the northeast of Lake Van, and there the Persian forces made their stand. Shah Ismail's army was only forty thousand men strong, almost all of them cavalrymen, but Argalia surveying their battle array knew that superior numbers did not always decide a fight. Like Vlad Dracula in Wallachia, Ismail had used a scorched earth strategy. Anatolia was bare and charred, and the advancing Ottomans marching from Sivas to Arzinjan found little to eat or drink. Selim's army was tired and hungry when it camped by the lake after its long march, and such an army is always beatable. Afterward, when Argalia was with the hidden princess, she told him why her erstwhile lover had been bested.

"Chivalry," she said. "Foolish chivalry, and listening to some stupid nephew of his and not to me."

The extraordinary fact is that the enchantress of Persia, along with her slave the Mirror, was present on the command hill above the field of battle, her thin veiling garment blowing against her face and breasts in the breeze so suggestively that when she stood outside the king's tent her body's beauty turned the Safavid soldiers' thoughts entirely away from war. "He must have been mad to bring you," Argalia told her when blood-filthy and kill-sick he found her abandoned at the death-heavy end of the day. "Yes," she said, matter-of-factly, "I drove him mad with love."

However, in the matter of military strategy not even her enchantments could make him heed her. "Look," she cried, "they are still building their defensive fortifications. Attack now, when they aren't ready." And, "Look," she cried, "they have five hundred cannons chained in a line and twelve thousand riflemen behind. Don't just gallop at them head-on or you'll be cut down like fools." And, "Don't you have guns? You know about guns. For pity's sake, why didn't you bring any guns?" To which the Shah's nephew Durmish Khan, the fool, answered, "It would not be sportsmanlike to attack them when they are not ready to fight." And, "It would not be noble to send our men to attack them from the rear." And, "The gun is not a weapon for a man. The gun is for cowards who do not dare to fight at close quarters. Yet however many guns they have we will take the fight to them until it is hand-to-hand. Courage will win the day, not—ha!—these '*arque-buses*' and '*muskets.*'" She turned to Shah Ismail in a kind of laughing despair. "Tell this man he is an idiot," she commanded him. But Shah Ismail of Persia answered, "I am not a caravan thief to go skulking in the shadows. Whatever is decreed by God will occur."

She refused to watch the battle, sitting, instead, inside the royal tent with her face turned away from the door. The Mirror sat beside her and held her hand. Shah Ismail led a charge down the right wing that smashed the Ottoman left but the enchantress had turned away her face. Both armies suffered terrible losses. The Persian cavalry cut down the flower of the Ottoman horsemen, the Illyrians, the Macedonians, the Serbians, the Epirots, Thessalians, and Thracians. On the Safavid side, the commanders fell one by one and as they died the enchantress in her tent murmured their names. *Muhammad Khan Ustajlu, Husain Beg Lala Ustajlu, Saru Pira Ustajlu,* and so on. As if she could see everything without looking. And the Mirror reflected her words, so that the names of the dead seemed to echo in the royal tent. *Amir Nizam al-Din Abd al-Baqi . . . al-Baqi . . .* but the name of the Shah who believed himself to be God was not spoken. The Ottoman center held, but the Turkish cavalry was on the verge of panic when Argalia ordered the artillery to be brought up. "You bastards," he screamed at his own Janissaries, "if any of you try to run I'll turn the fucking cannons on you." The Swiss giants, armed to the teeth, ran on foot along the Ottoman battle line to add emphasis to Argalia's threats. Then the thunder of the guns began. "The storm has started," the enchantress said, sitting in her tent. "The storm," the Mirror replied. There was no need to look as the Persian army died. It was time to sing a sad song. Shah Ismail was alive, but the day was lost.

He had fled the battlefield, wounded, without coming for her. She knew it. "He has gone," she told the Mirror. "Yes, he has gone," the other assented. "We are at the enemy's mercy," the enchantress said. "Mercy," the Mirror replied.

The men posted outside the tent to guard them had run away

as well. They were two women alone upon a field of dreadful blood. That was how Argalia found them, sitting unveiled and straight-backed and alone, facing away from the door of the royal tent at the end of the battle of Chaldiran, and singing a sad song. The princess Qara Köz turned to face him, making no attempt to shield the nakedness of her features from his gaze, and from that moment on they could only see each other and were lost to the rest of the world.

He looked like a woman, she thought, like a tall, pale, black-haired woman who had glutted herself on death. How white he was, as white as a mask. Upon which, like a bloodstain, those red, red lips. A sword in his right hand and a gun in his left. He was both things, swordsman and shootist, male and female, himself and his shadow as well. She abandoned Shah Ismail as he had abandoned her and chose again. This pale-faced woman-man. Afterward he would claim her and her Mirror as spoils of war and Selim the Grim would agree, but she had chosen him long before, and it was her will that moved everything that followed.

"Don't be afraid," he said in Persian.

"Nobody in this place knows the meaning of fear," she replied, first in Persian and then again in Chaghatai, her Turkic mother tongue.

And beneath those words, the real words. *Will you be mine. Yes. I am yours.*

—⁂—

After the sack of Tabriz, Selim wanted to stay in the Safavid capital for the winter and conquer the rest of Persia in the spring, but Argalia told him that the army would mutiny if he insisted on this. They had won the victory and annexed much of eastern Anatolia and Kurdistan, almost doubling the size of the Ottoman empire. It was enough. Let the line reached at Chaldiran be the new border between Ottoman and Safavid power. Tabriz was empty anyway.

There was no food for the men or the cavalry horses or baggage camels. The army wanted to go home. Selim understood that an ending had been arrived at. Eight days after the Ottoman army entered Tabriz, Selim the Grim led his men out of the city and turned toward the west.

A defeated god ceases to be divine. A man who leaves his consort behind on the field of battle ceases to be a man. Shah Ismail returned broken to his broken city and spent the last ten years of his life steeped in gloom and drink. He wore black robes and a black turban and the standards of the Safavids were dyed black as well. He never rode into battle again and swung between profound sadness and debauchery on a scale that showed everyone his weakness and the depths of his despair. When he was drunk he would run through the rooms of his palace looking for someone who was no longer there, who would never be there again. When he died he was not yet thirty-seven years old. He had been Shah of Persia for twenty-three years but everything that mattered had been lost.

When she undressed Argalia and found tulips embroidered on his underclothes she understood that he was addicted to his superstitions, that like any man whose work is death he did what he could to ward off the last day. When she removed his undergarments and found them tattooed on his shoulder blades and buttocks and even on the thick shaft of his penis she knew for certain that she had met the love of her life. "You don't need those flowers anymore," she told him, caressing them. "Now you have me instead to be your good luck charm."

He thought, *Yes, I have you, but only until I don't. Only until you choose to leave me as you left your sister, to change horses again as you changed from Shah Ismail to me. A horse is only a horse, after all.* She read his mind, and seeing that he needed further reassurances she clapped her hands. The Mirror came into the flower-heavy bedchamber. "Tell him who I am," she said. "She is the lady who loves you," the Mirror said. "She can charm the snakes from the ground and the birds from the trees and make them fall in love and she has fallen in love with you, so now you can have anything you desire." The enchantress made a small movement of her eyebrow and the Mirror let her clothes fall to the floor and slipped into the bed. "She is my Mirror," the enchantress said. "She is the shadow that shines. Who wins me, gets her as well." At this point Argalia the great warrior admitted defeat. In the face of such an outflanking assault the only course left to a man was unconditional surrender.

He was the one who renamed her "Angelica." Defeated by "Qara Köz," with its glottal stop and unfamiliar progression of sounds, he gave her the seraphic name by which her new worlds would know her. And she, in turn, passed the name on to her Mirror. "If I am to be Angelica," she said, "then this guardian angel of mine will be an Angelica too."

For many years he had had the honor of being permitted, as a recipient of the Sultan's favor, to reside in chambers in the Abode of Bliss, the Topkapi, instead of the spartan accommodation at the Janissary barracks. Now that the chambers had the added grace of a woman's touch, they began to feel like a true home. But home was always a troubled, dangerous idea for men like Argalia to allow themselves to believe in. It could catch at them like a noose. Selim the Grim was not Bayezid or Mehmed, and did not think of Argalia as his indispensable right-hand man but as a probable, and dangerous, rival for power, a popular general who could lead his Janissaries into the inner sanctum of the palace, just as he had done once before, when he killed the Grand Vizier. A man capable of murdering the Vizier was also capable of regicide. Such a man had perhaps outlived his usefulness. As soon as they were back in Stamboul, the Sultan, while publicly lavishing praise on his Italian commanding officer for his part in the famous victory of Chaldiran, began secretly to plot Argalia's destruction.

News of Argalia's precarious position came to his ears on account of Qara Köz's decision to continue to satisfy his love for tulips. There were gardens all around the Abode of Bliss, walled gardens and sunken gardens, woodland areas where deer wandered freely, and waterside lawns sloping down to the Golden Horn. The tulip beds were to be found in the Fourth Court, and on the low hill at the northern end of the Topkapi complex, the highest point in the entire Abode of Bliss, where there were small wooden pleasure pavilions called kiosks. The tulips grew around them in great numbers and created an air of fragrant serenity and peace. The princess Qara Köz and her Mirror, demurely veiled, often walked in these gardens and rested in the kiosks, drinking sweet juices, speaking gently to the many palace *bostancis,* the gardeners, to get them to gather flowers for Lord Argalia, and to prattle idly, as women will, about the innocent gossip of the day. Soon all the garden staff from the lowliest weed-puller to the Bostanci-Basha, the head gardener himself, were deeply enamored of the two ladies and consequently loose-tongued as only true lovers are. Many of them remarked how swiftly the two foreign ladies had become proficient in the Turkish language, almost overnight, or so it seemed. As if by magic, the gardeners said.

But Qara Köz's true purposes were far from innocent. She knew, as all new residents of the Abode of Bliss swiftly came to know, that the one thousand and one *bostancis* were not only the Sultan's gardeners but his official executioners as well. If a woman was convicted of a crime, it was a *bostanci* who sewed her, still alive, into a sack weighted down with stones and threw her into the Bosphorus. And if a man was to be killed, a group of gardeners grabbed him and performed an act of ritual strangulation. So Qara Köz befriended the *bostancis* and learned what they called, with dark humor, the tulip news. And soon enough the stink of betrayal began to overpower the fragrance of the flowers. The gardeners warned her that her lord, the great general, servant of three sultans, was in danger of being tried on trumped-up charges and sentenced to death. The head gardener himself told her so. The Bostanci-

Basha of the Abode of Bliss was the Sultan's executioner-in-chief, chosen not only for his horticultural skills but also for his running speed, because when a grandee of the court was condemned to death he was given a chance not granted to common men. If he could outrun the Bostanci-Basha he could live; his sentence would be commuted to banishment. But the Bostanci-Basha was famous for being able to run like the wind, so the "chance" was in reality no chance at all. On this occasion, however, the gardener was not happy about what he would have to do. "To execute such a great man would make me feel ashamed," he said. "Then," said the enchantress, "we must find a way out of the situation if we can."

"He will kill you soon," she came home and told Argalia. "The gardens are full of rumor." Argalia said gravely, "On what pretext, I wonder?" The princess took his pale face in her hands. "I am the pretext," she said. "You have taken a Mughal princess as a spoil of war. He did not know that when he gave you leave, but he knows it now. To capture a Mughal princess is an act of war against the Mughal king, and, he will say, by placing the Ottoman empire in such a position you have committed treason and must pay the price. Such is the news the tulips have to tell."

Forewarned, Argalia had time to make plans, and on the day they came for him he had already sent Qara Köz and the Mirror, under cover of night, along with many treasure chests holding the wealth he had amassed on many successful military campaigns, and protected by the four Swiss giants and the entire company of his most loyal Janissaries, some one hundred men in all, to wait for him at Bursa to the south of the capital. "If I run away with you," he said, "Selim will hunt us down and murder us like dogs. Instead, I must stand trial, and after I am condemned I must win the Gardener's Race." It was what Qara Köz had known he would say. "If you are determined to die," she told him, "I suppose I will have to allow it." By which she meant, she would have to save his life, and it would be hard, because she would not be present at the scene of the great race.

As soon as Selim the Grim in the throne room of the Abode of Bliss pronounced the sentence of death on the traitor Argalia, the warrior, knowing the rules, spun on his heel and began to run. From the throne room to the Fish-House Gate it was about half a mile through the palace gardens, and he had to get there before the Bostanci-Basha in his red skull-cap, white muslin breeches, and bare chest, who was already in hot pursuit and gaining on him with every stride. If he was caught he would die at the Fish-House and be thrown into the Bosphorus where all the dead bodies went. As he ran between the flower beds he saw the Fish-House Gate ahead, heard the footsteps of the Bostanci-Basha close behind him, and knew he could not run fast enough to escape. "Life is absurd," he thought. "To survive so many wars and then be strangled by the gardener. Truly is it said, there are no heroes who do not learn the emptiness of heroism before they die." He remembered how as a young boy he had first discovered the absurdity of life, alone in a small rowboat in the middle of a naval battle in a fog. "All these years later," he thought, "I am having to learn the lesson all over again."

No satisfactory explanation was ever given of why Sultan Selim the Grim's fleet-footed head gardener suddenly fell down clutching his stomach just thirty paces from the end of the Gardener's Race, or why he then succumbed to a bout of the foulest farting anyone had ever smelled, releasing blasts of wind as loud as gunshots, and crying out in pain like an uprooted mandrake, while Argalia ran past the finishing post at the Fish-House Gate, mounted the horse waiting for him, and galloped on into exile. "Did you do something?" Argalia asked his beloved when he met her at Bursa. "What could I have done to my dear little Basha?" she answered, wide-eyed. "To send him a message thanking him in advance for slaying you, my vile abductor, along with a jug of Anatolian wine to demonstrate my gratitude, that is one thing, yes; but to calculate exactly how long a certain potion stirred into the wine would take before it had its effect on his stomach, why, that would be quite impossible, of course." When he looked into her eyes he saw no sign of any subterfuge there, no indication that she, or her Mirror, or both of them together, might have done anything to persuade the gardener to fail in his duty, perhaps even to take the drink at a time specified in advance, in return for a moment of bliss that would last such a man a lifetime. No, Argalia told himself, as Qara Köz's eyes drew him deeply into their spell, nothing of that sort could have happened. Behold the eyes of my beloved, how guileless they are, how full of love and truth.

—\\\\—

Admiral Andrea Doria, captain of the fleet of Genoa, lived, when he was on dry land, in the suburb of Fassolo outside the city walls, in front of the San Tomasso gate at the northwest entrance to the harbor. He had bought a villa here from a Genoese noble called Jacobo Lomellino because it made him feel like one of the ancient toga-wearing, laurel-wreathed Romans who lived in grand sea villas like the one at Laurentinum described by the younger Pliny, and also on account of the harbor view that allowed him to keep an eye on exactly who was coming to or going from the city at any given time. His galleys were moored right outside the house in case quick action was required. So naturally he was one of the first people to see the ship from Rhodes that was bearing Argalia back to Italy, and through his spyglass he made out the large number of heavily armed men on board wearing the uniforms of Ottoman Janissaries. Four of them were apparently albino giants. He sent a messenger down from the terrace where he sat to instruct his lieutenant Ceva to sail out to meet the Rhodes vessel and find out what the new visitors might have in mind. This was how Ceva the Scorpion came face to face again with a person he had abandoned in enemy waters.

The man whom Ceva did not yet recognize as Argalia had positioned himself before the mast of the Rhodes ship dressed in the spreading turban and flowing brocade robes of a wealthy Ottoman prince. His Janissaries were behind him, fully armed and at the ready, and standing beside him, appearing to draw all sunlight toward themselves so that the rest of the world seemed dark and cold, were the two most beautiful women Ceva had ever seen, their beauty unveiled for all to behold, their loose black locks blowing like the tresses of goddesses in the breeze. As Ceva came aboard the Rhodes transport ship with a detachment of the Band of Gold right behind him the women turned to face him and he felt his sword drop from his hand. Then there was a gentle but inexorable downward pressure on both his shoulders, a pressure he discovered he had no desire whatsoever to resist, and suddenly he and all his men were kneeling at the visitors' feet and his mouth was uttering unaccustomed words of greeting. *Welcome, good ladies, and all these who watch over you.*

"Be careful, Scorpion," said the Ottoman prince in perfect Florentine Italian, and then, imitating Ceva's own speech, " 'cause if a fellow don't look me in the eye I tears their liver out and feeds it to the gulls."

Now Ceva understood who was standing before him and began to rise, groping for his weapon; but found that for some reason he was stuck down there on his knees, and so were all his men. "But then again," Argalia went on, thoughtfully, "right now your eye is only high enough to stare at my fucking cock."

The great *condottiere* Doria, his beard and mustache flooding down from his face in mighty waves, was posing as the sea-god Neptune for the sculptor Bronzino, standing naked on the terrace of his villa holding a trident in his right hand while the artist sketched his nudity, when to his considerable consternation a heavily armed band of scoundrels marched up from his private jetty to confront him. At their head, quite amazingly, was his own man Ceva, the Scorpion, behaving like a lickspittle toady, and in the center of the group, wearing hooded cloaks, were what appeared to be two female persons, whose identity and nature he could not at once determine. "If you think a bunch of brigands and their whores can take Andrea Doria without a fight," he roared, grabbing his sword in one hand and brandishing the trident in the other, "let's see how many of you leave this place alive."

At this point the enchantress and her slave threw back their hoods and Admiral Doria was suddenly reduced to blushing stammers. He retreated from the advancing group in search of his breeches, but the women appeared to pay his nakedness no attention at all, which was, if anything, more demeaning still. "A boy you left for dead has returned to claim his due," said Qara Köz. She spoke perfect Italian, Doria could hear that, though plainly this was no Italian girl. This was a visitor for whom a man could lay down his life. This was a queen to worship and her associate, who looked like a mirror image of the royal lady, only faintly inferior to the original in pulchritude and charm, was also a beauty to adore. It was impossible to think of battle in the presence of such wonders. Admiral Doria, clutching a cloak around himself, stood open-mouthed as the strangers approached, a sea-god in thrall to nymphs arising from the waters.

"He has returned," said Qara Köz, "as he promised himself he would, like a prince, with a fortune to his name. He has cleansed himself of the desire for revenge, so your safety is assured. However, he asks you for that reward which, in the light of his past service and his present mercy, must plainly be his due."

"And how much might that be?" Andrea Doria asked.

"Your friendship," said the enchantress, "and a good dinner, and safe conduct through these lands."

"Safe conduct in what direction," the Admiral asked. "Where does he propose to go with such a cut-throat band?"

"Home is the sailor, Andrea," said Argalia the Turk. "Home is the man of war. I have seen the world, had my fill of blood, made my packet, and now I'm going to rest."

"You haven't stopped being a child," Andrea Doria told him. "You still think that home, at the end of a long journey, is a place where a man finds peace."

III

{ 16 }

As if all Florentines were cardinals

[244]

As if all Florentines were cardinals, the despised poor of the city pre-empted the red-clothed eminences sealed in the Sistine Chapel and lit bonfires to celebrate the election of a Medici Pope. The city was so full of flame and smoke that from a distance it seemed to be burning down. A traveler coming this way at sunset—this traveler, coming this way now, along the road from the sea, his narrow eyes, white skin, and long black hair giving him the look not of a returning native but of an exotic creature out of some Far Eastern legend, a *samouraï,* perhaps, from the island of Chipango or Cipangu, which was to say Giapan, a descendant of the redoubtable Kiushu knights who once defeated the invading forces of the Chinese emperor Kubilai Khan—might believe himself to be arriving at the scene of a calamity, and might very well pause in his tracks, reining in his horse and holding up a general's imperious hand, a hand accustomed to being obeyed, to take stock. Argalia would remember that moment often enough in the coming months. The bonfires had been lit before the cardinals' decision had been taken, but their prophecy proved to be correct and a Medici Pope, Cardinal Giovanni de' Medici, Leo X, was indeed elected that night to join forces with his brother Duke Giuliano in Florence. "Considering that those bastards were back in the saddle, I should have stayed in Genoa and gone off sailing with Doria on his fighting ships until the world came to its senses," he told il Machia when he saw him, "but the truth is I wanted to show her off."

"A man in love becomes a fool," the emperor told Mogor dell'Amore. "To show your beloved's beauty bare-faced to the world is to take the first step toward losing her."

"No man ordered Qara Köz to bare her face," said the traveler. "Neither did she order her slave to do so. She freely made her own decision, and the Mirror made hers."

The emperor fell silent. Across time and space, he was falling in love.

At the age of forty-four Niccolò "il Machia" was playing cards in the tavern of Percussina in the late afternoon with Frosino Uno the miller, the butcher Gabburra, and Vettori the innkeeper, who were all yelling insults at one another, but, carefully, not at the lord of the hamlet, even if he was sitting down boozily at their raucous table and behaving like their equal, thumping his fist twice when he lost a hand and three times when he won, using bad language the same as the rest of them, drinking as hard as any man there and calling them all his beloved lice, when Gaglioffo the foulmouthed good-for-nothing woodcutter came in at high speed, wild-eyed and pointing and badly out of breath. "One hundred men or more," he shrieked, pointing through the doorway and gulping down air. "Fuck me twice in the rear if I'm a liar. Heavily armed, with giants on horseback, and heading this way!" Niccolò rose to his feet, still holding his cards. "Then, my friends, I am a dead man," he said. "The great Duke Giuliano has decided to do away with me after all. I thank you for these evenings of pleasure that have helped me scrape the mold from my brain at the end of a hard day, and must go now and say goodbye to my wife." Gaglioffo was doubled up, panting and holding his sides to ease the pain of the stitch. "Sir," he gasped, "perhaps not, sir. They do not wear our livery, sir. Fucking foreigners, sir, from fucking Liguria, maybe, or even further away. And there are women along for the ride, sir. Women with them, foreign women, sir, that when you lay eyes on the pair of witches the desire to fuck them comes upon you like swine fever. Fuck me if I lie. Sir."

These people were good people, thought il Machia, these few people of his own, but in general the people of Florence were traitors. It was the people who had betrayed the republic and invited the Medici back. The people whom he had served as a true republican, as secretary of the Second Chancery, traveling diplomat, and founder of the Florentine militia, had betrayed him. After the fall of the republic and the dismissal of the *gonfaloniere* Pier Soderini, the chief of the republic's governing body, il Machia too had been dismissed. After fourteen years of loyal service the people had shown that they did not care about loyalty. The people were fools for power. They had allowed il Machia to be taken down into the underground bowels of the city where the torturers waited. Such a people did not deserve to be cared for. They did not deserve a republic. Such a people deserved a despot. Perhaps this was what all people were like, everywhere, always excepting these rustics with whom he drank and played cards and *triche-tach,* and a few old friends, Agostino Vespucci, for instance, thank God they had not tortured Ago, he was not strong, he would have confessed to anything, everything, and then they would have killed him, unless he died during the torture, of course. But they had not wanted Ago, who was il Machia's junior. It was il Machia they had wanted to kill.

They did not deserve him. These rustics deserved him but in general the people deserved their cruel beloved princes. The pain that had coursed through his body was not pain but knowledge. It was an educative pain that broke the last fragments of his trust in the people. He had served the people and they had paid him in pain, in that lightless subterranean place, that place without a name in which nameless people did nameless things to bodies that were also nameless because names did not matter there, only pain mattered, pain followed by confession followed by death. The people had wanted his death, or at least had not cared if he lived or died.

In the city that gave the world the idea of the value and freedom of the individual human soul they had not valued him and cared not a fig for his soul's freedom, nor his body's integrity neither. He had given them fourteen years of honest and honorable service and they had not cared for his sovereign individual life, for his human right to remain alive. Such a people were to be set aside. They were incapable of love or justice and therefore did not signify. Such a people no longer mattered. They were not primary but secondary. Only despots mattered. The love of the people was fickle and inconstant and to pursue such a love was folly. There was no love. There was only power.

By slow degrees they had taken his dignity from him. He had been forbidden to leave the territories of Florence, and he was a man who loved to travel. He had been forbidden to enter the Palazzo Vecchio, where he had worked for so many years, where he belonged. He had been interrogated by his successor, a certain Michelozzi, a Medici lickspittle, a toady of toadies, regarding possible embezzlement. But he had been an honest servant of the republic and no trace of wrongdoing could be detected. Then they found his name on a piece of paper in the pocket of a man he did not know and locked him up in the nameless place. The man's name was Boscoli, a fool, one of four fools whose plot against the Medici had been so foolish that it was crushed almost before it had begun. In Boscoli's pocket was a list of two dozen names: enemies of the Medici in the opinion of a fool. One of the names was *Machiavelli*.

Once a man has been in a torture chamber his senses never forget certain things, the wet darkness, the cold stink of human ordure, the rats, the screams. Once a man has been tortured there is a part of him that never stops feeling the pain. The punishment known as the *strappado* was among the most agonizing torments that could be inflicted on a human person without killing him outright. His wrists were fastened behind his back, and the rope that bound them passed over a pulley hanging from the ceiling.

When he was lifted off his feet by that rope the pain in his shoulders became the whole world. Not just the city of Florence and its river, not only Italy, but all God's bounty was erased by this pain. Pain was the new world. Just before he stopped thinking about anything, and in order not to think about what was about to happen, il Machia thought about the other New World, and about Ago's cousin Amerigo, Gonfaloniere Soderini's friend, Amerigo the wild man, the wanderer who had proved, with Columbus, that the Ocean Sea didn't contain monsters that could bite a boat in half, and didn't turn to fire when it reached the Equator, and didn't become a sea of mud if you sailed too far west, and who, even more importantly than all of that, had had the wit to realize what that dolt Columbus never grasped, namely that the lands on the far side of the Ocean Sea were not Indies; they had nothing to do with India, and were, in fact, an entirely new world. Would that New World now be denied by order of the Medici, would it be canceled by decree and become just another ill-fated idea—like love or probity or freedom—to fall along with the fallen republic, dragged down by Soderini and the rest of the losers, including himself? Lucky sea-dog, il Machia thought, to be safely in Seville, where even the Medici's arms could not reach him. Amerigo might be old and sick but he was safe from harm and at least he could die in peace after all his wanderings, il Machia thought; and then the rope hoisted him up for the first time and Amerigo and the New World disappeared, and the old world too.

They did it six times and I confessed to nothing because I had nothing to confess. After they stopped torturing him they locked him in the jail cell again and pretended they would forget him and let him die there slowly in the rodent dark. Then, eventually, and unexpectedly, release. Into ignominy, oblivion, married life. Release into Percussina. He walked in the woods with Ago Vespucci and looked for mandrake roots but they were not children now. Their hopes lay behind them in ruins instead of luminously up ahead. The time for mandrakes was past. Once Ago had tried to get La Fiorentina to fall in love with him by dropping mandrake powder into her drink but smart Alessandra was not going to be caught that way, she was impervious to mandrake magic, and devised for Ago a dreadful punishment of her own. On that night after drinking the mandrake potion she broke the fastidious habits of a lifetime and let Ago the lowly wretch into her haughty bed, but after he experienced forty-five minutes of the undiluted bliss of Paradise she had him thrown out unceremoniously, reminding him before he left of the secret curse of the mandrake, which was that any man who made love to a woman under the power of the root would die within eight days, unless she saved his life by allowing him to stay with her for a whole night, "of which," she told him, "there is simply no possibility, my dear." Ago, the superstitious scaredy-cat, as obsessed by magic as everyone else in the world, spent eight days convinced that the end was imminent, began to feel death creeping through his limbs, caressing him with cold fingers, squeezing slowly, slowly around his testicles and heart. When he woke up alive on the ninth morning he was not relieved. "A living death," he told il Machia, "is worse than the death of the dead, because the living dead can still feel the pain of a broken heart."

Niccolò knew something now about living death, because although he had narrowly avoided the death of the dead he was a dead dog now, as dead a dog as poor Ago, for they had both been dismissed from life, from their jobs, from grand salons like Alessandra Fiorentina's, from what they had had every reason to think of as their real existence. Yes, they were broken-hearted dogs, they were less than dogs, they were married dogs. He stared at his wife over the dinner table every night and found nothing to say to her. Marietta, that was her name, and here were his children, their children, their many, many children, so, yes, he had certainly married and had children like a proper person, but that was in another age, the age of his neglectful grandeur, when he was fucking a different girl every day to stay vigorous and alive, and fucking his wife too, of course, six times, at least. Marietta Corsini, his wife, who sewed his undershirts and towels, and knew nothing about anything, who didn't understand his philosophy or laugh at his jokes. Everyone else in the world thought he was funny, but she was a literalist, she thought a man meant whatever he said, and allusions and metaphors were just the tools men used to deceive women, to make women think they didn't know what was going on. He loved her, that was true. He loved her like a member of his family. Like a sibling. When he fucked her he felt faintly *wrong.* He felt *incestuous,* as if he were fucking his sister. As a matter of fact that notion was the only thing that could arouse him when he lay with her. *I am fucking my sister,* he told himself, and came.

She knew his thoughts, as any wife knows her husband's mind, and they made her unhappy. He was courteous to her and cared for her deeply in his way. Madonna Marietta and her six children, his mouths to feed. Absurdly fertile Marietta: touch her and she ballooned with child, and popped out a Bernardo, a Guido, a Bartolomea, a Totto, a Primavera, and the other boy, what was his name, Lodovico, it seemed there was no end to fatherhood, and these days the money was so tight. Signora Machiavelli. Here she was coming into the tavern in a hurry, looking as if her house was burning down. She wore a frilled mob-cap and her hair hung down in uncontrolled ringlets around that egg-shaped face with its small, full mouth and her hands flapped like the wings of a duck; indeed, on the subject of ducks, it had to be admitted that she waddled. His wife waddled. He was married to a waddling wife. He could not imagine touching her private places ever again. There was really no reason to touch her anymore.

"*Niccolò mio,*" she cried in that voice that, yes, did sound just a little too much like a quack, "have you seen what's coming down the road?"

"What is it, my dear spouse," he replied, solicitously.

"Something bad for the neighborhood," she said. "Like Death himself on horseback and his ogres too, and his queen demonesses by his side."

The arrival in Sant'Andrea in Percussina of the woman who would become famous, or perhaps notorious, as *l'ammaliatrice Angelica,* the so-called enchantress of Florence, brought men running from the fields, and women from their kitchens, wiping doughy fingers on aprons as they came. Woodcutters came from the forests and the butcher Gabburra's son ran out from the slaughterhouse with bloody hands and potters left their kilns. Frosino Uno the miller's twin brother Frosino Due emerged floury from the mill. The Janissaries of Stamboul were a sight to behold, battle-scarred and leathery, and a quartet of Swiss albino giants on white horses was not a thing seen every day in that neck of the woods, while the imposing figure at the head of the cavalcade, with his white, white skin and his black, black hair, the pale captain whom Signora Machiavelli had identified as the Reaper himself, was undoubtedly alarming, and children shrank from him as he passed, because whether he was the exterminating angel or not he had plainly seen too much of dying for his own good or anyone else's. But even if he was the Angel of Death he also seemed strangely familiar and spoke perfectly the dialect of the region, and that made people wonder if Death always came in a local manifestation, so to speak, using your slang and knowing your secrets and sharing your private jokes even as he carted you away to the shadow world.

But it was the two women, Marietta Corsini Machiavelli's "devil-queens," who quickly captured everyone's attention. They were riding as men rode, straddling their mounts in a manner that made their female audience gasp for one reason while the watching men's gasps were of another kind, and their faces shone with the light of revelation, as though in those early days of their unveiling they were capable of sucking light in from the eyes of all who looked upon them and then flinging it out again as their own personal brilliance, with mesmeric, fantasy-inducing effects. The

Frosino brothers, twins themselves, acquired faraway expressions as they imagined a double wedding sometime in the near future. In spite of their delusions, however, they were keen-eyed enough to see that the astonishing ladies were not quite identical, and probably not even related. "The first lady is the mistress and the other the servant," said flour-dusted Frosino Due, adding, because he was the more poetic of the two brothers, "They are as the sun and the moon, the sound and the echo, the sky and its reflection in a lake." His sibling was the direct type. "So I'll take the first lady, and you'll have number two," said Frosino Uno. "Because the second, she is beautiful, sure, you won't be getting a bad deal, but next to the first one she becomes invisible. You have to shut one eye, to blind yourself to my girl, in order to notice that yours is pretty too." As the older twin by eleven minutes he assigned to himself the prerogative of having first pick. Frosino Due was about to protest, but just then the first lady, the mistress, turned to look directly at the brothers and murmured to her companion in perfect Italian.

"What do you think, my Angelica?"

"My Angelica, they are not without their certain simple charms."

"It's forbidden, of course, my Angelica."

"My Angelica, of course. But maybe we will visit them in their dreams."

"Both of us, visiting both of them, my Angelica?"

"My Angelica, the dreams will be better that way."

They were angels, then. Not devils but mind-reading angels. No doubt their wings were folded away neatly beneath their clothes. The Frosino brothers reddened and cringed and stared wildly around them, but it seemed that only they had heard what the angels on horseback had said. That was impossible of course and so it was further proof that something of a divine nature had occurred. A divine or an occult nature. But these were angels, angels. "Angelica," the name they apparently shared, was no handle for a demon. They were dream angels who had promised the millers joys of which men like them could truly only dream. The joys of Paradise. Their mouths suddenly full of giggles, the brothers turned away and ran toward the flour mill as fast as their legs would take them. "Where are you going?" Gabburra the butcher called after them, but how could they tell him that they needed, with great urgency, to lie down and close their eyes? How to explain exactly why it was so important, why it had never been more important, to sleep?

The procession came to a halt outside Vettori's tavern. A silence fell, broken only by the neighing of tired horses. Il Machia was staring at the women like everyone else so when he heard Argalia's voice coming out of the mouth of the pale warrior he felt as if he had been dragged from a place of beauty into a stinking cesspit. "What's the matter, Niccolò," the voice was saying, "don't you know that when you forget your friends it means you have also forgotten yourself?" Marietta clutched at her husband in fright. "If Death has become your friend today," she hissed in his ear, "then your children will be orphans before night falls." Il Machia shook himself as if shrugging off the effects of an intoxicating draft. He looked the rider in the eye, steadily and without warmth. "In the beginning there were three friends," he said softly. "Niccolò 'il Machia,' Agostino Vespucci, and Antonino Argalia. Their boyhood world was a magic wood. Then Nino's parents were taken by the plague. He left to seek his fortune and they never saw him again." Marietta looked back and forth from her husband to the stranger and a slow comprehension spread across her face.

"Then," Niccolò concluded, "after long years of treasonous deeds against his country and his God, which damned his soul to Hell and rendered his body deserving of the rack, Argalia the Pasha—Arcalia, Arqalia, Al-Ghaliya, even his name became a lie— came back to what was no longer his home."

He was not a deeply religious man, il Machia, but he was a Christian. He avoided mass, but he believed all other religions to be false. He held popes responsible for most of the wars of the period, and thought of many bishops and cardinals as criminals, but cardinals and popes liked what he had to say about the nature of the world better than princes. He would rant to his tavern companions about how the corruption of the Curia had driven Italians away from faith, but he was not a heretic, certainly not, and though there were aspects of the rule of the Mussulman Sultan that he was prepared to learn from and even to praise, the idea of entering such a potentate's service was a nauseating one.

And then there was the matter of the memory palace, that beautiful girl, Angélique Coeur of Bourges, the angelic heart, who on account of what had been done to her mind and body had jumped through a window to her death. For obvious reasons this matter could not be raised in his wife's presence, his wife being the jealous type, and himself being guilty of causing this fault in her character, of being an old man full of love, not for his wife, or not in that way, but, in point of fact, for the girl Barbera Raffacani Salutati, the contralto, who sang so sweetly, who performed so many things so well, and not only on a stage, yes, Barbera, Barbera, yes!, not as young as she once was but still far younger than he, and prepared, unaccountably, to love a gray man throughout the years of her beauty's greenness . . . so, in sum, having considered the consequences of doing otherwise, it was better to concentrate for the present on questions of blasphemy and treason.

"Sir Pasha," he greeted his boyhood friend, his bat-wing eyebrows crushed together in jagged disapproval, "what business can a heathen have here, on Christian land?"

"I have a favor to ask," Argalia replied, "but not for myself."

The two boyhood friends were alone in il Machia's writing room, surrounded by books and heaps of paper, for more than an hour. The sky darkened. Many of the villagers dispersed, having their own business to attend to, but many stayed. The Janissaries remained motionless on their mounts, and so did the two ladies, accepting only an offering of water from the Machiavellis' maid. Then as night fell the two men came out again and it was plain that some sort of truce had been made. At a sign from Argalia the Janissaries dismounted and Argalia himself helped Qara Köz and her Mirror down from their mounts. The soldiers were to camp on the property for the night, some in the little field near Greve, others in the *poderi* of Fontalla, Il Poggio, and Monte Pagliano. The four Swiss giants would remain at the La Strada villa, camped in a tent on its grounds, to act as guardians of the residents' safety. Once the men had rested and refreshed themselves, however, the company would move on. But it would leave something of great value behind.

The women were coming to stay, Niccolò informed his wife, the foreign ladies, the *Mogor* princess and her servant girl. Marietta received the news as if it were a sentence of death. She was to be killed by beauty, burned at the stake of her husband's interminable lustfulness. The most beautiful and desirable females anyone in Percussina had ever seen—the queen demonesses—were to be housed under her roof, and as a consequence of their presence she, Marietta, would simply cease to exist. Only the two ladies would exist. She would be her husband's nonexistent wife. Food would appear on the table at mealtimes and the laundry would be done and the house kept in order and her husband would not notice who was doing these things because he would be drowning in the eyes of the foreign witches whose overwhelming desirability would simply erase her from the scene. The children would have to be moved, maybe into the house at the eight canals, along the Roman Road, and she would have to stretch herself between that place and La Strada, and it would be impossible, it could not happen, she would not permit it.

She began to scold him, right there in public, beneath the eyes of the whole village and the albino giants and the figure of Death who was Argalia returned from the dead, but il Machia held up a hand and for a moment he looked once more like the grandee of Florence he had so recently been, and she saw that he meant business, and fell silent.

"Okay," she said. "It's not a princess's palace we have to offer, so they better not complain, that's all."

After eleven years of marriage to her philandering husband Signora Marietta's temper had frayed, and now he shamelessly blamed her irritability for driving him away, into, for example, the harlot Barbera's boudoir. That shrieking Salutati, whose plan was quite simply to outlive Marietta Corsini and then usurp her kingdom, following her into the master bedroom at the villa of La Strada, where La Corsini was mistress and mother to Niccolò's children. It made Marietta determined to live to a hundred and eleven, to see her rival buried, and to dance naked on her pauper's grave under a gibbous moon. She was horrified by the vehemence of her dreams but had stopped denying the truths they contained. She was capable of rejoicing in another woman's death. Perhaps she was even capable of expediting its arrival. It might have to be murder, she reflected, because she knew little of witchcraft, and so her spells usually failed. Once she rubbed her entire body with a holy unguent before having sex with her husband, which was to say before forcing him to have sex with her, and if she had been a better witch it would have bound him to her forever. Instead he headed off to Barbera's as usual the next afternoon and she swore at his retreating back, calling him a godless whoremaster who didn't even respect the sanctity of the blessed oil.

He didn't hear her, of course, but the children did, their eyes were everywhere, their ears heard everything, they were like the whispering consciences of the house. She might have thought of them as her holy ghosts except that she had to feed them and mend their clothes and put cold compresses on their foreheads when they had a fever. So they were real enough; but her anger and jealousy were more real than they were and pushed them, her own children, into the back of her mind. The children were eyes and ears and mouths and sweet breathing in the night. They were peripheral. What filled her vision was this man, her husband, so saturnine, so learned, so attractive, such a failure, this expelled, exiled man, who still hadn't understood what was truly of value in life, even the *strappado* hadn't taught him the value of love and simplicity, not even the repudiation of his whole life and work by the citizenry to whose service he had dedicated himself had taught him that it was better to give his love and loyalty to those close to home, and not to the public in general. He had a good wife, she had been a loving wife to him, and yet he chased after cheap young cunt. He had his dignity and erudition, and his small but sufficient estate, and yet he wrote degrading letters to the Medici court every day, begging in servile fashion for some kind of public work. They were sycophantic letters, unworthy of his dark skeptical genius, soul-lessening words. He scorned what he should have treasured: this humble patrimony, this soil, these houses, these woods and fields, and the woman who was the humble goddess of his corner of the earth.

The simple things. The snaring of thrushes before dawn, the burdened vines, the animals, the farm. Here he had time to read and write, to allow the power of his mind to rival that of any prince. His mind was the best of him, and in it he still possessed everything that mattered, and yet all he seemed to care about in his wild disappointment, his painful unhousing, was to find new lodgings for his cock. Or just to lodge in that one special resting place, that Barbera, the singing tart. When they performed his new play about the mandrake root in this town or in that one he made them give her work singing in the intermission to entertain the waiting public. It was a wonder the audience didn't walk out with earache, in disgust. It was a wonder his good wife hadn't put poison in his wine. It was a wonder that God allowed hussies like Barbera to prosper while good women rotted and aged.

"But maybe now," Marietta told herself, "that howling cow

and I have something in common. Maybe now we have to discuss this new question of the witches who have come to destroy our happy Florentine way of life."

———※———

It was Niccolò's habit to commune every evening with the mighty dead, here in this room in which he now stood face to face with his boyhood friend to see if he could set aside the hostility surging through his body, or if they were fated to be enemies for life. Silently he asked the dead for advice. He was on close terms with most of the heroes and villains, the philosophers and the men of action, of the ancient world. When he was alone they crowded around him, arguing, explaining, or else they took him away with them on their immortal campaigns. When he saw Nabis, prince of the Spartans, defending that city against Rome and the rest of Greece as well; or witnessed the rise of Agathocles the Sicilian, the potter's son who became King of Syracuse by wickedness alone; or rode with Alexander of Macedon against Darius the Great of Persia; then he felt the curtains of his mind part, and the world became clearer. The past was a light that if properly directed could illumine the present more brightly than any contemporary lamp. Greatness was like the sacred flame of Olympus, handed down from the great to the great. Alexander modeled himself on Achilles, Caesar followed in Alexander's footsteps, and so on. Understanding was another such flame. Knowledge was never simply born in the human mind; it was always reborn. The relaying of wisdom from one age to the next, this cycle of rebirths: this was wisdom. All else was barbarity.

And yet barbarians were everywhere, and everywhere victorious. The Swiss, the French, the Spaniards, the Germans, all of them trampling over Italy in this age of incessant wars. The French invaded and fought the Pope, the Venetians, the Spaniards, and the Germans on Italian soil. Then in the blinking of an eye it was the French and the Pope and the Venetians and Florence versus the Milanese. Then the Pope, France, Spain, and the Germans against Venice. Then the Pope, Venice, Spain, and the Germans against France. Then the Swiss in Lombardy. Then the Swiss against the French. Italy had become a carousel of war, war played as a dance of changing partners, or as a game of "Going to Jerusalem," which was to say musical chairs. And in all these wars no army of purely Italian troops had ever proved competent to stand against the hordes from beyond her borders.

This, in the end, was what had reconciled him to his revenant friend. If the barbarians were to be expelled then Italy perhaps needed a barbarian of her own. Perhaps Argalia, who had lived among barbarians for so long, and grown into so ferocious a barbarian warrior that he looked like the very incarnation of Death, would be the redeemer the country needed. There were tulips embroidered on Argalia's shirt. "Death among the tulips," the great dead whispered in his ear, approvingly. "Perhaps this Florentine Ottoman will be the city's good luck flower."

Slowly, after long thought, il Machia held out a hand of welcome. "If you can redeem Italy," he said, "maybe your long journey will turn out to be an act of Providence, who knows."

Argalia objected to the religious resonances of il Machia's hypothesis. "All right," il Machia readily conceded. "'Redeemer' is the wrong title for you, I agree. Let's just say 'son of a bitch' instead."

In the end Andrea Doria had persuaded Argalia that there was no point dreaming about going home to put his feet up and rest. "What do you think Duke Giuliano is going to say," the older *condottiere* asked him, " *'Welcome home, Signor Armed-to-the-teeth Pirate Traitor Christian-Killer Janissary, with your one hundred and one battle-hardened fighters and your four albino giants, I believe you when you say you come in peace, and obviously all those gentlemen will be working as gardeners and butlers and carpenters and house painters from now on'*? Only a baby would swallow that fairy tale. Five minutes after you show up looking ready for war he'll send the whole militia hunting for your head. So you're a dead man if you go to Florence, unless." Unless what, Argalia was forced to ask. "Unless I tell him he should hire you to be the military commander-in-chief he very badly needs. It's not as if you have many other choices," the older man said. "For men like us, retirement is not an option."

"I don't trust the Duke," Argalia told il Machia. "Come to that, I don't fully trust Doria either. He was always a total bastard and I'm not convinced that his character has improved with age. Maybe he sent Giuliano a message saying, kill Argalia as soon as he sets foot inside the city walls. He's cold blooded enough to do that. Or maybe he was feeling generous and he really did recommend me, for old times' sake. I don't want to take the women into the city until I know how things stand."

"I'll tell you precisely how they stand," Niccolò bitterly replied. "The absolute ruler of the city is a Medici. The Pope is a Medici. People round here say that probably God is a Medici and as for the Devil, he's definitely one, beyond any doubt. On account of the Medici I'm stuck here making a pittance raising livestock and farming this patch of land and selling firewood to make a living, and your friend Ago is out in the cold too. That's our reward for staying in the city and serving it faithfully all our lives. Then you show up after a career of blasphemy and treason, but because the Duke will see in your cold eyes what everyone can see there, namely that you're good at killing men, you will in all probability be given command of the militia that I built, the militia I created by persuading those miserly penny-pinching fellow-citizens of our rich city that it was worth paying for a standing army, the militia I trained and led into success in battle at the great siege and reconquest of our old possession of Pisa, and that militia, my militia, will be your prize for leading a wicked, profiteering, and dissolute life, and it is difficult, is it not, in such a situation to believe what faith teaches us, that virtue is inevitably rewarded and sin invariably cast down?"

"Look after the two ladies until I send for them," Argalia said, "and if I am fortunate and gain preferment I will see what I can do for you, and for little Ago too."

"Perfect," il Machia said. "So you're doing *me* a favor now."

— ⁀⁀ —

Life had hit Agostino Vespucci hard, and he was different these days, less cheerful, cleaner-tongued, defeated. Unlike il Machia he had not been exiled from the city so he spent his days in the Ognissanti house or working in the oil, wool, wine, and silk businesses he detested so much, but often he made his way out to Sant'Andrea in Percussina to lie in the mandrake wood alone, watching the movements of leaves and birds, until it was time to join Niccolò in the tavern for drink and *triche-tach*. His shining golden hair had whitened prematurely and thinned as well, so that he looked older than his years. He had not married, nor did he frequent whorehouses with anything like the regularity or enthusiasm of old. If the loss of his job had destroyed his ambition, then his humiliation at the hands of Alessandra Fiorentina had ruined his sex drive. He dressed shabbily now and had even begun to be stingy with money, quite unnecessarily, because in spite of the loss of his salary there was plenty of Vespucci wealth to pay his way. On the night before il Machia left Florence for Percussina, Ago threw a dinner party, and at the end of it he presented each guest, even Niccolò himself, with a bill for fourteen *soldi*. Il Machia didn't have that much cash on him, and only handed over eleven. Nowadays Ago still reminded him with quite unseemly frequency that there were still three *soldi* to pay.

Il Machia didn't hold his friend's new parsimoniousness against him, however, because he believed that Ago had been hit even harder than himself by the city's rejection of their years of hard work, and the loss of the beloved could manifest itself in the jilted lover in all manner of strange symptoms. Ago was the one of the three friends who had never needed to travel, the one for

whom the city had been all he needed and more. So if il Machia
had lost a city, then Ago had come unstuck from the world. Sometimes he even spoke about leaving Florence forever, following
Amerigo to Spain, and crossing the Ocean Sea. When he mused
about such journeyings he did so without pleasure; it was as if he
were describing a passage from life into death. News of Amerigo's
death deepened his cousin's gloom. Ago seemed readier than ever
before to contemplate a death under an alien sky.

Other old friends had grown quarrelsome. Biagio Buonaccorsi
and Andrea di Romolo had broken up with each other, and with
Ago and il Machia too. But Vespucci and Machiavelli had remained
close, and that was why Ago showed up on horseback before dawn
just to go birding with il Machia and almost died of fright when
four enormous men rose up all around him in the morning mist
and demanded to know his business. However, once il Machia,
wrapped in a long cloak, had emerged from the house and established his friend's identity, the giants became affable enough. In
fact, as Argalia well knew, the four Swiss Janissaries were inveterate
gossips, loose-tongued as any fishwife on market day, and while
they were waiting for il Machia, who had gone back indoors to finish spreading birdlime on elm twigs in little cages, Otho, Botho,
Clotho, and D'Artagnan gave Ago so much vivid information
about the situation that he felt, after a long neutered time, the first
renewed stirrings of sexual desire. Those women sounded like they
were worth a look. Then Niccolò was ready, looking, with the
empty cages strapped to his back, for all the world like a bankrupt
peddler, and the two friends set off into the woods.

The mist was lifting. "When the thrush migration is over," il
Machia said, "the two of us won't even have this to look forward
to." But there was a light in his eye which hadn't been there for a
while, and Ago said, "So, they're really something, eh?"

Il Machia's grin was back, too. "Here's a strange thing," he
said. "Even the wife has suddenly stopped bitching about things."

The moment the princess Qara Köz and her Mirror entered
the Machiavelli home Marietta Corsini had commenced to feel

foolish. A delicious bittersweet fragrance preceded the two foreign women into the house, and quickly spread along the corridors, up the stairs, and into every cranny of the place, and as she inhaled that rich smell Marietta started thinking that her life was not as hard as she had erroneously believed it to be, that her husband loved her, her children were good children, and these visitors were after all the most distinguished guests it had ever been her privilege to receive. Argalia, who had asked to rest for one night before leaving for the city, was to sleep on the couch in il Machia's study; Marietta showed the princess the guest bedroom and asked, awkwardly, whether her lady-in-waiting would wish to occupy one of the children's rooms for the night. Qara Köz placed a finger across her hostess's lips and murmured into her ear, "This room will be perfect for us both." Marietta went to bed in a strange state of bliss and when her husband slipped in beside her she told him about the two ladies' decision to sleep together, without sounding at all shocked about it. "Never mind those women," her husband said, and Marietta's heart leapt for joy. "The woman I want is right here within my grasp." The room was full of the princess's bittersweet perfume.

As for Qara Köz, however, when the door closed behind her and her Mirror she found herself unexpectedly drowning in a flood of existential dread. These sadnesses came over her from time to time, but she had never learned to be on her guard against them. Her life had been a series of acts of will, but sometimes she wavered and sank. She had built her life on being loved by men, on being certain of her ability to engender such love whenever she chose to do so, but when the darkest questions of the self were asked, when she felt her soul shudder and crack under the weight of her isolation and loss, then no man's love could help her. As a result she had come to understand that her life would inevitably ask her to make choices between her love and her self and when those crises came she must not choose love. To do so would be to endanger her life. Survival must come first.

This was the inevitable consequence of having chosen to step away from her natural world. The day she refused to return to the Mughal court with her sister Khanzada she had learned not only that a woman could choose her own road, but that such choices had consequences that could not be erased from the record. She had made her choice and what followed, followed, and she had no regrets, but she did, from time to time, suffer the black terror. The terror buffeted and shook her like a tree in a storm and the Mirror came to hold her until it passed. She sank onto the bed and the Mirror lay with her and held her, tightly, her hands hard upon Qara Köz's biceps, held her not as a woman holds a woman but as a man does. Qara Köz had learned that her power over men would permit her to shape her life's journey but she had also understood that that act of shaping would entail great loss. She had perfected the arts of enchantment, learned the world's languages, witnessed the great things of her time, but she was without family, without clan, without any of the consolations of remaining within one's al-lotted frontiers, inside her mother tongue and in her brother's care. It was as if she were flying above the ground, willing herself to fly, while fearing that at any moment the spell might be broken and she would plummet to her death.

What scraps of news she had of her family she hugged to her bosom, trying to squeeze from them more meaning than they contained. Shah Ismail had been her brother Babar's friend, and the Ottomans had their own ways of knowing what was happen-ing in the world. So she knew that her brother was alive, that her sister had been reunited with him, and that a child, Nasiruddin Humayun, had been born. Beyond that all was uncertainty. Fer-ghana, their ancestral kingdom, had been lost and perhaps it would never be regained. Babar had set his heart on Samarkand but in spite of the defeat and death of Shaibani Khan, Lord Wormwood, the Mughal forces didn't seem able to hold on to the fabled city for any length of time. So Babar, too, was homeless, Khanzada was homeless, and the family had no permanent foothold on any patch of God's earth. Maybe this was what it was to be a Mughal, to roam, to scavenge, to depend on others, to fight without success, to be lost. Despair claimed her for a moment. Then she shrugged it off. They were not the victims of history but its makers. Her brother and his son and his son after him: what a kingdom they would establish, the glory of the world. She willed it, foresaw it, brought it into being by the ferocity of her need. And she would do the same, against impossible odds in this alien world she would make her own kingdom, for she, too, was born to rule. She was a Mughal woman and as fearsome as any man. Her will was equal to the task. Quietly, to herself, she recited in Chaghatai the verses of Ali-Shir Nava'i. Chaghatai, her mother tongue, was her secret, her link to her true, abandoned self, which she had chosen to replace with a self of her own making, but which would of course be a part of that new self, its bedrock, its sword and shield. Nava'i, "the Weeper," who once in a faraway land had sung for her. *Qara ko'zum, kelu mardumlug' emdi fan qilg'il. Come, Qara Köz, and show me your kindness.* One day her brother would rule an empire and she would return as a queen in triumph. Or her brother's children would greet her own. The blood ties could not be broken. She had made herself anew but what she had been, she would remain, and her heritage would be hers and her children's to reclaim.

The door opened. The man came in, her tulip prince. He had waited for the household to be asleep and now he had come to her, to them. The darkness did not leave her but it shuffled to one side and made room for her beloved in the bed. The Mirror, feeling her relax, released her and attended to Argalia's garments. He was leaving for the city in the morning and everything, he said, would soon be arranged. She was not deceived. She knew that things would either go well or, if not well, then very badly indeed. Tomorrow night he might be dead and then she would have to make another survivor's choice. Tonight, however, he was alive. The Mirror was preparing him for her with caresses and oils. She watched in the moonlight as his pale body flowered under her servant's touch. With his long hair he might almost be a woman himself, his hands so long, his fingers so slender, his skin so improbably soft. She closed her eyes and could not tell which of them was touching her, his hands as gentle as the Mirror's, his hair as long, his tongue as expert. He knew how to make love like a woman. And the Mirror with her brutal fingers could stab at her like a man. His sinuousness, his slowness, the lightness of his touch, these were the things that made her love him. The shadow was pushed into a corner now and the moon shone down on the three moving bodies. She loved and served him. She loved the Mirror but did not serve her. The Mirror loved and served them both. Tonight it was love that mattered. Tomorrow, maybe another thing would be more important. But that was tomorrow.

"My Angelica," he said. "Here is Angelica, Angelica's here," the two women replied. Then soft laughter, and groans, and one overloud shout, and little cries.

She awoke before the dawn. He slept heavily, the deep sleep of one from whom much will be demanded when he wakes, and she watched him as he breathed. The Mirror, too, was asleep. Qara Köz smiled. My Angelica, she whispered in Italian. The love between women was more durable than the thing between women and men. She touched their hair, so long, so black. Then she heard noises outside. A visitor. The Swiss giants confronted him. Then she heard the man of the house go out and explain matters. She could see him for what he was, this Niccolò, a great man in the hour of his defeat. Maybe he would rise again, be pre-eminent again, but the house of defeat was no place for her. The defeated man's greatness communicated itself readily, greatness of intellect and perhaps also of soul, but he had lost his war, so he was nothing to her, he could not be anything. She relied on Argalia completely now, counted on him to succeed, and if he did so she would rise with him and take wing. But if she lost him, she would grieve wildly, she would be inconsolable, and then she would do what she had to do. She would find her way. Whatever happened today, she would make her journey to the palace soon enough. She was meant for palaces, and kings.

The birds hopped into the cages and stuck to the lime on the elm sticks. Ago and il Machia caught them up and broke their little necks. They would eat a delicious songbird stew later that day. Life still afforded them some pleasures, at least until the thrush migration ended. They returned to La Strada with two sacks full of birds and found happy Marietta waiting for them with glasses of good red wine. Argalia and his men had already departed, leaving behind Konstantin the Serb, with a dozen Janissaries under his command, to defend the ladies should the need arise; so Ago would have to wait to be reunited with the wanderer. Briefly he felt a pang of disappointment. Niccolò had described their old friend's transformation into an almost effeminate but also utterly ferocious Oriental incarnation of Death—"Argalia the Turk," the villagers were already calling him, just as he had prophesied long ago on the day he set out as a young boy to seek his fortune—and Ago had been anxious to see the exotic sight for himself. That Argalia had actually come home with the four Swiss giants he had dreamed up was already incredible enough.

Then there was a footfall on the stair and Ago Vespucci looked up and it was as though Argalia had ceased to exist. He heard himself telling himself that no beautiful women had ever existed in the world up to that moment, that Simonetta Vespucci and Alessandra Fiorentina were the plainest of Janes, because the women coming down toward him were more beautiful than beauty itself, so beautiful that they redefined the term, and banished what men had previously thought beautiful into the ranks of dull ordinariness. A fragrance preceded them down the stairs and wrapped itself around his heart. The first woman was slightly lovelier than the second but if you closed one eye and blotted her out then the second woman looked like the greatest beauty on earth. But why would one do that? Why obliterate the exceptional merely in order to make the outstanding look finer than it was?

"Damnation, Machia," he whispered, sweating lightly, the curse escaping his lips under the pressure of his emotions, after a long period during which he had forsaken swearing entirely, and the sack of dead thrushes fell from his hand. "I think I just rediscovered the meaning of human life."

{ 17 }

The Duke had locked up his palace

The Duke had locked up his palace, afraid of an invasion by the rampant crowd, because in those days after the election of the first ever Medici Pope the city was in an ecstasy that hovered on the edge of violence. "People were playing the fool," Argalia told il Machia afterward, "without respect of age or sex." The noise of church bells sounding *glorias* was incessant and deafening and the bonfires threatened to ruin whole sectors of the town. "In the Mercato Nuovo," Argalia reported, "young bucks ripped up boards and planks from the silk stores and the banks. By the time the authorities moved to stop it even the roof of the cloth merchants' guild, the old Calimala, had been broken for firewood and burned. There were fires burning, they told me, up on the campanile of Santa Maria Fiore. This kind of nonsense went on for three days." Noise and smoke choked the streets. There was fucking and buggery in every side alley and nobody gave a damn. Every evening a garlanded cart of victory was pulled by oxen from the Medici gardens in Piazza San Marco to the Palazzo Medici in the Via Larga. Outside the shuttered palace the citizenry sang songs in praise of Pope Leo X, and then set the cart and its flowers ablaze. From the upstairs windows of the Medici palace the new rulers hurled bounty down upon the crowd, maybe ten thousand gold ducats and twelve large napkins of cloth of silver which the Florentines tore to bits. In the streets of the city there were barrels of wine and baskets of bread, free for all to use. Prisoners were pardoned and whores grew rich and male babies were named after Duke Giuliano and his nephew Lorenzo, or after Giovanni who had become Leo, and female children were baptized Laodamia or Semiramide after the family's female grandees.

It was impossible at such a moment to enter the city with a hundred armed men and seek an audience with Duke Giuliano. Sybaritism and firestarters ruled the streets. At the city gate Argalia presented his papers to the guards, and was relieved to learn that they had been told to expect him. "Yes, the Duke will see you," they said, "but, you comprehend, not right now." The Janissary force camped under the city walls until the fourth day, when the Florentine party for the Pope finally ran out of steam. Even then Argalia was not allowed to enter the city. "After dark tonight," said the captain of the guard, "expect a noble visitor."

He knew how to make love like a woman and how to kill men like a man, but Argalia had never before faced a Medici duke in his pomp. However, when Giuliano de Medici rode into his encampment that night, with a hood over his head for secrecy, Argalia understood at once that the new ruler of Florence was a weakling, and so was that young nephew of his, riding by his side. Pope Leo was known to be a man of power, a Medici of the old school, inheritor of the authority of Lorenzo the Magnificent, his father. How concerned he must be to have entrusted Florence to the care of these second-raters! No true Medici duke would have skulked out of his own city like a thief just to meet a possible employee. That Duke Giuliano had chosen to do so proved he needed a strong man at his side to give him confidence. A military man. A tulip general to defend the City of Flowers. There was unquestionably a job vacancy here.

In his tent, Argalia studied the noblemen by flickering yellow lamplight. This lesser spawn of Lorenzo de Medici, Duke Giuliano, was in his middle thirties, had a sad long face, and looked like he was in poor health. He would not make old bones. No doubt he was a lover of literature and art. No doubt he was a man of culture and wit. A liability on the field of conflict, then. It would be better if he stayed home and left the battle to those who were competent to fight, for whom fighting was their culture, killing their art. The nephew, another Lorenzo, was dark skinned, fierce of face, swaggering of manner; just one of a thousand twenty-year-old Florentine braggarts, Argalia decided. A boy, full of sex and himself. Not a man to be trusted in a scrap.

Argalia had prepared his arguments. At the end of his long travels, he would say, he had learned this much: that Florence was everywhere and everywhere was Florence. Everywhere in the world there were omnipotent princes, Medici who ran things because they had always run things, and who could make the truth what they wanted it to be merely by decreeing it to be so. And there were Weepers everywhere too (Argalia had missed the time of the Weepers in Florence but news of the monk Savonarola and his followers had traveled a long way), Weepers who wanted to run things because they were convinced that a Higher Power had shown them what the truth really was. And everywhere there were also people who thought they ran things whereas in fact they did not, and this last group was so large that it could almost be called a social class, the class of Machias, perhaps, of servants who believed themselves to be masters until they were shown the bitter truth. This class could not be trusted, and the greatest threats to the prince would invariably flow from it. Therefore the prince must be sure of his ability to overpower the servants' uprisings as well as the foreign armies, the assaults of the enemy within as well as attacks from outside. Everywhere on earth a state that wished to survive both these threats was in need of a puissant lord of war. And he, Argalia, perfectly represented the union of Florence with the rest of creation, because he was that necessary warlord, who could ensure his own city's calm and security, as he had done in other cities, in the service of other masters far away.

The Medici had returned to power a few months earlier with the assistance of Spanish mercenaries, "white Moors," under a certain General Cardona. Outside the beautiful town of Prato they had faced the Florentine militia, il Machia's pride, which was actually superior in numbers, but inferior in courage and leadership. The Florentine militia broke ranks and fled, and the city fell on the first day, after no more than the shadow of a struggle. After that the "white Moors" sacked the town with a ferocity that terrified Florence into dismantling its republic, getting down on its knees, and inviting the Medici back. The sack of Prato went on, and on, for three weeks. Four thousand men, women, and children died, burned to death, raped, cut in half. Not even the convents were safe from the lechery of Cardona's men. In Florence, the Prato gate of the city was struck by lightning, and the omen was impossible to ignore. However—and this was the crux of Argalia's argument—the Spaniards were now so hated by every Italian that it would be unwise for the Medici ever to rely upon them again. What they needed was a cadre of war-hardened warriors to take control of the militia of Florence and give them the backbone and organization they so plainly lacked, the fighting spirit which Niccolò, a bureaucrat by nature and not a man of war, had so patently failed to instill in them.

Thus carefully distancing himself from his disgraced old friend, Argalia the Turk argued his way into the post of *condottiere* of Florence. He was pleasantly surprised to hear that he was being offered a permanent-service contract rather than one with a fixed term of a few months. Some of his fellow warriors in that time of the *condottieri*'s decline were hired for periods as brief as three months, and their pay was tied to their success in military ventures. By contrast, Argalia's pay was good by the standards of the time. In addition, Duke Giuliano gave his new captain-at-arms a substantial residence on the Via Porta Rossa, with a full staff and a lavish household allowance. "Admiral Doria must have recommended me highly," he said to Duke Giuliano, readily accepting the generous terms. "He said you were the only barbarian motherfucker he wouldn't want to come up against on land or at sea even if you were naked as an uncircumcised baby with just a kitchen knife in your hand," the Duke elegantly replied.

—⁓—

According to legend the Medici family possessed a magic mirror whose purpose was to reveal to the reigning Duke the image of the most desirable woman in the known world, and it was in this mirror that the earlier Giuliano de Medici, the uncle of the present ruler, who was murdered on the day of the Pazzi plot, first saw the face of Simonetta Vespucci. After her death, however, the mirror darkened and stopped working, as though unwilling to sully the memory of Simonetta by offering up lesser beauties in her place. During the family's exile from the city the mirror remained for a time in its place on the wall of what had been Uncle Giuliano's bedchamber in the old house on the Via Larga, but because it resolutely refused to function either as an instrument of revelation or as an ordinary mirror it was eventually taken down and placed in a storage closet, no more than a mere broom cupboard, concealed in the bedroom wall. Then all of a sudden after the election of Pope Leo the mirror had begun to glow again, and a servant girl was reported to have fainted when she opened the broom closet to find a woman's face shining back at her from a cobwebbed corner, a stranger who looked like a visitor from another world. "In the whole city of Florence there is not such a face," said the new Duke Giuliano when he was shown the miracle, and his health and demeanor seemed to improve visibly as he gazed into the magic glass. "Hang the mirror on the wall again, and I will give a golden ducat to any man or woman who can bring this vision of loveliness before me."

The painter Andrea del Sarto was summoned to look into the magic mirror and paint the likeness of the beauty within, but the mirror wasn't that easily tricked, a magic mirror that allowed its occult images to be reproduced would soon be out of work, and when del Sarto looked into the glass he saw nobody there but himself. "Never mind," said Giuliano, disappointed. "When I find her, you can paint her from life." After del Sarto departed, the Duke wondered if the problem might be that the mirror didn't have a sufficiently high opinion of the artist's genius; but he was the best one available, because Sanzio was in Rome quarreling with Buonarroti in the Vatican, and old Filipepi who had been so besotted with dead Simonetta that he wanted to be buried at her feet—he wasn't, obviously—was dead himself, and long before he died he had become poor and useless anyway, unable to stand without the help of two walking sticks. Filipepi's pupil Filippino Lippi was popular with the *festaiuoli* who organized the city's parades and street carnivals, a crowd-pleaser of a painter, but unsuitable for the job Duke Giuliano had in mind. That left del Sarto, but the point was academic, because from then on the magic mirror only worked when Duke Giuliano was alone in the room. For the next few days he began to find excuses to retreat to his bedchamber several times a day so that he could gaze on that unearthly beauty, and his courtiers, already worried about his generally poor health and his neurasthenic airs, began to fear a deterioration and to look in the direction of his probable successor Lorenzo with increased sycophancy and alarm. Then the enchanting creature rode into the city at the side of Argalia the Turk, and the time of *l'ammaliatrice* began.

———m———

She was just twenty-two years old, almost a quarter-century his junior, and yet when she asked il Machia if he would walk with her in his woods he leapt up with the alacrity of a moonstruck youth. Ago Vespucci leapt to his feet as well, which irritated Niccolò; what, was that indolent fellow still here? And he expected to accompany them on their outing? Tiresome, very tiresome, but, in the circumstances, probably unavoidable. Then came the first indication that the princess possessed exceptional gifts. Niccolò's wife Marietta, customarily the most jealous of shrews, agreed enthusiastically with the proposal, in tones that amazed her husband. "But of course, you must show the girl around," she cooed sweetly, and quickly provided a picnic basket and a flask of wine to increase the pleasure of the outing. The astonished il Machia was at once convinced that his wife must have been placed under some sort of spell, and found the words *foreign witches* forming in his thoughts, but, remembering the proverb about the gift horse, he dismissed such speculation, rejoiced in his good fortune. He set out with Ago in tow within the half-hour, followed at a discreet distance by Konstantin the Serb and his detachment of guardians, and escorted the young princess and her lady-in-waiting to the oak wood of his childhood. "Here, once," Ago told her, and il Machia could see he was trying in his rather pathetic way to impress her, "I actually found a mandrake root, the magic thing of fable, I found it, yes!, somewhere around here." He looked energetically about him, unsure in which direction he should point. "Oh, the mandrake?" Qara Köz replied in her immaculate Florentine Italian. "Look over there, there's a whole bed of the dear things."

And before anybody could stop them, before anybody could warn them that they had to block their ears with mud before attempting such a thing, the two ladies had run over to the mass of impossible plants and commenced to uproot them. "The screaming," Ago shrieked, with much flapping of incompetent hands. "Stop, stop! It will drive us all mad! Or deaf! Or else we'll all be . . ." *Dead,* he was going to say, but the two ladies were looking at him with puzzled expressions on their faces, with an uprooted mandrake in each hand, and there was no deadly scream to be heard. "It is poisonous if taken in excess, of course," Qara Köz said reflectively, "but there's no need to be afraid." When they saw that they were in the presence of women for whom the mandrake root would give up its life without protest the two men marveled mightily. "Well, just don't use it on me," Ago blustered, trying to cover up his fear of a few moments earlier, "or I'll just have to be in love with you forever, or at least until one of us dies." Then he blushed brightly, the redness going all the way down the collar of his shirt and emerging from his sleeves to change the color of his hands as well; which went to show, of course, that he was already hopelessly and forever amorous. No occult plant's power was necessary to ensure his love.

—⁓—

By the time Argalia and the Swiss giants returned to escort Qara Köz to her new home in the Palazzo Cocchi del Nero, the entire village of Sant'Andrea in Percussina had fallen under her spell, down to the last man, woman, and child. Even the hens seemed happier, and were certainly laying more eggs. The princess did nothing, by all accounts, to encourage the growth of this adoration; yet it grew. During the six days of her sojourn at the Machiavelli home, she walked in the woods with the Mirror, she read poetry in a variety of languages, she met and befriended the children of the household, and was not above offering to help in the kitchen, an offer which Marietta refused. In the evenings she took pleasure in sitting with il Machia in his library and allowing Niccolò to read to her divers passages from the works of Pico della Mirandola and Dante Alighieri, and also many cantos from the epic poem *Orlando in Love,* by Matteo Boiardo of Scandiano. "Ah," she cried as she learned of Boiardo's heroine's many vicissitudes, "poor Angelica! So many pursuers, so little power with which to resist them, or to impose her own will upon them all."

In the meanwhile the village as one person began to sing her praises. The woodcutter Gaglioffo no longer crudely referred to Qara Köz and the Mirror as "witches" to "fuck" and spoke of them instead with a wide-eyed, deferential awe that plainly did not permit him even to dream of having carnal relations with the great ladies. The Frosino brothers, the village gallants, daringly declared that they were suitors for her hand, it being unclear whether she and Argalia the Turk were actually legally married—and of course if that proved to be the case then the two millers conceded that they would not challenge his rights in the matter—but on the chance that she was single they were definitely interested, and had even agreed, in the interests of brotherly love, that they would be prepared to share her and her lady-in-waiting between them, turn and turn about. Nobody else was quite as foolish as Frosino Uno and Due, but the general opinion of Qara Köz was high, and women as well as men declared themselves "enchanted."

But if this was sorcery it was of the most benign kind. All Florentines were conversant with the rapacious procedures of the dark enchantresses of the period, their invocations of demons to force chaste men to engage in libidinous acts, their use of effigies and pins to torment their enemies, their ability to make good men abandon their home and work, just to be their willing slaves. In the household of il Machia, however, neither Qara Köz nor her lady-in-waiting gave any indication of practicing the black arts, or, at least, for some reason those indications they did give were not considered problematic. Witches liked wandering in woods, everybody knew that, but the sylvan perambulations of Qara Köz and the Mirror were, in the opinion of the good people of Percussina, no more than "charming." The incident of the mandrake bed did not become widely known, and, strangely enough, il Machia never found it again, nor were the plants uprooted by the two ladies ever displayed by them, so that it was easy for Niccolò and Ago to doubt whether the incident had ever happened.

Witches were widely held to possess strong Sapphic inclinations, but nobody, not even Marietta Corsini, was at all perturbed by the two ladies' decision to share a bed. "Why, it's only for companionship," Marietta told her husband in a sluggish voice, and he nodded heavily, as if under the soporific influence of an excess of afternoon wine. As for the celebrated enthusiasm of witches for copulating with the Devil, why, there were simply no devils to be found in Percussina, and none rose up from the inferno to cackle in fireplaces or to sit like gargoyles on the roofs of the tavern or the church. It was an age of witch-hunts and in the courts of the city women were heard confessing to dire deeds, of capturing the hearts and minds of good citizens by the use of wine, frankincense, menses, and water drunk from the skulls of the dead. But while it was true that everyone in Percussina was in love with the Princess Qara Köz, the adoration she inspired—except, perhaps, in the highly sexed Frosino twins—was entirely chaste. Not even Ago Vespucci, the romantic moon-calf who would love her, as he had said, "until one of them was dead," at that time entertained any thoughts of becoming her carnal lover. To worship her was delightful enough.

Those who afterward charted and analyzed the career of the enchantress of Florence, most notably Gian Francesco Pico della Mirandola, the great philosopher Giovanni's nephew and the author of *La strega ovvero degli inganni dei demoni* ("The Witch, or the Deceptions of Demons"), concluded that the miasma of approval which Qara Köz created around Percussina, and which quickly spread throughout the neighborhood, across San Casciano and Val di Pesa, Impruneta and Bibbione, Faltignano and Spedaletto, had been the product of a deliberate enchantment of immense potency, its purpose being to test her powers—those same powers she subsequently proceeded to use to such remarkable effect in and upon the city of Florence itself—and to smooth her entry into what might otherwise have been hostile surroundings. Gian Francesco records that when Argalia the Turk returned with the Swiss giants he found a substantial crowd gathered outside the Machiavelli residence, as if a miracle had occurred, as if the Madonna had materialized in Percussina and everyone had assembled to see her. And when Qara Köz and the Mirror emerged from the house, arrayed in their finest brocades and jewels, the assembled populace actually fell to its knees, seemingly asking for her benediction; which, without words, with a smile and a gently raised arm, she gave them. Then she was gone, and Marietta Corsini, as if awaking from a dream, yelled at the people trampling on her property to be off about their business. In the words of Gian Francesco, "the rustics came to their senses and were amazed to discover where they found themselves. Scratching their heads in wonder, they returned to their homes, fields, mills, woods, and kilns."

Andrea Alciato, who believed that witches and their adherents should be treated with herbal remedies, ascribed the mysterious "Percussina event" to the locals' bad eating habits, which rendered them vulnerable to fantasies and hallucinations, while Bartolomeo Spina, author of *De Strigibus,* written a decade after these manifestations, went so far as to suggest that Qara Köz might have whipped up the villagers into a Satanic frenzy and led them in a large-scale, orgiastic Black Mass, a defamatory supposition for which there is no evidence whatsoever in the historical records of the time.

—⟋⟍—

The entry into Florence of the new *condottiere* of the city and commander of the Florentine militia, Antonino Argalia, called "the Turk," was greeted by the excessive, hedonistic celebrations for which the city was renowned. A wooden castle was constructed in the Piazza della Signoria, and a mock-siege was staged, with one hundred men defending the edifice and three hundred attacking it. Nobody wore armor, and they fought so ferociously, stabbing one another with lances and hurling unbaked bricks at one another's heads, that many of the actors had to go to the hospital of Santa Maria Nuova, where some of them unfortunately died. There was also a bull-hunt in the Piazza, and the bulls, too, sent many revelers to the hospital. Two lions were released to hunt a black stallion, but the horse responded so nobly to the first lion's attack, kicking him hard all the way from outside the Mercantantia, the home of the Tribunal of the Merchants' Guild, to the center of the Piazza, that the king of the beasts ran away and hid in a shadowed corner of the square, and after that neither lion was prepared to rejoin the affray. This was interpreted as a grand omen, the horse being Florence, obviously, and the lions her foes from France, Milan, or any other damnable place.

After these preliminaries the procession entered the city. Eight *'dfici,* or platforms on wheels, came first, with actors upon them portraying scenes from the victories of the great warrior of antiquity, Marcus Furius Camillus, Censor and Dictator, the so-called Second Founder of Rome, depicting the many prisoners he had taken at the siege of Veii almost two thousand years ago, and suggesting how rich had been the spoils of war, weaponry and clothing and silver. And then there were men singing and dancing down the streets, and four caparisoned squadrons of men-at-arms, with their lances at the ready. (The Swiss giants, Otho, Botho, Clotho, and D'Artagnan, had been put in charge of pike training, for all the world feared the Swiss infantry's skill with pikes, and the improvement of the militia's lancework even after one or two preliminary training sessions was already plain for all to see.) Finally, Argalia entered through the great gate, flanked by the four Swiss gossips, with Konstantin the Serb immediately behind, riding between the two foreign ladies, and then the hundred Janissaries whose appearance struck terror into the hearts of all who saw them. *Now our city is safe,* the cry went up, *for our invincible protectors are come.* That was the name—*Invincibles*—that stuck to the new guardians of the city. Duke Giuliano, waving from the balcony of the Palazzo Vecchio, seemed pleased that his appointment had gone down so well with the public; by contrast Lorenzo, his nephew, was sullen and resentful. Argalia, looking up at the two Medici potentates, understood that the younger one would need careful watching.

Duke Giuliano at once recognized Qara Köz as the woman in the magic mirror, the object of his incipient obsession, and his heart leapt for joy. Lorenzo de' Medici saw her too, and in his concupiscent heart at once began to dream of possessing her. As for Argalia, he knew the dangers of bringing his beloved into the city so flamboyantly, right under the nose of the Duke whose name-sake his uncle had shamelessly stolen the city's previous great beauty from her husband, Horned Marco Vespucci, whose self-hood had been so eroded by her loss that when she died he sent all her clothes and all the paintings of her he possessed across to the Palazzo Medici so that the Duke could have what remained of her, after which he went down to the Bridge of the Graces and hanged himself. But Argalia was not the suicidal type and calculated that the Duke would not wish to antagonize the military strongman whom he had only just appointed and whose entry to the city he was at this moment celebrating. "And if he does try to take her from me," Argalia thought, "he'll find me waiting with all my men, and to capture her against that kind of opposition he'll have to be a Hercules or Mars, which, as anyone can see, this sensitive soul is not."

In the meantime, he was happy to show her off.

As the crowds caught sight of Qara Köz a whisper began to spread through the city, becoming a murmur that had the effect of hushing all the riotous sounds of the day, so that by the time Argalia and the ladies arrived at the Palazzo Cocchi del Nero an extraordinary silence had fallen, as the people of Florence con-templated the arrival in their midst of physical perfection, a dark beauty to fill the hole left in their hearts by Simonetta Vespucci's death. Within moments of her coming she had been taken to the city's heart as its special face, its new symbol of itself, the incarna-tion in human form of that unsurpassable loveliness which the city itself possessed. The Dark Lady of Florence: poets reached for their pens, artists for their brushes, sculptors for their chisels. The com-mon people, the noisiest and most rambunctious forty thousand souls in all Italy, honored her in their own fashion, by becoming still and silent as she passed. As a result everyone heard what hap-pened when Duke Giuliano and Lorenzo de' Medici met Argalia's party at the entrance to their new four-story home, three high arched doorways in a façade of *pietra forte*. Above the doorway, in the center of the façade, was the coat of arms of the Cocchi del Nero family, which had lately fallen on hard times and sold the place to the Medici. It was the greatest architectural masterpiece on that street of masterpieces, which also boasted the grand residences of some of the city's oldest families, the Soldanieri, the Monaldi, the Bostichi, the Cosi, the Bensi, the Bartolini, the Cambi, the Arnoldi, and the Davizzi. Duke Giuliano wanted to make clear to Argalia and to everyone else exactly how generous he was being, and chose to do so by addressing his remarks, with many flourishes and even a little bow, not to Argalia but to Qara Köz.

"I am pleased," he said, "to give this exquisite jewel a setting that befits its charms."

Qara Köz replied in ringing tones. "Sir, I am no bauble, but a princess of the blood royal of the house of Timur and Temüjin—that is Chinggis Qan, whom you call Genghis—and I expect to be addressed in a manner befitting my rank."

Mongol! Mogor! The glamorous, alien words ran round the crowd engendering an almost erotic combination of excitement and terror. It was Lorenzo de' Medici, red-faced with self-importance, who said what some were feeling, thus confirming Argalia's assessment of him as a vain, second-rate boy. "Argalia, you fool," Lorenzo shouted. "By abducting this insolent daughter of the Mogor you will bring the Golden Horde down upon our heads." Argalia replied gravely, "That would indeed be quite an achievement, more particularly as the Horde was vanquished and its power broken forever by the princess's own ancestor, Tamerlane, over one hundred years ago. In addition, my lords, I have abducted no one. The princess was formerly the prisoner of Shah Ismail of Persia, and I freed her after our victory over that lord at the battle of Chaldiran. She comes here of her own free will, in the hope of forging a union between the great cultures of Europe and the East, knowing she has much to learn from us and believing, too, that she has much to teach."

This statement went down well with the listening mob—which was also mightily impressed by the news that their new protector had been on the winning side in that already legendary battle—and loud cheers rose up in honor of the princess, making any further objections to her presence impossible. Duke Giuliano, recovering skillfully from his surprise and discomfiture, held up a hand for silence. "When such a great visitor comes to Florence," he cried out, "Florence must rise to the occasion, and Florence will."

The Palazzo Cocchi del Nero possessed one of the most magnificent grand salons in the city, a room twenty-three feet wide and fifty-three feet long with a ceiling height of twenty feet, lit by five immense leaded-glass windows, a room in which to entertain on the most lavish scale possible. The principal bedroom, the so-called Nuptial Chamber, boasted a frescoed frieze on all four walls illustrating a romantic poem by Antonio Pucci based on an old Provençal love story, and was a room in which two (or even three) lovers might while away entire days and nights without ever feeling the need to rise or leave the house. In other words, this was a mansion in which Qara Köz could have behaved like all the great ladies of Florence, remaining apart from the common people, sequestering herself from all but the finest folks in town. This was not, however, how the princess chose to spend her time.

It was plain that both she and her Mirror were relishing their new unveiled existence. By day the princess went out to walk the thronging streets, going to market or simply seeing the sights, with the Mirror as her companion and only Konstantin the Serb to protect her, deliberately making herself visible as no great lady of Florence had ever allowed herself to be. The Florentines loved her for it. "Simonetta Due," they called her at first, Simonetta the Second, and then, after hearing the name she and the Mirror used for each other, interchangeably, "Angelica the First." They threw flowers at her feet wherever she went. And slowly her fearlessness shamed the city's young women of breeding into following her out of doors. Breaking with tradition, they began to come out of an evening to promenade in twos and fours, to the delight of the city's young gentlemen, who finally had good reason to stay away from the bordellos. The city's whorehouses began to empty, and the so-called "eclipse of the courtesans" began. The Pope in Rome, appreciating the sudden shift in the public morality of his hometown, wondered aloud to Duke Giuliano, who was paying a visit to the Eternal City, whether the dark princess, who claimed not to be a Christian, might actually be the Church's newest saint. Giuliano, a religious man, repeated this to a courtier and then the pamphleteers of Florence recounted the anecdote to the whole town. No sooner had Leo X speculated in this fashion about Qara Köz's possibly divine nature than reports of her miracles began.

Many of those who saw her walking the streets claimed to have heard, playing all around her, the crystal music of the spheres. Others swore that they had seen a halo of light around her head, bright enough to be visible even in the hot glare of the day. Barren women came up to Qara Köz and asked her to touch their bellies, and then told the world how they had conceived children that very night. The blind saw, the lame walked; only an actual resurrection from the dead was missing from the accounts of her magical deeds. Even Ago Vespucci joined the ranks of the miracle-mongers, claiming that her blessing upon his vineyards, which she had graciously visited, had brought forth the finest vintage his family had ever produced; and he undertook to bring a free supply of the wine to the Palazzo Cocchi del Nero once a month.

In short, Qara Köz unveiled—as "Angelica"—had come into the fullness of her womanly powers and was exerting the full force of those capacities upon the city, misting the air with a benevolent haze which filled the thoughts of Florentines with images of parental, filial, carnal, and divine love. Anonymous pamphleteers declared her to be the reincarnation of the goddess Venus. Subtle perfumes of reconciliation and harmony filled the air, people worked harder and more productively, the quality of family life improved, the birth rate rose, and all the churches were full. On Sundays in the Basilica of San Lorenzo the Medici clan heard sermons extolling the virtues not only of the heads of their mighty family but of their new visitor as well, *a princess not only of faraway Indy or Cathay, but of our own Florence too.* It was the bright time of the enchantress. But the darkness would come soon enough.

People's heads were full of imaginary enchantresses in those days, for example Alcina, the evil sister of Morgana le Fay, in alliance with whom she persecuted her other sister, the good witch Logistilla, the daughter of Love; and Melissa the enchantress of Mantua; and Dragontina the captor of the knight Orlando; and Circe of ancient times, and the unnamed but fearsome Sorceress of Syria. The witch as ugly old monster, the hag, had given way, in Florentine fancy, to these gorgeous creatures, their wild hair denoting their loose morals, their powers of seduction well-nigh irresistible, their magic used sometimes in the service of Good, at other times to do harm. After the arrival of Angelica in the city the idea of the good enchantress, the beneficent, supranormal being, who was both goddess of love and guardian of the people, took firm hold. There she was in the Mercato Vecchio, after all, large as life—"Try these pears, Angelica!"—"Angelica, these plums are succulent!"—no fiction, but a flesh and blood woman. So she was adored, and believed to be capable of great things. But the distance between *enchantress* and *witch* was still not so great. There were still voices that suggested that this new incarnation of the Woman-wizard through whom the occult powers of all women were unleashed was a disguise, and that the true faces of such females were still the fearsome ones of old, the lamia, the crone.

Those skeptics who by virtue of their sour temperament resist a supernatural account of events may prefer more conventional explanations for the time of golden contentment and material prosperity that Florence enjoyed in those days. Under the benignly tyrannical aegis of Pope Leo X, Florence's true master, and either a man of genius or a fatuous fool, depending on how you saw it, the city's fortunes thrived, its enemies retreated, etc., etc., quite so. Were you a naysayer of such jaundiced stripe, the Pope's meeting with the King of France after the battle of Marignano, his alliances and treaties, the new territories he carved out or purchased and gave into Florentine care, from which the city benefited greatly; or his naming of Lorenzo de' Medici as Duke of Urbino; or his arrangement of Giuliano de' Medici's wedding to Princess Filiberta of Savoy, after which the King of France, François I, awarded him the Dukedom of Nemours, and perhaps whispered in his ear that Naples, too, would soon be his . . . all this would be at the forefront of your thoughts.

Let it be conceded to such dry-as-dust quibblers: yes, undoubtedly the power of the papacy was very great. As was the power of the King of France, and the King of Spain, and the Swiss army, and the Ottoman Sultan, and all of these were constantly engaged in conflicts, marriages, reconciliations, renunciations, victories, defeats, machinations, diplomacies, purchases and sales of favors, tax levies, intrigues, compromises, vacillations, and the devil knows what else. All of which activity is, fortunately, quite beside the point.

After a time Qara Köz showed signs of physical and spiritual enervation. Perhaps the Mirror was the first to recognize these signs, for she watched her mistress every minute of every day: so she would have noticed the faintest tightness in the corners of that sensuous mouth, seen the tension clutching at the muscles of her dancer's arms, tended to the headaches, uncomplainingly suffered the moments of irritability. Or perhaps it was Argalia the Turk who first worried about her, because for the first time in their romance she started turning away from his advances, asking the Mirror to pleasure him instead. *I don't feel like it. I'm too tired. My sexual urges have ebbed. Don't take it personally. Why can't you understand that. You are already who you are, mightiest of warlords, you have nothing to prove. Whereas I am just trying to become what I have it in me to be. How can you love me and not understand. That is not love, it is selfishness. Love's banal declension through squabbling toward an end.* He did not want to believe their love might be failing. He did not believe it. He put it out of his mind. Theirs was the love story of the age. It could not end in pettiness.

Duke Giuliano also noticed something amiss in his magic mirror, into which he still stared every day, to the intense annoyance of his wife, Filiberta of Savoy. His union with Filiberta had been wholly political. The Savoyard lady was not young; neither was she beautiful. After their wedding Giuliano continued to adore Qara Köz from a distance, though it should be said, in fairness to that frail and godly man, that he never attempted to seduce her away from his great general, contenting himself with throwing, in her honor, a *festa* comparable only to the celebrations at the time of the Pope's visit to Florence. Filiberta on her arrival in Florence heard the legend of the festivities for the princess of the Mogor and demanded that her new husband do at least as well by his new bride, to which Giuliano replied that such a carnival would be more appropriate when she gave him an heir. He rarely visited her bedroom, however, and his only son would be a bastard, Ippolito, who became a cardinal, as bastards sometimes do. After that rejection Filiberta hated Qara Köz deeply and when she learned of the existence of the magic mirror she hated that as well. When she heard Giuliano one day lamenting the ill health of the dark princess, Filiberta had had enough. "She isn't well," he said to her mournfully when she found him mooning into the magic mirror as usual. "Look at the poor girl. She ails." Filiberta shouted, "I'll make her ail," and threw a silver-backed hairbrush at the magic mirror, smashing the glass. "*I'm* not well," she said. "To tell you the complete truth, I have never felt so terrible in my life. Be as solicitous of my health as you are of hers."

The truth was that Qara Köz was overdoing it, that no woman

could sustain so immense an effort for long. The enchantment of forty thousand individuals, month after month, year after year, was too much, even for her. There were fewer reports of miracles, and then they ceased entirely. The Pope no longer mentioned sainthood.

And over life and death, unlike Alanquwa the sun-goddess, she had no power. Three years after she came to Florence, it was Giuliano de' Medici who fell ill and died. Filiberta packed her possessions, including her entire, immensely valuable trousseau, and returned at once, without ceremony, to Savoy. "Florence has fallen under the sway of a Saracen whore," she said when she got home, "and is no place for a good Christian woman to remain."

{ 18 }

The incident of the lions and the bear

The incident of the lions and the bear had occurred during the *festa* for Qara Köz. On the first day there was the running of the *palio* and the fireworks. On the second day wild beasts were released into the Piazza della Signoria, bulls, buffaloes, stags, bears, leopards, and lions, and men on horseback and lancers on foot as well as men concealed inside a giant wooden tortoise, and a wooden porcupine also, did battle with them. One man was killed by a buffalo.

At one point the biggest male lion seized a bear by the throat and was on the point of killing him when, to general astonishment, a lioness intervened on the bear's side and bit the male lion so hard that he released his grip on the bear. After that the bear recovered, but the other lions and lionesses ostracized the lioness who had saved him, and she wandered the crowded square disconsolately, attacking nobody, ignoring the taunts and cries of the hunters, seemingly heartbroken. In the succeeding days and months there were many disputes over the meaning of this strange event. By general consensus the lioness stood for Qara Köz, but who was the bear and who the lion? The explanation that eventually found favor, and became established as the truth, was circulated in an anonymous pamphlet whose author, unknown to all but a few Florentines, was Niccolò Machiavelli, popular playwright, disgraced man of power. The lioness had shown herself willing to interpose herself between her own species and another in the cause of peace, wrote the pamphleteer. So also the princess Qara Köz had come among them to reconcile forces that might appear irreconcilable, even if she had to oppose her own people to do so. "But unlike the lioness in the Piazza, this human lioness is not alone. She has and will always have many true friends among the bears."

So she became a symbol of peace, of self-sacrifice in the name of peace, for many people. There was much talk of her "Eastern wisdom," which she dismissed when it reached her ears. "There is no particular wisdom in the East," she said to Argalia. "All human beings are foolish to the same degree."

—✺—

Once Qara Köz and her Mirror had left his home il Machia felt the advent of a bitter sadness that would stay with him for all his thirteen remaining years. Friends had vanished when power evicted him from its mansions, and glory was a distant memory, but the departure of great beauty from his life was the last straw. Now that the enchantress's spell over Percussina had been broken, he saw his wife once again as a waddling duck and his children as financial burdens. He would go on making occasional excursions to other women, not only to singing Barbera but to another lady in the neighborhood, whose husband had run off without so much as a word of farewell. These visits did not cheer him up. He thought enviously more than once about that runaway husband and seriously considered disappearing himself one night, and letting his family believe that he was dead. If he had been able to formulate any sort of idea of what to do with his life after such a desertion, perhaps he would even have gone through with it. Instead, abjectly, he poured his lifetime of thought and knowledge into the short book he was writing in the hope of regaining favor at court, his little mirror-of-princes piece, such a dark mirror that even he feared it might not be liked. But surely wisdom would be prized higher than levity, and clear sight would be judged more valuable than flattery? He dedicated the book to Giuliano de'

Medici, writing the whole text out in his own hand, and when Giuliano died he did the whole thing over again for Lorenzo instead. But in his heart it was the knowledge that beauty had left him forever, that the butterfly did not settle on the withered flower, that preoccupied him the most. He had looked into her eyes and she had seen his withering, and had turned away from it. It had felt like a sentence of death.

He had spent twenty minutes alone with Argalia in his library when the new general of Florence came to fetch his lady love. "All my life," Argalia told him, "ever since I was a boy, my motto was, do whatever you have to do to get where you have to go. I survived by learning what served me best and following that star, beyond loyalty, beyond patriotism, beyond the borders of the known world. Myself, myself, always and only myself. This is the way of the survivor. But she has tamed me, Machia. I know what she is, because she is still the way I was. She loves me until it no longer serves her to love me. She adores me, until the time not to adore me arrives. So it is my business to make sure that time is long in coming. Because I do not love her in that way. The love I have for her knows that the well-being of the beloved matters more than that of the lover, because love is selflessness. She does not know that, I think. I would die for her, but she would not die for me."

"Then I hope you do not have to die for her," Niccolò told him, "because that would be a waste of your good heart."

He had had a moment alone with her too, or alone with her and her Mirror, from whom she was inseparable, and who might be, il Machia surmised, her real love. He did not talk to her about matters of the heart. That would have been inappropriate, discourteous. Instead he said, "This is Florence, my lady, and you will live well here, for Florentines know how to live well. But if you are sensible, you will always know where the back door is. You will plan your escape route and keep it in good working order. For when the Arno floods all those without boats are drowned."

He looked out of his window and could see the red dome of

the Cathedral across the fields where his tenant farmer was working. A lizard basked on a low boundary wall. He heard a golden
oriole crying *whee-la-whee-lo.* There were oak trees and chestnut
trees, cypresses and umbrella pines punctuating and organizing the
landscape. In the distance, high in the sky, a buzzard banked and
wheeled. Natural beauty remained, that was undeniable; but to
him the bucolic scene looked like a prison yard. "For me," he said
to Qara Köz, "alas, there is no escape."

He wrote to her often after that day, but he never dispatched the
letters, and he only saw her once more before he died. Ago, however—Ago who still had the freedom of the city—went to call on
her once a month in the Palazzo Cocchi del Nero, and she did him
the favor of receiving him in the so-called Room of the Orioles
next to the *grand salon,* so named because of the birds painted all
around its formally afforested walls. He sent the wagon with the
wine to the tradesmen's entrance down the narrow lane at the
back of the house but he did not enter the house as a tradesman.
He put on his finest clothes, his court clothes, for which he had little use nowadays, and he strode down the Via Porta Rossa like an
aging beau visiting his sweetheart, his hair, once yellow, now white
and thinning, plastered down over his head, and flowers in his
hand. He looked a little ridiculous, he could see that fact reflected
in her overly honest eyes, but it was the best he could do. He expected nothing of her but she did ask something of him, a secret.
"Will you do this for me?" she asked, and he said, "Whenever you
wish." Only the Mirror and the orioles knew what had been said.

Giuliano de' Medici died, Lorenzo de' Medici became ruler of
Florence as Lorenzo II, and things began to change. For three
years, however, the change was not apparent. Lorenzo needed Argalia as badly as his uncle had. It was Argalia who led the men of
Florence into battle against Francesco Maria, the Duke of Urbino,

whom Leo X was in the process of betraying. During the Medici's time of exile it was Francesco Maria who had sheltered them, but now they had turned upon him to seize his dukedom. He was a powerful man leading well-trained forces and even with all Argalia's Janissaries it took three weeks to defeat him. At the end of this engagement nine of his hardened Ottoman warriors were dead. D'Artagnan, one of the four Swiss giants, was among the fallen, and the wailing grief of Otho, Botho, and Clotho was terrible to behold. After that Argalia put down the revolts of a number of barons loyal to Francesco Maria in the Marches of Ancona; and then he, Argalia the Turk, was simply too powerful for Lorenzo to be able to move against him openly.

It was in this period that il Machia submitted his little book to Lorenzo's court. He never heard a word of thanks, appreciation, criticism, or even simple acknowledgment of receipt, nor was any copy of the book found among Lorenzo's effects after his death. A story briefly made the rounds about how Lorenzo had laughed contemptuously when the book was handed to him and thrown it to one side. "The failure presumes to lecture the prince on how the prince should succeed," he said with heavy sarcasm. "Obviously, this is a book I must commit to memory at once." Then, after his courtiers' laughter subsided he added, eliciting a second wave of deferential guffaws, "Of one thing we may be sure. If this Niccolò Mandragola's name is remembered at all, it will be as a comedian, not a thinker." This story reached Ago Vespucci's ears, but he was too kind to repeat it to his friend. As a result Niccolò hoped for a reply for many months. When it became clear that no reply would be given, il Machia entered a steeper decline. As for the little book, he put it to one side, and did not offer it for publication in his lifetime.

In the spring of 1519 Lorenzo made his move. He sent Argalia off to chase the French around Lombardy, where the Turk of Florence engaged François I's men in battle in various parts of the province of Bergamo. In Argalia's absence Lorenzo staged a great joust in the Piazza di Santa Croce, an event closely modeled on the joust in honor of Simonetta Vespucci at which the elder Giuliano de' Medici had carried a banner extolling the loveliness of *la sans pareille*. Qara Köz was invited to sit in the place of honor on the royal platform, beneath a blue canopy decorated with golden lilies, and Lorenzo rode up to her and unfurled a new banner, this one bearing her likeness painted by del Sarto; but the words were the same. *La sans pareille*. "I dedicate these events to our city's queen of beauty, Angelica of Florence and Cathay," Lorenzo proclaimed. Qara Köz remained impassive, declining to throw him any sort of scarf or kerchief as a favor for him to wear, and the rising color in the Duke's cheeks betrayed his humiliated anger. There were about sixteen jousters, soldiers who had remained behind to guard the city, and there were two prizes, a *palio* made of gold brocade and another of silver. The Duke did not enter the lists, but came to sit beside Qara Köz and did not speak to her until after the prizes had been won.

There was a banquet at the Palazzo Medici after the games, at which there was *zuppa pavese* to drink, and peacocks to eat, and pheasants from Chiavenna, and Tuscan partridges, and oysters from Venice. There was pasta made in the Arab way with much sugar and cinnamon, while all dishes involving the flesh of the swine, such as *fagioli* with pork skins, were avoided out of consideration for the sensibilities of the guest of honor. There was quince jam from Reggio, marzipan from Siena, and good Florentine *caci marzolini,* that is to say, March cheese. Great heaps of tomatoes made the finest of table decorations. After the feasting there were orations by poets and intellectuals on the subject of love, as there had been at Agathon's feast, which was recorded in the *Symposium* of Plato. Lorenzo concluded this part of the festivities by reciting certain choice words from the *Symposium* itself. "Love will make men dare to die for their beloved—love alone," he declaimed, "and women as well as men. Of this, Alcestis, the daughter of Pelias, is a monument to all Hellas; for she was willing to lay down her life on behalf of her husband, when no one else would." When he sat down with a thump Qara Köz asked him about his selection. "Why speak of death," she said, "when we are in the midst of pleasant life?"

Lorenzo shocked her by addressing her in the harshest language possible. He had been drinking heavily, and it was well known that he had no head for wine. "Death, madam, is never so far away as you imagine," he said. "And who can say what may be asked of you before long." She became very still and silent then, understanding that her destiny was about to speak to her through her loutish youth of a host. "Before a flower dies," he said, "its perfume fades. And your aroma, madam, has faded considerably, has it not." It was not a question. "There is little talk now of heavenly music playing in your vicinity, or of glorious healings, or wonderful pregnancies in barren wombs. Not even our most credulous citizens, not even the starving ones who eat bread flavored with herbs that cause hallucinations just to take their mind off their hunger, not even the beggars who eat rotten food and poisonous plants so often that they see demons every night, are talking about your magical powers anymore. Where are your spells now, madam, where now your intoxicating perfumes that turned all men's minds to amorous thoughts? It seems that the enchantments of even the most beautiful woman may fade with, how should one put this?— with age."

Qara Köz was twenty-eight years old, but there was an exhaustion in her that had dimmed her light, and a tautness, too, for private reasons which Lorenzo identified correctly and brutally. "Even at home," he whispered theatrically, "things may have dwindled, eh. Six years together in Florence and some before, and yet you have no children. People wonder about your own barrenness. Physician, heal thyself." Qara Köz began to rise. Lorenzo II's hand came down hard on her forearm, pinning it to the arm of her chair. "How long will your protector protect you if you do not give him a son?" he asked. "That is to say, if he even returns from the wars."

In that instant she understood that an act of treachery had been planned, that some individual or group under Argalia's command had agreed to betray him in return for some promised preferment, which might turn out to be a secret knife in the ribs or a public execution. One betrayal often deserved another. "You will never kill him while his own men are around him," she said faintly, and at that moment there rose up before her eyes, like a prophecy, the face of Konstantin the Serb. "What did you promise him," she asked, "that after all these years of friendship he should agree to do so foul a thing?" Lorenzo leaned forward to whisper in her ear. "Everything he could imagine," he cruelly replied. So she had been the bribe, and Konstantin, who had guarded her so closely for so long, had been corrupted by that proximity into hungering after a more intimate nearness, and there it was. She was Argalia's doom. "He won't do it," she said. Lorenzo's hold on her forearm grew tighter. "Well, even if he does, princess," he said, "he need not get his reward." Yes, she understood. Here it was then, her fate. "Let's just suppose that the men come from battle bearing their dead commander on his shield," the man beside her was murmuring. "Dreadful tragedy, of course, a burial among the city's heroes, and at least a month of mourning. But just suppose that by the time of his return we had moved you and your lady-in-waiting and all your possessions from the Via Porta Rossa to the Via Largo. Just suppose you were here, as my guest, seeking consolation in your time of horrible grief. Imagine what I would do to the coward who murdered the champion of Florence, your beloved, my friend. You could describe to me the tortures you would prefer us to use, and I would guarantee that he would be kept alive until he had experienced them all to the full."

Music struck up. There was to be dancing now. She was to dance a pavana with the assassin of her hopes. "I must think," she said, and he bowed. "Of course," he said, "but think quickly, and before you think, you will be brought to my private rooms tonight, so that you may understand what it is you have to think about." She stopped dancing and stood facing him. "Madam, please," he chided her, holding out his hands until she began to step in time once again. "You are a princess of the blood royal of the house of Tamerlane and Genghis Khan. You know how the world works."

She returned home with the Mirror that night after demonstrating that she did indeed understand the workings of the world. "Angelica, what had to be done has been done," she said. "Now, Angelica, let us be ready to die," the Mirror replied. This was the code phrase which she and the princess had settled on long ago, and its meaning was that it was time to move on, to shed one life and find the next, to use the escape plan and disappear. To set the plan in motion, the Mirror in a long hooded cloak would have to slip out by the tradesmen's entrance after the city was asleep, and make her way down the narrow lane behind the Palazzo Cocchi del Nero, and then wind her way through the city to the Ognissanti district, until she found herself at Ago Vespucci's door. But to her surprise Qara Köz shook her head. "We will not leave," she said, "until my husband comes home alive." She had no power over life and death, and was relying instead on a power she had never trusted before: that of love.

—⁓⁓—

The next day the river had run dry. The city was full of the news that Lorenzo de' Medici was mortally ill, and even though nobody said it aloud everybody knew that the illness was the dreadful *morbo gallico,* which was to say syphilis. The lack of water in the Arno was seen as a dire omen. Lorenzo's doctors were attending to him around the clock, but so many Florentines had died of this disease since it had first appeared in Italy twenty-three years earlier that few people expected their Duke to survive. As usual, half the city blamed the sickness on French soldiers while the other half held that Christopher Columbus's sailors had brought it home from their voyages, but Qara Köz wasn't concerned about such tittle-tattle. "This has happened more rapidly than I foresaw," she told the Mirror, "which means it is only a matter of time before suspicion falls on me." This would have struck many people as a strange remark, because Qara Köz was not syphilitic, as a medical examination would have proved, nor did she contract syphilis at any later date. But the fact was that nobody had suspected Lorenzo II of having been infected either, which made the sudden onset of the illness in its most aggressive form all the more remarkable. And so it was a suspicious case, and in such a case a suspect—or at the very least a scapegoat—had to be found. Who knows how things would have worked out, if Argalia the Turk had not come home alive.

The night before he returned she slept poorly but when sleep did come she dreamed of her sister. On a blue carpet edged in a pattern of red and gold, with a red and gold diamond at the carpet's center, inside a large tented pavilion of red and gold cloth, Khanzada Begum sat staring at a man whom she did not recognize, dressed in cream silk clothes with a pink and green shawl thrown across his shoulders and on his head a turban in pale blue and white and a little gold. I am your brother Babar, the stranger said. She looked into his face but her brother was not there. I don't think so, she said. The man turned to a second man sitting a little to one side. Kukultash, he said, who am I? Sire, the second man said, you are Zahiruddin Muhammad Babar, as surely as we are sitting in Qunduz. Khanzada Begum answered, why should I believe him any more than you? I know no Kukultash. The brother and sister continued to sit in that tent, she waited upon by her maidservants, he guarded by soldiers carrying spears and bows. There was no emotion displayed. The lady did not know her brother. She had not seen him for ten years. Qara Köz understood even while she was dreaming that she was all the people in the dream. She was her sister who, having been torn away from her family, could not find the pathways of memory and love that would allow her to return. She was her brother Babar, who was both ferocious and poetic, who could sever men's heads and extol the beauty of a woodland glade on the same afternoon, but who had no country, no land to call his own, who was still wandering the world, battling for space, taking places, losing them again, now marching in triumph into Samarkand, now into Kandahar, and now he was chased out of them again; Babar running, running, trying to find the ground upon which he could stand still. And she was Kukultash, Babar's friend, and the maids-in-waiting, and the soldiers, she was floating outside herself and watching her own story as if it were happening to someone else, without feeling anything, without permitting herself to feel. She was her mirror as well as herself.

Then the dream changed. The canopies and cupolas of the tent hardened into red stone. What was transient, portable, mutable was all of a sudden permanent and fixed. A stone palace on a hill and her brother Babar taking his ease on a stone dais at the center of a rectilinear pool, a beautiful pool, a pool without peer. He was so rich that when he felt generous he could empty the pool and fill it with money instead and let his people come and scoop up his largesse. He was rich, and at ease, and had not just a pool but a kingdom. But he was not Babar. He was not her brother. She did not recognize him. He was a man she did not know.

"I have seen the future, Angelica," she told the Mirror when she awoke. "The future is set in stone, and my brother's descendant is an emperor beyond compare. We are water, we can turn into air and vanish like smoke, but the future is wealth and stone." She would wait for the future to arrive. Then she would return to her old life, be rejoined to it, and made whole. She would do better than Khanzada. She would not fail to recognize the king.

There had been a woman in the dream, seen from behind, a woman with long yellow hair worn loose about her shoulders, seated opposite the king, talking, wearing a long garment made up of lozenges of many different colors. And another woman indoors, who never saw the sunlight, who wandered the palace corridors like a shade, now fading, now strengthening, now fading again. This part of the dream was unclear.

—m—

Qara Köz understood about suppressing the emotions. Ever since she had been taken to Lorenzo II's private quarters she had permitted herself no feelings. He had done what he had intended to do and she too had carried out her intentions, in cold blood. After her return to the Palazzo Cocchi del Nero she remained perfectly cool and calm. The Mirror scurried about packing up a couple of *cassoni,* the large chests in which women normally packed their trousseaux, getting ready for a quick departure, even if her mistress was determined to stay. Qara Köz waited by an open window in the *grand salon,* allowing the city's talk to drift up to her on the breeze. It was not long before she heard the word she had known would be spoken, the word that made it unsafe for her to remain. Still she made no attempt to depart.

Witch. She bewitched him. He lay with the witch and sickened and died. He was not sick before. Witchcraft. She gave him the Devil's disease. Witch, witch, witch.

Lorenzo II was dead by the time the militia returned from the victory at Cisano Bergamasco, marching in good order in spite of the consternation caused in the ranks by Konstantin the Serb's attempt to murder the *gran condottiere* General Argalia in the heat of the battle. Along with six of his fellow Janissaries, armed with matchlock muskets, pikes, and swords, Konstantin made a cowardly attack on the general's position from the rear. The first bullet caught Argalia in the shoulder and unhorsed him, accidentally saving his life, because after that there were horses all around the fallen captain and the mutineers could not reach him. The three remaining Swiss giants turned away from the enemy in front to do battle with the traitors behind, and after strenuous hand-to-hand combat the insurgency was quelled. Konstantin the Serb was dead, with a Swiss pike through his heart, but Botho had fallen too. By nightfall the battle against the French had been won but Argalia took no pleasure from the victory. Of his original band of men fewer than seventy remained alive.

As they approached the city they saw flames rising everywhere, as they had on the day of the Pope's election, and Argalia sent a rider ahead at speed to find out what was happening. The scout returned with the news that the Duke was dead and the leaderless citizens were inclined to blame Qara Köz for having cursed him with a hex of such potency that it had eaten his body away like a hungry animal, starting with the genitals and working outward from there. Argalia instructed Otho, one of the two remaining, broken-hearted Swiss brothers, to lead the militia back to its barracks at a quick march. Gathering Clotho and the remaining Janissaries around him, and ignoring his wounded right arm in its sling, he galloped home upon the wind. For indeed there was a wind that night, and they saw olive trees uprooted by it, and oaks flung aside as though they were little saplings, and walnut trees, cherry trees, and alders, so that as they rode it seemed that a forest was flying through the air alongside them; and as they neared the city they heard a great tumult, such as only the people of Florence knew how to make. However, this was no tumult of joy. It was as if every man in the city had turned werewolf and was howling at the moon.

What a short journey from *enchantress* to *witch*. Only yesterday she had been the city's unofficial patron saint. Now there was a mob gathering at her door. "The back door is still open, Angelica," the Mirror said. "Angelica, we will wait," she replied. She was sitting in an upright chair by the side of a window in the *grand salon,* looking out at an angle, seeing without being seen. Invisibility was her fate. She remained calm. Then she heard the horses' hoofs and rose to her feet. "He is here." And he was.

Outside the Cocchi del Nero palace the Via Porta Rossa

widened into a little square around which the Davizzi palace and the tower houses of the Foresi also stood. Argalia and the Janissaries, riding toward the square, were slowed by the gathering throng of witch-hunters. But they were determined, and heavily armed, and people let them pass. When they reached the palace façade the Janissaries cleared a space and when they were sure it was secure the doors were opened. A voice in the crowd shouted out, "Why do you protect the witch?" Argalia ignored it. Then the same voice shouted, "Who do you serve, *condottiere,* the people or your own lust? Do you serve the city and its hexed Duke, or are you in thrall to the hag who hexed him?" Argalia wheeled his horse around to face the crowd. "I serve her," he said, "as I always have and will." Then with around thirty men he rode into the inner courtyard, leaving Clotho in charge of operations outside. The riders halted around the well in the center of the courtyard, and the silent palace was full of noises, the whinnying of animals, the clatter of weapons and clamor of men shouting orders and replies. The servants of the household rushed out to offer drink and nourishment to the riders and their mounts. And now Qara Köz, like a woman waking from sleep, all of a sudden understood her danger. She stood at the head of the flight of stairs rising up from the courtyard and Argalia stood below her looking up. His skin was as white as death.

"I knew you lived," she said. She did not mention his wounded arm.

"And you must live too," he said. "The crowd is growing larger." He said nothing of the aching of the wound in his right shoulder, or of the flame radiating outward through his body from it. He said nothing of the pounding in his heart when he looked at her. He felt short of breath after his long ride. His white skin felt hot to the touch. He did not use the word "love." For the last time in his life he wondered if he had wasted his love on a woman who only gave her love until it was time to take it back. He set the thought aside. He had given his heart this once in his life and counted himself blessed to have had the chance to do so. The question of whether she was worthy of his love had no meaning. His heart had answered that question long ago.

"You will protect me," she said.

"With my life," he replied. He had begun to shiver a little. When he fell at the battlefield of Cisano Bergamasco his grief at the treason of Konstantin the Serb had been followed swiftly by the realization of his own folly. He had been caught out exactly as he had once caught out Shah Ismail of Persia at the battle of Chaldiran. The swordsman would always fall to the man with a gun. In the age of the matchlock musket and the light, swiftly movable field cannon, there was no room for knights in armor. He was a figure from the past. He had deserved that bullet as the old deserves to be destroyed by the new. He was a little light-headed.

"I could not leave," she said. There was a note of surprise in her voice, as if she had learned something extraordinary about herself.

"You must leave now," he replied, panting a little. They did not move toward each other. They did not embrace. She went away and found the Mirror.

"Now, Angelica, let us be ready to die," she said.

The night was on fire. Flames rose everywhere into the brilliant sky. The moon was full, low on the horizon, tinged with red, huge. It looked like God's cold, mad eye. The Duke was dead and only rumor ruled. According to rumor the Pope had damned "Angelica" for a murderous whore and was sending a Cardinal to take charge of the city and deal with its wild witch. The memory of the burning at the stake of the three head Weepers, Girolamo Savonarola, Domenico Buonvicini, and Silvestro Maruffi, in the Piazza della Signoria had not faded, and there were those who looked forward to the stench of incandescent female flesh. But it is in the nature of mobs to be impatient. By midnight the crowd had perhaps tripled in size and its mood was uglier. Stones were thrown at the Cocchi del Nero palace. The phalanx of Janissaries under Clotho the Swiss still held the entrance but even Janissaries tire, and some were nursing wounds. Then in the small hours as the mob bayed came fatal news. The militia of Florence, goaded by the unsubstantiated reports of the Pope's fiat against the witch Angelica, had risen up to join the enraged masses and was marching to the Via Porta Rossa, fully armed. When Clotho heard this he knew that all three of his brothers were now dead, and he decided that he was ready to finish things.

"For the Swiss," he shouted, and launched himself at the crowd with all his might, swinging a sword with one hand and a spiked ball on the end of a length of chain with the other. His fellow Janissaries looked at him in amazement, because the men in the crowd carried nothing more harmful than sticks and stones, but Clotho could not be stopped. The killing mist was upon him. People fell below his horse's hoofs and were trampled to death. The crowd was wild with fear and anger, and at first everyone retreated from the maddened albino giant on his horse. Then a strange moment came, a moment of the kind that determines the fate of nations, because when a crowd loses its fear of an army the world changes. All of a sudden the crowd stopped retreating, and right then Clotho on his horse with his sword raised to strike knew that he was done for. "Janissaries, to me," he shouted, and then the crowd came at them like a flood, thousands upon thousands of screaming voices and grabbing hands and pounding fists, a rain of stones fell upon the soldiers, and men leapt at them like cats, pulling down the horses, dying under the warriors' lashing weapons, but coming forward still, clawing, dragging, clutching, pulling, until the soldiers were all unhorsed, and still the trampling feet of the people came on, the crushing force of the swollen, swelling crowd, and all the world was blood.

Even before the militia arrived, the crowd parting like the sea to allow the armed men through, the Janissaries outside the Palazzo Cocchi del Nero were no more, and with the axes taken from the fallen warriors the crowd was attacking the three great wooden doors of the palace. In the courtyard behind those doors, Argalia the Turk and his remaining fighters, mounted on their horses and wearing full battle armor, had set themselves to make their last stand. "The greatest shame of all is to die at the hands of men you have captained in war," Argalia thought, "but at least my oldest companions will die with me, and there's honor in that." Then matters of honor and shame fled from his mind because Qara Köz was leaving, and it was time for last words to be spoken.

"It's lucky that mobs are so stupid," she said, "otherwise Ago and the Mirror wouldn't have been able to get to the back door down the lane. It's lucky that I took your friend Niccolò's advice, or there would be no plan, and nobody would be outside with empty wine barrels to hide us in and a cart and fresh horses to take us away."

"In the beginning there were three friends," said Argalia the Turk, "Antonino Argalia, Niccolò 'il Machia,' and Ago Vespucci. And at the end, too, there were three. Il Machia will have faster horses waiting for you. Go." The fever had taken hold of him now, and the pain of the wound was very great. He had begun to shake. The end would not be slow in coming. It would be hard to remain mounted very long.

She paused. "I love you," she said. *Die for me.*

"And I you," he answered. *I am already dying, but I will die for you.*

"I have loved you like no other man," she said. *Die for me.*

"You have been the love of my life," he replied. *My life is almost gone, but what remains I give up for you.*

"Let me stay," she said. "Give me up. That will end it all." Again, in her voice, the note of surprise at what she was allowing herself to say, to offer, to feel.

"It's too late for that," he said.

The last fight of the Invincibles of Florence, their final defeat and destruction in the Riot of the Via Porta Rossa, took place in the courtyard of what was afterward known as the Bloody Palace. By the time the battle was over the witch and her assistant were long gone, and when the people of Florence discovered their flight their anger seemed to vanish, and like men waking from a dreadful dream they lost their appetite for death. They *came to themselves,* and were no longer a mob, but a crowd of individual sovereign entities, all of whom went mumbling back to their homes, looking ashamed, and wishing they didn't have blood on their hands. "If she has flown," somebody said, "then begone to her and goodbye." There was no attempt at pursuit. There was only shame. When the Pope's Regent arrived in Florence the Palazzo Cocchi del Nero was locked and shuttered, and the seal of the city was placed upon it, and no one lived there for over one hundred years. And once Argalia the Turk had fallen, rendered unconscious by the septicemia blazing through his body, once he had been stabbed through the neck, as he lay dying of the infection, by a militiaman's ignoble pike, the age of the great *condottieri* came to an end.

And the River Arno, as if cursed by a witch, remained dry for a year and a day.

—⁓—

"She had no child," the emperor observed. "What do you say to that?"
"There's more," the other replied.

—⁓—

Niccolò saw Ago in the distance as the dawn was breaking, Ago at the reins of the cart with the two wine barrels on the back, and he gave up his plan of catching thrushes, set down the birdcages, and went to prepare the horses himself. He could ill afford the gift of two horses, but he would make it nevertheless, and without regret.

Maybe this was how he would be remembered, as the man who assisted in the escape from her pursuers of the Lady of the *Mogor,* the princess of the blood royal of the house of Tamerlane and Genghis Khan, the erstwhile enchantress of Florence. He shouted upstairs to his wife and told her to prepare food and wine at once, and to pack more that could be eaten on a journey; and, hearing the note of crisis in his voice, she leapt out of bed, did as he asked, and did not argue, even though it was not pleasant to be woken from an unusually deep sleep and given unceremonious orders. Then Ago clattered up in front of the Machiavelli house, breathless, frightened. Argalia was not with him. Silently il Machia's eyebrows interrogated Ago Vespucci, who drew a finger across his neck, and then burst into tears of fear, excitement, and grief. "Open the barrels, for God's sake," Marietta Corsini came out of doors to say. "They must be bruised half to death inside there."

Ago had put cushions and bolsters inside the barrels and made hinged doors in their sides, and little ventilation holes, but in spite of his efforts the two women emerged from their hiding places in bad shape, red-faced, gasping and in pain. They accepted water gratefully but refused food on account of the effects of the journey on their stomachs. Then without further ado they asked for a room where they could change their clothes, and Marietta showed them into the main bedchamber. The Mirror followed Qara Köz, carrying a small bag, and when the two women emerged half an hour later they were men, dressed in short tunics—red and gold for Qara Köz, green and white for the Mirror—with belts knotted around their waists, wearing woolen hose for riding, and boots of chamois leather. Their hair had been hacked short and tucked under close-fitting skull-caps. Marietta breathed in sharply when she saw their legs in the tight hose, but said nothing about it. "Will you not eat a little before you go?" she asked, but they would not. They thanked her for the bag of bread, cheese, and cold meat she had prepared for them. Then they went outdoors and found il Machia and Ago waiting. Ago still sat up on his cart. The barrels were no longer aboard, but the two chests of the ladies' possessions were there, and another bag, containing Ago's clothes and all the money he had had to hand, including several large-denomination bills of exchange. "I'll get more when we reach Genoa," he said. "I have my checks." He looked Qara Köz in the eyes. "You ladies can't travel alone," he said. Her eyes widened. "So," she replied, "at a moment's notice, when asked for your help, and seeing our predicament, you are ready to step away from your home, your work, your life, and flee with us into an unknown future, out of one peril and, who knows, into many others?" Ago Vespucci nodded. "Yes, I am." She went over to him and took his hands in hers. "Then, sir," she said, "we are yours now."

Il Machia said goodbye to his old companion. "In the beginning there were three friends," he said, "Antonino Argalia, Niccolò 'il Machia,' and Ago Vespucci. Two of the three loved to travel, the third loved to stay at home. Now, of the two travelers, one has gone forever, and the other is marooned. My horizons have shrunk and I have only endings to write. And it's you, my beloved Ago, you, the homebody, who are setting out to find a new world." Then he reached out his hand and put three *soldi* into Ago's palm. "I owe you these," he said. A few minutes later, as the two riders and the man in the cart disappeared round a bend in the road, the early morning sunlight kissed Ago Vespucci's hair, which was so thin now, so white. But in that yellow light it looked as if he possessed once again the golden hair of boyhood, when he and il Machia first went hunting in the Caffagio oak wood, and the *vallata* grove near Santa Maria dell'Impruneta, and also in the forest around the castle of Bibbione, hoping to find a mandrake root.

{ 19 }

He was Adam's heir, not Muhammad's

He was Adam's heir, not Muhammad's or the caliph's, Abul Fazl told him; his legitimacy and authority sprang from his descent from the First Man, the father of all men. No single faith could contain him, nor any geographical territory. Greater than the king of kings who ruled Persia before the Muslims came, superior to the ancient Hindu notion of the Chakravartin—the king whose chariot wheels could roll everywhere, whose movements could not be obstructed—he was the Universal Ruler, king of a world without frontiers or ideological limitations. What followed from this was that human nature, not divine will, was the great force that moved history. He, Akbar, the perfect man, was the engine of time.

The sun had not yet risen, but the emperor was up and about. Sikri in shadow seemed to embody the great mysteries of life. It felt to him like an elusive world of questions to which he must find responses. This was his time of day for meditation. He did not pray. Once in a while he would go to the great mosque he had built around Chishti's shrine, for appearances' sake, to still the gossip of sharp tongues. Badauni's tongue. The tongue of the Crown Prince, who was even less godly than his father but who allied himself with the god-botherers just to spite him. Mostly, however, the emperor liked to use these early hours, before the sun came to heat the stones of Sikri and the emotions of its citizens, to think things through, the high things, not the low quotidian irritations like Prince Salim. He meditated again at noon, and in the evening, and at midnight, but the early meditation was the one he liked best. Musicians came to play religious hymns quietly in the background. Often he waved them away and allowed the silence to caress him. The silence broken only by the dawn cries of the birds.

Sometimes—for he was a man of many desires—his high considerations were interrupted by images of women: dancing girls, concubines, even the royal wives. In the old days, he had most often been distracted by thoughts of Jodha, his imaginary queen; her sharp tongue, her beauty, her sexual expertise. He was not a perfect man, he knew that in his heart, but for a long time he had thought of her as his perfect woman. Companion, helpmeet, erotic tiger, no man could wish for more. She was his masterpiece, or so he had thought for a long time, a dream made flesh, a traveler from the world of *khayal,* fancy, whom he had brought across the frontier of the real. Lately, however, things had changed. Jodha no longer had the power to interrupt his musings. A different woman visited him instead. Qara Köz, Lady Black Eyes, the hidden princess: for a long time he refused to recognize her, refused to understand in which direction his heart was being drawn, for it was leading him toward an impossibility, a passion that could never be consummated, that was, in every sense of the word, improper. He was bent on the sounds of the future and she was an echo from the distant past. Perhaps that was what lured him, her nostalgic gravity; in which case she was indeed a dangerous sorceress, who would drag him backward in time, and consequently backward in every way, in his ideas, his beliefs, his hopes.

She would be bad for him. She would entice him into the delirium of an impossible love and he would sink into her and away from the world of law and action and majesty and destiny. Maybe she had been sent to do this. Perhaps Niccolò Vespucci was an enemy—the queen mother Hamida Bano was one of the proponents of this theory—an agent of the Christian otherworld from which he had emerged, an assassin sent to destroy him by planting this scarlet woman, this deracinated renegade, in his mind. No man could capture Sikri by force of arms but the hidden princess could perhaps defeat him from within himself. She was bad for him. Yet she was the one who came, more and more often, and there were things she understood that Jodha had never grasped. She understood, for example, silence. When the hidden princess came to him she did not speak. It was not her way to chide or tease. She did not speak or giggle or sing. She brought with her a scent of jasmine, and simply sat down beside him, did not touch him, and watched the day begin, until the eastern horizon was rimmed with red, and a sweet breeze got up, and in that instant they became a single person, he was united with her as he had never been with any woman, and then, with infinite delicacy, she left him, and he waited alone for the first, loving touches of the dawn.

No, she was not bad for him, and he would defy all who said so. He could not see evil in her, or in the man who had brought her here. How could such an adventuresome spirit be condemned? Qara Köz was a woman such as he had never met, a woman who had forged her own life, beyond convention, by the force of her will alone, a woman like a king. This was a new dream for him, an undreamed vision of what a woman might be. It alarmed him, aroused him, intoxicated him, possessed him. Yes, Qara Köz was extraordinary; and so, the emperor believed, was Vespucci, or Mogor dell'Amore. The emperor had tested him and found great merit there. He was not an enemy. He was a favorite. He deserved to be praised, not blamed.

Akbar forced his thoughts back onto their proper path. He was not a perfect man, that was a flatterer's phrase, and Abul Fazl's flatteries led him into what Mogor dell'Amore had called the webs of paradox. To elevate a man to near-divine status, and to allow him absolute power, while arguing that human beings and not gods were the masters of human destinies contained a contradiction that would not survive much examination. Besides, the evidence of the interference of faith in human affairs was scattered all around him. He had not been able to forget the suicide of the angel-voiced sisters Tana and Riri for whom death had been preferable to compromising their faith. He did not wish to be divine. If there had never been a God, the emperor thought, it might have been easier to work out what goodness was. This business of worship, of the abnegation of self in the face of the Almighty, was a distraction, a false trail. Wherever goodness lay, it did not lie in ritual, unthinking obeisance before a deity but rather, perhaps, in the slow, clumsy, error-strewn working out of an individual or collective path.

Again, at once, he was mired in contradictions. He did not wish to be divine but he believed in the justice of his power, his absolute power, and, given that belief, this strange idea of the goodness of disobedience that had somehow slipped into his head was nothing less than seditious. He had power over men's lives by right of conquest. That was the inevitable conclusion to which any realistic prince must come, that might was right and all the rest, this endless meditation on virtue, for example, was decoration. The victor was the man of virtue, that was all that needed to be said. Difference existed, there would be executions and suicides, but discord could be quelled, and it was his fist that could quell it. But what, then, of the voice within, that whispered every morning about harmony, not the foolish all-men-are-one nostrums of the mystics, but this stranger idea. That discord, difference, disobedience, disagreement, irreverence, iconoclasm, impudence, even insolence might be the wellsprings of the good. These thoughts were not fit for a king.

He thought of the faraway dukes in the foreigner's tale. They did not claim a divine right to their lands either, but only the right of the victor. Their philosophers too portrayed the human being standing at the center of his time, his city, his life, his church. But foolishly they ascribed man's humanity to God, they required divine sanction to support their case in this matter, the higher matter of Man, even though they dispensed with the need for such a sanction in the lower matter of power. How confused they were and how little they were too, ruling a mere city in Tuscany and a

Roman bishopric to go with it, and how much they thought of themselves. He was the ruler of the frontierless universe and he saw more clearly than they. No, he corrected himself, he did not, and was indulging in mere bigotry if he asserted it. Mogor had been right. *The curse of the human race is not that we are so different from one another, but that we are so alike.*

Daylight spilled across the carpeted floor and he stood up. It was time to show himself at the *jharokha* window and accept the adoration of the people. The people were in celebratory mood today—this, too, they had in common with the populace of that other city whose streets he walked in dreams, this talent for merrymaking—because it was their emperor's solar birthday, the fifteenth of October, and His Majesty would be weighed, twelve times each, against, among other things, gold, silk, perfumes, copper, ghee, iron, grain, and salt, and the ladies of the harem would send each household its share of the largesse. The breeders of livestock would each receive as many sheep, goats, and chickens as the king had years. A quantity of other animals, intended for the slaughterhouse, would be freed to run wild and take their chances. Later, in the harem, he would take part in the ceremony of the tying of the knot in the string of his life, the string that kept the record of his age. And today, also, he had a decision to make, concerning the foreigner who claimed to be a "Mughal of Love."

The emperor had experienced many feelings concerning this individual: amusement, interest, disappointment, disillusion, surprise, amazement, fascination, irritation, pleasure, perplexity, suspicion, affection, boredom, and increasingly, it was necessary to admit it, fondness and admiration. One day he understood that this was also the way in which parents responded to their children, except that in his own sons' case his moments of fondness were rare, while disappointment, disillusion, and suspicion were constants. The Crown Prince had been plotting against him almost from the cradle, and all three boys were degenerates, but the man with the story of Qara Köz to tell was invariably respectful, undeniably intelligent, plainly fearless, and he wove quite a yarn. Of late Akbar had begun to entertain an almost scandalous notion concerning this increasingly amiable Vespucci, who had settled in so well to court life at Sikri that almost everyone now treated him as if he belonged there by right. Prince Salim loathed him, and so did the religious fanatic Badauni, whose secret book of poisonous attacks on the emperor grew fatter and fatter every day while its author grew thinner and thinner, but those enmities redounded greatly to his credit. His mother and Queen Mariam-uz-Zamani, his senior, actually existing wife, detested him too, but they lacked imagination and opposed all intrusions of dream-worlds into the real.

The almost scandalous notion concerning Vespucci had nagged at Akbar for some time now, and to put it to the test he had started involving the foreigner in matters concerning affairs of state. The yellow-haired "Mughal" had mastered, almost at once, the complex details of the *mansabdari* system by which the empire was governed and upon which its survival depended, the pyramid of rank-holders who were expected to maintain troops and horses according to their seniority and who received, in return, personal fiefdoms which were the source of their wealth. Within days he had memorized the names of every *mansabdar* in the empire—and there were thirty-three ranks of these officers, from the royal princes who commanded ten thousand men to the lowly commanders of ten—and, in addition, he had briefed himself on the rank-holders' performance, and put himself in a position to advise the emperor on which *mansabdars* merited promotion and which of them were failing in their tasks. It was the foreigner who proposed to Akbar the fundamental change in the structure of the system that would guarantee the stability of the empire for a hundred and fifty years. Originally most of the *mansabs* were either Turanis, Central Asians of Mughal ethnic stock whose family origins lay in the vicinity of Ferghana and Andizhan, or else Persians. Persuaded by Mogor, however, Akbar began to include large numbers of other peoples, Rajputs, Afghans, and Indian Muslims, until no group formed a majority. The Turanis were still the largest group but after the great reform they held only one-quarter of the posts. As a result no single group could dictate terms to the rest, and all of them were obliged to get along and co-operate. *Sulh-i-kul.* Complete peace. It was all a question of organization.

So he was a man with talents other than magic tricks and story-telling. The emperor, very favorably impressed, began to test the young man's athletic and military skills, and discovered that he could ride a horse bareback, hit a target with an arrow, and wield a sword with more than adequate aplomb. Off the fields of play and combat, his gift of tongues was already renowned, and he rapidly became an expert at the court's most popular indoor games, such as the board game *chandal mandal,* and the card game of *ganjifa,* which he enlivened by trying to identify the color cards with the grandees of Sikri. *Ashwapati,* the Lord of Horses, the highest card in the game, must of course be the emperor himself. *Dhanpati,* the Lord of Treasures, was obviously the finance minister Raja Todar Mal, and *Tiyapati,* the Queen of Ladies, was, naturally, Jodha Bai. Raja Man Singh was *Dalpati,* the Lord of Battle, and Birbal, beloved above all others, first among equals, should probably be *Garhpati,* Lord of the Fort. Akbar was hugely amused by these conceits. "And you, my Mughal of Love," he said, "you must be *Asrpati,* I think." That was the Lord of the Genii, the magicians' and sorcerers' king. Then the foreigner dared to say, "And *Ahipati,* the Lord of Snakes, *Jahanpanah* . . . might that be the Crown Prince, Salim?"

In short, this was a man with qualities, which was the first re-quirement for becoming a man of quality. "Stories can wait," the emperor told him. "You need to improve your knowledge of how things are around here." So Mogor dell'Amore was apprenticed first to Raja Todar Mal and then to Raja Man Singh, to be initiated into the mysteries of finance and governance, and when Birbal rode west toward the fortresses of Chittorgarh and Mehrangarh, Amer and Jaisalmer, to check up on the empire's subjects and allies in those parts, the foreigner accompanied him in the role of a senior aide, and returned wide-eyed with wonder at the emperor's power, having seen those impregnable fortress palaces whose princes had all bowed the knee to the king of kings. As the months lengthened into years it became clear to everyone that the tall yellow-haired man was no longer to be considered a foreigner. The "Mughal of Love" had become the Grand Mughal's adviser and confidant.

"Look out for that snake lord, by the way," the emperor warned Mogor. "The knife he dreams of planting in my back may find its way into yours."

Then Birbal died.

The emperor blamed himself for acquiescing in his friend's wish to be given a military command. But Birbal had taken the uprising of the Raushanai cult, the Afghan Illuminati, surprisingly person-ally—on, so to speak, the emperor's behalf. Their leader, Bayazid the Prophet, had stirred Hinduism and Islam together and come up with a pantheist stew of amorality. Birbal was disgusted. "Because God is in everyone and everything, it follows that all acts are divine acts, and therefore, because all acts are godly, there is no difference between right and wrong, good deeds and evil ones, and so we may do exactly as we please?" he scoffed. "*Jahanpanah,* forgive me, but this petty warlord is laughing at you. He has taken the beauty of your desire to find the one faith within all faiths, and turned it into ugliness, to taunt you. For that temerity alone he should be brought down, even if he were not pillaging and plundering like a barbarian. Plunder, of course, is in his opinion permissible—ha!—because the Raushanai are the chosen people, destined by God to inherit the earth, so if they want to grab their inheritance a little ahead of time, who can say they are not entitled?"

The idea of pillage becoming a religious duty, by means of which the elect acquired that which was theirs by divine gift, ap-pealed strongly to the tribes in the Afghan mountains, and the cult grew rapidly. Then Bayazid suddenly died and was replaced as the leader of the Raushanai by the sixteen-year-old Jalaluddin, his

youngest son. Birbal's anger at this development was uncontrol-
lable, for "Jalaluddin" was also the emperor Akbar's given name,
which coincidence greatly compounded the insolence of the
Raushanai. "*Jahanpanah, it is time to answer these insults as they
deserve to be answered*," he said. Akbar, amused by such nonmil-
itary rage, agreed that Birbal could have his way. But the foreigner
Mogor dell'Amore did not accompany Birbal. "He's not ready for
an Afghan war," the emperor pronounced, to general laughter, in
the House of Private Audience. "He should be here, at court,
keeping us company."

However, the uprising was no joke. The mountain routes had
become well-nigh impassable. And not long after Birbal arrived in
the region to teach the Illuminati a lesson he was ambushed in the
Malandrai Pass. There were malicious stories afterward about how
the great minister tried to save his skin by running away from his
troops, but the rumors the emperor believed spoke of betrayal. He
suspected that the Crown Prince had somehow been involved but
was never able to prove it. Birbal's body was never found. Eight
thousand of his men were slaughtered.

After the calamity of the Malandrai Pass the emperor was
wretchedly miserable for a long time, refusing food and drink, utterly bereft. He wrote a verse in his fallen friend's honor. *You gave
the helpless whatever you could, Birbal. Now I am helpless, but you have
nothing left for me.* He wrote for the first and last time in the first
person, not as a king would, but as a man singing a lament for his
beloved. And while he mourned Birbal he sent first Todar Mal and
then Man Singh to bludgeon the Raushanai into submission. In
the palaces of Sikri he saw voids everywhere, empty spaces where
three of his Nine Jewels had been, and which no lesser men could
fill. He drew Abul Fazl ever closer and relied on him more and
more. And then he had his notion, the almost scandalous notion
which he was still weighing carefully eight months after Birbal's
death, on the day of his forty-fourth solar birthday, when he himself was on his way to the royal balance to be weighed.

This was the question to which he was trying to find the answer: should he make the foreigner, Mogor dell'Amore, also known as Niccolò Vespucci, the teller of tall tales who outrageously claimed to be his uncle, who was proving himself to be such an adept administrator and counselor, and to whom he had taken such an unexpected liking, into his honorary son? The rank of *farzand* was among the least-bestowed, most-coveted honors in the empire, and anyone who was awarded the title was at once admitted into the emperor's inner circle. Was this young rogue, who was more like his younger brother than his child (or his uncle), worthy of so great an accolade? And—just as important—how would such an appointment be received?

He showed himself at the *jharokha* and the crowd cheered mightily. This Mughal of Love, Akbar reflected, was also popular with the masses. His popularity, the emperor suspected, had as much to do with the success of his house of courtesans down by the lake, the House of Skanda where the Skeleton and Mattress held sway, as with the tale of Qara Köz, but it was undeniably the case that the story of the hidden princess had become part of the lore of the capital, and the people's interest in it refused to fade away. The people knew, too, that the king's sons were a disappointment. The future of the dynasty was consequently a problem. According to legend the Mughals' ancestor Timur, at the time a minor bandit, was traveling in the guise of a camel-herder when he was accosted by a mendicant *faqir* and asked for food and water. "If you give me nourishment, I'll give you a kingdom," promised the *faqir,* a fellow who had renounced Islam in favor of Hinduism. Timur gave him what he wanted, whereupon the *faqir* threw his cloak over him and began to spank Timur on the behind with the palm of his hand. After eleven blows Timur cast off the cloak in anger. "If you had tolerated more spanking," the *faqir* said, "your dynasty would have lasted longer. Instead, it will end with your eleventh descendant." The emperor Akbar was the eighth descendant of Timur the Lame, so, if the legend was to be believed, the

Mughals were safe on the throne of Hindustan for three generations more. But the ninth generation was a difficulty. At eighteen,
fifteen, and fourteen they were all drunkards, and one of them had
the falling sickness, and the Crown Prince, what was there to say
about the Crown Prince, he was a horror, that was all.

The emperor on his birthday, seated in the scales of life, being
weighed twelve times in rice-milk, contemplated the future. Later
he visited the art workshops but his mind was elsewhere. Even in
the harem where the women closed around him, their softnesses
engulfing him, he was distracted. He felt that he had arrived at a
turning point, and that this decision about the foreigner was somehow at its heart. To allow him into the family would be a sign that
he was indeed pursuing Abul Fazl's idea of becoming the World-
King, that he could incorporate into his line—into himself—persons, places, narratives, possibilities from lands as yet unknown,
lands which might, in their turn, also be subsumed. If one foreigner could become a Mughal then so, in time, could all foreigners. Additionally, it would be a further step in the creation of a
culture of inclusion, that very culture which the Raushanai cult
satirized merely by existing: his true vision come to life, in which
all races, tribes, clans, faiths, and nations would become part of the
one grand Mughal synthesis, the one grand syncretization of the
earth, its sciences, its arts, its loves, its differences, its problems, its
vanities, its philosophies, its sports, its whims. All of which encouraged him to conclude that to honor Mogor dell'Amore with
the title of *farzand* would be an act of strength.

Yet might it not also look like weakness? Like sentimentality,
self-deception, gullibility? To fall for a smooth-talking stranger
about whom nothing was known save what he himself proffered as
the incomplete, chronologically problematic tale of himself? For
to give him official standing would be, in effect, to say that the
truth was no longer considered significant, that it no longer mattered if his tale was just a clever lie. Should not a prince avoid making his contempt for the truth so clear? Should he not defend that

value, and then lie when it suited him under cover of that defense? Should not a prince, in short, be colder, less susceptible to fantasies and visions? Perhaps the only vision he should allow himself was power. Did the elevation of the foreigner serve the emperor's power? Maybe it did. And maybe not.

And beyond these questions lay deeper inquiries still, questions from that world of magic which everyone lived in as passionately as they inhabited the world of tangible materials. When Akbar was glimpsed each day at the *jharokha* window he was feeding this belief; there were devotees below him, members of a burgeoning Cult of the Glimpse, who afterward began to spread stories of miracles. The sick, the dying, the injured were brought there each day, and if Akbar's eye fell upon them, if he Glimpsed them even as they Glimpsed him, then a cure was the inevitable result. Glimpsing transferred the emperor's potency to the Glimpsed. Magic invariably flowed from the more magical person (the emperor, the necromancer, the witch) to the lesser: that was one of its laws.

It was important not to offend against the laws of magic. If a woman left you it was because you did not cast the right spell over her, or else because someone else cast a stronger enchantment than yours, or else because your marriage was cursed in such a way that it cut the ties of love between husband and wife. Why did So-and-so rather than Such-and-such enjoy success in his businesses? Because he visited the right enchanter. There was a thing in the emperor that rebelled against all this flummery, for was it not a kind of infantilization of the self to give up one's power of agency and believe that such power resided outside oneself rather than within? This was also his objection to God, that his existence deprived human beings of the right to form ethical structures by themselves. But magic was all around and would not be denied, and it would be a rash ruler who pooh-poohed it. Religion could be rethought, re-examined, remade, perhaps even discarded; magic was impervious to such assaults. This, finally, was why the story of Qara Köz had so easily possessed the imagination of the people of

Sikri. She had taken her magic, "their" magic, into other worlds, worlds with their own occultisms, and her sorcery had proved more potent than theirs. Her sorcery. Which not even he, the emperor, could resist.

The magical issues regarding the foreigner Niccolò Vespucci, the self-styled Mughal of Love, could be stated as follows: was his presence among them a blessing or a curse? Would his elevation to high rank result in the empire being blessed, or would it, by offending against some dark law of Fortune, bring down disaster upon the realm? Was foreignness itself a thing to be embraced as a revitalizing force bestowing bounty and success upon its adherents, or did it adulterate something essential in the individual and the society as a whole, did it initiate a process of decay which would end in an alienated, inauthentic death? The emperor had taken advice from the guardians of the unseen realms, the palmists, astrologers, soothsayers, mystics, and assorted divines who were in plentiful supply in the capital, particularly in the vicinity of Salim Chishti's tomb, but their advice had been contradictory. He had not asked the foreigner's fellow Europeans Fathers Acquaviva and Monserrate for their opinions, for their hostility to the storyteller was well known. And Birbal, oh, his beloved, wise Birbal was gone.

He was left, in the end, with himself. Only he could choose.

The day ended. He had not decided. He was meditating at midnight beneath a crescent moon. She came to him, all in silver, silently, and shone.

—✳—

Things had reached the point at which Jodha had become invisible to many people. The household staff allocated to her service could see her, naturally, because their livelihoods depended upon it, but the other queens, who had always resented her presence, could no longer make her out. She knew something bad was happening to her, and was filled with fear. She felt fainter, and even, from time to time, intermittent, as if she came and went, as if the candle of her being were being snuffed out, relit, then snuffed out and relit again. Birbal was dead, and she was fading, she thought. The world was changing for the worse. The emperor visited her much less these days and when he did he seemed distracted. When he made love to her she had the impression that he was thinking about somebody else.

The spying eunuch, Umar the Ayyar, who could see everything, including some things that hadn't happened yet, found her resting in the heat of the afternoon in the Chamber of the Winds, the breezy second-story room which had *jalis,* stone filigree-work screens, filling three of the four walls. It was the day after the emperor's birthday and there was a curious urgency about his movements. Normally he was all languid grace and fluid gestures. Today, however, he was almost flustered, as if the news he had to impart was bouncing around inside him and knocking him off balance. "Okay," he announced, "a big moment for you. Mary of Eternity and Mary of the Mansion—the wife and mother of the Divine Caliph, the Unique Jewel, and the Khedive of the Age—are personally coming to call."

Mary of Eternity was Mariam-uz-Zamani, Prince Salim's real mother, Rajkumari Hira Kunwari, a Kachhwaha Rajput princess of Amer. Mary of the Mansion, Mariam Makani, was the emperor's mother Hamida Bano. (The Caliph, the Jewel, and the Khedive were all the emperor himself.) If these two great ladies, who had never given the nonexistent queen the time of day before, were coming to see her in her private rooms, something of great significance was afoot. Jodha gathered herself and stood in the position of humility, with folded hands and downcast eyes, to await their arrival.

Minutes later they swept in, their faces expressing both amazement and contempt. Bibi Fatima, the queen mother's echo of a lady-in-waiting, was absent on this occasion, having recently died, and in any case the ladies had intentionally come unaccompanied by courtiers, except for Umar the Ayyar, whose ability to keep secrets was not in doubt. They looked around in confusion and then turned to the Ayyar for assistance. "Where is she?" Hamida Bano hissed. "Has she left the room?" Umar inclined his head in Jodha's direction. The queen mother looked perplexed, while the younger royal lady snorted crossly and turned to face in the general direction indicated by the spy.

"I am here, to my considerable astonishment," said Queen Mariam-uz-Zamani, speaking too loud and too slowly, as if conversing with a stupid child, "talking to a woman who does not exist, whose image cannot be reflected by any mirror, who looks to me like an empty space on a carpet. I am here with the emperor's mother, Widow of the Cupola of Absolution, Beloved Former Consort to the emperor Humayun, Guardian of the World, whose Nest is Paradise, because we fear that something worse than you may be about to possess the emperor, my august husband, her illustrious son. It is our view that an enchantment has been cast upon him by the foreigner Vespucci, who has been sent here as a black-hearted functionary of the Infidel or the Devil, to destroy our tranquillity and bring us low, and that this enchantment has ensnared the emperor's manhood, thus endangering his sanity, which in turn imperils the entire kingdom, and therefore, it follows, all of us as well. It is an enchantment of which you will have heard—it seems everyone in Sikri knows about it already! It takes the form of an apparition of the so-called hidden princess, Qara Köz.

"We, we recognize"—and here Mary of Eternity faltered, for what she had to say was offensive to her pride—"that for reasons of his own the emperor prefers you to any other female companion"—she refused to say *queen*—"and it is our hope that, understanding the peril he is in, you will see where your duty lies. To be plain, we wish you to exert all your powers over him so that he can be rescued from his hexed condition—from his lust for this hell-demon in female form—and we are therefore here to assist you, by teaching you every means by which any woman has ever retained her power over any man, things the emperor, as a man, could not know, and therefore was unable to impart to you, his somewhat absurd and now, it seems, almost imperceptible creation. We know you have read many books and, I have no doubt, learned well what they have to teach. But there are things that have never been written down in books, but preserved only in the oral lore of women, passed in whispers from mother to daughter since the beginning of time. Do these things, and he will be your slave once more, and the demon's victory over the master of Fatehpur Sikri may be prevented. For she is, we are certain, a malicious ghost from the past, a vengeful ghost that resents its long exile and that seeks to suck the emperor back in time to possess and unmake him, to the detriment of all. And in any case it would be better to be spared, if at all possible, the spectacle of the Emperor of Hindustan, the King of Manifestation and Reality, Inhabiter of the Untainted Body, Master of the Faith and the Firmament, becoming infatuated with the phantom of his renegade, and also deceased, great-aunt."

"Remember what happened to the painter Dashwanth," the queen mother said.

"Quite so," Mariam-uz-Zamani concurred. "We may find it acceptable to mislay an artist in that way, but the Shelter of the World we cannot lose."

They genuinely couldn't see the woman to whom they were speaking, yet they were willing to arrange themselves on her carpets, lounge against her bolsters, drink the wine her servants offered, and tell the sexual secrets of women throughout history to the empty air. After a while they stopped feeling that they had lost their minds, and acted as if they were alone, just the two of them talking to each other, speaking openly about what had always been closed, laughing helplessly at the shocking comedy of desire, the absurd things men wanted and the equally absurd things women would do to please them, until the years dropped away from them and they remembered their own youth, and recalled how they had been told these secrets by other stern, ferocious women, who had also dissolved, after a time, into guffaws of joy, remembering, in their turn, how the knowledge had been given to them, and by the end of it the laughter in the room was the laughter of the generations, of all women, and of history.

They spoke in this fashion for five and a half hours and when they finished they thought it had been one of the happiest days of their lives. They began to have kinder thoughts toward Jodha than ever before. She was one of them now, part of the women's relay; she was no longer the emperor's creation alone. In part, she was theirs as well.

Dusk was falling. The palace candle-maids came in with camphor candles in silver candlesticks. Iron flambeaux on the room's rear wall were lit, and the cottonseed and oil inside them burned merrily, so that the two ladies' shadows danced over the red stone *jalis.* Then in another part of Sikri the emperor's fancy, his *khayal,* changed finally and forever, and consequently in the Chamber of the Winds Umar the Ayyar caught his breath, and a moment later Mary of Eternity and Mary of the Mansion saw what he had seen: not only the shadow of a third woman among the *jalis,* but the solid outline of a woman forming in thin air, becoming sharper, clearer, filling in, until the woman stood facing them with a curious smile on her lips. "You're not Jodha," the queen mother faintly said. "No," said the apparition, whose black eyes were sparkling. "Jodhabai has gone, because the emperor no longer has need of her. I will be his companion from now on." They were the phantom's first spoken words.

In spite of the two queens' precautions, news of the replacement of the imaginary queen Jodhabai by the phantom of Qara Köz spread through the city at high speed. For some this was the final proof that the hidden princess had really existed, that she belonged to the realm of fact not fable, because no woman who had never lived and died could end up having a ghost. For others it gave further credence to Abul Fazl's claim of divine status for the emperor, since now he had to his credit not only the creation of an entirely imaginary woman who could walk, talk, and make love in spite of not existing, but also the return of a real woman from the dead. The many families who had been entranced by the stories of the hidden princess, which had rapidly become tales that parents liked to tell their children at night, were exhilarated at the possibility that she might actually be seen in public. A few scandalized conservative voices were heard insisting that on all occasions when she left the royal women's quarters she must wear the veil; the kind of bare-faced shamelessness in which she had indulged in Western streets would not be acceptable among the decent folk of the Mughal capital.

The familiarity with which the supernatural occurrence was received was of course the consequence of such occurrences being normal at that time, before the real and unreal were segregated forever and doomed to live apart under different monarchs and separate legal systems. More surprising was the lack of sympathy for the unfortunate Jodhabai, so unceremoniously discarded by the emperor, so humiliatingly supplanted in the Chamber of the Winds under the eyes of the queen mother and the senior queen. Many citizens had formed an unfavorable impression of Jodha because of her refusal ever to leave the palace. To these people her dematerialization was a well-deserved punishment for being excessively arrogant and lacking the common touch. Qara Köz had quickly become the people's princess, whereas Jodha had always been an aloof and distant queen.

Umar the Ayyar reported all this to the emperor, but added a note of warning. By no means all reactions to the news were positive. In the Turani colony, in the Persian sector, and in the quarter where the Indian Muslims lived, there was a degree of restlessness. Among the non-Islamic polytheists whose gods were too numer-

ous to count, the arrival of one more miraculous being was of little concern, because the divine population was already too big a
crowd to comprehend, everything contained gods, trees contained
spirits, and so did rivers, and heaven alone knew what else, there
was probably even a god of garbage and a god of the toilet, so if a
new spirit was abroad it was scarcely worth discussing. In the
streets of monotheism, however, there was some shock. A low
murmur had begun, a murmur that only the most finely tuned ears
could detect, concerning the emperor's mental well-being. In the
secret journal of Badauni which Umar was still memorizing
nightly while the leader of the *manqul* party was asleep the question of blasphemy had been raised, for while it might just possibly
be argued that if men could turn their dreams into reality there was
no divine law against it, so that the creation of Jodha could just
possibly be exempted from opprobrium, but only the Almighty
had power over the living and the dead, and to bring a woman
back from the afterlife just for one's personal enjoyment was to go
much, much too far, and there was no excuse for it.

What Badauni wrote in private his followers were beginning
to mumble to each other. This mumbling was being conducted at
a very low level because, as the old saying had it, in the court of the
Grand Mughal only the humble did not stumble. Nevertheless
there was, in the Ayyar's opinion, some cause for concern, because
underneath the low-level mumble, at an even lower level, he had
heard a darker rumble, a deeper condemnation of the new relationship between Akbar and Qara Köz. At this deep level Umar
had picked up some faint sounds, sounds that hardly dared to be
sounds, spoken by lips that barely moved and were terrified at the
notion of a listening ear. These almost pre-aural vibrations contained a word so powerful that it could severely damage the esteem
in which the emperor was held, and maybe even rock his throne.

The word was *incest*. And Umar's warning was timely, because
a short time after the appearance of Qara Köz in Fatehpur Sikri
the Crown Prince Salim left the capital and raised the standard of

rebellion in Allahabad, and *blasphemy* and *incest* were the accusations with which he justified his revolt. The rebellion was a feeble affair, even though Salim had managed to raise an army of thirty thousand men. For several years he galloped around northern Hindustan claiming to desire his father's overthrow without ever daring to engage the great king in an actual battle. But he did achieve one terrible triumph, when he successfully arranged for the murder of the emperor's closest remaining adviser, whom he blamed for *perverting his father's mind,* encouraging him to perform blasphemous acts, and making him turn his love away both from God and his Holy Prophet, and also, by *always making snide remarks,* turning the emperor against the Crown Prince, his heir, his son. Abul Fazl died in an ambush, as Birbal had. Prince Salim had sent word to an ally, Raja Bir Singh Deo Bundela of Orchha, through whose territory the Jewel of Sikri was traveling, to *dispatch him to nonexistence,* with which request the Raja readily complied, decapitating the unarmed minister and sending his head to Salim in Allahabad, where Salim, displaying his usual sense of taste and appropriate behavior, threw it into a field latrine.

Akbar was reclining on a bolster in the Chamber of the Winds, having drunk perhaps too much wine, listening to the evening phantom of Qara Köz singing sad love songs while accompanying herself on a *dilruba,* when Umar the Ayyar came in with the news of Abul Fazl's death. This awful information served to bring the emperor to his senses. He rose to his feet and left Qara Köz's rooms at once. "From now on, Umar," he vowed, "we are going to go back to acting like the ruler of the universe and stop behaving like a spotty, infatuated boy."

The laws by which a prince was bound were not those of friendship or revenge. A prince had to consider the good of the kingdom. Akbar knew that two of his three sons were unfit to succeed to the throne, as they were so deep in drink and disease that they might actually die. So there was only Salim; no matter what he had done the continuity of the line must be assured. Akbar therefore sent messengers to Salim promising not to be avenged upon him for Abul Fazl's death and declaring his undying love for his firstborn child. Salim took this to mean that his murder of Abul Fazl had been justified. Now that that fat weasel had been dispatched his father had opened his arms once again. Salim sent Akbar a gift of elephants, three hundred and fifty of them to pacify the Elephant King. Then he agreed to go to Sikri, and at the house of his grandmother Hamida Bano he fell at the emperor's feet. The emperor raised Salim up, took off his own turban, and put it on the Crown Prince's head to show there were no hard feelings. Salim wept. He really was a pathetic young man.

As for Salim's mentor Badauni, however, he was thrown into the dirtiest cell of the deepest dungeon of Fatehpur Sikri, and no man or woman except his jailers ever saw him alive again.

After the death of Abul Fazl the emperor became stern. It fell to him to define how his people should live and for too long he had been derelict in carrying out that duty. He banned the sale of liquor to the common people unless it was prescribed by a doctor. He moved against the great prostitute swarms buzzing around the capital like locusts and had them all taken to an encampment called Deviltown some distance away and ordered that any man going to the devil should be obliged to write down his name and home address before entering that zone. He discouraged the eating of cow meat, onions, and garlic, but recommended that people eat tiger to gain courage from its flesh. He declared that religious observance was to be free of persecution irrespective of the religion being observed, temples could be built and *lingams* washed, but he was less tolerant of beards, because beards drew their nourishment from the testicles, which was why eunuchs didn't have them. He forbade child marriages and disapproved of widow-burning and slavery. He told people not to bathe after having sex. And he summoned the foreigner to the Anup Talao, whose waters had grown choppy and uncalm even though there was no breeze, an augury which meant that things that should have been at peace had become disturbed.

"There are still too many mysteries around you," the emperor said, irritably. "We can't rely on a man whose life story doesn't add up. So tell us everything, let's have it all out in the open right now, and then we can decide what's to be done with you, and which way your destiny leads, up to the stars or down into the dust. Clearly, now. Leave nothing out. Today is judgment day."

"It may be that what I have to say will not find favor, sire," Mogor dell'Amore replied, "because it concerns *Mundus Novus,* the New World, and the erratic nature, in that half-uncharted territory, of Time."

—∞—

Across the Ocean Sea in *Mundus Novus* the ordinary laws of space and time did not apply. As to space, it was capable of expanding violently one day and then shrinking the next, so that the size of the earth seemed either to double or halve. Different explorers brought back radically different accounts of the proportions of the new world, the nature of its inhabitants, and the way in which this new quadrant of the cosmos was prone to behave. There were accounts of flying monkeys and snakes as long as rivers. As for time, it was completely out of control. Not only did it accelerate and slow down in utterly wanton fashion, there were periods—though the word "periods" could not properly be used to describe such phenomena—when it did not move at all. The locals, those few who mastered European languages, confirmed that theirs was a world without change, a place of stasis, *outside time,* they said, and that was the way they preferred it to be. It was possible, and there were philosophers who argued the point vociferously, that time had been brought to *Mundus Novus* by the European voyagers and settlers, along with various diseases. This was why it didn't work properly. It had not yet adapted to the new situation. "In time," people in *Mundus Novus* said, "there will be time." For the present, however, the fluctuating nature of new world clocks simply had to be accepted. The most alarming effect of this chronological uncertainty was that time could run at different speeds for different people, even within families and households. Children would age faster than their parents until they looked older than their progenitors. For some of the conquerors, sailors, and settlers there never seemed to be enough time in the day. For others, there was all the time in the world.

The emperor, listening to Mogor dell'Amore as he told his story, understood that the lands of the West were exotic and surreal to a degree incomprehensible to the humdrum people of the East. In the East men and women worked hard, lived well or badly, died noble or ignoble deaths, believed in faiths that engendered great art, great poetry, great music, some consolation, and much confusion. Normal human lives, in sum. But in those fabulous Western climes people seemed prone to hysterias—such as the Weeper hysteria in Florence—that swept through their countries like diseases and transformed things utterly without warning. Of late the worship of gold had engendered a special type of this extreme hysteria, which had become their history's driving force. In his mind's eye Akbar pictured Western temples made of gold, with golden priests inside, and golden worshippers coming to pray, bringing offerings of gold to placate their golden god. They ate gold food and drank gold drinks and when they wept the molten gold ran down their shining cheeks. It was gold that had driven their sailors even further west across the Ocean Sea in spite of the danger of falling off the edge of the world. Gold, and also *India,* which they believed to contain fabulous hoards of gold.

They did not find *India,* but they found . . . a further west. In this further west they found gold, and searched for more, for golden cities and rivers of gold, and they encountered beings even less probable and impressive than themselves, bizarre, unknowable men and women who wore feathers and skins and bones, and named them *Indians*. Akbar found this offensive. Men and women who made human sacrifices to their gods were being called *Indians!* Some of these otherworld "Indians" were little better than aborigines; and even the ones who had built cities and empires were lost, or so it seemed to the emperor, in philosophies of blood. Their god was half bird, half snake. Their god was made of smoke. Theirs was a vegetable god, a god of turnips and corn. They suffered from syphilis and thought of stones and the rain and stars as living beings. In their fields they worked slowly, even lazily. They did not believe in change. To call these people *Indians* was in Akbar's emphatic opinion a slight to the noble men and women of Hindustan.

The emperor knew that he had reached a kind of boundary in his mind, a frontier beyond which his powers of empathy and interest could not journey. There were islands here that afterward metamorphosed into continents, and continents that proved to be mere islands. There were rivers and jungles and promontories and isthmuses and to the devil with them all. Maybe there were hydras in those climes, or griffins, or dragons guarding the great treasure heaps that reputedly lay in the jungles' depths. The Spanish and the Portuguese were welcome to it all. It had begun to dawn on these foolish exotics that they had not discovered a route to *India* but somewhere entirely other, neither East nor West, somewhere that lay between the West and the great Gangetic Sea and the fabled isle of treasures, Taprobane, and beyond that the kingdoms of Hindustan and Cipangu and Cathay. They had discovered that the world was larger than they believed it to be. Good luck to them as they wandered in the Islands and Terra Firma of the Ocean Sea and died of scurvy, hookworm, malaria, consumption, and yaws. The emperor was tired of them all.

And yet this was where she had gone, the delinquent princess of the house of Timur and Temüjin, Babar's sister, Khanzada's sister, blood of his blood. No woman in the history of the world had made a journey like hers. He loved her for it and admired her too, but he was also sure that her journey across the Ocean Sea was a kind of dying, a death before death, because death too was a sailing away from the known into the unknown. She had sailed away into unreality, into a world of fantasy which men were still dreaming into being. The phantasm haunting his palace was more real than that flesh-and-blood woman of the past who gave up the real world for an impossible hope, just as she had once given up the natural world of family and obligation for the selfish choices of love. Dreaming of finding her way back to her point of origin, of being rejoined to that earlier self, she was lost forever.

The way east was closed to her. The corsairs in the waters made the sea passage too risky. In the Ottoman world, and in the kingdom of Shah Ismail, she had burned her boats. In Khorasan she feared capture by whoever had filled the gap left by Shaibani Khan. She did not know where Babar was, but the way back to him was barred. In Genoa, at the home of Andrea Doria by the water's edge, where she had asked Ago Vespucci to take her, she decided she could not go back the way she had come. Nor, fearing the wrath of Florence, could she stay. The grizzled old sea-dog Doria, who was frankly shocked by, but forbore to remark upon, the new, mannish appearance of Qara Köz and her Mirror, gallantly made them welcome—for Qara Köz was still capable of inducing gallantry in men, even men with reputations for callousness and brutality—and assured them that while they were under his protection no Florentine harm could come to them. Doria was the one who first mentioned the possibility of making a new life across the Ocean Sea.

"If I didn't have so many Barbary pirates to kill," he said, "I might consider the trip myself, following in the footsteps of Signor

Vespucci's celebrated cousin." By this time he had killed quite a few such pirates, and his personal fleet, mostly made up of boats seized from the corsairs, now numbered twelve vessels, whose crews' loyalty was to nobody but Doria himself. Yet he no longer considered himself a true *condottiere,* because of his uninterest in fighting on land. "Argalia was the last of us," he declared. "I'm just a watery hangover." In his spare time, when he wasn't at war, he was doing political battle in Genoa with his rivals in the Adorni and Fregosi families, who kept trying to exclude him from power. "But I have the ships," he said, and added—unable to restrain himself even though there were ladies present—perhaps because the ladies were disguised as young men—"and they don't even have penises, do they, Ceva?" Ceva the Scorpion, his tattooed ox of a lieutenant, actually blushed before replying awkwardly, "No, Admiral, none that I have ever been able to make out."

Doria took his guests into his library and showed them a thing which none of them had ever seen, not even Ago, whose blood relation it concerned: the *Cosmographiae Introductio* by the Benedictine monk Waldseemüller of the monastery of St. Dié-des-Vosges, which came with a vast map that unfolded to cover the floor, a map whose name was almost as big, the *Universalis Cosmographia Secundum Ptholoemaei Traditionem et Americi Vespucii Aliorumque Lustrationes,* the Geography of the World According to the Tradition of Ptolemy and the Contributions of Amerigo Vespucci and Other People. On this map Ptolemy and Amerigo were depicted like colossi, like gods gazing down upon their creation, and upon a large segment of *Mundus Novus* there appeared the word *America.* "I see no reason," Waldseemüller wrote in his *Introductio,* "why anyone could properly disapprove of a name derived from that of Amerigo, the discoverer, a man of sagacious genius."

When Ago Vespucci read this he was deeply moved and understood that destiny in the form of his cousin must have been leading him toward the new world all his life, even though he had always been a stick-in-the-mud who thought of wild Amerigo as a hot-air merchant whose accounts of himself needed to be taken with a pinch of salt. He had not known Amerigo very well and had never really tried to know him better, for they had had little in common. But now the voyaging Vespucci was a sagacious genius and had put his name to a new world, and that was worthy of respect.

Slowly, shyly, with much trepidation, and repeating many times that he was not by nature a traveling man, Ago began to discuss his cousin's voyages of discovery with Admiral Doria. The words *Venezuela* and *Vera Cruz* were spoken. In the meanwhile Qara Köz had been studying the map of the world. She reacted to the new place names as if she were hearing an incantation, a charm that could bring her her heart's desire. She wanted to hear more, more. *Valparaiso, Nombre de Dios, Cacafuego, Rio Escondido,* Ago said. He was down on his hands and knees, reading. *Tenochtitlán, Quetzalcoatl, Tezcatlipoca, Montezuma, Yucatán,* Andrea Doria added, and also *Española, Puerto Rico, Jamaica, Cuba, Panama.* "These words which I have never heard," said Qara Köz, "are telling me my way home."

Argalia was dead—"At least he died in his hometown, defending what he loved," Doria said by way of a gruff epitaph, and raised a glass of wine in salute. Ago was a poor substitute for such a man, but Qara Köz knew he was all she had. It was Ago with whom she would make her last journey, Ago and the Mirror. These would be her last guardians. They learned from Doria of the conviction of most westward mariners, and of the rulers of Spain and Portugal too, that a passage to *India* would soon be found, an opening, suitable for shipping, through the landmasses of *Mundus Novus* into the Gangetic Sea. Many people were urgently searching for this middle passage. In the meanwhile the colonies of Española and Cuba were safe to live in, and the new place, Panama, was probably getting safer. In these places the *Indians* were for the most part under control, one million of them in Española, over two million in Cuba. Many of them were Christian converts even though they spoke no Christian tongue. The coastlines were secure at any rate, and even the interiors were being opened up. It was possible, if one had the money, to obtain a cabin on a caravel leaving from Cadiz or Palos de Moguer.

"Then I will go," announced the princess, gravely, "and wait. And the opening in the new world, for which so many fine men are searching so hard, will undoubtedly be found." She stood upright with her arms turned outward at the elbows, and her face was illumined by an unearthly light, so that she reminded Andrea Doria of Christ himself, the Nazarene performing His miracles, Christ multiplying loaves and fishes or raising Lazarus from the dead. On Qara Köz's face was the same strained expression it had acquired in the time of her enchantment of Florence, darkened further by grief and loss. Her powers were failing but she intended to exercise them one last time as they had never been exercised before, and force the history of the world into the course she required it to take. She would enchant the middle passage into being by the sheer force of her sorcery and her will. Andrea Doria looked at the young woman in her olive-green tunic and hose, her cropped black hair standing out from her head like a dark halo, and was overcome. He fell to his knees before her and bent down to touch his hand to her chamois leather boot and remained there with bowed head for a minute or perhaps more. In the years that followed, Doria, who lived to a great old age, thought every single day about what he had done, and was never certain whether he had knelt to receive a blessing or to give one, whether he had felt the need to worship her or protect her, to admire her in her last glory or to seek to dissuade her from her doom. He thought of Christ in Gethsemane and how He must have looked to His disciples as He prepared Himself to die.

"My ship will carry you to Spain," he said.

On a morning of white mist the *Cadolin,* the legendary corsair fighting ship, set sail from her new master Andrea Doria's dock at

Fassolo with three passengers and Ceva the Scorpion at the helm, and flying the flag of Genoa, the Cross of St. George. When he was saying his farewells Andrea Doria had managed to hold back the emotion that had earlier brought him to his knees. "The library of a man of action is little used," he told Qara Köz, "but you have given meaning to my books." He had the feeling that after reading the *Cosmographiae Introductio* and inspecting Waldseemüller's great map the princess was actually entering the book, moving out of the world of earth, air, and water and entering a universe of paper and ink, that she would sail across the Ocean Sea and arrive not at Española in *Mundus Novus* but in the pages of a story. He was sure he would never see her again in this world or the new one because death was sitting on her shoulder like a falcon, death would travel with her for a while until it grew impatient and tired of the journey.

"Goodbye," she said, and faded into white. Ceva brought the *Cadolin* back to Fassolo in due course, looking as if the last vestiges of joy had just left his life forever. Almost two years later Doria heard the news of Magellan's discovery of a stormy strait that would allow lucky sailors to pass around the southern tip of the new world. He had nightmares in which the beautiful princess perished in Magellan's strait along with her companions. No definite news of her whereabouts or fate was ever received in Genoa during his long lifetime. However, fifty-four years after the hidden princess set sail from Italy, a young yellow-haired rogue, no more than twenty years of age, presented himself at the gate of the Villa Doria, claiming to be her son. By this time Andrea Doria had been dead for thirteen years, and the house was owned by his great-nephew Giovanni, prince of Melfi, founder of the great house of the Doria-Pamphilii-Landi. If Giovanni had ever known the story of the lost princess of the house of Timur and Temüjin, he had long forgotten it, and had the ragamuffin chased away from his door. After that the young "Niccolò Antonino Vespucci," named after his father's two best friends, set forth to see the world, taking ship hither and yon, sometimes as a member of the crew, on other occasions as a carefree stowaway, learned many languages, acquired a wide variety of skills, not all of them within the boundaries of the law, and accumulated his own tales to tell, tales of escapes from cannibalism in Sumatra and of the egg-sized pearls of Brunei and of fleeing from the Great Turk up the Volga to Moscow in winter and of crossing the Red Sea in a dhow held together with string and of the polyandry of that part of *Mundus Novus* where women had seven or eight husbands and no man was allowed to marry a virgin and of making the pilgrimage to Mecca by pretending to be a Muslim and of being shipwrecked with the great poet Camoens near the mouth of the Mekong River where he saved the *Lusiads* by swimming ashore naked with the pages of Camoens's poem held in one hand above his head.

About himself he would only say to the men and women he met on his voyages that his story was stranger by far than any of these tales, but that it could only be divulged to one man on earth, whom he would face one day in the hope of being given what was his by right, and that he was protected by a mighty spell that blessed all those who aided him and cursed those who did him harm.

"Shelter of the World, the plain fact is that on account of the variability of chronological conditions in *Mundus Novus*," he told the emperor Akbar by the waters of the Anup Talao, "which is to say, on account of the unsettled nature of time in those parts, my mother the enchantress was able to prolong her youth, and might have lived for three hundred years had she not lost heart, had she not lost her belief in the possibility of a homecoming, and permitted herself to catch a fatal sickness so that she could at least join her deceased family members in the hereafter. A falcon flew in through her window and settled on her deathbed as she drew her last breaths. It was her final enchantment, the manifestation in the new world of this glorious bird from across the Ocean Sea. When the falcon flew out of the window we all understood that it was her soul. I was nineteen and a half years old at the time of her death and as she slept she looked more like my older sister than my parent. But my father and the Mirror had continued to age normally. Her magic was no longer strong enough to help them resist the temporal forces, just as it was not strong enough to change the geography of the earth. No middle passage was found, and she was trapped in the new world until she decided to die."

The emperor was silent. His mood was impenetrable. The waters of the Anup Talao continued to be disturbed.

"This finally is what you ask us to believe," the emperor said at length, heavily. "At last, and after everything, this. That she learned how to arrest time."

"In her own body," the other replied, "and for herself alone."

"That would indeed be a prodigious feat, if it were possible," Akbar told him, and rose, and went indoors.

—ɯ—

That night Akbar sat alone on the topmost story of the Panch Mahal and listened to the darkness. He did not believe the foreigner's tale. He would tell himself a better one instead. He was the emperor of dreams. He could pluck the truth from the darkness and bring it into the light. He had lost patience with the foreigner, and was left, in the end, as always, with himself. He sent his fancy across the world like a messenger bird and in the end the answer came. This was his story now.

Twenty-four hours later he summoned Vespucci back to the Best of All Possible Pools, whose waters still roiled in perplexity. Akbar's expression was grim. "Sir Vespucci," he asked, "are you familiar with camels? Have you had a chance to observe their ways?" His voice was like low thunder rolling across the troubled waters of the pool. The foreigner was at a loss for words.

"Why such a question, *Jahanpanah*?" he asked, and the emperor's eyes flashed at him angrily.

"Do not presume to question us, sir. We ask again, are there camels in the new world, camels such as we have here in Hindustan, are camels to be found among all those griffins and dragons?" Akbar asked, and seeing the other shake his head, held up a silencing hand and went on, his voice gathering force as he spoke. "The physical freedom of the camel, we have always thought, offers a lesson in amorality to mere human beings. For between camels nothing is forbidden. A young male camel, soon after he is born, will seek to fornicate with his mother. An adult male will feel no qualms about impregnating his daughter. Grandchildren, grandparents, sisters, brothers, all these are fair game when a camel seeks a partner. The term *incest* has no meaning to this animal. We, however, are not camels, isn't that right? And against incest there are ancient taboos, and harsh penalties are levied against couples who disregard them—rightly levied, as we hope you will agree."

A man and a woman sail into the mists and lose themselves in a formless new world where nobody knows them. In all the world they have only each other and the servant girl. The man is a servant too, the servant of beauty, and the name of his journey is love. They arrive in the place whose name does not matter just as their names do not. The years pass and their hopes die. All around them are energetic men. A wild world to the south and another to the north are slowly, slowly being tamed. Shape, law, form is being given to what was inchoately unchanging, but the process will be long. Slowly, slowly, the conquest moves ahead. There are advances, retreats, and again advances, small victories, small defeats, and then again larger gains. No man asks whether this is a good process or a bad one. It is not a legitimate question. God's work is being done, and gold is being mined as well. The greater the hubbub around them, the more dramatic the victories, the more dreadful the defeats, the bloodier the revenge of the old world upon the new, the stiller they become, the three unimportant people, the man, the woman, the servant. Day by day, month by month, year by year they grow smaller and less significant. Then illness strikes and the woman dies, but she leaves behind a child, a baby girl.

The man has nothing on earth now except the child and the servant, his dead wife's mirror. Together they raise the child. Angelica. The magic child. The servant's name has become Angelica too. The man watches the girl grow up and become a second mirror, the image of her mother, her mother to the life. The servant as she ages sees the uncanny likeness in the growing girl, the rebirth of the past, and sees, in addition, the father's burgeoning desire. How lonely they are, the three of them, in this world that has not yet fully taken shape, in which words can mean what you wish them to mean, and so can deeds; in which new lives must be made as best they can. There is complicity between the man and the servant for in the old days they used to lie together, the three of them, and they miss the departed third. The new life, the life reincarnate, grows to fill the hollow in the air where the old life used to be.

Angelica, Angelica. There is a point at which the language they use is changed, a point beyond which certain words lose their meaning, the word father, for instance, is forgotten, as are the words my child. They live in a state of nature, a state of grace, an Eden in which the fruit of the tree has not been eaten, and so good and evil are unknown. The young woman grows up between the man and the servant and what happens between them, naturally happens, and feels pure, and she is happy. She is a princess of the blood royal of the house of Timur and Temüjin and her name is Angelica, Angelica. One day a passage will be found and with her beloved husband she will enter into her kingdom. Until then they have their invisible home, their anonymous lives, and this bed, in which they move, so sweetly, so often, for so long, the three of them, the man, the servant, and the girl. Then a child is born, their child, the offspring of three parents, a boy with yellow hair like his father. The man names his son after his closest companions. Once there were three friends. By bringing their names across the Ocean Sea, he feels, he has brought them across also. His son is his friends reborn. The years move on. The girl sickens for reasons unknown. Something is wrong with her life. Something amiss with her soul. She becomes delirious. Who is she, she asks. In her last conversation with her son she tells him to find his family, to be rejoined, to remain joined always to what he is and never leave it, never after that set forth into the world for love or adventure or self. He is a prince of the blood royal of the Mughal house. He must go and tell his story. A falcon flies in through the window and flies out with her soul. The young man with the yellow hair goes down to the harbor to look for a ship. The old man and the servant stay behind. They are not important anymore. Their deed is done.

"That is not what happened," said Mogor dell'Amore. "My mother was Qara Köz, your grandfather's sister, the great enchantress, and she learned how to stop time."

"No," said the emperor Akbar. "No, she did not."

—⁂—

Lady Man Bai, niece of Mariam-uz-Zamani, sister of Raja Man Singh, married her long-time sweetheart Crown Prince Salim on the date specified by the court astrologers, the fifteenth of Isfandarmudh of that year according to the new solar calendar introduced by the emperor, which is to say the thirteenth of February, at her family's fortress palace of Amer, in the gracious presence of His Majesty the *padishah* Akbar, the Shelter of the World. When she was alone with her husband on their wedding night, after the usual application of unguents and massaging of the princely member, she made two stipulations before she allowed him to enter her. "In the first place," she said, "if you ever visit that whore the Skeleton again you had better start sleeping with your penis encased in armor every night, because you won't know which will be the night of my revenge. And in the second place, you need to attend to the yellow-haired foreigner, the Skeleton's poxy lover, because while he's in Sikri your father might just be crazy enough to give him what by right belongs to you."

After the events at the Anup Talao the emperor gave up the idea of raising Niccolò Vespucci to the rank of *farzand* or honorary son. Firmly convinced of, and a little disgusted by, the correctness of his version of the foreigner's story, he concluded that such a child, the offspring of an amoral liaison, could not be recognized as a member of the royal family. In spite of Vespucci's own obvious innocence in the matter, and indeed his ignorance of his true origins, and no matter how great his charms or talents, that one word, *incest,* placed him beyond the pale. Work could certainly be found for so able a person at Sikri if he wanted it, and the emperor issued instructions for such employment to be identified and offered, but their own intimacy would have to come to an end. As if to confirm the rightness of these decisions the waters of the Anup Talao resumed their habitual serenity. Niccolò Vespucci was informed by Umar the Ayyar that he was permitted to remain at the capital, but must immediately cease to refer to himself by the sobriquet "Mogor dell'Amore." The ease of access to the emperor's person that he had enjoyed was also, he should understand, a thing of the past. "From today," the Ayyar informed him, "you will be considered a common man."

Of the vindictiveness of princes there is no end. Even so great a fall from grace as Vespucci's did not satisfy Lady Man Bai. "If the emperor's mind can move this swiftly between fondness and rejection," she reasoned, "it can swing back in the other direction just as fast." While the foreigner remained in the capital the succession of Prince Salim was not guaranteed. But to her great vexation the Crown Prince did not move against his fallen rival, who had refused the bureaucratic post found for him by Akbar's functionaries, choosing instead to remain in the House of Skanda with the Skeleton and Mattress, and devoting himself to the pleasure of its guests. Man Bai was contemptuous. "If you could kill a great man like Abul Fazl without a qualm, what's stopping you from dealing with this pimp?" she demanded. But Salim feared his father's displeasure, and stayed his hand. Then Man Bai gave him a son, Prince Khusraw, and that changed things. "Now it's your heir's future you need to safeguard as well as your own," said Lady Man Bai, and this time Salim had no answer for her.

And Tansen died. The music of life was stilled.

The emperor took his friend's body back to his hometown of Gwalior, buried him next to the shrine of his master, the *faqir* Sheikh Mohammed Ghaus, and returned to Sikri in despair. One by one his bright lights were going out. Maybe he had wronged his Mughal of Love, he mused on his journey home, and Tansen's death was his punishment. A man was not responsible for the misdeeds of his progenitors. Moreover, Vespucci had proved his loyalty to the emperor by refusing to move away. So he was not simply a traveling opportunist. He had come to stay. More than two long years had passed. Perhaps it was time to rehabilitate him. As the emperor's procession moved past the Hiran Minar and up the hill toward the palace compound he made up his mind, and sent a runner to the House of Skanda to ask the foreigner to present himself at the pachisi courtyard the next morning.

Lady Man Bai had set up a network of informants in every quarter of the city to guard against just such an eventuality, and within an hour of the runner's arrival at the Skanda house the wife of the Crown Prince had been informed of the change in the wind. She went immediately to her husband and scolded him as a mother scolds an errant infant. "Tonight," she told him, "is the night to play the man."

Of the vindictiveness of princes there is no end.

—⁓⁓—

At midnight the emperor sat quietly atop the Panch Mahal and remembered the famous night when Tansen had sung the *deepak raag* at the House of Skanda and set alight not only the oil lamps but himself as well. At the very moment when this memory was in his mind a red flower of flame sprang up at the water's edge far below him, and after a dull moment of incomprehension he realized that a house was on fire in the darkness. When he discovered soon afterward that the House of Skanda had been burned to the ground he had a fleeting moment of alarm, wondering if the fire in his mind's eye had somehow caused this other, more lethal blaze. He was filled with grief by the thought that Niccolò Vespucci must be dead. But when the smoking ruin was searched no trace of the foreigner's body was found. Nor were the bodies of the Skeleton and Mattress among the charred remains; indeed, all the ladies of the house appeared to have escaped, and their clients too. Lady Man Bai was not the only person in Fatehpur Sikri who kept a precautionary ear close to the ground. The Skeleton had feared her former employer for too long.

On hearing of the disappearance of the foreigner, of his mysterious dematerialization from the middle of a burning house, which was making many of the capital's citizens talk about him as a sorcerer, the emperor feared the worst. "Now we will find out," he reflected, "whether all that talk of curses had anything to it."

The morning after the fire the flat-decked ice transportation boat the *Gunjayish* was found scuttled on the far side of the lake, with a great hole in the bottom created by an angry axe. Niccolò Vespucci the Mughal of Love was gone for good, having escaped by boat not by sorcery, and he had taken his two ladies with him. The ice consignment arrived from Kashmir and there was no boat to take it across the lake to Sikri. The more luxurious royal passenger craft *Asayish* and *Arayish* had to be pressed into service, and even the little skiff *Farmayish* was loaded to the water-line with ice blocks. "He is punishing us with water," the emperor thought. "Now that he has gone he will leave us thirsty for his presence." When Prince Salim came to him at Lady Man Bai's insistence to accuse the vanished trio of having set fire to their own house the emperor saw his son's guilt sitting on his forehead like a beacon but said nothing. What was done was done. He gave orders for the foreigner and his women to be allowed to depart. He would not have them pursued and brought back to answer for the sunken boat. Let them go. He wished them well. A man in a coat of particolored leather lozenges, a woman as thin as a knife, and another like a bouncing ball. If the world was just it would find a peaceful corner even for people as hard to accommodate as those three. Vespucci's story was concluded. He had crossed over into the empty page after the last page, beyond the illuminated borders of the existing world, and had entered the universe of the undead, those poor souls whose lives terminate before they stop breathing. The emperor at the lakeside wished the Mughal of Love a gentle afterlife and a painless ending; and turned away.

Man Bai hated the incomplete nature of what had transpired and howled in vain for blood. "Send men after them to kill them," she screamed at her husband, but he silenced her, and for the first time in his petty life gave a sign of the excellent king he would grow up to become. The events of recent days had disturbed him profoundly and new things were stirring inside him, the things which would enable him to leave his petulant youth behind and become a fine and cultured man. "My killing days are done," he said. "From now on I will consider it a greater act to preserve a life than to destroy one. Never ask me to commit such a wrong again."

The Crown Prince's change of heart had come too late. The destruction of Fatehpur Sikri had begun. The next morning the sounds of panic rose early toward the emperor's bedchamber and when he had had himself carried down the hill past the uproar at the waterworks and the louder cacophony in and around the caravanserai he saw that something had happened to the lake. Slowly, moment by moment, retreating at a man's walking pace, the water was receding. He sent for the city's leading engineers but they were at a loss to explain the phenomenon. "The lake is leaving us," the people were screaming, the golden life-giving lake, which once a traveler arriving at sunset had mistaken for a pool of molten gold. Without the lake the ice blocks from Kashmir could not bring fresh mountain water to the palace. Without the lake the citizens who could not afford Kashmiri ice would have nothing to drink, nothing to wash or cook with, and their children would soon die. The heat of the day was mounting. Without the lake the city was a parched and shriveled husk. The water continued to drain away. The death of the lake was the death of Sikri as well.

Without water we are nothing. Even an emperor, denied water, would swiftly turn to dust. Water is the real monarch and we are all its slaves.

"Evacuate the city," the emperor Akbar commanded.

———ᴡᴍ———

For the rest of his life the emperor would believe that the inexplicable phenomenon of the vanishing lake of Fatehpur Sikri was the doing of the foreigner he had unjustly spurned, whom he had not decided to take back into his bosom until it was too late. The Mughal of Love had fought fire with water and he had won. It was Akbar's most shattering defeat; but it was not a fatal blow. Mughals had been nomads before and could be nomads again. The tent army was already assembling, those artists of the collapsible home, two and a half thousand of them, and their camels and elephants too, preparing to march wherever he commanded and build their pavilions of fabric wherever he chose to rest. His empire was too immense, his pockets too deep, his army too strong to be unmade by a single blow, even a blow as powerful as this one. In nearby Agra there were palaces and a fort. In Lahore, another. The wealth of the Mughals was beyond counting. He must abandon Sikri, must leave his beloved red city of shadow and smoke to stand alone in a place made suddenly dry, to stand for all time as a symbol of the impermanence of things, of the suddenness with which a change can overtake even the most potent of peoples and mightiest of men. Yet he would survive. This was what it meant to be a prince, to be able to ride the metamorphoses. And as a prince was only his subjects writ large, a man elevated to the ranks of the near divine, then this too was what it meant to be a man. To ride the metamorphoses and go on. The court would move and many of its servitors and nobles would come too, but for the peasants there was no place on this, the last caravan to leave the caravanserai. For the peasants there was what there always would be: nothing. They would scatter into the immensity of Hindustan and their survival would be their own business. *Yet they do not rise up and slaughter us,* the emperor thought. *They accept their paltry fate. How can that be? How can it be? They see us abandon them, and they serve us still. This, too, is a mystery.*

It took two days to prepare the grand migration. There was enough water for two days. At the end of that time the lake had emptied and there was only a muddy hollow where once that sweet water had glittered. Even the mud would be caked and dry in two days more. On the third day the royal family and its courtiers departed on the Agra road, the emperor sitting upright on his steed, the queens lustrous in their palanquins. Following the royal procession were the nobles, and after them the immense cavalcade of their servants and dependents. Bringing up the rear were bullock-carts on which the skilled workers had loaded their goods. Butchers, bakers, masons, whores. For such people there was always a place. Skills could be transported. Land could not. The peasants, tied as if by ropes to land that was arid and dying, watched the great procession leave. Then, seemingly determined to have one night of pleasure before the misery of the rest of their lives, the abandoned masses walked up the hill to the palaces. Tonight, for this one night, the common people could play human pachisi in the royal courtyard and sit like the king atop the great stone tree in the House of Private Audience. Tonight a peasant could sit on the highest story of the Panch Mahal and be monarch of all he surveyed. Tonight if they wished they could sleep in the bedchambers of kings.

Tomorrow, however, they would have to find ways not to die.

—⁂—

One member of the royal household did not leave Fatehpur Sikri. After the fire at the House of Skanda, Lady Man Bai entered a state of mental confusion, at first shrieking and screaming for blood, and then, after Prince Salim rebuked her, falling into a profound melancholy, a loud grief that abruptly became silent. While Sikri was dying her life ended too. In the confusion of those last days, perhaps overcome by guilt, by her responsibility for the death of the capital of the Mughal empire, she found a moment of solitude, and in a corner of her palace when none of her maids was within sight she ate opium, and died. Prince Salim's final act before joining his father in grief at the head of the great exodus was to bury his beloved wife. In this way the story of the long enmity of Man Bai and the Skeleton came to a tragic end.

And as Akbar rode past the crater where the life-giving lake of Sikri had been he understood the nature of the curse under which he had been placed. It was the future that had been cursed, not the present. In the present he was invincible. He could build ten new Sikris if he pleased. But once he was gone, all he had thought, all he had worked to make, his philosophy and way of being, all that would evaporate like water. The future would not be what he hoped for, but a dry hostile antagonistic place where people would survive as best they could and hate their neighbors and smash their places of worship and kill one another once again in the renewed heat of the great quarrel he had sought to end forever, the quarrel over God. In the future it was harshness, not civilization, that would rule.

"If that is your lesson for me, Mughal of Love," he silently addressed the departed foreigner, "then the title you gave yourself is false, for in this version of the world there is no love to be found anywhere."

But that night in his brocade tent the hidden princess came to him, Qara Köz, her beauty like a flame. This was not the mannish shorn-haired creature she had become to escape from Florence, but the hidden princess in all her youthful glory, the same irresistible creature who had entranced Shah Ismail of Persia and Argalia the Turk, the Florentine Janissary, Wielder of the Enchanted Lance. That night of Akbar's retreat from Sikri she spoke to him for the first time. *There is a thing,* she said, *about which you were wrong.*

She was barren. She had been the lover of a king and a great warrior and there had been no issue in either case. So she had not given birth to a young girl in the new world. She had had no child.

Who was the foreigner's mother, then, the emperor in wonder demanded. On the walls of the brocade tent the mirrorwork panels caught the candlelight and the reflections danced in his eyes. I had a Mirror, the hidden princess said. She was as like to me as my own reflection in water, as the echo of my voice. We shared everything, including our men. But there was a thing she could be that I could never become. I was a princess but she became a mother.

The rest of it was much as you imagined, said Qara Köz. The Mirror's daughter was the mirror of her mother and of the woman whose mirror the Mirror had been. And there were deaths, yes. The woman who stands before you now, whom you have brought back to life, was the first. After that the Mirror raised her child to believe she was the thing she was not, the woman the girl's mother had once reflected and also loved. The blurring of generations, the loss of the words *father* and *daughter,* the substitution of other, incestuous words. And the thing you dreamed her father did, yes, that was so. Her father who became her husband. The crime against nature was committed, but not by me, and no infant of mine was thus defiled. Born of sin, she died young, not knowing who she was. Angelica, Angelica, yes. That was her name. Before she died she sent her son to find you to ask for what was not his to demand. The criminals remained silent by her deathbed, but when the Mirror and her master went to stand before their God, then all their deeds were known.

So the truth of it is this. Niccolò Vespucci who was raised to believe that he was born of a princess was the child of a Mirror's child. Both he and his mother were innocent of all deception. They were the deceived.

The emperor fell silent and considered the injustice he had done, for which the ruination of his capital city had been his punishment. The curse of the innocent had been visited upon the guilty. Humbled, he bowed his head. The hidden princess, Qara

Köz, Lady Black Eyes, came to sit at his feet, and softly touched his hand. The night fled. A new day was beginning. The past was meaningless. Only the present existed, and her eyes. Under their irresistible enchantment, the generations blurred, merged, dissolved. But she was forbidden to him. No, no, she could not be forbidden. How could what he felt be a crime against nature? Who would dare forbid the emperor what the emperor permitted himself? He was the arbiter of the law, the law's embodiment, and there was no crime in his heart.

He had raised her from the dead and granted her the freedom of the living, had freed her to choose and be chosen, and she had chosen him. As if life was a river and men its stepping stones, she had crossed the liquid years and returned to command his dreams, usurping another woman's place in his *khayal,* his god-like, omnipotent fancy. Perhaps he was no longer his own master. What if he tired of her?—No, he would never tire of her.—But could she be banished in her turn, or could she alone decide to stay or go?

"I have come home after all," she told him. "You have allowed me to return, and so here I am, at my journey's end. And now, Shelter of the World, I am yours."

Until you're not, the Universal Ruler thought. *My love, until you're not.*

BIBLIOGRAPHY

BOOKS

Ady, Cecilia M. *Lorenzo de Medici and Renaissance Italy*. London: English University Press, 1960.

Alberti, Leon Battista. *The Family in Renaissance Florence*. Columbia, S.C.: University of South Carolina Press, 1969.

Anglo, Sydney. *The Damned Art: Essays in the Literature of Witchcraft*. Boston: Routledge & Kegan Paul, 1977.

Ariosto, Ludovico. *Orlando Furioso*. New York: Oxford University Press, 1966.

Birbari, Elizabeth. *Dress in Italian Painting, 1460–1500*. London: John Murray, 1975.

Boiardo, Matteo. *Orlando Innamorato*. West Lafayette, Ind.: Parlor Press, 2004.

Bondanella, Peter, ed. *The Portable Machiavelli*. Translated by Mark Musa. New York: Penguin, 1979.

Brand, Michael, and Glenn Lowry, eds. *Fatehpur-Sikri*. Bombay: Marg Publications, 1987.

Brebner, John Bartlet. *The Explorers of North America: 1492–1806*. London: A. & C. Black, 1933.

Brown, Judith, and Robert Davis. *Gender and Society in Renaissance Italy*. London: Longman, 1998.

Brucker, Gene. *Giovanni and Lusanna: Love and Marriage in Renaissance Florence*. Berkeley: University of California Press, 1986.

———. *Renaissance Florence*. Berkeley: University of California Press, 1969.

———, ed. *The Society of Renaissance Florence: A Documentary Study*. Toronto: University of Toronto Press, 2001.

———. "Sorcery in Early Renaissance Florence." *Studies in the Renaissance,* Vol. 10 (1963), pp. 7–24.

Burckhardt, Jacob. *The Civilization of the Renaissance in Italy*. Vol. I. New York: Harper & Row, 1958.

Burke, Peter. *The Italian Renaissance: Culture and Society in Italy*. 2nd ed. Princeton, N.J.: Princeton University Press, 1986.

———. *The Renaissance*. New York: Barnes & Noble, 1967.

Burton, Sir Richard. *The Illustrated Kama Sutra*. Middlesex, U.K.: Hamlyn Publishing Group, 1987.

Calvino, Italo. *Italian Folktales*. Translated by George Martin. New York: Harcourt Brace Jovanovich, 1980.

Camporesi, Piero. *The Magic Harvest: Food, Folklore and Society*. Cambridge, U.K.: Polity Press, 1993.

Cassirer, Ernest, ed. *The Renaissance Philosophy of Man.* Chicago: University of Chicago Press, 1948.

Castiglione, Baldesar. *The Book of the Courtier.* Translated by George Bull. New York: Penguin, 1967.

Cohen, Elizabeth S., and Thomas V. Cohen. *Daily Life in Renaissance Italy.* Westport, Conn.: The Greenwood Press, 2001.

Collier-Frick, Carole. *Dressing Renaissance Florence.* Baltimore: Johns Hopkins University Press, 2002.

Creasy, Sir Edward S. *History of the Ottoman Turks from the Beginning of Their Empire to the Present Time.* Ann Arbor, Mich.: UMI, Out-of-Print Books on Demand, 1991.

Curton, Philip D. *Cross-Cultural Trade in World History.* New York: Cambridge University Press, 1984.

Dale, Stephen Frederic. *Indian Merchants and Eurasian Trade, 1600–1750.* New York: Cambridge University Press, 1994.

Dash, Mike. *Tulipomania.* New York: Random House, 2001.

de Grazia, Sebastian. *Machiavelli in Hell.* Hertfordshire, U.K.: Harvester Wheatsheaf, 1989.

Dempsey, C. *The Portrayal of Love: Botticelli's Primavera and Humanist Culture at the Time of Lorenzo the Magnificent.* Princeton, N.J.: Princeton University Press, 1992.

Dubreton-Lucas, J. *Daily Life in Florence in the Time of the Medici.* New York: Macmillan, 1961.

Eraly, Abraham. *Emperors of the Peacock Throne: The Age of the Great Mughals.* New Delhi: Penguin Books India, 2000.

Fernandez-Armesto, Felipe. *Amerigo: The Man Who Gave His Name to America.* New York: Random House, 2007.

Findly, Ellison B. "The Capture of Maryam-uz-Zamani's Ship: Mughal Women and European Traders." *Journal of the American Oriental Society,* Vol. 108, No. 2 (April 1988).

Finkel, Caroline. *Osman's Dream: The Story of the Ottoman Empire, 1300–1923.* London: John Murray, 2005.

Gallucci, Mary M. "'Occult' Power: The Politics of Witchcraft and Superstition in Renaissance Florence." *Italica,* Vol. 80 (Spring 2003), pp. 1–21.

Gascoigne, Bamber. *The Great Mughals: India's Most Flamboyant Rulers.* London: Constable & Robinson, 2002.

Goodwin, Godfrey. *The Janissaries.* London: Saqi Books, 1997.

Goswamy, B. N., and Caron Smith. *Domains of Wonder: Selected Masterworks of Indian Painting.* San Diego, Calif.: San Diego Museum of Art, 2005.

Grimassi, Raven. *Italian Witchcraft: The Old Religion of Southern Europe.* Woodbury, Minn.: Llewellyn Publications, 2006.

Gupta, Ashin Das, and M. N. Pearson, eds. *India and the Indian Ocean, 1500–1800.* Calcutta: Oxford University Press, 1987.

Hale, J. R. *Florence and the Medici: The Pattern of Control.* London: Thames & Hudson, [1977].

Horniker, Arthur Leon. "The Corps of the Janizaries." *Military Affairs,* Vol. 8, No. 3 (Autumn 1944), pp. 177–204.

Imber, Colin. *The Ottoman Empire, 1300–1650: Structure of Power.* New York: Palgrave Macmillan, 2002.

Jones, Dalu, ed. *A Mirror of Princes: The Mughals and the Medici.* Bombay: Marg Publications, 1987.

King, M. *Women of the Renaissance.* Chicago: University of Chicago Press, 1991.

Klapisch-Zuber, Christine. *Women, Family and Ritual in Renaissance Italy.* Chicago: University of Chicago Press, 1985.

Kristeller, Paul Oskar. *Renaissance Concepts of Man and Other Essays.* New York: Harper & Row, 1973.

Lal, Ruby. *Domesticity and Power in the Early Mughal World.* New York: Cambridge University Press, 2005.

Landucci, L. A. *Florentine Diary from 1450 to 1516.* New York: Arno Press, 1969.

Lawner, Lynne. *Lives of the Courtesans: Portraits of the Renaissance.* New York: Rizzoli, 1987.

Lorenzi, Lorenzo. *Witches: Exploring the Iconography of the Sorceress and Enchantress.* Translated by Ursula Creagh. Florence: Centro Di, 2005.

Machiavelli, Niccolò. *The Discourses.* New York: Penguin Putnam, 1998.

Manucci, Niccolao. *Mogul India, 1653–1708, or Storia do Mogor.* Translated by William Irvine. Vols. I–IV. New Delhi: Low Price Publications, 1996.

Masson, Georgina. *Courtesans of the Italian Renaissance.* New York: St. Martin's Press, 1976.

McAlister, Lyle N. *Spain and Portugal in the New World: 1492–1700.* Minneapolis: University of Minnesota Press, 1984.

Mee, Charles L. *Daily Life in Renaissance Italy.* New York: American Heritage Publishing Co., 1975.

Morgan, David. *Medieval Persia, 1040–1797.* Essex, U.K.: Pearson Education, 1988.

Mukhia, Harbans. *The Mughals of India.* Malden, Mass.: Blackwell Publishing, 2004.

Nath, R. *Private Life of the Mughals of India: 1526–1803.* New Delhi: Rupa & Co., 2005.

Origo, Iris. "The Domestic Enemy: Eastern Slaves in Tuscany in the 14th and 15th Centuries." *Speculum* 30 (1955), pp. 321–66.

Pallis, Alexander. *In the Days of the Janissaries.* London: Hutchinson & Co., 1951.

Penrose, Boies. *Travel and Discovery in the Renaissance, 1420–1620.* Cambridge, Mass.: Harvard University Press, 1952.

Pottinger, George. *The Court of the Medici.* London: Croom Helm, 1978.

Raman, Rajee. *Ashoka the Great and Other Stories.* Vadapalani, Chennai: Vadapalani Press, n.d.

Rizvi, Saiyid Athar Abbas, and Vincent John Adams Flynn. *Fathpur-Sikri.* Mumbai: Taraporevala Sons & Co., 1975.

Rogers, Mary, and Paolo Tinagli. *Women in Italy, 1350–1650: Ideals and Reality.* Manchester, U.K.: Manchester University Press, 2005.

Rosenberg, Louis Conrad. *The Davanzati Palace, Florence, Italy: A Restored Palace of the Fourteenth Century.* New York: Architectural Book Publishing Company, 1922.

Ruggiero, Guido. *Binding Passions: Tales of Magic, Marriage, and Power at the End of the Renaissance.* New York: Oxford University Press, 1993.

Sachs, Hannelore. "Women Slaves, Beggars, Witches, Courtesans, Concubines," in *The Renaissance Woman,* pp. 49–53. New York: McGraw-Hill, 1971.

Savory, Roger. *Iran Under the Safavids.* New York: Cambridge University Press, 1980.

Seed, Patricia. *Ceremonies of Possession in Europe's Conquest of the New World: 1492–1640.* New York: Cambridge University Press, 1995.

Sen, Amartya. *The Argumentative Indian: Writings on Indian History, Culture and Identity.* New York: Farrar, Straus & Giroux, 2005.

Seyller, John. *The Adventures of Hamza: Painting and Storytelling in Mughal India.* Washington, D.C.: Freer Gallery of Art and Arthur M. Sackler Gallery, Smithsonian Institution, 2002.

Sharma, Shashi S. *Caliphs and Sultans: Religious Ideology and Political Praxis.* New Delhi: Rupa & Co., 2004.

Symcox, Geoffrey, ed. *Italian Reports on America: 1493–1522.* Turnhout, Belgium: Brepols, 2001.

Thackston, Wheeler M., ed. and trans. *The Baburnama: Memoirs of Babar, Prince and Emperor.* New York: Oxford University Press, 1996.

———, ed. and trans. *The Jahangirnama: Memoirs of Jahangir, Emperor of India.* New York: Oxford University Press, 1999.

Treharne, R. F., and H. Fullard, eds. *Muir's Historical Atlas: Medieval and Modern.* 10th ed. New York: Barnes & Noble, 1964.

Trexler, R. *Public Life in Renaissance Florence.* New York: Academic Press, 1980.

Trexler, Richard. "Florentine Prostitution in the Fifteenth Century: Patrons and Clients," in *Dependence and Context in Renaissance Florence.* Binghamton, N.Y.: Medieval and Renaissance Texts and Studies, 1994.

Turnball, Stephen. *Essential Histories: The Ottoman Empire, 1326–1699.* Oxford, U.K.: Routledge, 2003.

Viroli, Maurizio. *Niccolò's Smile: A Biography of Machiavelli.* Translated by Antony Shugaar. London: I. B. Tauris, 1998.

Weinstein, D. *Savonarola and Florence: Prophecy and Patriotism in the Renaissance.* Princeton, N.J.: Princeton University Press, 1970.

Welch, Evelyn. *Shopping in the Renaissance: Consumer Cultures in Italy, 1400–1600.* New Haven, Conn.: Yale University Press, 2005.

WEB SITES

al-Fazl ibn Mubarak, Abu. *Akbar-namah (The Book of Akbar).* Translated by H. Beveridge. Packard Humanities Institute: Persian Literature in Translation. Available online: http://persian.packhum.org/persian.

———. *Ain-i-Akbari (Akbar's Regulations).* Translated by H. Blockhmann and Colonel H. S. Jarrett. Packard Humanities Institute: Persian Literature in Translation. Available online: http://persian.packhum.org/persian.

Bada'uni, Abd al-Qadir. *Muntakhab ut-tawarikh.* Translated by W. Haig, G. Ranking, and W. Lowe. Packard Humanities Institute: Persian Literature in Translation. Available online: http://persian.packhum.org/persian.

Bréhier, Louis. Entry for "Andrea Doria" in *The Catholic Encyclopedia,* Vol. V. New York: Robert Appleton Company, 1909. Available online: www.newadvent.org/cathen/05134b.htm.

Cross, Suzanne. *Feminae Romanea: The Women of Ancient Rome.* 2001–2006. Available online: web.mac.com/heraklia/Dominae/imperial_women/index.html.

Encyclopaedia Britannica, 2007; see entry for "Doria, Andrea." Available online: Encyclopaedia Britannica Online, http://www.britannica.com/eb/article-9030969.

Gardens of the Mughal Empire; see page for Brian Q. Silver, "Introduction to the Music of the Mughal Court." Smithsonian Productions. Available online: www.mughalgardens.org/html/music01.html.

Von Garbe, Richard. *Akbar, Emperor of India.* Translated by Lydia G. Robinson. Project Gutenberg eBook, 23 Nov. 2004. Available online: www.gutenberg.org.

A NOTE

This is not a complete list of the works I consulted. If I have inadvertently omitted any source from which material has been used in the text, I apologize. Any such omissions will be rectified in future editions if I'm notified.

ACKNOWLEDGMENTS

I would like to thank Vanessa Manko for her help in compiling the bibliography, and also for her invaluable assistance with the research for this novel, which was made possible, in part, by a Hertog Fellowship at Hunter College, New York. My gratitude, too, to my editors Will Murphy, Dan Franklin, and Ivan Nabokov; to Emory University; and to Stefano Carboni, Frances Coady, Navina Haidar, Rebecca Kumar, Suketu Mehta, Harbans Mukhia, and Elizabeth West. Also to Ian McEwan, with whom, many years ago, I improvised a song called "My Sweet Polenta."

ABOUT THE AUTHOR

SALMAN RUSHDIE is the author of nine previous novels: *Grimus; Midnight's Children* (which was judged to be the "Booker of Bookers," the best novel to have won that prize in its first twenty-five years); *Shame* (winner of the French Prix de Meilleur Livre Etranger); *The Satanic Verses* (winner of the Whitbread Prize for Best Novel); *Haroun and the Sea of Stories* (winner of the Writers Guild Award); *The Moor's Last Sigh* (winner of the Whitbread Prize for Best Novel); *The Ground Beneath Her Feet* (winner of the Eurasian section of the Commonwealth Prize); *Fury* (a New York Times Notable Book); and *Shalimar the Clown* (a Time Book of the Year). He is also the author of a book of stories, *East, West*, and four works of nonfiction—*Imaginary Homelands, The Jaguar Smile, The Wizard of Oz*, and *Step Across This Line*. He is co-editor of *Mirrorwork*, an anthology of contemporary Indian writing.

ABOUT THE TYPE

This book was set in Bembo, a typeface based on an old-style Roman face that was used for Cardinal Bembo's tract *De Aetna* in 1495. Bembo was cut by Francisco Griffo in the early sixteenth century. The Lanston Monotype Company of Philadelphia brought the well-proportioned letterforms of Bembo to the United States in the 1930s.